ONCE DEAD

Also by Richard Phillips

The Rho Agenda: The Second Ship
The Rho Agenda: Immune
The Rho Agenda: Wormhole

ONCE DEAD

A RIPPER/RHO AGENDA NOVEL

RICHARD PHILLIPS

47NORTH

The characters and events portrayed in this book are fictitious. Any similarity to real persons, living or dead, is coincidental and not intended by the author.

Published by 47North, Seattle

www.apub.com

ISBN-13: 9781477824108
ISBN-10: 1477824103

Cover design by Cyanotype Book Architects

Library of Congress Control Number: 2014932945

Printed in the United States of America

Dedicated to my wife, Carol, whose love and encouragement has made writing such a pleasure

PROLOGUE

Jack Gregory felt strong hands shove him into the moonlit alley, only dimly aware of the half-dozen men that encircled him as his focus shifted to the man that waited in the center of that ring. These self-appointed referees had brought them together here for two reasons: to watch a death match between Americans and to make sure Jack wasn't the one who walked away. And if that was how things went down, that was fine with him. Priest Williams wouldn't be walking away either.

The Calcutta slums bred hard men and women. By the time children reached the age of thirteen, they'd already experienced more work and hardship than most Americans would endure in their lifetimes. The residents of this particular neighborhood bore no love for Americans in general or CIA operatives in particular. Carlton "Priest" Williams, an ex–Delta Force mercenary, fell into the first category. Jack fit the second.

As he looked at the mercenary's muscular torso, shimmering with sweat in the moon's pale glow, Jack's hatred for the man filled his veins with ice. Airborne Ranger, Green Beret, Delta Force. Priest's mere existence screamed betrayal of all that America's Special Forces stood for. Because of Priest, Jack's brother's body lay in an unmarked grave somewhere in Waziristan. Not his head, just his body. A burlap bag containing Robert's decaying head had been left on Jack's hotel room pillow. That delivery had propelled him into this alley, into this night.

Priest launched himself at Jack, moving with surprising speed and agility for a man his size, but his right cross failed to land. Shifting his weight left, Jack's side kick buckled Priest's right leg, bringing him to his knees. Immediately Jack was behind him, his right arm encircling Priest's throat. Struggling to prevent Jack's left arm from completing the choke hold, Priest rolled forward, throwing Jack over his head onto the sewage-strewn ground, coming to rest straddling Jack's body.

As heavy blows rained down onto his face and neck, Jack grabbed Priest's left hand, whipping his right leg up to lock beneath Priest's chin. Levering Priest's arm outward against the pressure of his leg, Jack felt the arm break, sending Priest's gargling scream echoing through the alley. Shifting his weight, Jack continued to twist the broken arm, rolling the bigger man onto his side as Jack's feet sought their fatal lock around Priest's neck.

The slash of twin blades across his back took Jack by surprise, sending him rolling to his feet to face his new attackers. All six men who formed the circle around the two combatants held the foot-and-a-half-long, boomerang-shaped knives called Khukuri. It was the signature weapon of the local Nepalese gang who called themselves the Ghurkaris. Blood dripped from the blades of the two men to his left.

With a rage-filled scream, one arm dangling uselessly at his side, Priest bull-rushed him. Although Jack sidestepped this new attack, the movement brought him too close to those that encircled them and he suffered a new cut higher up on his back. As he spun away, two more slashed across his chest. The wounds weren't deep enough to be dangerous, the bloodletting intended to weaken, not to kill. The vision of a Madrid bullfight swam through his head. Picadores.

Priest's left hook caught him high on the head, sending Jack staggering backward, taking another cut on his right side before he recovered. Priest followed up with a spinning side kick aimed at his head, a mistake that allowed Jack to hook Priest's foot beneath his right arm. The leg sweep that followed dropped Priest onto his broken arm.

Lifting the leg, Jack put all his power into a kick that caught Priest in the groin. As a knife again sliced at his back, Jack released Priest and lunged sideways, catching the knife wielder by the wrist and thumb, his motion twisting the arm over and back, opening the man's throat to the blow that crushed his windpipe. Before the knife could slip from the dying man's fingers, Jack redirected it into a second gang member's stomach.

There are moments when surprise and shock are your only allies and Jack embraced this one, falling upon the other four, wielding a Khukuri in each hand. Taking another cut across his chest, he slashed the throat of the nearest gangster and spun under another thrust, his long knife removing the attacking hand at the wrist. His subsequent thrust spilled the man's guts onto his dying friend.

Sensing movement to his left, Jack twisted sideways, but not quite fast enough. A razor-sharp blade pierced his left side below his ribcage, just before Jack's counter-thrust dropped the man on his face.

The last of the Ghurkaris stepped backward, but when Jack staggered, the Ghurkari lunged to fill the opening, a look of shock widening his eyes as Jack's right heel caught him in the throat, crushing his trachea and dropping him to the ground. The blow left the man gagging, vainly struggling to draw breath through his broken air passage. Jack watched as his battle came to a rattling, wheezing end, then returned his attention to Priest.

But Priest was gone.

Taking a half-dozen steps forward, Jack swept the alley with his gaze, but there was no sign of the man. A wave of frustration engulfed him, sapping the last of his strength and dropping him to his knees. Then, as the Nepali knives slipped from his bloody fingers, the ground rose up to kiss him good night.

~ ~ ~

Sister Mary Judith limped slowly through the darkened slum that had been her home the last forty-eight years of her fading life. Her right shoe hurt her foot more than usual tonight. But her bunions weren't likely to get better. And compared to the poor people whose souls she sought to save and whose bodies her clinic treated, she had no complaints.

Tonight that clinic had failed a three-year-old child and the woman whose tears still dampened Sister Mary Judith's shoulder. Malaria had taken the little girl from her mother's arms and into God's. Salara. Such a beautiful name. A name that had been repeatedly sobbed into her left ear as the mother wept in her old arms.

She was so lost in the memory that she failed to notice the running man until he staggered into her, knocking Sister Mary Judith to the ground. Although pain lanced through her left hand, she did not cry out. But the cry of pain from the running man followed him into the darkness.

Rubbing her wrist, the sister flexed her fingers. It wasn't broken. She'd always been blessed with strong bones and, thankfully, her advancing years had failed to rob her of that blessing. Apparently, the Lord needed her bones strong so she could continue to aid these people.

Struggling back to her feet, Sister Mary Judith glanced in the direction the man had disappeared. What had he been running from? Not really running. More of a barely controlled stagger, with one arm hanging limply at his side. Something had so terrified him that he had forced himself to flee despite injuries that would have curled a strong man into a fetal ball.

Turning to look in the direction from which the man had come, a new thought occurred to her. He couldn't have come that far from whoever had injured him. If it had been a gang fight, perhaps others lay injured or dying.

Sister Mary Judith turned her steps in that direction. Despite their appallingly violent deeds, she had no fear of the gangs. She moved among them every day, an old nun who posed no threat to anyone, so unattractive that rape never crossed their minds, her clinic so undersupplied and futile that it offered nothing worth stealing. A doctor to set bones and sew up open cuts, boiled rags for bandages, boiled water for washing wounds, a few old surgical instruments, a surgical table, some basic antiseptics, some cots, and an old woman's faith and hardworking hands. Nothing more.

At the entrance into the alley, she smelled death before she saw it, a smell that overwhelmed this place's underlying stench. The smell propelled the old nun forward, adding an increased urgency to her shuffling steps. Over the years her eyes had become accustomed to the darkness night brought to these backstreets and alleys, but tonight's moonlight eliminated the need for that talent, bathing the alley in its ghostly glow. And in the midst of that pale light, seven bodies drained their life's blood into the mud.

Sister Mary Judith moved among them, kneeling briefly beside each victim to place a finger on the carotid artery. One man had fallen facedown several steps from the cluster of bodies, as if he had tried to pursue the one who had fled the alley. And like the fleeing man, this one was shirtless, although, in the moonlight, it seemed he wore a shirt of blood. There was so much of it that the nun gasped when she felt a faint pulse in his throat.

Despite her advancing years, Sister Mary Judith was strong. Nevertheless, the thin layer of skin that covered the hard muscles beneath was so slick with warm blood she had difficulty turning the man onto his back. When she achieved it, her hope that she could save him withered within her soul. Like his back, his chest and arms were covered in shallow cuts. Worse, a deep wound penetrated his left side. Removing her scarf, the sister wadded it into a tight ball, pressing it as deeply into the wound as she could manage before rising to her feet and rushing back the way she had come.

Dr. Jafar Misra's house was less than a block away, but Sister Mary Judith felt the weight of all her years as she hurried along, holding tight to the hope that God would allow her to accomplish one good thing on this sorrow-filled evening. When she reached the narrow door, it took more than a minute for Jafar to open it to her insistent knock. It took another half-hour to help Jafar load the man onto a rickshaw and deliver him to the darkened clinic.

By the time they had laid him on her surgery table, she could barely feel any pulse at all. She took the fact that he still lived as an indication that the Lord was not yet done with this man. If the man's will was as strong as his jawline and lean musculature seemed to indicate, perhaps there was yet hope.

Dr. Misra, working by lamplight, with Sister Mary Judith assisting, bathed the wounds in Betadine and sewed them closed. Then, as she tied off the last knot, as if mocking their feeble attempts to save him, their patient shuddered and passed from this world into the next.

~ ~ ~

There was no tunnel with a beautiful light to beckon him forward. Jack Gregory hadn't expected one. But he hadn't expected this either.

A pea-soup fog cloaked the street, trying its best to hide the worn paving stones beneath his feet. It was London, but this London had a distinct, nineteenth-century feel. Not in a good way either. For some reason it didn't really surprise him. If there was a doorway to hell, Jack supposed a gloomy old London backstreet was as appropriate a setting as any.

While his real body might be bleeding out somewhere in Calcutta, here Jack suffered from no such wounds. He stepped forward, his laced desert combat boots sending wisps of fog swirling around them. Long, cool, steady strides. A narrow alley to his left beckoned him and he didn't fight the feeling. He hadn't started this journey by running away and he'd be damned if he was going to end it running away from whatever awaited him.

The fog wasn't any thicker in the alley. The narrowness just made it feel that way. Jack didn't look back, but he could feel the entrance dwindle behind him as he walked. To either side, an occasional door marred the walls that connected one building to the next, rusty hinges showing just how long it had been since anyone had opened them. It didn't matter. Jack's interest lay in the dark figure that suddenly blocked his path.

The man's face lay hidden in shadow, although it wasn't clear what dim light source was casting the shadows. Still, Jack could see his lips move, could hear the gravel in his voice.

"Are you certain you wish to walk this path?"

Jack paused. "Didn't think I had much choice."

"Not many do."

"I'm listening."

"You've thought about death?"

"Figured it was just a big sleep."

The shadowy figure hesitated.

"Nothing so easy."

"Heaven and hell, then? Enlighten me."

"Keep walking this path and you'll find out. I offer you something different."

"Ahhh. My soul for my life, is it?"

The laugh rumbled deep inside the other's chest. "I've been around a very, very long time, but I'm not your devil."

"Then what are you?"

For several seconds, silence hung in the fog between them.

"Think of me as a coma patient, living an eternity of sensing the things going on around me, unable to experience any of them. I know what's happening, what's about to happen, but I feel nothing. Such immortality is its own special kind of hell. Humanity offers me release from that prison."

"I'm not interested in being your vessel."

"I have limitations. I can only send back one who lingers on death's doorway, not someone who is beyond natural recovery. There are rules. My host must willingly accept my presence and the host remains in control of his or her own being. His nature is unchanged. I, on the other hand, get to experience the host's emotions for the duration of the ride. I can exist in only one host at a time and, once accepted, I remain with that host until he dies."

Jack stared at the shadowed figure's face. Had he seen a flicker of red in those seemingly empty eye sockets?

"No thanks."

"I don't deny that there's a down side. As I said, I don't change a host's nature in any way. But what he feels excites me and some of that excitement feeds back to my host. The overall effect is that he still loves what he loves and hates what he hates, but much hotter. He's the same person he always was, just a little bit more so. And because my intuitions also bleed over, my hosts find themselves drawn to situations that spike their adrenaline. Because of that, few of them live to a ripe old age."

"So you ride these people until they die, then move on to the next person."

"I never said anything about this being a random selection. I have certain needs, and those can't be fulfilled by inhabiting some Siberian dirt farmer or his wife. With all my limitations, I have a very clear sense of those who stride the life and death boundary, fully immersed in humanity's greatest and most terrible events. I always choose a host from this group."

"Such as?"

"Alexander, Nero, Caligula, Attila, Joan of Arc, Napoleon, and hundreds of others, including another Jack who once roamed these London alleys."

"Not a great references list."

"It's not about your notions of good or evil. Whether you want it or not, you are a part of it."

"So my choice is to die now or to open myself to evil?"

"As I said, I can't make you anything you aren't. Hosting me merely amps up your inner nature."

"And you expect me to believe that?"

Again the demon paused. "You pride yourself on your highly developed intuition, your ability to know if someone is lying to you. What is that inner sense telling you now?"

The truth was that, at the moment, it wasn't telling him shit. Or maybe it was, and Jack was just too damn tired to listen. Jack stared at the shadowy figure before him, inhaled deeply, failed to feel a real breath fill his lungs, and decided.

"I guess I can live with that."

~ ~ ~

Doctor Misra had filled out and signed the death certificate for one Jack Gregory, the name on the identification card in the man's wallet. Sister Mary Judith watched as he took one last look at the chiseled face of the dead man on the table, shook his weary head, and departed.

Having swabbed up most of the blood that dripped from her surgery table, Sister Mary Judith straightened, placed her right hand in the small of her back and pressed, as if that simple act could drive away the pain that hard work and old age had placed there. Glancing up at the table and the stitched up corpse that lay atop it, she grabbed a white sheet from the freshly laundered stack, flapped it out, and let it fall through the air to slowly drape the body. As the sheet settled over the dead man's face, she saw something that sent a shiver up her spine, a shallow billowing in the sheet where it covered his mouth.

Leaning close, she peeled back the cotton cloth, once again placing her finger on the carotid artery. One strong pulse brought her erect. Then the man's eyes fluttered open. And as Sister Mary Judith stared into those deep brown orbs, a fleeting red glint within those pupils froze her soul. Unable to deal with the vision that engulfed her, her mind skittered to a safer place, leaving her lips repeating a single phrase, a mantra that would follow her through the remainder of her days.

"Dear Lord, The Ripper walks the earth."

CHAPTER 1

Jack had always craved danger's adrenaline rush. But in the year since his Calcutta deathbed experience and his subsequent rebirth atop the old nun's surgery table, that craving wrapped him like an anaconda, hard enough to make him question the nature of his near-death encounter. Whether the demon was a hallucination or had just left out a few key details, it had changed the way he experienced this world. And if he didn't get control of it, that craving was going to render him every bit as dead as most of the world thought he already was.

As he sat at one of the outdoor tables, sipping cappuccino and gazing out across the Heidelberg marktplatz, he forced himself to relax into the moment. He wasn't the only American in the plaza, but this morning most of the tables beneath the red, blue, green, and white umbrellas were filled with Germans out enjoying a sunny Saturday morning. From where he sat, he could see the

Heidelberg Castle ruins over the tile rooftops of the buildings that lined the square's southeastern edge.

It was ten o'clock in the morning and, outside the Max Bar, a slender fraulein was busy setting frothy glasses of Römer Pils in front of the four men at the table closest to Jack's. From the volume of their conversation and laughter, it was clear this wasn't their first round and wasn't likely to be the last.

Wiping his cappuccino mustache onto a paper napkin, Jack pushed back his chair and began a leisurely stroll across the cobblestones, his path carrying him toward his ten-thirty appointment on the Alte Brücke, Heidelberg's picturesque old bridge across the Neckar River. Officially it was the Karl-Theodor-Brücke, but nobody called it anything but the Old Bridge. The beauty of the nine red-brick arches that supported the walking bridge made it a favorite for both tourists and locals alike. It was a perfect spot for the type of conversation Jack would soon be having.

Jack stopped five meters south of Karl Theodor's statue, leaned up against the stone railing, and looked out over the Neckar to the east. The stunning blond woman who stepped up beside him was tall and slender. Her hair, held back in a French braid, reached halfway down her back.

"Herr Frazier, is it?" Her soft German accent enhanced the tonal quality of her voice.

Jack nodded. "Frau Koenig. You can call me Jack."

She leaned over the stone wall to look down at the water flowing beneath the bridge, then snuggled up close to him, as if they were two lovers standing side by side, taking in the sights.

"You received my package?"

"Yes."

"Did you find it acceptable?"

The stress in her whispered query carried a desperation she failed to hide. Jack had felt that sort of desperation in the voices of all of his recent employers, although the reasons behind that desperation were as varied as the people involved. Alleviating that pain was as important in his choice of employers as the money that came with it.

He smiled. "Your offer was fine."

Her breath released with an audible sigh and, when she leaned her face against his, Jack felt her tears dampen his cheek.

"Thank you, Jack. For the first time in weeks, I feel some hope."

Jack enfolded her in his powerful arms, feeling her fall into the protective embrace. "Hang on to that feeling."

Taking a big breath, Rachel leaned back to stare directly into his eyes. "How should I arrange payment?"

"I only take payment when the job is done."

Recovering her equilibrium, Rachel Koenig wiped her eyes and gazed up into his face.

"Unusual business practice."

"It works for me."

"From what I've heard, that's not surprising. It's why I sought you out. We—I needed the best."

Taking her two delicate hands in his, Jack gave them a firm squeeze and smiled.

"So, now you can relax."

Then, with one last look into her blue eyes, he turned and strolled back along the bridge in the direction from which he'd come.

~ ~ ~

From the corner of his eye, Klaus Diebert watched the couple leaning against each other as he pretended to take in the sights from the opposite side of the bridge. For the last ten days, he'd shadowed Rachel Koenig's every move outside her estate, but this was the first time she'd met someone he didn't know. The way she leaned her head into his as they talked, then dabbed away tears as they parted—they could have been secret lovers. But Klaus knew everything there was to know about the former supermodel and wife of Rolf Koenig, founder and CEO of Hamburg Technautics. Klaus knew she had no current lovers, male or female, not even her husband.

Watching the lean man with the short, spiked-up blond hair slide through the crowd as he walked back toward the southern bridge towers, a sense of familiarity seized Klaus. He didn't know the man, yet he did. One predator's recognition of another. And this one made his skin crawl.

No doubt about it. Rachel Koenig had called in a heavy hitter.

As Rachel turned in the opposite direction, Klaus fought the choice that suddenly confronted him. His job was to stay on Rachel. But this might be his best chance to find out just who had decided to involve himself in Rachel's business. Right now, Klaus badly wanted to know the answer to that question.

Making up his mind, Klaus began casually strolling along the bridge after the stranger, letting Rachel disappear among the pedestrians behind him.

CHAPTER 2

Jack had spotted Rachel's unwanted tail as she approached him. Now, as he walked away from her along the Alte Brücke, he felt the man's indecision. Predictably, the tail disengaged from Rachel and attached itself to his backside. Feeling anticipation rise up inside, Jack damped it back down. Self-discipline had become his obsession, the only way to master his newfound addiction.

Passing through the tower-gate on the Alte Brücke's south side, Jack crossed the street and entered the Wirtshaus Zum Nepomuk, taking a seat by the window. It was one of Jack's favorite spots in Heidelberg, good food, good drink, and good atmosphere, all in a small package. Right now it was giving his tail a problem. Following Jack inside would be a dead giveaway, and standing out on the street wouldn't do either. Also, since the gasthaus was situated on the corner across from the Alte Brücke, there were no convenient shops or bars from which a watcher could casually maintain surveillance while Jack ate lunch. And he planned a leisurely repast. Might as well start this new relationship on his terms, especially since it wasn't likely to last.

Holding up a finger, Jack signaled the waitress. "Die speisekarte, bitte?"

In moments, she returned with the leather-bound menu, took his drink order, and departed. Although Jack knew the menu by heart, he took his time, using the menu and the fact that the restaurant interior was darker than the street outside to mask his study of his opponent. The man was a couple of inches taller than Jack, about six-foot-three, flaxen hair tied back in a short pony tail, with weightlifter musculature. He wore a tan blazer over khaki pants. Although no bulge gave it away, the way his left arm moved told Jack he wore a holstered gun beneath that shoulder.

The man stopped on the opposite side of the street and looked around, letting his gaze casually sweep the gasthaus before moving off to the west. Taking a seat beneath a tree alongside Neckerstaden, he leaned back, just a man enjoying a leisurely summer day. There were two problems with that approach. It placed him in the open where Jack could watch him and ensured the tail could only see the gasthaus entrance, not the man within.

Jack ordered his meal, then sipped his beer until his plate arrived. As usual, the Jaeger Schnitzel was to die for. But he wouldn't be the one dying today.

Across the street, the man beneath the tree stood up, looked toward the gasthaus, and raised his cell phone to his ear. In so doing, he was weighed, measured, and found wanting. An impatient man.

Jack signaled the waitress.

"Ich möchte zahlen."

She handed him the check and he handed her fifteen euros. Waving away the change, he stepped through the door and out into the bright sunlight.

Jack turned left, letting his feet carry him back onto the Alte Brücke and across the Neckar, before cutting diagonally across Neuenheimer Landstrasse. As he turned up the narrow Schlangenweg trail, he felt his stalker pick up the pace, trying to keep Jack in sight. With the houses dropping away behind him, the walking trail wound its way up the densely wooded hill. Rounding a bend, Jack stepped behind a tree, stopped, and waited. He didn't have to wait long.

As the bigger man rounded the bend in the trail, Jack's flying elbow caught him flush on the nose, dropping him to the ground as if he'd been pole-axed. Before the fellow could roll to his knees, Jack kicked him in the side of the head and dragged him into the dense underbrush.

Laying the man on his back, Jack took a cell-phone photo of his face and then fished his wallet, passport, and phone from his pockets. Plugging a small attachment into his phone, Jack swiped each of the man's credit cards through the slot in the device, also swiping the magnetic strip on the man's ID card. Klaus Diebert.

Jack opened the passport, taking more photos as he flipped through its pages. Then, attaching a cable between his cellphone and Klaus's, he copied the contents of Klaus's phone to his.

Without bothering to wipe away his own prints, Jack returned everything to Klaus's pockets. The sooner the bad guys found out exactly who they were dealing with the better. Leaving the Glock 17 in its shoulder holster and the ankle knife in its sheath, Jack turned Klaus on his side so he wouldn't drown in the blood draining from his broken nose.

Then, with a quick check to verify that no passersby were visible on the Schlangenweg trail, he began the leisurely stroll back to his motorcycle.

CHAPTER 3

Thirty kilometers southeast of Heidelberg, Rachel drove the winding road to the castle known as Königsberg, the thirty-meter-high granite walls giving way to the towering edifice that rose above the vineyard-draped hillsides, the castle's spires rising like the pikes of ancient knights doing their best to thrust back the modern world. As she passed through the arched gateway into the inner grounds, she let the Mercedes idle down, paused to admire the engine's low thrum, then switched it off, stepped out, and tossed the keys to the groom. Not really a groom. It just felt like she should be tossing her horse's reins to a groom. The baroness returning to her lord baron's keep.

Bypassing the butler holding open the massive door into the great hall, she felt the familiar feeling. Despite the best efforts of the priceless carpets and tapestries, the cold leached in through the granite floors and walls to freeze her soul. No matter how many servants her husband placed at her disposal, she still felt trapped. A prized bird in a gilded cage. Nothing more.

Stepping into the small elevator that would carry her to the living quarters on the fourth floor, Rachel pressed the button. When she stepped out into the south hallway, she paused before the huge painting of the first Baron Koenig, ridiculously garbed in tights and a ruffled red jacket, seated in a chair that looked like a throne. In the soft lighting, his eyes seemed to follow her disapprovingly, as if to imply that she should have used the stairs.

A vision of the man she had just hired leapt into her mind. Jack Gregory. A.k.a. Jack Frazier. A.k.a. The Ripper. The reputedly dead ex-CIA agent turned enforcer for hire seemed to be everything she had hoped. Just over six feet tall, he moved like an Olympic athlete. His short, spiked blond hair framed an angular face with brown eyes that drilled into her soul. Snake charmer's eyes. When she'd leaned against him, she'd felt lean, hard muscle ripple beneath his skin. But she'd detected something else in the man, an otherworldly energy, as if his body could barely contain the force within. Like one of those plasma globes with electrical arcs crawling around its interior, perpetually seeking release, Jack exuded an aura of caged, deadly electricity.

What had he said to her?

"So, now you can relax."

Something in his voice, something in the way he'd looked deep into her eyes made her believe. And dear God, she wanted to believe.

She hadn't always been so vulnerable. The daughter of Hans and Crista Veigert, she'd been the favorite child. The popular girl. It had not surprised her when *Sports Illustrated* had asked her to do its swimsuit shoot. It was the level of competition she'd been born for. After that, the magazine covers, the money, and the fame had come so easily. Nothing surprised her. Not even when the famed industrialist playboy, Rolf Koenig, had fallen under her spell. After all, she was the chosen one. It was her destiny.

What a massive double-handful of crap.

She'd been a spring lamb, primed for slaughter. But Rolf hadn't slaughtered her. He'd placed her on a very public pedestal. And in so doing, he'd imprisoned her more thoroughly than if he'd chained her in Königsberg's deepest dungeon, a prime tribute to the Koenig Barony's medieval roots.

Walking down the south hallway, Rachel entered her private chambers. Private chambers. A vivid description of her marital status. Rolf's true love had always been technology. Technology brought money and money bought power. Once legally married, he'd lost all interest in his trophy wife. She was just one more checkmark on Rolf's to-do list. Power was what he wanted. It was what Vladimir Roskov wanted. And unlike Rachel, the Russian mobster had Rolf by the balls. Unfortunately, that meant he owned her, too.

Stripping out of her clothes, Rachel let them fall to the floor, turning to stare at her reflection in the full-length, mirrored closet doors. It had been five years since the *Sports Illustrated* cover and, as far as Rachel could tell, she still looked just as good. Turning to look over her shoulder at the reflection of her Pilates-tightened ass, Rachel pursed her lips, slipped between her sheets, squeezed her eyes closed, and hugged a fluffy pillow to her chest. Whether Rolf appreciated it or not, she still had a very nice ass.

Hopefully The Ripper could save it.

CHAPTER 4

Rolf Koenig stepped off the corporate jet's bottom stair onto the dark surface of the Yubileiny Airfield and stretched his tall, slender body, feeling the anticipation of the upcoming event leach from the taxiway through the soles of his Italian shoes, directly into his soul. He shook hands with Igor Laskov, the Russian charged with ensuring that the mating of his special payload with the Proton launch vehicle went smoothly. And although the launch date was still a few weeks away, the importance of this mission meant that Koenig had the scientist's full attention.

This wasn't Rolf's first trip to the Baikonur Cosmodrome, but it was the first time he'd arrived at sunset. Behind Igor, the great orange ball of the sun settled to the surface of the vast, flat expanse, seeming to grow larger as it silhouetted the distant towers and buildings of Proton Launch Pad 39 against a blood-red sky. Of all the lonely spots on earth, this one had an otherworldly feel all its own.

"Stunning, yes?" Igor's voice broke through Rolf's reverie.

"We could be standing on another planet."

"If governments learn to listen to men like us, we will."

"Even governments can be brought to heel by those of sufficient vision."

Rolf stepped toward the black limousine, its right rear door held open by a Russian security guard. As Igor climbed in the other side, the sedan's engine rumbled to life.

Igor looked inquiringly at Rolf. "Would you like to go to the hotel and get a night's sleep after your long trip?"

"No. Take me to see it."

Building 92A-50 occupied a spot on the cosmodrome's northwest corner, the Proton rocket preparation and payload mating facility positioned adjacent to Launch Pads 24 and 39. Bigger than two football fields, the building currently housed two pieces of equipment that Rolf cared about deeply. By the time the car pulled up near the entrance that would grant him access to that staging area, only the twin floodlights above the door pushed back the darkness.

Although he knew exactly where the XLRMV-1 payload rested while his engineers performed final checks, Rolf let Igor lead the way. The Russian hardly looked the part of Russia's most brilliant rocket scientist. He could have played the stereotypical Soviet era general in a remake of an old Cold War movie. But beneath that gruff exterior beat the heart of a man in love with his work. He had known that Rolf had no interest in freshening up at the hotel because Igor himself would have had no such interest.

Any spacecraft launch was exciting stuff, but this one would be special. A previous launch had carried aloft the other half of this mission, the lander that would gently set this payload on the surface of the moon. Once released, Rolf's module would dock with that lander and the mated pair would begin their history-making journey. After landing, the Experimental Lunar Robotic Mining Vehicle dubbed XLRMV-1 would embark on its four-year mission to prove the viability of remotely mining rare earth metals and staging them for transport back to earth. The duration and required power for this mission mandated the most sophisticated nuclear power generator ever created for a space vehicle.

Getting prepped for the clean room took time, but Rolf had done it so often over the years it had become routine. Once suited up and inside, he walked directly to the nuclear generator that sat on its own cradle, not scheduled for mounting on the Proton launch vehicle until the six plutonium power cells were attached, and that wouldn't happen until shortly before launch. The man that strode to meet him was Heinrich Glatch, his lead engineer in charge of the night shift.

"Herr Koenig. It's good to see you got in okay. How was your flight?"

"Long."

No need for small talk or briefings. His team had learned long ago that Rolf despised these corporate wastes of time. He already knew that things were progressing precisely on schedule.

Moving up beside the generator, Rolf placed a gloved hand atop it. It was Rolf's design from top to bottom, a design that would provide all the power the XLRMV-1 would require. He walked around the gleaming engineering marvel, his familiar presence ignored by his team. Comparing what he was seeing to his clear mental image of the design specifications, Rolf felt a slow smile lift the corners of his mouth.

There was no doubt in his mind that this power package would enable the most advanced mining robot ever constructed to prove that companies could make money mining the moon—vast hordes of it. He would be the modern Queen Isabella, launching Columbus on the first of many missions to funnel riches back from a new world.

Unfortunately, neither this power package nor this mining robot was going to get the opportunity to accomplish that mission.

Despite how exquisitely the power package had been designed and constructed, it had been primarily designed for rapid replacement by its doppelganger. That replacement package was currently undergoing final assembly and testing inside a warehouse in Kyzylorda, two hundred and fifty kilometers to the southeast, a warehouse owned and operated by Vladimir Roskov. And that package was going to pave the way for all the extraterrestrial claims Rolf and others would stake.

The raft of international treaties that currently restricted extraterrestrial body claimant rights prevented profitable exploitation. So, before he proved just how incredibly profitable it could be for corporations to stake claim to huge sections of the moon, asteroids, and planets, those rules had to be rewritten. And that meant casting aside their shortsighted author, the United States of America. In the end, all advances sprouted from the seeds of exploitation these shortsighted, politically-correct rules were designed to poison.

As Rolf stepped back to gaze proudly at his creation, he knew that it and each of the engineering marvels that would follow owed their future existence to the evil twin that was about to be born in Kyzylorda. Without a doubt, that beautiful-ugly baby would change the world. And just like in Isabella's day, the spread of mankind across vast, dark seas was about to commence, to the greater glory of all.

CHAPTER 5

"Tell me what you've got."

That voice, even if only through the phone, always gave Rita Chavez a cold thrill, like the man had just slipped a sweating ice cube along the small of her bare back, arching her body at precisely the right moment. It was a bright Riviera memory, courtesy of a hot summer evening, the InterContinental Carlton Cannes, and the fascinating CIA killer known as Jack Gregory.

But even though he clearly wasn't as DECEASED as his official file labeled him, Jack wasn't CIA anymore. And Rita shouldn't be giving him shit. Then again, a girl had to make a living. And through a series of offshore bank accounts, Jack was paying her very, very well. That was okay. She was worth every euro.

"Klaus Diebert, a.k.a. Karl Weiden, a.k.a. James Reirdon. A record as long as your arm, but never more than two consecutive years in the slammer. Interesting thing, that. All those prosecuting attorneys suddenly losing their courtroom mojo when they went after Klaus."

"Why is that?"

"Nothing to do with him. He works for an organization that reports to Vladimir Roskov."

"Ahh."

"You know him?"

"I know his dossier."

"His CIA dossier?"

"Yes."

"Interested in his complete Interpol file?"

"That's what I'm paying you for."

"And if I could provide his FSB file?"

"That'd be worth a little extra."

"Define a little."

"Worth your while."

A smile spread across Rita's face. She just wished he was in Paris right now so she could deliver the package in person.

"Jack. You know you'll always be my only love."

"That won't get you more."

Rita laughed her deep, throaty laugh and then clicked the button on her MacBook Pro.

"Okay, Jack. Here it comes."

CHAPTER 6

Vladimir "Vlad" Roskov had little tolerance for failure. Little as in *none*. As he stared at the big man strapped to the chair in the center of the warehouse, anger pulsed through the veins that lined the sides of his forehead, making them writhe like tiny purple snakes. Normally he left failure's punishment to his lieutenants, but not today. Today he would make a very public example of what lay in store for one of his people should they choose to violate his specific orders and go off mission.

To his right, Gregor Lins angled his video camera to frame the scene to max effect, so that the glare from the high windows lining the west wall provided optimal lighting. Most of the time, cell-phone video was good enough, but not today. Today Vlad wanted the video quality only an expensive camera could provide.

When Vlad shoved the Sig Sauer's muzzle into Klaus Diebert's mouth, the man's pleading came to a gagging end, his eyes rolling in wild terror. Grabbing a handful of Klaus's blond hair, Vlad turned his head to the right, facing directly toward the camera, twisted the Sig, and pulled the trigger. The bullet carried several teeth and part of Klaus's jawbone out through the ragged hole in his left cheek, spraying blood in an arc that would look spectacular on the internet. Klaus's screams mingled with the gunshot's dying echo to add just the right acoustic touch.

Releasing his hold on Klaus's hair, Vlad stepped back to admire his handiwork. To his credit, unlike many others who had been the subject of Vladimir Roskov's art, Klaus didn't pass out. That was good. Maybe they could get through this in one clean take, instead of having to pause every few minutes to revive his star performer.

Due to the bullet taking a large part of Klaus's tongue out through his cheek, the man's noises had devolved into a gargling, bestial keening. Setting the Sig on the metal table to his rear, Vlad picked up the five-pound, ball-peen hammer and turned back toward the man whose face had become a horrible parody of an evil clown's.

Placing a hand on Klaus's head, Vlad stared into the gargling man's eyes before dropping to a knee to remove Klaus's shoes and socks. Then, with the grace of a London Symphony Orchestra conductor alerting his musicians, he raised the hammer above his head. Whereas the opening act had been strictly for show, the main act was all about the sound.

By the time the video recording stopped, the sun had sunk below the horizon, sunset's red glow bathing the scene in a fitting, bloody light. Vladimir laid the slippery hammer back on the table, stripped off his clothes and walked across the concrete floor to the industrial shower on the north wall, feeling the satisfaction that only a good day's work could bring. Without waiting for the water to warm up, Vlad stepped beneath the sprinkler showerhead, grabbed the half-used yellow soap bar and lathered up, letting the red swirls carry the blood and flesh away from his body and down the drain.

When he stepped out to take the towel Gregor held for him, he took his time, making sure his body and hair were completely dry before putting on the new Armani suit that hung from a rack along the near wall. By the time he stepped out of the warehouse and into the black Mercedes, he looked like he'd just walked out of the Berlin Opera.

He had no worries. With Gregor directing the cleanup team, the warehouse would soon be returned to its normal state. Vlad took the camera from Gregor's outstretched hand and, with the push of a button, raised the rear window. Then with a one-handed signal to his driver, he launched the powerful automobile into the night.

CHAPTER 7

He was ten minutes late. He wasn't trying to make a statement; it was just how this day had started.

Deputy Director Nolan Trent's steps took him directly across the sixteen-foot diameter of the Central Intelligence Agency seal, over its eagle bearing the familiar spiked gray compass rose, between the gunpowder gray and off-white columns, and across the gray and off-white tiles toward this morning's meeting. The many shades of gray found in the lobby of the original CIA headquarters entered his eyes, the ghost of a forthright past, a haunting reminder of his agency's glory years.

The new, adjacent CIA headquarters, with its artistic lines, colors, and airy courtyard, wept false openness and civility. It made Nolan's skin crawl. It was one of the reasons he was using the old 233C conference room for this morning's meeting. But there were more important reasons he didn't want this meeting conducted in his executive conference room.

Stepping off the elevator, Nolan turned down a hallway lit by the same white lights that illuminated the ground-floor lobby, his leather shoes extracting small squeaks of outrage from the immaculately clean tiles. Opening the door to the small conference room, the deputy director stepped inside, closed the door, and moved to take his seat at the head of the table. Seeing that the other three participants were present, Nolan touched a button on his console, activating the room's electronic lock, an action that also illuminated the *CLASSIFIED MEETING IN PROGRESS* sign outside the room.

Raising his blue eyes, Nolan scanned the faces of those around the six-foot conference table. Christie Parson sat immediately to his left, her taut face and throat elegantly framed by her shoulder-length brown hair, her pinstriped gray pantsuit more expensive than anything Nolan owned, except for his car and house. At thirty-four, Christie looked as good as she had at twenty-eight. Better, actually. There was something to be said for the twin C's of confidence and competence that only came through repeated success.

Next to her, a balding Craig Faragut, broad of shoulder and waist, had failed to manage the transition from field operative to desk jockey with anything approaching elegance, something his rumpled, black, off-the-rack suit screamed to the rafters, or in this case, to the hidden steel beams supporting the building's upper levels. But what Faragut lacked in the public graces, he more than made up for in intelligence and loyalty. That combination of qualities made him Nolan's go-to guy.

On the right side of the rectangular oak table, as isolated from the others as he was from humanity in general, Jacob Knox leaned back in the Herman Miller chair until it appeared ready to tip over, his eyes as dark as his short, cropped black hair, seemingly all pupil. Those eyes stared directly at Nolan, as inscrutable as the man himself.

Together, this group formed his core team.

Nolan nodded at Craig and the big man rose from his chair, extracted a small handheld electronic device from his satchel, turned it on, and made a pass around the room. After a glance at the display, Craig nodded in satisfaction and returned to his seat.

"We're good."

Although the CIA regularly swept all offices for transmitting devices, Nolan believed in taking his own precautions, especially when it came to meetings like this, where lines of political correctness were certain to be crossed and where the restraining bands of legality would be stretched, if not broken.

Nolan leaned forward so that his elbows rested on the table, his fingers intertwined. He didn't yet know the subject of this meeting and that bothered him. The fact that Craig had requested it without telling him didn't bode well. Yet it emphasized the sensitivity of the information to be conveyed and the importance of the decisions required.

"Okay, Craig. What've you got?"

Picking up the remote control from the table in front of him, Craig powered on the monitor that took up a significant portion of the wall opposite Nolan. The face that stared out of the photograph exuded power and malice, a scarred, angular visage that could only belong to one man. Vladimir Roskov. The man headed one of the world's most violent crime syndicates, the infamous Russian Mafia. He was also one of the CIA's most important sources of intelligence, a man referred to in top secret communications as Asset Zulu.

"This morning I received a message from our man in Kazakhstan. It seems that someone has placed a contract on Roskov."

Nolan laughed. "What an idiot."

"That's what I thought. Then I got a look at the attached documents."

Craig thumbed a button on the remote and Roskov's image was replaced by an assortment of documents spread across a gray steel desktop. As Craig cycled through the pictures that followed, Nolan found himself staring at identification documents, credit cards, and passport pages, all apparently belonging to a man named Klaus Diebert.

"Who is he? The hitter or the idiot who placed the contract?"

"Neither. He was one of Roskov's men, someone who got himself rousted by our hitter. Roskov was displeased enough to post a video of Diebert's punishment on the web."

"Then why am I looking at his documents?"

Craig advanced to the next image, a tight zoom of a Visa card showing the swirl of several fingerprints. As the display moved from one image to the next, each document continued to show a number of fingerprints, but the picture page from Klaus's passport slapped Nolan in the face. There, so clearly defined that they seemed to be acid etched into the document, a complete set of right-hand fingerprints. There could be no doubt. The page had been turned sideways. Then the man had pressed all four fingers firmly down on the right three quarters and followed up by rolling his right thumb across the space just to the left of those prints. Nolan had seen the pattern too often, having performed the action after placing his fingers on an ink blotter. This wasn't an announcement of the man's identity, it was a threat. The meaning could not be clearer.

I'm coming for you.

"You've got to be kidding me," Nolan said. "Someone has the balls to call out Roskov?"

"More interesting than that, Roskov passed this along to us."

Nolan rose from his chair and walked around the conference table to stare at the image on the screen from a foot away, reaching out to trace those prints with his own fingers, as if that act could grant him some psychic insight into their owner's mind.

"So who is it?"

The photograph that appeared on the screen so surprised Nolan that he stepped back, his left hip bumping roughly into the conference table's sharp corner.

"Impossible!"

"I've confirmed the identification." Christie Parson's smooth voice brought Nolan's head around. "Those are Jack Gregory's prints."

Nolan turned to stare at the monitor once more. The photograph showed Jack Gregory's naked body stretched out on a bloody table, his upper torso covered in crudely stitched wounds. Beneath the table, between the footprints made by the doctor and the old nun who had assisted him, pools of blood reflected the camera flash. On the screen beside the photograph was a signed and witnessed copy of Gregory's Calcutta death certificate, the text printed in both Hindi and English, India's official and semi-official languages.

As Nolan stared at the screen, his mind worked to reconcile this new information. Jack Gregory had been dead for a year now. Nolan had never liked anyone who failed to follow procedure and Gregory had set the standard for ignoring operational protocols. After the death of his brother, Robert, the agent had become impossible to control. Even though he had maintained his fan club within the agency, the time had come to pull the plug. Given the opportunity to offer up Priest Williams, the man Gregory blamed for his brother's death, Nolan had acted. There, on the monitor, lay the proof of that operation's success. One less rogue agent polluting his agency.

"How was Gregory's death verified?" asked Christie.

Craig shrugged. "After taking the photograph and filling out the death certificate, the doctor left the old nun to finish cleaning up. Our people got to the clinic the next morning. Place was still a mess. The nun had lost it. Apparently she had some sort of stroke or something, because she never finished the cleanup. They found her sitting, huddled in a corner, rocking back and forth, muttering rubbish. Gregory's body was gone, but there was plenty of his blood on the floor. Nobody could have survived that kind of blood loss. And yes, we verified it was Gregory's blood."

"So where was the body?"

"We figured the Ghurkari gang took it. Probably played a grand football game with his head."

Returning to his seat, Nolan pursed his lips. "Then why are Gregory's fingerprints all over Diebert's documents?"

Getting no response, Nolan asked another question. "Why did Roskov send this to us?"

Craig Faragut answered. "I think he wants us to know he's about to clean up our mess."

Nolan nodded. That normally would have worked for him. But not now. Not with Rolf Koenig about to bring all these years of preparation to fruition in Kazakhstan. Right now he just couldn't afford to have Roskov distracted by Jack Gregory.

He turned to look at the only person who hadn't yet spoken.

"Whether Roskov wants our help or not isn't important. Make the problem go away. Any means available."

Jacob Knox's lips shifted into what might have been a smile.

"I'm on it."

CHAPTER 8

Because Jack craved action, he refused to yield to that constant desire, forcing himself to sleep at least six hours when he could get it. It was why he maintained his rigorous schedule of deep meditation and tai chi. It was why he played a chess variant called Brazilian Bullet Chess. As in combat, the key to this game was to get inside your opponent's decision cycle, making him react to what you were doing, rather than the reverse. It was about anticipating your opponent's move, responding with ever increasing pressure, using your opponent's speed against him, or letting the clock break him if he countered with deep thought.

Jack had always followed his gut, but his intuition had taken a remarkable turn for the better. Whether it was chess or physical combat, under the influence of that enhanced state of awareness, he could sense his opponent's coming move as they made the decision. His intuition had its benefits. Unfortunately, he couldn't trust it.

Not that it was wrong. Far from it. The problem was one of targeting rather than accuracy.

Following his gut could take him down an alley to his target or divert him from his true mission, just because of what he sensed along that path. He could smell danger and it drew him like blood pulled a shark through dark waters. He never knew exactly what waited; only that he hungered for it.

Watching the clock run out on his latest opponent, Jack reached across the chessboard, shook the woman's hand, and stood up. The venue for today's match was a park bench along the southeastern side of the Neckar River. His opponent, a university professor, had just been the latest to succumb to his peculiar skill. The intellectuals always fell hardest, as their memorized opening sequences gave way to thoughtful incredulity and, finally, to slack-jawed disbelief.

Making his way back to the two-room, third-floor apartment he had rented under the name Greg Hollywell, Jack hung his jacket on the rack just inside the door, stripped off his shoulder holster, and set the nine-millimeter H&K P30S on the chrome-legged kitchen table, right next to his laptop. When he logged in, a new email with an encrypted attachment awaited his attention. The sender address read *WatfordElephant87654@gmail.com*, a temporary user account that had been set up for this exchange and would never be used again.

Jack right-clicked the attachment, selected *Save As*, renamed the file to Roskov.exe, and saved it to his desktop. Running the new executable file brought up a window with a blank text box containing a blinking cursor and an OK button on the bottom right. Opening his browser, Jack navigated to the Wikipedia page for Baker Street and Waterloo Railway, copied the second paragraph, pasted it into the empty text box, and then clicked the OK button. He was rewarded with a spinning hourglass cursor above a message that read:

"Decrypting contents . . . "

Jack walked to the fridge, took out a diet soda, popped open the tab, and tilted it to his lips, savoring the carbonated beverage's mild burn on his tongue before swallowing. When he returned to the laptop, the window and its spinning cursor had disappeared, leaving a folder labeled Roskov on his desktop. By the time Jack finished examining its contents, the sun had set, leaving the apartment swathed in a darkness that was pushed back by the laptop's eldritch glow.

Locking the laptop screen, Jack flipped on the kitchen light, made himself a bratwurst and mustard sandwich, and chased it down with a German beer chilled American cold. Then, stripping off his clothes, he stepped into the tiny shower, positioned the handheld shower head to its topmost mounting post, and let the hot spray wash away another day in a counterclockwise spiral through the small round hole of the shower drain.

CHAPTER 9

The mind worm had been called by many names, among them, Anchanchu. Loosely translated, it meant *The Rider*. Although humans thought of it as a demonic being from their various religious traditions, the truth was something far stranger. It was an entity beyond the four dimensions that compose space-time, able to observe all possible timelines but, until it had discovered the human race, unable to experience any of them, its existence a frustrating hell from which humanity's arrival on the cosmic stage had offered release.

Anchanchu learned that, as a human straddled the life–death threshold, it could establish a parasitic link to that person's limbic system. The mind worm required the host's cooperation but, once accepted, it could stimulate the human's physical responses far more effectively than a doctor's adrenaline injection or electric paddles. If the body was not too badly damaged, Anchanchu could shove its host back across that life–death boundary.

The mind worm's limbic attachment enabled it to feel human emotion, to experience the world through its host's senses, to amplify its host's feelings and bodily responses. But Anchanchu's lack of connection to the higher brain functions meant it was unable to sense its host's thoughts.

While humans offered the mind worm the experiences it craved, they had induced within it a deep and abiding fear of the loss of its playthings. Unfortunately, an alarmingly small fraction of humanity's timelines lasted beyond their notion of the twenty-first century AD, most terminating with the humans destroying themselves or attracting the attention of advanced species that had no interest in the preservation of primitive cultures.

Anchanchu knew its hosts better than they knew themselves. It understood what drove them. And with its ability to sense what was coming, it was easy to see the paths along which their amplified passions would carry them. Breaking a new mount to rein was different in every case. With some it was as simple as amping-up specific desires. Though some struggled to resist its siren call and to maintain their sense of self-control; even the most strong-willed succumbed within months.

But Jack Gregory was different. He crawled a chaotic web of possible futures, his choices determined by such a complex mixture of passion, self-discipline, and his own intuitive sense of what lay just around the next corner that the mind worm found itself unable to determine where those choices would lead.

It was new. It was disconcerting. It was thrilling.

Anchanchu had always searched for such a human, one whose actions produced inflection points where humanity's fate hung in the balance, one who walked paths that might extend mankind's future. And although it couldn't foretell which of those paths this mount would take, Anchanchu was certain of one thing. It was in for one hell of a ride.

CHAPTER 10

The room opened off the southeast end of the short, second-story hallway. Here in Gasthaus Traurig, in the heart of the medieval walled city of Rothenburg, while the other guests were out on the Night Watchman's tour or sampling the local cuisine, Jack sat on the double bed in his three-by-four-meter room with the laptop propped across his folded legs, as his vision of the mission fractured into a five-hundred-piece puzzle.

The picture Rachel Koenig had painted was of her politically connected industrialist husband being blackmailed by a ruthless crime boss, forced to pass along confidential insider information to the Russian Mafia, with threats against Rachel used for additional leverage.

As Jack worked his way through the latest data from the lovely and talented Rita Chavez, the strands of Rachel's story unraveled before his eyes. While Roskov had interests that could make significant money from the type of financial information Rolf Koenig was privy to, his recent activity hinted at something far more troubling. Jack stared at a timeline of Roskov's travels over the past several months, something he'd specifically asked Rita to research, something she'd initially resisted. It was a search with too much potential to attract attention for information of little value. But Jack had anteed up a bonus and, as usual, Rita delivered.

Up until six weeks ago, Roskov spent most of his time in Kazakhstan, with frequent trips to Russia and, to a lesser extent, to the former Soviet republics of Georgia, Latvia, and Lithuania. Only occasionally did his travels take him to Western Europe and only for a few days at a time. But lately he'd taken up residence in Berlin, supposedly to oversee operations at Gottfried Transport, a trucking company recently purchased by Keigel Holdings, one of Roskov's shell corporations. His move to Berlin also corresponded to the commencement of his intimidation of the Koenigs.

There were other pieces that didn't fit. Rolf Koenig, for one. The man was more than the CEO of a major space technology company. He was intricately connected with top power brokers within the Deutscher Bundestag and rumored to have parliamentary political ambitions, his future possibly even involving a run at the German chancellorship. Why would he jeopardize that by associating with Roskov?

Jack leaned back against the headboard. This was normally the phase of an operation where he developed a detailed understanding of his opponent. It was what the military referred to as intelligence preparation of the battlefield. Know your enemy. Know the terrain. Know the conditions under which the battle will be fought. During this process, Jack moved about randomly, picking his locations without establishing any perceptible pattern to his movements, never staying in one location longer than twenty-four hours. Right now he should be touching up the fine details of his plan, not figuring out why his employer had lied to him, not deciding if this was a setup.

On the Alte Brücke in Heidelberg, Rachel hadn't been aware of the man tailing her. Of that Jack was certain. And Klaus Diebert hadn't been expecting Jack. If Rachel had been setting him up, Jack would have sensed it, and a setup would have involved more and better men than Klaus. That meant Rachel didn't really know what was going on. Just enough to be very, very scared.

And from what Jack was learning, she had damn good reason to be.

CHAPTER 11

The ICE train departed Munich's Hauptbahnhof at 12:36 p.m., beginning the five hour and forty-eight minute trip to Berlin precisely on time. The Intercity-Express comfort car featured first class seats with available WiFi, individual video screens, and sockets for personal laptops, tablets, or cell phones. Jack stowed his travel bag in the overhead rack, then took a solo seat next to the window.

Outside the window, the city, with its half-timbered houses, gave way to the rolling hills of the Bavarian countryside, the red-striped, white train picking up speed as it snaked its way along the winding track.

His attention shifted to the brunette couple seated three rows up on the left. They'd entered the car after Jack had taken his seat and had passed him by, taking no notice, the man in a two-piece charcoal-gray business suit, the woman wearing a navy skirt and blazer over a chiffon blouse. Two business people discussing an important upcoming presentation. The man placed their bags in the overhead rack and removed and folded his jacket, placing it atop his travel case before sliding into the seat beside her. Since their departure from the station, they'd focused on the contents of a folder they passed back and forth, never once glancing in Jack's direction. They weren't bad.

Jack was certain of two things. These two didn't work for Roskov and they weren't business executives or salesmen. Sophisticated agency training illuminated their movements, giving them an aura of lethal competency not required for selling widgets. Clearly, they weren't armed. Or at least they had no firearms on their persons. In their bags, probably, but nothing readily available. That meant they weren't on this train to take him down, just to make sure he reached his scheduled destination. Whatever was going down would happen there.

The fact that he was under surveillance puzzled him. He hadn't been tailed to Munich and nobody else knew his travel agenda. The fact that at least two agents were on this train eliminated the possibility that he'd been recognized by someone at the Munich train station. That meant some agency was actively hunting him, using all the sophisticated means at its disposal, specifically facial recognition technology. As prolific as video cameras were in the U.S., Germany had a camera density that made that laughable. But for the CIA or the German BfV to access that footage on a broad scale indicated a high-profile operation.

So someone had figured out Jack wasn't really dead. Not surprising. He hadn't exactly tried to stay invisible. But his private contractor work had only involved making his high-profile clients' problems disappear, nothing that should have ruffled either agency's feathers. With headquarters in Cologne and Berlin, the BfV seemed the most likely party to appear, but these two felt like CIA.

Since this was a high-speed, non-stop train, getting off early wasn't a great option. Besides, it would just serve to let his hunters know he was onto them. They'd realize that soon enough. Removing his laptop from his case, Jack woke it from sleep mode, plugged it into his seat's power receptacle, typed in his twenty-character password, and launched the wipe utility that would perform the multi-pass digital shredding of all data on the encrypted hard drive. A dialogue box popped up, center screen.

If you are certain you wish to permanently destroy all data on this system, type YES at the prompt.

Jack typed *YES* and pressed the ENTER key. He watched the program begin its work, then closed the laptop lid and set it on the floor by his feet. With the limited amount of data on its solid-state drive, it would finish its task long before the train arrived in Berlin. Despite the hardware encryption on the SSD, redundancy never hurt.

Leaning back in his seat, Jack closed his eyes, using the train sounds to slide into restful meditation. John and Jane Doe couldn't surprise him. But they'd set the cosmic dice tumbling and his next chance for rest might be a very long time coming. Feeling the thrill of anticipation surge through his body, Jack refocused on his meditation.

He would enforce self-control. Every day, he was getting better and better at it. And as Jack focused on that mantra, repeating it over and over while he sank deeper into meditation, he almost found himself believing it.

CHAPTER 12

Dr. Denise Jennings stared at the computer screen, her detailed mind working to comprehend what Big John was trying to tell her.

Most people believed the NSA actively monitored American citizens, keeping a vast collection of private information in its Utah data center. The truth was something far different, something the public would find infinitely more frightening. In her classified briefings to the president and to the appropriate congressional oversight committees, Denise described the system as a sophisticated data-mining cyber-structure, hence the name Big John, after the legendary miner in the old Jimmy Dean ballad.

The truth was that even Denise didn't understand how Big John did what he did. No data center could hold the information that coursed through Big John's synaptic system, a system that encompassed an estimated sixty-eight percent of the earth's computing power.

The fact that Denise, who had designed the software that formed Big John's core underpinning, didn't understand how he worked wasn't surprising. An outgrowth of the most advanced parallel computing research from Los Alamos and Lawrence Livermore, supplemented by work from MIT, Caltech, Carnegie Mellon, and others, Big John was a collection of genetic algorithms operating on a vast, polymorphic neural net.

It was fed by a software kernel Denise had developed in the latter part of the twentieth century under a secret government program designed to support and encourage the hacker subculture. With the rise of computer viruses, Trojan horses, worms, and their endlessly evolving variants, everyone found themselves needing antivirus protection. And unknown even to the antivirus companies that arose to fill that need, Denise's software kernel was incorporated into almost every one of the antivirus applications. And with each software update, her kernel got better.

Big John operated on too much data to ever transmit across the internet to a central data center. He needed to touch everything. The elegance of Denise's solution provided the answer. Each system's antivirus software scanned every bit of data stored locally, along with all data coming or going over the internet. Best of all, the antivirus software needed to regularly update itself with the latest definitions, and, when it did, her kernel updated itself and delivered its encrypted node weights using the same mechanism. Her kernel didn't transmit raw data across the network. Each instance on an individual computing platform formed a synaptic patch of neurons, a tiny slice of a much larger brain, an insignificant piece of the vast neural net that was Big John.

Computers, cell phones, and tablets came and went, were turned on and off, were replaced by newer ones, and Big John shifted and evolved with that changing capability. The information that each synaptic patch analyzed acquired shifting weight patterns in Big John's correlative data web, a web so vast no databank could store it. The world was Big John's data bank.

Denise wasn't sure when computing systems would become intelligent, but she was pretty sure we wouldn't recognize it when it happened. Dr. Turing had created the test that most computer scientists thought of as defining artificial intelligence. It postulated that if a person in one room had a conversation with a computer in another room and couldn't tell that he wasn't conversing with a human, the computer met the definition for artificial intelligence. The problem with that scenario was that intelligent, self-aware computing systems would probably have no interest in emulating humans.

Big John didn't. And he didn't mine data. He experienced it. To Denise it seemed that finding correlations among disparate data excited him. He didn't care that the individual data points might seem to have nothing in common. Denise didn't really believe Big John was artificially intelligent, but she wouldn't bet her life on it. What Big John did was pure magic.

When someone with the right authorization entered a Big John query, it initiated a new correlative data search with each available node contributing its weight. Queries often led Big John down unexpected paths. It was one of those dark paths that Denise now found herself traversing.

Picking up the phone on her desk, she dialed a memorized extension.

"Riles." The NSA director's voice carried the quiet confidence of its owner.

"Sir, this is Dr. Jennings."

"Yes, Denise?"

"I've got some Big John data you'll want to see."

"The subject matter?"

"We've picked up some anomalous activity in Germany."

Admiral Riles paused. "I'll round up David and Levi. How soon can you have your briefing ready in my conference room?"

Denise glanced at the clock on her computer screen: 9:43 a.m.

"I can be ready by ten thirty."

"Ten thirty then."

Riles ended the call and Denise turned her attention to preparing for her upcoming presentation.

The shimmering black glass structure nicknamed Crypto City housed many things. One of them was a small conference room currently owned by Vice Admiral Jonathan Riles. The NSA director was a stocky man with an open, friendly face that served as an unlikely platform for his icy-gray eyes. Number one in his class at the Naval Academy, Rhodes Scholar, all-American football player, he exuded an easy self-confidence that filled the small conference room.

Dr. David Kurtz sat to his left, the NSA's wild-haired chief computer scientist's gaze fixed on Denise as if he expected her to pull a gun from her case. Opposite him, fingers interlaced beneath his narrow chin, sat Levi Elias, the finest analyst the NSA had.

Admiral Riles nodded at Denise. Clearing her throat, she clicked a button that brought the flat-screen monitor opposite Riles to life.

"Sir, as you know, along with the specific priority intelligence requests we issue to Big John, there are a set of long-standing correlative data searches that remain active at all times. Recent activity within Germany triggered a security alert of sufficient significance for me to request this briefing."

Jonathan Riles interrupted. "What's the category?"

"Counter-intelligence activity."

"Correlation coefficient?"

"Point nine three seven."

Dr. Kurtz frowned. "That high?"

"It's Big John's estimate, not mine."

Admiral Riles nodded. "Okay, Denise. Take us through it."

Denise brought up the first chart. "Two days ago, Big John noticed a change in intelligence activity in Germany that triggered one of his standing correlative searches."

She clicked a button and a graph replaced the data on the first image. "Throughout yesterday and continuing today, the level of that activity continued to increase. It started with remote access of official police reports and progressed to streaming camera data. The camera access was centered in a hundred-and-sixty-kilometer radius around Heidelberg."

"A hundred-mile radius?"

Denise suppressed a smile. Riles was quick. "That's right. Big John tagged it as a U.S. search pattern. It's definitely CIA, but it's odd."

Moving to the next chart, Denise used a red laser pointer to circle a sharp spike in communications data on an isolated portion of the graph. "Knowledge of this operation seems to be isolated to a very small group within CIA. Based upon what we're seeing, it's highly unlikely that this has come to Director Rheiner's attention, most likely an off-the-grid action designed to maintain plausible deniability."

As she sequenced through a series of charts and graphs, Denise continued. "Then, this morning, Big John identified a new hot spot in Munich. As you can see, this shows a spike in interest in street camera data, culminating in extensive data access from the Munich Central Train Station."

Levi Elias shifted forward in his chair. "I assume Big John identified the target of the facial recognition search."

"That's why I asked for this meeting." Denise pressed a button on the remote and a photograph replaced the graphical display. "Meet Jack Gregory, formerly a CIA operative, special task unit."

"Formerly?" Admiral Riles voiced the obvious question.

"Jack Gregory, credited with thirteen high-value target deactivations, was killed in Calcutta last year. His body was never recovered."

"And the CIA was hunting him in the Munich train station today?"

"Yes. Quite vigorously."

"And?"

Denise switched to a grainy image of a man walking along a crowded platform. "And it looks like they found him. Just after noon, Munich time, he boarded the 12:36 Intercity-Express to Berlin. It's scheduled to arrive about a half-hour from now."

"Ideas, Levi?"

The analyst turned to face Admiral Riles. "I won't know for sure until we get more data, but it looks like someone at CIA is set on bending some rules. If an ex-agent posed a high-profile security threat in Germany, they are required to share that information with us and DIA. Unless Denise left something out from the Big John data, there's no indication the DCI's been briefed, much less the Director of National Intelligence."

"I left nothing out."

Levi cleared his throat. "No offense. I'm just making a point. Something big's going down in Germany and it's being kept very close."

Jonathan Riles's gray eyes narrowed. "Denise. Are we monitoring that Berlin train station?"

"I added several specific Big John search directives. If anything's happening electronically, we own it."

Riles stood up and the other two at the table rose with him.

"Okay, Levi."

"Yes sir?"

"Get me everything there is to know about Jack Gregory."

CHAPTER 13

The ICE train within the north–south Tiergarten Tunnel slowed to a crawl, halting at one of the five island platforms that occupied the lowest level inside the glass shell of Berlin's central train station. Jack remained in his seat, watching the other passengers rise en masse to reach for belongings, then shoulder their way toward the doors that offered release onto the platform. John and Jane Doe mirrored the other passengers' movements, their uncaring glances passing over him as if his seat was empty. Good, but just a touch too little interest to be natural. The sudden adrenaline rush told him the rest. Others waited outside the railcar to make sure Jack Gregory never left this station alive.

A crowded train station was one of the better spots for an assassination, allowing the hunters to blend into the milling mob. But there were ways to illuminate those who lurked within a crowd.

"Bomb!"

Jack's yell momentarily froze the people moving through the crowded railcar. The explosion that followed had nothing to do with C4. An eruption of humanity spewed onto the platform, a coronal mass ejection that grew as the mob picked up his yell, repeating it again and again. And as the milling throng became a stampede, the five that didn't join that rush for the exits might as well have been limo drivers holding up boldly lettered "Jack Gregory" signs.

Jack didn't make the same mistake. He rushed along within the crowd, one more panicked traveler shoving toward the exit, except Jack's path took him steadily toward the killer standing just to the right of the broad stairway that led up to ground level. The large man in the blue ball cap shoved aside the river of humanity that flowed around him, frustration painted on his face as he fought to find his target in the midst of the maelstrom.

Jack's side kick crushed the hunter's kneecap, wiping the frustration from his face as it toppled him sideways into the knife edge of Jack's inner palm. The blow crushed his windpipe, bringing his cry of pain to a gargling end.

Ducking below the level of those shouldering past him, Jack dragged the dying man around the side of the stairs. Putting on the man's cap and sun glasses, Jack shrugged into the loose fitting tan jacket, then lifted the Glock from the fellow's shoulder holster and slid it into his waistband at the small of his back.

These thugs weren't CIA and they weren't German BfV. That meant they were Roskov's men. So why were they getting CIA intel?

Blood thrumming through his temples, Jack's attention was drawn toward the tunnel to his right. The danger down that passageway pulled him like a swordfish on a thousand-pound test line. Fighting the nearly irresistible, soulless call that sought to drag him in that direction, he stepped around the stairway and shrugged back into the panicked throng. Moving with the crowd, his eyes once again found his remaining hunters—three men and a hawkish blond woman wearing a navy blue pantsuit. As he let himself be pushed up the stairs and out onto the street, Jack committed their faces to memory.

Then, amidst the blare of sirens and the flashing lights of arriving emergency vehicles, Berlin opened its mouth and swallowed him whole.

CHAPTER 14

Admiral Jonathan Riles looked across the small conference table at the slender, beak-nosed man, glad that the analyst worked for him instead of the competition.

"Take me through it, Levi."

Levi nodded and brought the ninety-inch flat-panel monitor on the far wall to life. "This is the first of a sequence of images from cameras in the Berlin Hauptbahnhof, captured just as the Intercity-Express train carrying Jack Gregory arrived at the platform, taken at 5:38 p.m. Berlin local time . . . rush hour."

The image showed a train platform crowded with passengers, many reading newspapers, listening to music on their smart phones, or lost in their eBooks while they waited for their train. As far as Jonny Riles could tell, there was nothing out of the ordinary.

Levi Elias clicked a button and the image changed. "Here is Gregory's train just prior to opening its doors to let the arriving passengers off. Now, in this next image you can see the first passengers exiting onto the platform from the first class car carrying Gregory and the two CIA field agents that we have identified as Pamela Scherrer and Roger Macon. This is where things get dicey."

The next image sent an electric thrill through Admiral Riles. It was as if someone had waved a magic wand and transformed the bored crowd within the train station into a completely different entity, gripped by fear that froze a thousand faces. Another button press from Levi put the crowd in motion as the recorded video feed from another camera played out on screen.

"Someone yelled 'Bomb!' and this is the result. Pure panic. Everyone racing for the exit, trampling those that got in their way." Levi froze the video, the red dot of his laser pointer circling a large man not moving with the crowd, but facing back toward the train. "As you can see, not quite everyone was running."

Levi started the video again, then stopped it once more, this time circling a dark suited woman struggling through the crowd in the wrong direction.

Admiral Riles leaned forward, his attention zeroed in on yet another man, this one of medium build and wearing khaki pants and a multi-colored linen shirt. "How many in the hit squad?"

Levi shook his head. "From the available footage, I've only been able to identify these three, but there was at least one more."

"How do you know?"

"Along with those injured in the stampede, one man was killed." The image on the screen was replaced by a morgue photo. "This is from the coroner's report. Crushed trachea produced by an open-hand blow. Definitely not accidental. The man's real name is Renee Balkman, a thug in the employ of Stadich Transport, one of Vladimir Roskov's companies."

"Gregory?"

"Almost certainly his handiwork. Didn't catch it on camera though."

"Why not?" Admiral Riles felt his anticipation rise.

"It appears Jack Gregory used the panicked mob to mask his departure. We just got him in a couple of frames. As you can see in this one where he is exiting the train, he looks like any other frightened passenger, shoving his way toward the exit. Here's another from a different camera that caught his approach to the stairs. There were two live video cameras with wide angle shots, but it seems Gregory knew where all the cameras were positioned. He just ducked a little and moved with the crowd. Invisible."

Riles glanced down at the open file in front of him, its contents spread across the table. As impressive as Jack Gregory's dossier painted him, Riles had a feeling it didn't do the ex-CIA operative justice.

"What about the dead man? Do we have him on film?"

"Not alive. He was by the stairs, but had positioned himself out of the field of view of any of the cameras. My guess is he was the primary shooter and didn't want the kill recorded. The others were just there to make sure Gregory didn't make a break for it."

"So Gregory spotted the shooter and took him down on his way out."

"He used the crowd to get in close. The way people were getting pushed around, the person right next to those two probably just thought someone else had gotten knocked down. Gregory probably looked like he was trying to help an injured man by dragging him out of the rush."

Riles looked back down at the documents, shuffling through the pages until he found what he was looking for.

"Levi, I believe you know the CIA's senior trainer of field agents, Garfield Kromly."

"We dated the same girl. Pam married him, but somehow, we all stayed friends through the years."

"When was the last time you saw him?"

Levi dropped his gaze, swallowed, then raised his dark eyes once again. "Pamela died almost a year ago. She'd fought cancer for a long time. Hell, we thought she'd beat it. But when it reemerged, it took her down so fast. I haven't seen Garfield since the funeral."

"And if I asked you to pay him a visit?"

"It would be awkward. Painful."

"It says here that Kromly trained Gregory. That Jack was his star pupil."

Riles watched as understanding dawned in Levi Elias's dark eyes. "I could talk to him myself, but I have a feeling he'll be more open with you."

Levi's mouth narrowed into a tight line. "I'll arrange it."

Admiral Riles rose to his feet and Levi Elias mirrored his action.

"Thanks, Levi. I look forward to your report."

Levi nodded, then turned and strode out, leaving Admiral Riles watching his back as he walked stiffly out the conference room door.

CHAPTER 15

What used to be known as East Berlin had long been the subject of exploitation by its richer, western namesake, but Jack liked it. Despite the advent of the Schickimicki, the wealthy yuppies who drove up prices and displaced the former occupants, it was still easier to disappear here than anywhere else in Germany. It was also easier to find the sort of characters that could provide anything imaginable to someone with ready cash and know-how. And Jack's imagination knew few limits.

The flat he'd rented had thus far escaped the upgrades that had accompanied East Berlin's absorption into a unified Germany, as had the neighborhood that surrounded it. Its seven hundred and fifty square feet contained a combination kitchen and dining room, a water closet with shower, toilet, and sink, and a bedroom just large enough for a twin bed, nightstand, and freestanding pine wardrobe. The flower-patterned wallpaper had seen its best days and Jack doubted those days had been all that good to begin with. It didn't really matter. He'd stayed in much worse and he wouldn't be here long.

Peter Weisen had served him well in the past, and today had been no exception. The portly German had a cheery disposition that endeared him to Rasthof Rhinesdorf's patrons, whether they dined and drank in the gasthaus restaurant or partook of beer and a game of nine pins in the two-lane bowling alley in the basement beneath the bar. But only a select few customers had been privy to the specialty shopping available in the sub-basement that lay below that kegelbahn. Peter was a man with access to a network that, given a sufficient combination of time and money, could acquire anything available to the CIA or FSB.

Jack had made a variety of off-the-shelf purchases and had left Peter with a list that would take a bit more effort to gather, along with specific instructions for where and how he wanted those items delivered . . . multiple deliveries to multiple locations. The agreed-upon price had widened Peter's usual smile, a large figure indeed, payment made via transfer from one numbered Credit Suisse account to another. Money well spent.

The new laptop was an upgrade from what Jack usually bought. In his line of work, laptops had a very limited shelf life. They certainly weren't the kind of things on which he stored essential information. For that he relied solely on his memory. But they did have their uses. Right now, seated at the metal-legged kitchen table, Jack found himself appreciating the high-end graphics card in this one.

Using readily available sketch artist facial composite software, he gradually brought the four faces in his mind's eye to life on the screen, images he could use to identify the surviving members of the hit team that had tried to ambush him inside the Berlin Hauptbahnhof. Two pots of coffee and another Swiss banking transaction later, he had electronic dossiers to go with the four faces.

Jack rose from the chair and rolled his neck, feeling it pop as his knotted muscles released. He glanced at the time displayed at the laptop's lower right corner: 1:48 a.m. Good. Just enough time to get in a workout while a fresh pot brewed. That would leave him three hours to commit the contents of the dossiers to memory, shower, and apply the prosthetics that would allow him to evade facial recognition.

Feeling adrenaline course through his system, he took a long, slow breath and forced his mind to a calmer place. The time for adrenaline was coming, but that time wasn't now.

CHAPTER 16

Of all the jobs Levi Elias had been asked to do throughout his years at the National Security Agency, he regarded this as the most distasteful. Pamela Meridith Kromly had been the one true love of his life. The fact that she had married his best friend hadn't changed that. Neither had the hurt from her rejection dampened his relationship with Garfield. Her death had done that.

It wasn't that he and Garfield Kromly didn't maintain their lifelong bond of friendship; it was that their mutual presence spawned an unbearable vortex of pain. So he and Garfield had maintained a respectful distance that honored their grief. For him to now set up a meeting to prod his friend's painful memories felt blasphemous. As he approached the base of the Washington monument where Garfield waited, the thought of what he was doing left Levi physically ill.

Still, he managed a smile as he gripped Garfield's extended hand. "Hello, Gar."

"Good to see you, my friend. It's been a while."

"Yes. Too long."

Levi let his gaze linger on Garfield's face. Despite the gray hair that showed the rapid approach of Garfield's sixtieth birthday, his jaw still bore the hard lines of an athlete. The CIA's top trainer of field operatives had always maintained a workout routine that left most of his recruits gasping for air, and Levi gathered that his routine hadn't eased since Pam's death.

Garfield's eyes narrowed slightly at the corners. "I take it you didn't arrange this meeting just to discuss old times."

Levi nodded, the two men picking up a casual stroll toward the distant Jefferson Memorial as they talked.

"I need to ask you about a former trainee of yours. Jack Gregory."

Garfield Kromly came to an abrupt halt, his jaw tightening as he turned to face Levi. "Jack's been dead more than a year."

Levi met the other's gaze, surprised at the antagonism in that stare. "So I've been told."

"Then why the sudden NSA interest?"

"Can you keep this strictly between the two of us?"

"That depends on the why."

Feeling a bit too exposed standing facing each other on the grass lawn of the National Mall, Levi inclined his head slightly and together they resumed their previous stroll. The Thursday mid-morning sun hung low in a clear blue sky, its warmth an early indication of the heat that was destined to follow.

"You know I loved her, too."

"I do."

"Then you know I would never take advantage of our friendship. Not for agency business. Not for anything."

"Armistead and Hancock?"

Levi felt a tightness grip his throat at the *Killer Angels* reference. "Just so."

"I'd still like to know why."

Having moved away from the tourists gathered near the base of the Washington Monument, Levi nodded. "Fair enough. We've picked up indications of some unusual CIA activity in Germany, the type of thing that we would expect to be kept in the loop on. We've linked yesterday's bomb scare in Berlin to what appears to be a high-priority, ongoing CIA operation."

"If it's sensitive enough, it's possible that notification to sister agencies could be delayed until the DCI is certain exactly what they are on to."

"Maybe, but as far as we can tell, Director Rheiner hasn't been informed about his own agency's involvement in the Berlin incident."

"I find that hard to believe."

Levi understood Garfield's doubt, but continued. "It wouldn't be the first time the DCI's been kept out of the loop to maintain plausible deniability."

Garfield's pace slowed ever so slightly. "You're implying that a senior CIA official is conducting an illegal operation."

"Like I said, it wouldn't be the first time."

A small grin lifted the corners of Garfield's mouth as he glanced over at Levi. "How does a dead man play into this?"

Levi formed his response carefully. He wasn't lying to Garfield, but not giving him the whole story sure felt like it. "We've picked up a number of references to Jack the Ripper in communications intercepts."

"Could be a code name."

"Not in this context. It sounds like he may be an operational target."

Garfield halted, turning to face Levi once more. "You're saying Jack Gregory's alive?"

"No. I'm saying the chatter indicates that someone thinks he's alive. It sounds like a group within CIA is going to considerable lengths to remedy that."

"Jack was more than one of my students. He was the best operative I've ever seen, and since I've trained almost every field agent that has come into the agency during the last thirty years, that's saying something. It's hard to describe him other than to say he was unique. A dynamic personality. He was quick, athletic, and highly skilled."

Levi studied his friend's face. Normally expressionless, strong emotion played behind those eyes. "You were close to him?"

"As with many of the top trainees, Pam and I had him over to the house on several occasions. But Jack was different. When he walked into a room it was like someone had just switched on the lights."

"Charismatic?"

Garfield laughed. "Jack Gregory exuded a love of life that bled into everyone around him. Pam loved him. Hell, I loved him. Jack was like the son we never had. When we heard he was dead, we couldn't accept it. I made a special trip to England to see the old nun who had watched Jack die in Calcutta. It was a waste of time. She was cloistered, lost in delusion and dementia, rocking back and forth on her bed, mumbling the same words over and over."

"The same words? What words?" Levi asked.

"*Dear Lord, The Ripper walks the earth.* That phrase and the fact that nobody ever found his body started the rumors that Jack was still alive. But it was all nonsense. I followed up with the Indian doctor that signed Jack's death certificate. He assured me he had made no mistake."

Garfield paused, taking in a deep breath and letting it out slowly.

"Pam was already fighting cancer and the news of Jack's death sapped her will to keep fighting. I remember what she said to me. *If a young god like Jack can face his mortality, maybe I can too.*"

Garfield's face hardened. "A part of me still wanted to believe he was alive. But when Jack didn't show up at Pam's funeral, I knew for certain he was dead. Dead to me anyway."

Despite the distress he heard in his old friend's voice, Levi felt compelled to ask the question this had all been leading up to.

"Okay, Gar, one last question. If Gregory is still alive, do you think it's possible he's gone rogue?"

Garfield Kromly's gray eyes locked with Levi's, the intensity of the gaze sending a chill through his body.

"Not a snowball's chance in hell."

CHAPTER 17

Levi Elias stared across the conference table at his boss. Admiral Riles's legendary silent interludes served dual purposes. They allowed his agile mind to rip apart, reassemble, and digest the information that had just been presented and they elicited extra information the briefer hadn't intended to reveal, an effect produced by the weight of the Admiral's extended silence. Riles had mastered the art of keeping his eyes fixed on the presenter, as if he expected the person to continue speaking, even as he wandered through the maze of his own thoughts.

Levi let that feeling wash over him, settled back in his chair, and waited.

When Admiral Riles finally spoke, his words startled Levi.

"I want you to send Janet Price to Berlin to make contact with Gregory."

"Isn't that stepping a bit outside our boundaries?"

Riles smiled. "Let me worry about that. This whole situation smells like a setup, one initiated without the DCI's approval. More important, I don't like the new Big John data. The damned machine has inferred a connection between events that should have no connection."

"Like what?"

"Rolf Koenig's space launch from the Baikonur Cosmodrome, the CIA surveillance of Jack Gregory, and some of Vladimir Roskov's operations in Kazakhstan."

"That could be just because Vladimir Roskov is putting pressure on both Gregory and Koenig."

"Not according to Dr. Jennings. Denise tells me this is a completely different correlation, although, aside from some gibberish about patterns of node weights in Big John's neural network, she can't give me a causal relationship. But even though I don't understand it, I'm not going to ignore a Big John correlation of point eight nine."

Levi couldn't argue with that, but he didn't like being forced to take the type of action that involved calling upon Janet's special skills without a thorough operational understanding of the battlefield. And, in his mind, that was exactly what Berlin had become, a battlefield where highly-trained foot soldiers from a variety of organizations, some criminal and some government sponsored, moved like pawns on a chessboard. Worse, he had no idea what underlying agendas drove the key players, or even who the key players were.

From what he'd learned from Garfield Kromly, Jack Gregory had been a uniquely qualified CIA asset. Now, someone high up at Langley had discovered Gregory was still alive and was desperately trying to correct that. But why kill Gregory? A couple of answers sprang to mind. Either the CIA had taken a hand in the original Calcutta attack on Gregory or he had subsequently stumbled onto something that threatened an ongoing CIA operation, or both. But that raised more questions. Riles must be thinking the same thing to consider sending Janet Price.

"Given recent circumstances, Gregory may not be in the mood for contact."

"Janet can make that call. Gregory's a dangerous man in a bad situation, one that's probably going to get a lot worse. I want to know who is setting him up and why? Don't worry. Janet can handle The Ripper."

Levi looked down at his steepled fingers. Perhaps Riles was right. The NSA had enticed Janet Price away from the CIA. She'd been the first woman to ever complete the Army's Ranger School and although it had been as a part of an unofficial CIA training class, she'd endured those nine weeks of starvation, sleep deprivation, and pressure-packed hell, succeeding where most of her classmates had failed.

At the CIA, Janet Price had broken Jack Gregory's thousand-meter marksmanship record. A dark-haired beauty who moved like a professional dancer, Janet could take a man's breath with a single glance. She could take his life with even less effort. She was the NSA's hidden treasure, an asset so valuable that Jonny Riles only assigned her to the highest-priority missions. But here and now, because The Ripper had returned from the dead, Riles was launching that asset into a German maelstrom on a hunch. The thought sent a cold shiver up Levi's spine.

Realizing that he'd remained silent even longer than Riles, Levi raised his eyes to meet his boss's gaze.

"Janet's in Cartagena. I'll have her on an agency jet to Berlin, tonight."

"You'll personally handle her briefing?"

"I'll assemble the mission briefing. It'll be waiting when she gets off the plane tomorrow, available for download when she settles in to her hotel."

Admiral Riles smiled. "That works."

Levi rose and walked back to his office, his thoughts on what his boss had ordered him to do. Riles never went off half-cocked. Based on the limited facts available, the Admiral had concluded that Jack Gregory had stumbled upon something that involved the CIA, Rolf Koenig, the Russian Mafia, and possibly the BfV, something all of those actors wanted desperately to keep secret.

And as he picked up his phone to make the required call, Levi realized he wanted answers just as badly as Admiral Riles did.

CHAPTER 18

Darkness filled the underground parking garage, a thick blanket that Jack's red LED penlight only managed to nudge back as he moved silently past the tightly parked Volkswagens, Citroëns, Audis, and BMWs. Having spent the last six hours watching the entrance, he had noted that no car had entered or left since 1:27 a.m. That was two hours ago.

The apartment complex above his head housed Kendra Armonis, a twenty-four-year-old exotic dancer from Lithuania, Carlo Veniti's current girlfriend. The dark-headed Italian hit man looked like a mixed martial arts heavyweight fighter. Six-foot-four, lean and hard muscled, Carlo enjoyed a reputation for killing people with his bare hands, preferring to take his time when the job offered that opportunity.

Carlo was a ladies' man, moving from relationship to relationship every few months. Those relationships quickly became so abusive that most of his women were too scared to run away and all refused to press charges or testify against him. With his peculiar tastes and skill set, it came as no surprise to Jack that Vladimir Roskov relied upon Carlo for high-priority eliminations. It was why he'd been the assassination team leader inside the Berlin train station.

Jack knew the type, a knowledge that stoked his inner fire. But soon, Kendra Armonis would find herself free to move on with her life. Except for Roskov, there weren't likely to be many mourners at Veniti's funeral.

Jack had spotted Carlo's license plate on the black Audi A8 as it entered the garage just after midnight. Seeing that same plate appear in his red flashlight beam, Jack stopped. Turning in a slow circle, he examined the surrounding spaces from floor to ceiling. Insulated boiler pipes crisscrossed the ceiling, reducing its height from six-and-a-half feet to a level that just allowed Jack's six-foot frame to pass beneath without stooping. The same wouldn't apply to Carlo when he made his way from Kendra's bed back to his car.

As Jack started to walk behind the car, he stopped. The scent of danger hung on the air, an invisible aura that thrilled him. But his innate sense of what was about to happen had become so amped up it was a distraction and, right now, he couldn't afford to be pulled off target just to investigate a feeling. Moving forward once again, Jack shined the penlight's red beam through the driver's side window, directly into Carlo Veniti's grinning face.

The door swung open with such force that it lifted him off his feet, launching his body onto the hood of the adjacent car, sending his flashlight flying. In the instant before it shattered on the concrete floor, as if in slow motion, Jack saw Carlo rise up, backlit by the Audi's interior lighting.

Jack felt Carlo's left hand close around his ankle, felt his body dragged across the hood as he pulled his SAS survival knife from its right ankle sheath. Instead of fighting the pull, Jack used Carlo's hold as an anchor to launch his body into his attacker, thrusting the black blade at the Italian's throat.

Recognizing his danger, Carlo thrust out his right hand to ward off the blow, but only succeeded in impaling his palm all the way to the hilt. With a grunt of pain, Carlo closed his injured hand, locking the blade in place, preventing Jack from pulling the knife free. He lunged backward, maintaining his grip on Jack's ankle as both men tumbled to the concrete floor. Jack locked himself to the hit man's body so that the two rolled across the floor as one.

Carlo hammered his forehead into Jack's, the head butt dislodging Jack's hold on the bigger man and sending a trickle of blood flowing from his eyebrow into his left eye. The big man attempted to wrap his thick left arm around Jack's neck, but Jack caught his thumb and twisted hard, the resultant crack and accompanying release of pressure providing him the opening to launch his elbow into the underside of Carlo's jaw.

Carlo twisted, seeking to roll Jack face down, a move Jack countered with an arm bar. Shifting his weight onto his right arm, Jack used the additional leverage to twist his knife, heard a bone snap within Carlo's palm, and felt the slick surge of hot blood. Reversing his previous opposition to Carlo's attempt to roll him over, Jack threw his weight into the movement.

Unable to stop their combined angular momentum, Carlo was thrown face down on the concrete as Jack whipped his feet under the big man's outstretched arms, locking both heels behind Carlo's neck in a leg full nelson. With a growl of desperation, Carlo struggled to break the hold, the muscles in his neck and arms cording like guitar strings. Attempting an alligator roll, he whipped Jack's body into the concrete floor but failed to dislodge his hold.

Jack leaned into it, using his entire core to strengthen the pressure his legs applied to Carlo's neck. For a long moment, Carlo intensified his resistance. Then, with a crack that echoed through the concrete space, Carlo's thick neck twisted and his body went limp. Giving Carlo's neck one last turn, Jack felt it flop unnaturally to the side. He released his leg lock and kicked the bigger man's body away.

Panting, as much from adrenaline overload as from exertion, Jack climbed back to his feet. The light shining from the open car door illuminated the scene, casting Jack's shadow across Carlo's body and onto the Volkswagen Jetta parked in the space opposite. Stepping across the corpse, Jack pulled his knife from Carlo's palm and wiped the blade on his white shirt. Jack tossed Carlo's wallet, cell phone, and pistol onto the Audi's passenger seat, then clicked the key fob button that opened the trunk latch.

Walking back to where Carlo's remains lay sprawled on the concrete, Jack grabbed his ankles and dragged him to the Audi. Jack heaved the corpse into the trunk, took a minute to arrange the body, then shut the lid with a solid thunk.

Wiping his bloody face on his shirt sleeve, Jack slid into the driver's seat, adjusted it and the mirrors to his liking, and then pressed the engine START button. The powerful vehicle rumbled to life and he backed out of the parking space, letting the headlight beams lead the way out of the garage and into Berlin's predawn darkness.

Sloppy.

His quest for self-control had caused him to ignore his intuition and had damn near gotten him killed. He'd been so busy fighting his amped up feelings he'd failed to pay attention to little details, like the smell of liquor as he'd approached Carlo's car, an indication Carlo had been drunk when he'd pulled into the parking spot and had passed out behind the wheel. Jack had assumed that the car was empty instead of going with his gut.

Right now he wanted to drop Carlo's car where it would have the most impact, but first he had a couple more errands to run. Before that, he needed some rest.

~ ~ ~

Back in his tiny apartment, Jack scrubbed his face, watching the counterclockwise swirl of red water make its way over scratched white porcelain and down the drain. As Tori Amos sang her haunting "Me and a Gun" from his laptop's speakers, he found himself wishing he'd been there to help her. But he hadn't been there. He hadn't been there for his own brother, either. Hell, he couldn't erase his own violation.

Looking at his reflection in the scratched bathroom mirror, the truth stared back at him through the red glint in his dark brown eyes. Jack Gregory wasn't anyone's hero.

He was just a dead man walking.

CHAPTER 19

Closing the bathroom door, Jacob Knox made his way back to his seat in the private jet. The luxurious leather seats faced each other separated by tables that facilitated mission planning. But tonight Jacob was the jet's only passenger. Sitting down, he pulled his specially equipped tablet from its pouch, propping it upright in its cover as he woke it up. He waited fifteen seconds while the camera performed the facial recognition that would grant him the opportunity to speak his private security phrase. There was another short wait as the computer validated his voice print before the primary display replaced the security screen.

Seeing that he had two messages waiting, both of them from Deputy Director Nolan Trent, Jacob activated the secure video chat session. Within seconds, Nolan's face filled the screen. Without bothering with a hello, Nolan got right to the point.

"There've been complications. This morning, in an alley between two of his Berlin warehouses, Roskov's people found a car with four bodies in the trunk, three men and a woman."

"Gregory?"

"Looks like his work. These four, plus the man killed in the Berlin train station made up the team Roskov sent to kill Gregory. Three of them had their throats cut. Carlo Veniti, the hit team leader, was laid out on top of the others. His body was face down, but his head was face up."

"So what did Roskov think of The Ripper's message?"

"You know I don't like that name."

"Gregory's then."

"He's not taking it well. It took me a half-hour of jawboning to convince him to stay focused on the Koenig job and leave Gregory to us. In the meantime he's doubling his personal security detail."

"Good idea."

"How far out are you?"

"A couple hours. I should be on the ground by 4 a.m. local time."

"Good. You'll find a diplomatic vehicle and the mission package waiting for you as planned. Let me know as soon as the job's done."

"Won't be a problem."

"That's why I sent you."

After signing off, Jacob leaned back in his chair to catch some sleep, a fog delay turning two hours into three. That was good. He didn't expect to sleep again until he finished what he'd come to do.

As Jacob stepped off the jet onto the Berlin airport tarmac, he patted the Sig Sauer in his left shoulder holster. Looking at the fog swirling around the hanger lights, he set his jaw.

Amateur hour was over.

CHAPTER 20

Releasing the aircraft door-locking lever, Janet Price opened the hatch and lowered the steps that would release her from the NSA Gulfstream G650 onto the fog-shrouded tarmac of Berlin's main airport. Clad in black jeans, a navy blue pullover, leather boots and polarizing Ray-Bans, she grabbed her duffel bag and headed toward the terminal building and Customs. Although it would have been possible for her to have arranged diplomatic transportation that would have allowed her to get her personal firearms around Customs, she didn't want that kind of attention, nor did she desire to announce her presence to the U.S. diplomatic corps. U.S. embassies were State Department and CIA territory, and right now it was possible they were part of the problem. At least that was what Janet was here to find out.

She'd always felt Berlin's airports provided a traveler-friendly customs experience when compared to the nightmares in Paris and Frankfurt. Today proved no exception and within an hour she found herself stepping into the cab that would ferry her to the Kempinski Hotel, where her room and mission package waited. By the time she tipped the cabbie and handed her bag to the bellboy, it was ten a.m. and she was ready to strip out of the wrinkled jeans and T-shirt to slide into a hot bath. After that she'd be ready for a full day of wading through the Jack Gregory mission briefing materials.

By noon, she felt she knew the man. By six p.m. she knew she didn't.

The information available in the thick electronic dossier Levi Elias had delivered was multi-layered but fragmentary. The deeper she dug into Jack Gregory's past, the more self-contradictory the mental profile she was erecting became. On the surface, he was the classic overachiever gone rogue, an Old-West gunfighter, hiring out to the highest bidder, but beneath that thin epidermal layer squirmed something far more complex.

Like all CIA field operatives trained in the last few decades, Jack Gregory had been administered the Myers-Briggs Jungian Type Indicator Test. His personality profile indicated that he was an Extroverted-iNtuitive-Feeling-Perceptive, or ENFP, commonly called the Champion personality. Marked by a highly developed intuition combined with great people skills and a love of adventure, those with Jack's personality type tended to be leaders and risk takers. Above all else, they hated to be controlled by others. They also tended to exhibit unpredictable behavior, following their inspiration wherever it might lead.

Janet had been familiar with Jack Gregory's legend since her training days at CIA. Garfield Kromly had practically worshipped the man—at least, that was how it had felt whenever he'd compared her efforts to that ultimate standard. It was the reason she'd been so happy to break Jack's thousand-meter marksmanship record. Stupid, really. She'd been more proud of that than of being the first woman to graduate from the U.S. Army Ranger School. Now that she thought about it, Jack had always been in her head, all because of Kromly.

As she paged through the dossier, that specter grew to new proportions. While the CIA killed hundreds of America's enemies using drones, it was a fraction of the targeted killings inflicted by a small group of special assets. And though some had more credited kills than Jack, through a unique combination of martial skills, charisma, and intuition, he had come to be regarded as the agency's deadliest assassin, something that failed to endear him to many of his compatriots.

Although it hadn't been proven, Janet believed that jealousy had led to the betrayal and killing of Jack's brother, Robert. That had been the tipping point that had sent Jack spiraling off mission. It had gotten him killed, or so most of the world's intelligence community still thought.

For the fifth time, Janet read Levi's summary of his visit with Garfield Kromly. Within the larger context of that report she'd glossed over a subtle comment that now acquired greater significance. Garfield Kromly had alluded to Jack's uncanny anticipation. Having spent the last several hours huddled with her laptop, reviewing everything known about Jack's classified operations, that description seemed understated. Janet didn't believe in extrasensory perception, but there was no doubt that Jack had always had a nose for finding trouble and the instincts to find his way through it.

But there was the incident that had led to his death in that Calcutta alley. That path hadn't been a particularly gifted choice.

Then again, maybe Jack hadn't planned to walk out of that alley alive. However, if he had been suicidal, why was she looking at a picture of him inside Berlin's Hauptbahnhof? Why was he still alive?

Janet stood, ran her fingers through her dark brown hair, and stretched, rolling her neck in a slow circle that popped her vertebrae. Walking to the coffee pot, she poured herself a cup, held it just below her nose and inhaled, letting the stout aroma clear her head. Even more than beer, the Germans knew how to make coffee. The Turks did too, but she'd always felt she was straining Turkish coffee through her teeth, an unappealing image.

Walking to the window, Janet looked out her seventh-story window as evening descended on Berlin. She sipped the hot beverage, and shifted her thoughts to the year that separated Jack's death from the present. Denise Jennings had run a query through Big John and the computer had delivered all the high-correlation Ripper rumors for that time period.

If Big John's data could be believed, The Ripper had been busy. Although there was nothing solid linking Jack to any specific act, the wealthy and politically connected persons on Big John's Ripper client list had each experienced a noted decrease in serious problems plaguing them during the period in question. Another interesting pattern Big John had uncovered linked those clients to large payments to offshore corporations that ceased to exist shortly after taking payment. While Janet lacked Denise's faith in Big John's arcane abilities, if even half of this list was accurate, Jack had acquired substantial financial resources over the last year.

Another troubling indicator was how dramatically Jack's patterns had changed since his reported death. Some of the incidents with the highest probability of involving The Ripper had nothing to do with money, power, or any logical client.

Right now she found herself staring at a police report of the killing of Ignacio Gomez, a two-bit pimp who got his girls from the misery of Cartagena's slums. A dark, pixelated security photo showed a man who could have been Gregory shooting a pistol at someone off camera. According to Elena Esteves, a hooker in Gomez's stable, Ignacio had been beating her with a stick in that dark alley when a man had stepped around the side of the liquor store, shot Ignacio in the head, and then disappeared into the night. Despite police attempts to get the woman to provide a description of the shooter, she had refused, claiming that it had been a ghost.

While that superstitious nonsense meant nothing to Janet, the pixelated low-resolution picture sure looked like Gregory. As she zoomed in on his face, she noticed the distinct red-eye shine produced by a camera flash. There was only one problem. There hadn't been any flash. This was a single still-frame from security camera video footage. If this was indeed Gregory, his eyes must have been reflecting some distant street light. Perhaps that reflection was what had made the hooker believe she'd seen a ghost. Or maybe she had lied to the police in order to protect the man who had come to her aid.

That wasn't what bothered Janet about the incident. It didn't fit Gregory's profile and it wasn't an isolated occurrence. Big John's data included three other recent instances of Jack involving himself in activities that violated his profile, all of them resulting in someone's violent death. The net effect of these aberrations was to cause Big John to lower its own correlation probability, thereby casting doubt on the conclusion that Jack had been associated with any of these killings.

Rubbing her eyes, Janet glanced at the clock on her computer desktop: 9:12 p.m. Rising from her seat, she decided it was time for room service, a hot bath, and bed. Maybe a good night's sleep would help her find some common thread that would give her a better sense of the man she was hunting. She hoped so. Because, without that understanding, she might as well be pursuing The Ripper through a pea-soup London fog.

CHAPTER 21

The thunder of horses' hooves shakes the ground beneath me as I lead the great wedge of the Companions into my enemy's left flank, the battleground awash in the screams of the wounded and dying as they fall before us. At the point of the wedge I lean forward, bracing for impact as my xyston pierces the nearest defender's chest. The wooden shaft twists in my sweaty grip and the muscles in my right arm knot with effort as I pull the spear free. My ragged breathing echoes in my ears, almost drowning out the cacophony of the battle that rages all around me.

As I select my next target, my warhorse stumbles, then lurches erect, as though, through sheer force of will, it can disregard the pike embedded in its heaving chest. When it falls, I feel myself launched from its back directly at the broad-chested soldier who just killed it. In slow motion I see the beginning of a triumphant grin crease his lips and the rage that rises up within me knows no bounds. I may die here today on this foreign field of battle, but it won't be at the hands of this grinning Persian bastard.

Meeting the ground with my left shoulder, I let my momentum propel me forward, coming out of the roll with my sword in hand. My gauntleted left arm deflects my enemy's thrust as I drive the tip of my sharp blade into the soft spot at the base of his throat. And as his hot, slick blood splashes my face, it is nothing compared to the battle heat that pulses through my veins.

For today, as I fight at the head of this mighty Greek army, truly, I am a god.

~ ~ ~

Jack sat bolt upright in bed, his naked body bathed in sweat, his labored breath still panting from his lungs. Tossing away the damp sheet, he rose to his feet, struggling to remember where he was and why he was here.

"Shit."

How long had it been since he'd awakened from a peaceful sleep? Jack couldn't remember. Always different, the dreams were so vivid they seemed more than memories, a past reexperienced. In his sleep, his inner demon worked overtime. Whatever dying had done to him, Jack couldn't recommend it.

He turned on the shower and stepped in, letting the cold water shock his system into full wakefulness. Without switching it to warm, Jack lathered up, leisurely rinsing away the night sweat as his mind focused on only one thought.

Discipline.

When all else failed, it was the one thing that might reestablish his sense of self-control. It was the one thing that might keep him sane.

Toweling himself dry, Jack tied the towel around his waist, walked to the kitchen table, awakened his laptop from its hibernation, and seated himself before it. Logging in, he glanced at the warning message box.

Virus definitions out of date. Press OK to update.

Jack pressed the OK button to allow the antivirus package to do its thing and began composing his next information request to Rita Chavez, knowing full well that, even more than his last request, this one was going to cost him.

CHAPTER 22

The warbling ring tone of her encrypted cell phone brought Janet Price from sleep to full alertness in a fraction of a second and identified the caller as Levi Elias. She touched the answer button and lifted the black device to her ear.

"Yes?"

"We've found Gregory."

Janet felt her pulse quicken. "How?"

"Big John identified him in a laptop camera image embedded in one of the Denise Jennings antivirus feeds. He's online right now."

Janet moved to her own laptop, put the cellphone on speaker, and logged in.

"Have you sent the location?"

"You should already have it."

"What about the video? Can you tie me in to his laptop?"

"I've embedded a link. Don't watch long though. Gregory might notice the increased bandwidth usage."

"Just want a quick look at what I'm about to step into."

"Fine. Elias out."

As Levi disconnected the call, Janet popped up the encrypted email, entered her unique key, and clicked the link. A small video window appeared in the upper right quarter of her screen. Janet maximized it and adjusted the video quality to the lowest frame rate, an action that gave her a sequence of freeze-frame images that changed once every second.

Although grainy, a semi-naked Jack Gregory appeared to stare directly out of the video window into her eyes as he typed on his own keyboard. Although she'd seen him in several photographs, they clearly hadn't done him justice. Short cropped, newly blond hair framed a lean, powerful face. Knife scars criss-crossed his naked upper torso that exhibited so little body fat that his muscles seemed to crawl beneath his skin with each slight movement. She turned her attention to his deep brown eyes. As she expected, they showed no hint of the red she'd seen in the Columbian photo.

Jack's image blocked most of her view of the room in which he sat, but she gathered it was a cheap hotel room or perhaps an apartment, the kind of place you'd rent if you weren't planning on a lengthy stay.

Switching off the video feed, Janet looked at the address provided in Levi's email, pulled up a satellite app to get a look at the building and the neighborhood, and then shut down the laptop. Twisting her long hair into a tight knot on the back of her head, Janet shoved the icepick-sharp metal hairpin through, securing it in place.

It didn't take her long to slide into a pair of jeans and a black pullover with the gun pocket that would secure the H&K

subcompact beneath her left arm. Shrugging into a black leather jacket, Janet walked from the room, letting the door snick closed behind her. She took the elevator directly to the parking garage, clicked the horn button on her key fob and followed the sound and flashing headlights to the jet-black BMW Z4 the NSA had arranged for her.

Sliding behind the wheel, Janet took a moment to adjust the seat and mirrors, and then let the roadster propel her into the night.

CHAPTER 23

Rolf Koenig walked through the Kazakh night, as alone as he could ever be, his security bubble barely glimpsed as they moved along with him. Being the creator of the greatest space technology company on the face of the planet had its advantages, one of which was the privacy app Rolf had designed for just this purpose. He merely had to say his desired destination and it simultaneously calculated the best routes and updated his team with the route he selected, allowing them to provide the optimum level of protection while staying out of Rolf's sight.

Lightning crawled across the western horizon, revealing the distant storm clouds, still hours away from the cosmodrome. Directly above his head, Jupiter almost touched the Cheshire moon that lighted his way toward the launch pad. Though the rocket that would carry his payload into space had not yet been moved to that launch pad, Rolf felt the need to go there, to stroll across the exact space where the huge vehicle would rest, to look up at the night sky.

Most people thought the vast Kazakh plains ugly, but if they were looking at the ground they were missing the view. Kazakhstan, especially this place, was all about the sky, and what a gorgeous sky it was. Rolf had fallen in love with it the first night he had spent here and that love had only grown stronger with each subsequent visit. It was why he slept the few hours he required during the day, just so he could soak in the night.

A fresh lightning tree sprouted in the distance as Mother Nature painted the sky in rapid strokes, strobed the results, and then erased her magnificent creation, leaving its after-image burned into Rolf's retinas. So beautiful. So fleeting. Like life itself.

The thought pulled him back to the news that had sent him on this head-clearing walk. Roskov reported trouble in Berlin. And although the crime boss had tried to hide it, Rolf had heard in Roskov's voice the undertones that told him the killer known as The Ripper had wrapped Roskov in a frenzy of fury and frustration.

Roskov, operating with CIA intel, had sent a five-person hit squad to kill the ex-CIA fixer, but The Ripper had killed one of their team before escaping from the train station. Then he'd hunted down the rest of the hit squad, leaving their corpses inside the trunk of a car parked outside one of Roskov's warehouses. It was a message intended to inspire fear. Intended to produce overreaction, exactly the kind of overreaction in which Roskov could lose himself. Rolf couldn't allow that, not with the mission entering its critical phase.

Rolf was seriously impressed. He'd always regarded Rachel as window dressing, a pretty face and body to escort him through the social activities his position required him to attend. Now she had refused to succumb to Roskov's intimidation and had taken it upon herself to hire her own enforcer. More than that, she had apparently chosen exceedingly well.

These were qualities Rolf hadn't imagined she possessed, qualities worthy of any Koenig matriarch. In a single bold action, Rachel had demonstrated that she—and by extension, her family—was not to be screwed with.

The thought sent a thrill shooting up Rolf's spine. Maybe he'd found his life partner buried within his trophy wife.

The feel of concrete beneath his feet brought Rolf out of his reverie, alerting him to his arrival on the launch pad. From this angle, without a rocket to fill the void between them, the steel framework of the launch towers framed the coming storm, the lighting seeming to connect the two superstructures. He almost expected to see Dr. Frankenstein step forward to draw upon that power to bring a new creature to life. But Rolf was the only doctor who would be bringing a monster to life in this place, and the monster he would unleash would make the Americans wish for Dr. Frankenstein's.

CHAPTER 24

Janet parked the car a block away from Jack's apartment building and walked directly to the entrance. She wasn't worried about the BMW. One way or another, she wouldn't be inside the building for that long. Besides, it was a rental.

She'd thought about her next actions during the twenty-three minutes it had taken her to get here from her hotel and she had settled on a crazy gamble. If her gamble went bad, she might just find herself dead or worse, spending the rest of her days behind bars in Fort Leavenworth. But from everything she'd read and heard, Jack Gregory had always exhibited an uncanny knack for spotting a tail, so watching from a distance probably wasn't going to produce acceptable results. And unlike Peter Sellers in the old classic movie *Being There*, Janet didn't like to watch.

The thing that had convinced her was Garfield Kromly's response to Levi Elias's question about whether he thought it was possible that Jack had turned. *Not a snowball's chance in hell.* Janet had always had faith in her old CIA trainer's judgment. Now she was about to put that judgment to the test.

She opened the door into an unadorned entryway. This room had no security guard, no comfortable waiting area, only a single elevator and a door to the stairwell. Janet took the latter, ascending to the third floor. It didn't surprise her that Jack would want to stay close to the bottom of the building, just in case he needed to make a hasty exit. Neither was she surprised to find the third-floor hallway almost completely dark, all but one of the light bulbs having burned out, that one illuminating a small circle near the hallway's far end. A sliver of light shone beneath the third door on the right and Janet already knew it would be Jack's.

Walking directly to the door, Janet knocked three times.

The door opened as her hand came away from the last knock and Janet found herself staring directly into the round black muzzle of a nine-millimeter H&K. She ignored it, extending her open right hand.

"Hello, Jack. Janet Price. NSA."

CHAPTER 25

A faint sound brought Jack to his feet, his H&K having filled his hand without his conscious awareness. No need to rack the slide, he kept a round constantly chambered. The presence of a manual safety was the only reason he preferred the H&K over a Glock. And despite the old Special Ops mantra that "My trigger finger is my safety," the clutching bush of the Amazon had long ago taught him that other things had trigger fingers as well. A flick of his thumb combined with a squeeze of the trigger sent a round downrange just as quickly as he could with the Glock's longer trigger pull.

The distant sound had been that of a door softly closing, but not one of the apartment doors. This had been the distinctive click of the metal stairwell door latching closed. Jack moved to the side of his door and leveled the weapon, ready for the booted feet that would soon kick it in. But he didn't hear any booted feet.

If someone moved down the hall, they did it so silently that even Jack's ears couldn't detect the movement.

Three loud raps surprised him, forcing Jack to change his plans on the fly. He jerked the door inward with his left hand as his right maintained the shooter's sightline, finger tightening ever so slightly on the trigger.

"Hello, Jack. Janet Price. NSA."

The woman who stood before him extended her right hand, holding it there in expectation of a welcoming handshake, no glimmer of fear in her dark brown eyes. Without taking his eyes away from her, his peripheral vision told him she was alone in the hallway. Jack ignored the extended hand, stepped back, and with a slight motion of the H&K, welcomed her into his apartment.

She stepped across the threshold as Jack closed the door with his foot, grabbed her arm, and spun her face against the wall, the muzzle of the H&K pressed firmly against her right temple. Kicking her feet shoulder width apart, he patted her down with his left hand. Reaching inside her black leather jacket, he extracted the subcompact from her undershirt's gun-pocket and tossed it onto the couch. Throughout the frisking, the woman remained calm, her lean, hard body offering no resistance.

Jack's gaze drank her in. Five foot ten, her body reminded him of a dancer he'd liked in the Broadway musical *Cats*. Tight jeans tucked into soft leather boots. If she hid a weapon there, she couldn't reach it before he killed her.

Releasing her, Jack stepped back, watching her turn to face him, her eyes sparkling with a hint of something. Certainly not fear. He felt no fear in her. Excitement.

Jack motioned her toward the kitchen table and she took a seat opposite the open laptop. Jack holstered the H&K, took a seat, and resumed his study of this fascinating young woman who, apparently with working knowledge of who and what he was, had calmly walked up to his apartment as if he'd invited her to dinner. Her long brown hair was tied up in a loose knot that enhanced the strong lines of her attractive face. But it was the ease with which she moved, the way her body relaxed into the chair, that Jack found so compelling. The way her eyes followed him reminded him of a cat watching a mouse. Hungry eyes.

Jack knew the feeling.

"So what brings Janet Price of the NSA to my apartment this many hours before dawn?"

"Do we have to continue speaking to each other in the third person or can we talk like real people?"

"Fine. Why are you here and how did you find me?"

Janet's eyes narrowed as she studied his face. Then, taking a breath that gave the first hint of stress he'd seen in this startling NSA operative, she nodded.

"Admiral Jonathan Riles sent me to find you. So here I am."

"That doesn't answer my questions."

Once again Janet Price paused, her gaze travelling to Jack's laptop. She gestured toward it with her hand, extending her index finger in a downward pointing gesture, touching the tip to the table in front of her and holding it there for several seconds. A light dawned in Jack's mind. Reaching for the laptop, he pressed the power key and held it down until the computer turned off.

"The NSA tracked me through the laptop? Mind telling me how they did that through a system I bought just a couple of days ago. A virus?"

"Let's just say the agency is adept at gaining access to someone's computer. By telling you, I'm putting my life in your hands."

"You did that when you walked up to my door."

"I'm well aware."

This time Jack paused, letting the silence hang in the air between them. He watched as Janet leaned back in her chair, watched as she let the tension drain from her body, re-establishing the utter calm she'd maintained up until the last few moments. As she watched him watch her, the hint of a smile returned to her lips. Jack liked what he was seeing and she knew it.

"You have my attention. Go on."

As Jack made a fresh pot of coffee, Janet told of how NSA analysts had identified unusual CIA activity in and around Germany, activity that correlated to Rolf Koenig, Vladimir Roskov, and a dead ex-CIA fixer named Jack Gregory. As he set a cup of the steaming black liquid in front of Janet and resumed his own seat, she wrapped up her narrative, explaining how Jonathan Riles had pulled her out of Cartagena with the mission of making contact with Jack. Once she'd gotten to Berlin, the NSA had found him, so here she was.

Jack sipped his coffee, letting the bold liquid linger on his tongue before swallowing.

"So Admiral Riles thought it was a good idea for you to walk right in on me."

"That was all me."

"Reckless."

"I'm still alive."

Jack closed the laptop, flipped it upside down, pulled the Swiss Army Knife from his pocket, and removed the screws which gave him access to the laptop internals. It took just three minutes to physically disconnect the built-in microphone and camera and reassemble the case. As he started to switch the laptop back on, Janet slid a tiny memory stick across the table toward him.

"Among other things, this has a clean Linux installation and a drive-wipe utility. Since the MAC address is compromised, you'll have to ditch that computer, but you can use the Linux install to clean your next one."

"And you think I'll take your word for that?"

"Garfield Kromly seems to think you're pretty good at deciding who and what to believe."

The sound of his old trainer's name slipping from this woman's lips sent an electric shock through his body. As close as Garfield and Pamela Kromly had been to him in his past life, Robert's death and its aftermath had robbed him of that relationship. Pam had died and been buried without him ever being aware of her illness. When Jack had learned of it, it had rocked him like the loss of his own mother. And as much as he'd wanted to contact Garfield to convey those feelings, he hadn't done it. Now that relationship was lost, forever. And maybe that was for the best.

"I used to be."

"Your choice."

Jack looked into Janet's eyes, watched her unblinking gaze meet his, and made his decision. Grabbing the memory stick, he plugged it in and then powered on the laptop. Bringing up the BIOS screen, he set the system to boot from the USB device and restarted it. When the initial options screen appeared, he selected the wipe utility, typed "YES" at the confirmation dialog, and let it run.

"Why me?"

"Riles thinks you've stumbled onto something bigger than what you signed on for. He believes you could be a valuable asset. It's why he sent me."

Jack laughed. "No thanks. Those days are over. Now I do what I'm paid to do and leave the big picture to you guys."

Janet leaned forward. "Going this one alone may not be such a good plan. The CIA activity I mentioned earlier is being kept off the DCI's radar. That can happen if the Director doesn't know or doesn't want to know about it, because then it's deemed a high-risk reward operation, one that requires plausible deniability."

"Or it could be a rogue Iran–Contra type operation."

"That thought occurred to us. Either way, they have way too many assets involved for any independent operator to handle. Even you. You're going to need backup."

"That hasn't always worked out well in the past."

Janet stared at him for several seconds, then leaned back. "Okay. What about a temporary partnership of convenience? No long-term strings attached. You stay on your mission, but if you come across something for us 'Big Picture' folks, you let me know about it. In the meantime, I feed you intel you can't get otherwise."

Jack considered. Janet was the smoothest operator he'd run across in recent memory. More than that, he knew she believed everything she was telling him. That combination made her very, very dangerous.

Noting his pause, Janet continued. "Also, on that memory stick, you'll find a special communications program. It will encrypt any document you want to send me. More than that, it monitors a number of high traffic, public websites, and can embed the encrypted message within public images. It will also identify, download, and decrypt any messages I've posted for you."

Jack shut down the laptop, packing it and the memory stick into its carrying case, and then stood up.

"I'll think about it."

"Good enough."

"I'm going to get dressed, grab my things, and walk out of this apartment. You're going to stay right here for twenty minutes after I'm gone."

"When will I know your decision?"

"If you don't get a message through your encryption program, then you'll know not to look me up again. If you get a message, I'll be asking for something to verify just how valuable you really are."

Janet nodded and then remained sitting as Jack walked across the room, dropped his towel on the floor and dressed. He packed his few belongings into a backpack that he slung over his left shoulder, stepped into the dark hallway, and shut the door behind him. By the time he secured his equipment to the motorcycle luggage rack, donned the black helmet, and stepped astride the Beemer that carried him out of the parking garage and into the night, he finally managed to purge the image of Janet Price relaxing at his kitchen table from the forefront of his thoughts.

~ ~ ~

Janet watched Jack unselfconsciously drop his towel and reach for his clothes. Once again she was struck by just how little body fat separated the killer's skin from the muscle that moved beneath it. Perfectly proportioned, marred only by the scar patterns on his chest, shoulders, and back, it was a body that put dangerous cravings in her head.

Janet pushed those thoughts aside and watched Jack walk out of the apartment, remaining seated long enough to allow him to enter the stairwell before walking over to the couch to retrieve her H&K. Sliding it into the gun-pocket, she moved to a more comfortable spot on the couch to wait. She'd give Jack thirty minutes before she took action, even though he'd only told her twenty. With Gregory, it was best not to rush.

Once the wall clock indicated she'd waited long enough, Janet took her encrypted cell phone from her jacket pocket and speed dialed the number. Levi answered on the third ring.

"Elias."

"First contact." Janet felt the two words roll off her tongue with just a hint of satisfaction.

"Target's response?"

"Guarded, but he's considering our proposal."

"Okay. Let me know when the situation changes."

"Wilco. Janet out."

Despite the security encryption provided, the call still went out over a cell-phone network instead of a direct SATCOM link. That meant it was vulnerable, so no specifics could be used in conversation. The short call also reduced the likelihood of a trace. But there was no use in hanging around Jack's old apartment longer than necessary.

When she reached the BMW, Janet was pleasantly surprised that it appeared as she had left it, not even a hubcap missing. Climbing in, she brought the powerful engine rumbling to life and pulled away from the curb. Giving one final glance at the run-down apartment building as it disappeared in her driver's side mirror, Janet switched on the radio. Yes, all in all, it had been a fine night indeed.

CHAPTER 26

"What you got for me?"

Jacob Knox spoke into the sat-phone with a voice that carried a hint of the growl that had been building inside him since he had landed in Berlin. He'd expected the resources available to Nolan Trent to have provided The Ripper's location on day one, but he'd been sitting on his ass in Berlin for three days now without one actionable piece of intel and he didn't like it. Gregory was the one who was supposed to be flying blind, not him.

Cunar Thane's response didn't greatly improve his mood.

"Nothing direct."

"Then give me some indirection."

"It's a little thin, but we've identified some recent unusual offshore banking transactions that might trace back to one of our analysts based out of our Paris consulate."

"Might trace back?"

"There's only an indirect link, nothing solid. We ran it up the chain and couldn't get any buy-in from higher."

"Okay. So who's the analyst?"

"One of the DCI's favorites, Rita Chavez. Rock solid reputation."

"So what's the link?"

"Three years ago she had a brief affair with Jack Gregory, when he was with the agency. The only other link is the timeline of the banking transactions. The accounts in question each received six-figure deposits over the last couple of weeks. But, like I said, we haven't been able to make a solid link between Rita and those accounts."

Inhaling deeply through his nose, Jacob held the breath for several seconds before slowly breathing it out. Cunar was right. This was pretty thin. But thin was better than nothing and, right now, Jacob had a fat fistful of nothing.

"Send me Rita's file."

The pause at the other end of the line punctuated the stress his request induced in Cunar Thane.

"Did I mention that Rita has close ties to the DCI?"

"I don't give a rat's ass. Get me the goddamned file! I'll take it from there."

Another pause ratcheted up Jacob's irritation, but he managed to hold it in.

"I'll see what I can do."

"You do that."

The phone went dead in Jacob's hand. Cunar was a chicken-shit son of a bitch, but he'd get Jacob the file he wanted, even if it took longer than usual to cover his tracks. He was way too smart to really piss Jacob off. Bad things happened to people who pissed him off.

Jacob set the phone on the hotel room desk and stood up to walk to the window. The fourteenth-floor suite looked out over

Potsdamer Platz, the square surrounded by high-rise buildings that proclaimed Germany's rise to Eurozone economic dominance. It was a beautiful sunny Berlin afternoon, one that would have made anyone else want to be out exploring the shops or sitting at an outdoor café sipping the froth on a pilsner. But Jacob wouldn't be partaking of alcohol until he put a bullet through The Ripper's brain pan. And since he currently had no other leads, he'd stay in the suite, alternately cleaning his weapons and pacing like a caged lion while he waited on Cunar Thane to produce. And even though Rita Chavez might turn out to be a false lead, it would set him in motion. Besides, a side trip to Paris wouldn't break his heart.

Even if Rita was clean, she had been Jack's lover. Perhaps there was still a little something between them. If so, that would be all Jacob needed to make The Ripper come to him. And pinning Rita's death on her ex-lover would be easy. Especially since Jacob would be the only surviving witness.

CHAPTER 27

On the opposite side of the room, Vladimir Roskov hurled his cell phone into the wall, following up with a kick to the wall-mounted television that tore it loose from its mounting bracket. The flat screen shattered as the corner struck the desk, sending a glittering spray of glass shards sliding across the tile floor.

Petor Kline had seen Roskov's temper flare many times before, but as he watched his employer destroy the east room of his own penthouse, he felt fear's knife edge slide into his brain. Vlad's just-ended conversation with Rolf Koenig had not gone well. From what he'd heard of the heated exchange, Koenig had ordered Roskov to cease work on any operation to find and kill The Ripper.

Breathing heavily, Roskov spun to face his lieutenant, fury bordering on madness shining in his eyes. "Screw Koenig. Does he think I'm a lapdog that can be ordered to sit, to stay? The bastard tells me to stay on target, to stay focused. You know what happens if I let someone kill my people and send their bodies to my warehouse in the trunk of one of my cars and then do nothing? Do you?"

Petor only nodded, unwilling to interrupt Vlad's rage with an insipid response.

"Sooner or later someone finds me in my own car's trunk."

"So Koenig wants us to do nothing?" Petor ventured.

Vlad's eyes finally focused on Petor. "Only with regard to The Ripper. He says unspecified government agencies will deal with that man. He wants me to increase my security and relocate to Kazakhstan by Monday."

The mention of moving into the operation's final phase one week earlier than planned quickened Petor's pulse. Time had become a crazy conductor on a bullet train, propelling them all toward Rolf Koenig's defining moment. He understood Koenig's demand that Roskov stay focused on the critical task that lay before him. For a mission this many years in the making to come off the rails now, just because of one man, was unthinkable. But The Ripper had gotten in Roskov's head, violating the man's self-image in a way that threatened his always tenuous sanity.

Of course Koenig had prepared for just such a contingency. It was the reason Rolf had inserted Petor into Roskov's operation three years ago. It was the reason Petor had put so much of himself into working his way into Roskov's inner circle. He'd killed his way in, not that he minded that. In fact, he regarded it as a bonus on a job that had already made him a rich man. And when all this was over, in addition to riches, he would have power such as only the likes of Rolf Koenig could bestow.

"There may be a way to get what you want without Koenig being any the wiser."

Now he definitely had Vlad's attention. "Talk to me."

Walking to the window, his shoes crunching broken glass, Petor let his gaze wander over the bustling Berlin streets.

"The problem is three-fold. First we need to get you secured in the Kazakh facility. Second, I'll target The Ripper, delaying and distracting him so he can't interfere with your mission, while I prep for the kill. Don't worry, I'll take The Ripper down."

"I want him alive."

"If I can't take him alive, I'll bring you his head in a sack."

Roskov moved up beside Petor, speaking with a voice that rumbled deep in his chest. "Not good enough."

Petor turned to face Roskov, his gaze locking with the mobster's. "Okay. But it'll cost you extra."

Roskov grinned. "Then I'll stay focused on the Koenig project. Afterward, bring me The Ripper and you can write your own check."

Petor nodded, then turned and walked toward the door.

"And Petor . . . "

Roskov's voice brought him to a halt, hand on the doorknob.

"Don't disappoint me."

CHAPTER 28

Jack banked the black Beemer hard around the corner of Rüdigerstrasse and Schottstrasse, letting the powerful motorcycle carry him away from the apartment and into the waning night.

Turning onto Frankfurter Allee, he left Berlin for the rural country to the east. Jack passed through Vogelsdorf and Tasdorf, letting the graying sky of the coming dawn welcome him to his next lodging. And although he didn't yet know whether he would choose to rent a room at a village gasthaus or at a farmhouse on the outskirts, he knew he would recognize the right place when he saw it.

The two-story farmhouse just outside Herzfelde, with its waterwheel and attached barn, pulled him into the cobbled driveway as if the bike had acquired a mind of its own. Dropping the kickstand, Jack switched off the Beemer and stepped clear.

Removing his helmet, he hung it from the handlebar, ran a hand through his hair, and walked up to the door.

The gray-haired woman that opened the door had the strong, matronly face of a farmer's wife, her clear blue eyes taking in the man before her with businesslike efficiency.

"May I help you?"

"Do you have a room free?"

"We always have a room for someone who is willing to pay."

"How much?"

"For one person, forty euros per night or two hundred a week, breakfast included, payment in advance."

Jack reached for his wallet and handed her two hundred-euro bills. Then, grabbing his things from the motorcycle, he followed her inside, up a narrow set of stairs to the second floor, and into a room at the far end of a narrow hallway. It was a clean but simple space—a single bed, a free-standing schrank by the door, a small desk beneath the window, and a sink.

Jack extended his hand. "I'm Karl Dietrich and this will do nicely."

"Frau Gensler. The water closet is down the hall on your left. Please make yourself comfortable. Breakfast is still available downstairs. I have some meats, cheeses, and breads set out. Also coffee."

"Thank you."

Jack watched Frau Gensler depart, then shut the door behind her.

Dropping his backpack onto the bed, Jack let his thoughts return to the fascinating young NSA agent who had confronted him in the Berlin apartment. To say that he found her exciting would be doing his inner demon a disservice. The confidence of that dark-haired beauty had set him on fire. He'd known that her pulse raced with a full load of adrenaline injected into her system by the dangerous encounter, yet she'd shown no outward indication of that internal tension. Sniper calm.

He had no doubt that Janet Price was one very special agent. And since Admiral Jonathan Riles had sent her to him, it meant the NSA director believed something big was about to go down and that Jack was right in the middle of it. Janet had made him a reasonable offer and he found himself wanting to accept it. That was exactly why he'd do no such thing.

After all, the thing he wanted most in the world was to track down Carlton "Priest" Williams and take his sweet time killing the man. But Jack continued to deny himself the object of his desire. Somehow he feared that if he let those inner urges control his actions, he would become a puppet of the beast within, a slave to his basest desires, no better than his nineteenth-century namesake, maybe something far worse. He already felt like a vampire thirsting for hot blood, all the while knowing that to give in to that craving would be to dive into a rip current that would sweep him into a roiling sea of addiction.

No. He would stay focused on the job at hand and keep his eye on the little picture. But first, he felt the need for a long, hard workout. Perhaps that, a cold shower, and some sleep would pluck Janet Price from his head.

CHAPTER 29

Rachel Koenig switched off her cell phone and set it on her nightstand, struggling to wrap her mind around the conversation she'd just had with her husband. At least she thought it was her husband, although she hadn't heard him speak to her like a real person since their wedding. Rolf had actually spent forty minutes talking to her as if she were a partner instead of a decoration. And he'd asked for her help. He hadn't demanded. He'd just asked.

Rachel rose from the bed and opened the French doors that let her step out onto the high balcony, feeling the gentle night breeze rustle her lacy white nightgown against her legs. Still low in the sky, the quarter moon dimly illuminated the castle walls far below, painting their long shadows across the courtyard.

As she replayed the conversation in her mind, Rachel understood one thing: Jack Gregory was everything she'd thought he'd be and more. As hard as it was for her to believe, The Ripper had cowed Vladimir Roskov. According to Rolf, Roskov had notified him that if Rachel would call off her attack dog, Roskov would end his intimidation campaign against Rolf and his family. In addition, Roskov had promised to have no more contact with the Koenigs or any of the many Koenig business concerns.

Stepping up to the stone railing, Rachel leaned over to look down into the moonlit courtyard. To think that just three weeks ago, she'd leaned across this railing and considered taking the fall onto those paving stones a hundred feet below. Now, it appeared her long nightmare was over. Rolf's voice had carried a very real note of respect as he'd thanked her for finding and hiring Jack Gregory. And although he hadn't overdone the praise, she sensed the feeling behind his words, a feeling that helped her believe. That, and the fact that Rolf hadn't ordered her to call off The Ripper. He'd asked her to.

Rachel walked back into her bedroom, shrugged into her warm cashmere robe, and walked out into the hallway. Turning left, she passed Rolf's bedroom on her left and the door to the ancient spiral stairway on her right, stopping before their private elevator to punch the call button. As the door slid open, Rachel stepped inside and pressed the button numbered two. When she stepped out of the elevator onto the office level, two floors above the grand entryway, Rachel noted the automatic increase in lighting as the motion sensor detected her arrival and walked directly to her private office.

While much smaller than Rolf's, it had all the toys that one would expect to be available to the wife of the founder of the world's second-largest technology conglomerate. But unlike Apple's legendary founder, Rolf Koenig was a multi-layered genius with personal designs that spanned technological realms from microprocessors to satellite communications systems and nuclear-powered, off-world mining robots.

Many people misjudged her husband, thinking he was primarily interested in building his family fortune. The truth was that Rolf regarded money as merely a tool that enabled him to move on to his next technological breakthrough. Rachel knew Rolf had ambitions far beyond mining the moon. Her husband believed he was a modern-day Queen Isabella, destined to release the riches of untapped worlds that others thought well beyond practical reach. More than that, he wanted to lay claim to vast stretches of those worlds. But that required changes to existing treaties that would enable companies to establish those land grants. That would open the floodgates, releasing the torrent of cash unproductively sitting in corporate vaults.

To do that he needed to prove to Europe and the emerging powers in Asia that America's time of technological leadership was past. America had set the world's rules for space exploration, had established the limits on its exploitation via outdated international treaties. But instead of protecting the solar system from exploitation, Rolf knew that those ill-considered agreements had prevented space development that would benefit all mankind.

America had lost its vision, relegating space exploration to an expensive hobby, subject to the inevitable federal budget cuts such a hobby deserved in tough fiscal times. But Rolf believed space held the key to untold wealth for the corporations that first commercialized its unlimited resources. The *how* was a technological problem, one that could only be solved by a visionary such as himself. Only Rachel knew that there were no visionaries like Rolf. That meant that if it was going to happen, Rolf Koenig would have to do it.

Rachel pulled her thoughts back to the present. It was time to make full payment into the three Caribbean bank accounts Jack Gregory had provided. Then, in the morning, when those transactions had been confirmed, she would send him an encrypted message that would thank him for a job exceptionally well done and notify him that his services were no longer required.

Remembering Heidelberg and how it had felt to stand next to The Ripper on the Alte Brücke, she again felt the surge of adrenaline she'd experienced on that fateful day. Of all the decisions she'd made in her life, hiring that man had certainly been her best.

CHAPTER 30

The moon rose over the Avenue des Champs-Élysées as Rita found herself stuck in traffic, staring out the windshield of her silver Citroën C-Zero at the famously lighted Arc de Triomphe. The environmentally friendly car allowed her to blend seamlessly into the politically correct French culture she had come to adore. Odd that. Rita had grown up in El Paso, Texas, ingrained with a southwestern conservative culture that sneered at European socialism. Yet, for the last five years she'd been firmly embedded, gradually learning to love every minute of it.

There were certainly parts of French culture that grated on foreigners, Americans in particular. But as she got to know them, the French people and their mores had wormed their way into her very soul. Not that there was only one French culture. The people in Normandy were far different from Parisians or from the Mediterranean folk of Nice or Cannes. But the fact that different regions of the country had very distinct feels held no surprise to Rita.

Despite the deep and enduring beauty of the scene, Rita was tired, and the traffic jam wasn't exactly making her day. She wanted to get home to her apartment, open a fine bottle of Bordeaux and swirl it in a broad-rimmed glass. Although she could now afford a much more luxurious place, Rita knew that her security lay in obscurity. While her apartment was small, it was homey, and it had the most wonderful little balcony with its view of the Seine. Just big enough for two chairs. But in this case it held one chair, an end table, and a hanging flower pot.

While some might have thought that sad, given the romantic nature of Paris, it fit Rita's life. Lovers were dangerous. Bringing them into your home was far more so. When she acquired a new lover, she always invaded their space rather than allow them into hers. The exception had been Jack Gregory. But that was in the past and, though she still loved him, she'd learned a lesson. Letting any man too deeply into your life was dangerous. Letting a dangerous man into your personal space could sweep you away in a passionate maelstrom that threatened a total loss of self. More than that, it threatened your life.

Rita looked at her reflection in the rearview mirror and swept her fingers through her long brown hair. Been there. Done that.

It took her another half-hour before she managed to work her way to the parking garage below her apartment. Stepping out of her car, she grabbed her briefcase and the small sack of groceries from her back seat, slamming the door with her knee as she fumbled with the key fob. A rustling noise behind her brought Rita's head around.

Nothing there. Christ, she was jumpy tonight. Probably just lingering tension from the brutal commute. Mix that with the poorly lit and cramped parking space and it was no surprise that she was hearing things. Rita thought about taking the elevator but decided that she could really use the exercise the climb to her third-floor flat would provide. But when she opened the door to the stairwell, the utter darkness that greeted her changed her mind. She'd have to call the manager about the light being out.

Rita hiked her grocery bag up tighter in her arm, walked around the corner to the elevator, and pressed the call button. Normally there were other people in the garage when she got home, but not tonight. Nine p.m. was one of those in-between hours when people were already settled in from work or had already headed out for dinner and an evening on the town.

Again she heard the shuffling sound and again she turned to look over her shoulder. The jolt from the taser dropped her to the concrete floor like she'd been kicked by a mule.

As she struggled to regain some control of her twitching body, a man knelt over her, shoved a needle into the side of her neck, and squeezed the contents of the syringe directly into her blood stream. As strong arms lifted her limp form, a black fog descended, smothering her consciousness along with the fear that tried to reawaken her. Then she drifted, that fear only one dream amongst many.

CHAPTER 31

Jacob Knox stared silently down at the woman seated before him, her hands bound to the steel chair's arms, her feet to the front chair legs, her rag-filled mouth duct-taped closed. She sat atop the chair on a twenty-foot-square sheet of clear plastic. Rita Chavez's long brown hair hung limply on her shoulders, her eyes locked on his face with a mixture of recognition, fear, and resignation to a fate she could only hope would come quickly. Unfortunately, he couldn't grant that wish.

Jacob thought that Rita had been feeding Jack Gregory back-door intelligence, although he wasn't certain of it. That didn't really matter to him. She had been one of Jack's past lovers and that was all that he needed.

Although Jacob despised the man, Gregory was every bit as good as Nolan Trent thought, perhaps even better. Not only was he unpredictable, but he had a highly refined knack for doing the right thing, part of which came as a natural consequence of paying attention to minor details in his surroundings. Jacob didn't know where the rest of that ability came from, but he didn't deny its existence. He made a habit of never underestimating a target.

Rita Chavez tried to say something, to at least get out a sound full of feeling, something to inspire sympathy within Jacob. But Jacob had no sympathy. Nor did he bear her any animus. It was what made Jacob the most accomplished killer the CIA had ever employed. Everyday human emotion was as alien to him as some bandy-legged green Martian. It was why he was going to kill The Ripper.

Because Rita was CIA and one of the DCI's favorites, Jacob would have to make certain that his setup was perfect. But that wouldn't be a problem. The Ripper wasn't the only one who paid attention to the fine details. It was why Jacob had spent the last day studying the little details of Vladimir Roskov's personal kills, the videos that ended up on the internet. Roskov liked blood, lots of it. He was fond of knives and hammers, as well as the creative use of guns to maim and injure. And although it was well known that Roskov was the artist behind those productions, there was never anything in the videos to prove that.

This video would have all of that, but with the deliberate insertion of an identifying mistake.

Jacob peeled off his shirt, revealing a lean, muscular chest, crisscrossed with scar tissue he had applied this morning in a pattern that reasonably matched that in the photo from Jack Gregory's file. That picture, taken in the Calcutta clinic, had been of Jack Gregory's naked corpse, the sutured wounds boldly apparent. Not many had access to that death photo, but the CIA did and Gregory would recognize them. Jacob intended to keep his back to the camera, except for one instance when an extended backswing would momentarily reveal the chest scars to the camera. That one moment was all he needed.

Pulling the plastic clown mask over his head, Jacob started the video recording, picked up his tool bag, and walked across the plastic sheeting toward the wide-eyed Rita Chavez.

It was show time.

CHAPTER 32

Jack finished re-reading Rachel's message for the third time, then, using the prepaid cellular wireless access point, he checked the balance in each of the three numbered Cayman Island accounts he'd given her. Paid in full for a job well done, or so she'd said. In fact, he'd been paid in full for a job half-done. But she was his employer and she was fully satisfied with the services he had provided. Time to pack it up and do what he did best, disappear.

The image of Janet Price sitting across from him at his kitchen table leapt, unbidden, into his mind, bringing with it the feeling that this wasn't over, that somewhere out there, something big was about to happen. It called to him on a primal level that he, once again, chose to ignore.

One good thing about reaching the end of a job was that he could relax for a while. For the moment, he had a safe spot to rest and recuperate before putting the word out that The Ripper was, once again, available for hire. No need to hurry into that, though. Right now, a hot shower sounded very good.

By the time he'd made his way down the hall, showered, and returned to his room, Jack felt at least half-human. He considered going downstairs for the continental breakfast, but the bed called to him louder than his stomach. Slipping the H&K beneath his pillow, Jack crawled beneath the thick German comforter and let his mind slip away.

He awoke in darkness, momentarily disoriented, as he tried to recall just where he'd settled in for this sleep. The feel of the H&K brought him all the way back to reality. A glance at his watch told him it was just past four a.m. He'd been dreaming, but for once he couldn't remember the content of those dreams. That was an improvement. He had enough blood in his life without wallowing in endless rivers of it while he slept.

By 6:30 a.m. Jack had worked out, showered, and downed a hearty breakfast of ham, cheese, and brötchen along with three cups of stout German coffee. Back in his room, he logged on to his laptop and checked the websites he monitored for special messages. Nothing. Glancing down at Janet's memory stick, he considered using the special program that would check to see if she had tried to contact him. But if she had, he didn't really want to know about it. No use opening himself up to the kind of manipulation an agency like the NSA could unleash upon you.

When he pulled up the CNN website, the picture of Rita Chavez and the accompanying headline slapped him in the face.

Torture Killing Video of U.S. French Consular Employee Posted on Web.

Jack read the article. Although CNN refused to provide a link to the gruesome terrorist video, it didn't take long to find it.

The video lasted an agonizing fifty-seven minutes, and Jack forced himself to watch every moment. Then he watched it again, occasionally freezing the playback to examine the tiniest details, locking each one firmly in his memory.

The man in the clown mask had known Vladimir Roskov's trademark technique and had applied it with a cold ruthlessness that kept Rita conscious throughout her drawn-out execution. As Jack watched, he felt the ice slide through his veins, only to vaporize under the heat of the rage that bubbled up from a deeper source. Giving himself completely to that rage, he felt it whet his focus into a glittering blade.

Despite the obvious connection to his Roskov mission, the video was clearly intended to weaponize Jack. It also painted him with a red CIA laser target dot. Although the briefly glimpsed scars on the clown's chest weren't a perfect match to those Jack bore and completely missed the scars on his back, they were close enough to fool someone who had only seen his face-up death photo.

Roskov may not have done the killing, but Roskov was at the heart of this, and the man who'd killed Rita wanted Jack to go for Roskov.

Jack shut down the laptop, walked to the sink, and dowsed his face with cold water. Drying it with the white hand towel, he stared at himself in the mirror. As he watched the dancing red reflection fill his pupils, Jack was certain of one thing: If Rita's killer had intended to activate The Ripper . . . *mission accomplished.*

~ ~ ~

Anchanchu felt the rush of Jack's rage course through his limbic system, using its special talent to amplify that emotional storm and feed it back to its host. As frustrating as this host could be in his determination to enforce self-control, when Jack's façade cracked, the intensity of his feelings went beyond any the mind worm had experienced. And it was oh-so-good when that happened.

It was only a matter of time before Jack's cravings for the adrenaline rush that only Anchanchu could provide controlled this hitherto unbreakable stallion. There could be no doubt. Eventually, Jack Gregory would yield to Anchanchu's bloody spurs.

CHAPTER 33

Frank Rheiner had one basic rule that he'd maintained since he'd been appointed Director of Central Intelligence a year and a half ago: Don't screw with my people. He didn't care if it was field agents, analysts, or the grounds maintenance crews at CIA Headquarters. Someone had just violated that rule, big time. Worse, the man had tortured to death an analyst Frank had known and liked. Now that prick was about to find out why pissing on the DCI wasn't a great plan.

Leaning forward so that his elbows rested on the smooth surface of his teak desk's gently curved top, Frank's eyes locked with those of his deputy, Nolan Trent.

"Talk to me, Nolan."

"We've got a man on the ground in Paris and he's already working a strong lead."

"Who is it?"

"Jacob Knox."

Frank nodded. That was good news. With Knox's special skills and the entire agency's resources at his disposal, Rita's killer was as good as dead.

"Roskov?"

"No sir. We've eliminated that possibility. Someone sure wanted us to think it was Roskov's work, though."

"A pretty slick plan. Kill one of my top analysts and use it to make us terminate one of our most important intelligence assets."

"Except it didn't work. The clown's going down."

"Make sure he does."

"Yes, sir."

The deputy director turned toward the door. As his hand touched the brass knob, Frank's voice brought him up short.

"And Nolan, tell Jacob it won't break my heart if this perp dies hard."

The hint of a smile creased Nolan Trent's lips.

"I'll pass it along."

CHAPTER 34

The Washington Mall was beautiful, a vast grassy expanse that stretched from the Capitol steps to the Lincoln Memorial, with the spire of the George Washington Monument rising up as a centerpiece. On opposite sides, the White House and the Jefferson Memorial flanked the national public space. Surrounded by the houses of government and the repository of U.S. history, the Smithsonian Institution, this beautiful space occupied a spot that had once been worthless swamp.

Nolan Trent walked along the mall, letting the sites he loved cleanse his soul. As hard as it was to conceive, most of the country thought of Washington, D.C., as a cesspool, a crime-ridden nation's capital, filled with corrupt lawyer-politicians, not worthy of the nation it symbolized. And while the caliber of its politicians was a legitimate concern, the beauty that a historic progression of those politicians had created here was beyond reproach. In this one magnificent spot, free to the public, lay a vast assortment of national treasures that those who hadn't visited could never appreciate.

It was a crime that this great country lost the will that had driven it to greatness. The fungus of apathy had crept in, an insidious infestation cloaked in self-satisfaction, a sense that things were good enough, that the country could rest on its laurels. Robbed of a unifying sense of purpose, it gradually surrendered its precious sovereignty to the nattering nabobs at the United Nations.

For a brief moment, he'd thought the Middle Eastern wars would provide that unifying purpose, but even there, the U.S. government had bowed its head to foreign masters until, at the end, it was forced to ask permission from the very governments it had installed, just to perform minor combat operations.

Disillusioned by the costs and sheer idiocy of nation-building, the American public had demanded withdrawal, and who could blame them? There was no path to victory when you couldn't attack into the heart of enemy territory for fear of collateral damage. Collateral damage! God help you if you killed some civilians, even if those were the very people supporting and enabling our enemies. Had that philosophy held sway in World War II, every American would now be speaking Japanese or German.

Feeling his blood pressure start to rise, Nolan stopped, removed the small pill bottle from his pocket, popped one in his mouth, worked up some saliva, and swallowed. Shit. Getting old sucked.

His thoughts turned from the crappy state of the union, to Rolf Koenig. He was the most brilliant man Nolan had ever met, but he was no saint. Thank heaven for that. Rolf had his own reasons for creating the event that was going to change everything, reasons that had nothing to do with the best interest of America. Rolf dreamed of corporations laying claim to the moon, the asteroids, eventually all the planets of our solar system. He dreamed of a space race fueled by the vast wealth out there begging to be exploited. He dreamed of the earth that could be, one that was the seat of robotic mining operations that spanned the solar system. More than that, he was going to make it happen.

To accomplish Rolf's dreams, he had to remove America from its position of dominance. And Nolan was going to help him do just that, although for a totally different set of reasons. Everything had unintended consequences and Nolan was convinced that if America was slapped down hard enough, the legendary American spirit would rise up, reviving the lost quest for U.S. ascendance.

Reaching the World War II Memorial, he paused to stare across the central pool at the Washington Monument framed by the many fountains. What would the warriors who had given their lives on foreign soil think of their mighty nation now? Nolan had no doubt. The United States of America was bleeding out on its deathbed.

The image of the reflective pool blurred, replaced by the memory of tears in his father's blue eyes as Nolan stood beside his wheelchair at the Pointe du Hoc Ranger Monument. Despite the years that had passed since he'd taken his dad to Normandy to pay a last tribute to fallen comrades, the memory of that lonely place was vivid, as crystal clear in his mind's eye as it had been on the day of his dad's funeral, when a soldier handed Nolan the triangular, folded flag.

But that moment hadn't just triggered memories. It had triggered Nolan.

Inhaling deeply, Nolan Trent turned away from that hallowed ground, letting his steps carry him back toward his car. If the jolt Rolf Koenig was about to deliver didn't restart the nation's pulse, then the America he loved was already dead.

CHAPTER 35

Fluent in Russian, Jack had to admit his Polish was a bit rusty. In a previous era, when the Soviet Union dictated how things were run, that would have made the border crossing an adventure. But EU membership had changed all that. Now the crossing was almost as uneventful as driving from New York to New Jersey.

It had taken Jack two hours of driving to get from Berlin to the Gryfia Shipyard in Szczecin. As he stepped off the black motorcycle and removed his helmet, swapping it for a blue baseball cap and sunglasses, he let his gaze roam the docks. It was nearing five p.m. and at this hour most of the workers were stowing gear in preparation for their home commute. In Jack's mind, this was what a shipyard should be, loading docks, cranes, big ships in dry-dock, the clank and roar of massive equipment, smelling of diesel fumes, paint, and sweat. It was an iron-bending world populated by hard men engaged in physically dangerous work.

Jack liked it.

For one thing, there were nowhere near as many web-enabled cameras here in Poland as existed in Germany. And though riding around masked by the motorcycle helmet's dark faceplate helped, it was nice not to have to constantly think about it.

Walking around the south side of the warehouse immediately to his left, Jack climbed the steps that led to a steel platform two dozen feet above the asphalt and stepped through a door that opened into a cluttered outer office. When he stopped in front of a gray steel-case desk, the heavyset blond woman looked up from her paperwork and removed her half-moon glasses, letting them fall to dangle from a silver chain around her neck. Her raised left eyebrow asked the question she didn't bother to voice.

Jack answered it. "I'm here to see Kazimer Wozniak."

The woman picked the hand-rolled cigarette from a broken gear casing that served as an ashtray and dragged the smoke deep into her lungs. Letting the gray swirl roll out of her mouth, she pulled it back in through her nose, a trick she seemed to think would impress him. It didn't.

When she spoke, her voice sounded like a cough.

"Who's asking?"

"Tell him Radoslaw Symanski wants to see him."

"Tell him yourself," she said, nodding toward the open door to Jack's right.

As Jack stepped through the door, a great black-bearded bear of a man wrapped him in arms strong enough to snap Jack's spine. Instead the big man planted a loud kiss on each cheek, slapped him hard on the back, and stepped away.

"Rado. Damn, it's good to see you. Why the hell didn't you tell me you were coming?"

"Was in the area so thought I'd drop by."

"Good timing. I was just straightening up some papers before knocking off for the day."

Jack glanced at the jumble of papers spread across the desk and grinned. "I can see that."

"Come on. Ludmina will shoot me if I don't bring you home for dinner. Wait. I better give her a call so she knows to cook extra. Kaszanka okay?"

"Nobody does blood sausage better."

The man picked up an old-style curly-corded phone, his huge hands making the green handset look like a child's toy. It had been four years since Jack had first seen Kazimer. He could still feel the sticky wetness, could still smell the blood that had bathed him as he'd struggled to lift the big man into his car. On that rainy night, three of Kaz's competitors had pumped a dozen rounds into the giant, yet he lived while they had not. Jack had made sure of that.

Odd how chance sometimes swept you up in its palm, rolling you across a giant, green-felt table as the players placed their bets. At those moments, Jack could almost hear a ghostly croupier yell . . . *New shooter coming out!*

Although Jack had been in Poland on business, it had been chance that arranged the meeting at the precise moment the hit had gone down. Perhaps it had been because the contract was for Kaz, or maybe because the man provided a bigger, more intimidating target that had made all three shooters aim their first several shots at him. Whatever the reason, it hadn't worked out all that well for them or for their boss. In Jack's experience, it never made sense to shoot a mobster's men, then leave him alive to hunt you down. So he hadn't.

In a way, Jack supposed that it had been Kaz who had saved his life that night, rather than the other way around. But that wasn't how Kaz and Ludmina saw it and it had made Jack family, at least as close to family as the head of a Polish syndicate and a

CIA killer could be. But that had happened in another life. In this one, the people he cared about got killed.

In fact, he wouldn't even be here if it hadn't been for Rita. The people behind her killing had inside information on Jack's resources. That meant he couldn't use any of his usual suppliers. But nobody except for himself, Kaz, and Ludmina knew about his Polish connection. So here Jack was, even though it meant putting another old friend in danger.

"My little wife says to make sure you don't get lost getting to the house. It's been so long she thinks you might have forgotten the way."

"I remember." Jack laughed. Only someone as large as Kaz would call Ludmina little.

"Yeah, well you follow me anyway. Wouldn't want one of my boys thinking you shouldn't be dropping by."

Jack nodded.

Kaz led the way out of the office, pausing at the outer door to turn back toward his secretary. "I'm leaving. You might as well close up here."

Without looking up from her papers, the woman waved him away.

At the bottom of the steps, the big man stopped.

"Where you parked?"

"Just around the corner."

"I'll swing around. Wait for me there."

"I'll be right on your ass. Black motorcycle."

By the time Jack stepped onto the Beemer, the black Mercedes pulled up beside him, pausing just long enough for him to strap on his helmet before heading away from the docks. A hard right turn onto Cementowa was immediately followed by a right that put them on Ludowa Street, headed north. Twenty-three minutes of fighting their way through rush-hour traffic brought them to the intersection of Szosa Polska and Na Wzgorzu. The Mercedes took a left turn and Jack closed up on its bumper while the residential neighborhood grew more prosperous around him, a collection of two-story houses separated by tree-lined green space.

Turning into a large, fenced compound, the Mercedes paused as two guards nodded to the driver and opened the electrically controlled gate. When the car rolled forward, Jack moved in after it. As he passed through, the guard on Jack's left attracted his attention. Something about the man's stance felt wrong, but before he had a chance to examine the man more closely, they went by, pulling into the large house's curved driveway.

The three-story house was painted white, its red tile roof sporting three separate chimneys, as one would expect in a house this size in this northwestern region of Poland. In winter, the winds off Dabie Lake blew in so cold and damp that multiple hearths were more of a requirement than a luxury.

As the triple garage door rumbled up along its track, Jack parked the Beemer in the driveway just to the left of the garage. Hanging his helmet over the handlebar, he stepped into the garage where Kaz waited. The driver, a muscular bald man with a Ruger strapped in a shoulder holster beneath his left arm, stepped around the rear of the car and opened the trunk. Once again, Jack felt that sense of wrongness. But here in the home of the man who ran Poland's third-largest seaport, it was unlikely that the mobster's enemies could threaten him, especially since a large portion of the city's police force was on his unofficial payroll.

When Jack stepped inside, the matronly woman in a blue-flowered dress and apron turned toward him, bread basket in hand, her shoulder-length blond hair framing a smiling face. As Jack started to greet her, he spotted the unusual bulge beneath the towels covering the dinner rolls.

Diving hard to his left, Jack saw the wood doorframe explode behind the spot where his head had been a second before. Firing twice as he finished his shoulder roll, he saw his first bullet punch a round hole in the center of Ludmina's forehead, the second catching her in the center of her chest. The dual impact hammered her backward into the stove, spilling the simmering kettle and sending blood sausages squirming across the tile floor like short red snakes.

Kazimer moved fast for a big man, his massive bulk crashing into Jack as he spun toward his host, the force of the blow sending Jack's H&K spinning across the floor, coming to rest beneath a cabinet. As the giant attempted the takedown, Jack went with it, using all his strength to increase the momentum Kazimer's flying body had imparted to him. It was like being shot from a cannon. Although it prevented Kaz from wrapping him in those massive arms, the impact with the kitchen cabinet knocked the air from Jack's body and opened a gash in the hairline on the left side of his head.

Jack spun, delivering a kick to the side of Kazimer's left knee that buckled the leg as he barely managed to dodge the grasping hand that sought to pull him into a fatal embrace. Seeing the big man reach for his own gun, Jack plunged toward the spot where Ludmina's body lay sprawled across the stove, fire now spreading from her dress into her hair, the Ruger still clutched in her plump right hand.

Grabbing her arm, Jack pulled and whirled, bringing her corpse around in front of him as the big man's pistol belched. The first bullet took her high on the shoulder, the second hammered into her stomach. Then Jack had the Ruger in his hand, raising the weapon and pulling the trigger as he let Ludmina's body fall away. Two head shots and the giant was down.

The driver came through the garage door, gun leveled, seeking a target. Jack's third shot sent him sprawling back into the garage. Reaching under the cabinet, Jack retrieved his H&K as a mental count started in his head. He didn't have long, maybe thirty seconds, before the two guards outside came for him. Or, if they were smart, one would come while the other called the cops. Either way, Jack didn't care to wait on them.

Striding rapidly out through the dining room, he moved into the spacious living room, staying away from the windows and close to the wall. Bypassing the staircase that led to the second floor, Jack reached a game room, replete with hardwood floors and tables for poker and billiards. A door opened out onto a back deck, beyond which a tree-lined path led down to a small pond.

The sound of the front door being kicked in got him moving. Avoiding the path, Jack stayed against the back wall. He paused briefly to check for more guards, then turned and sprinted along the east wall, coming to a stop just before he reached the front. All he had left to do was to turn that corner and sprint past the garage doors, start the motorcycle, and haul ass. But he felt that familiar tingle at the edge of his consciousness, a sense he'd been ignoring of late, and right now it was telling him that only one of the guards had gone inside.

Where would the other man be? Somewhere with a good line of sight to that front door, but with cover. Most likely right against the wall, pistol aimed and ready in case the wrong person stepped out of it. Having made his decision, Jack raised the H&K and spun around the corner, squeezing the trigger as his sightline cleared the side of the building. But this time the man wasn't where he was supposed to be, having crouched down behind the wall on the far side of the open gate.

The good news was that the guard was crouched behind the wall on the left side of the gate opening and would have to reveal himself to get a shot at Jack. The bad news was the Uzi he held in his hands. Jack ducked back around the corner as the submachine gun ate into the front of the garage. The brief glance had told him that this particular Uzi had an extended, forty-eight round clip and the guard had just used up about half the magazine repositioning himself behind the wall on the right side of the open gate.

Not wanting to allow the guard time to swap magazines, Jack put a couple of blind shots around the corner and then pulled back, rewarded with another burst of nine-millimeter slugs in his direction. As soon as the two quick bursts stopped, he fired again, then again.

When the guard didn't immediately fire back, Jack came around the corner at a dead run. The first bullet hit the metal gate. The man slammed home his second magazine and released the slide that would push a cartridge into the chamber. As the gun started to rise, Jack's next bullet lifted the guard and slammed him to the ground just beyond the gate. Seeing the guard struggle to rise, Jack squeezed the trigger twice more, the second shot sending a red plume out the back of the man's head.

At the motorcycle, Jack pressed the Beemer's start button and left it running behind him as he raced for the front door, coming to a stop in the spot he'd incorrectly anticipated the dead guard would wait. Now that the shooting had stopped and the motorcycle noise had started, it wouldn't be long. Kill zones did that. Pulled people to them like magnets. Psychology of war scholars had long observed this aspect of human nature. When a sniper shot one soldier in an open field, others would race to reach the downed man, and as more and more soldiers were drawn to the kill zone, their bodies would stack up. Leaders trained their men not to succumb to that deadly temptation, but many failed to resist that siren's call.

Jack waited for it and saw the concealed man swing the gun out through the open doorway. Grabbing the extended hand,

Jack twisted hard, feeling the bones crack as he heard the gunshot. With the gun spinning away onto the driveway, Jack pulled hard on the broken hand and kicked, whipping the legs out from beneath the shooter attached to it. A scream gargled from the man's mouth as he landed face down on the asphalt, and then it stopped as Jack pressed the H&K's muzzle to the fellow's head and squeezed the trigger.

As Jack got back to his feet, the sound of distant police sirens launched him back toward the motorcycle. With blood running down the left side of his face, Jack slid on the helmet, stepped onto the running motorcycle, and laid a trail of smoking rubber all the way back out to the street. Turning north onto Szosa Polska, Jack accelerated, letting the city fall away behind him.

An image burned itself into his head, an image of himself blowing the brains out of two people he'd cared about, two people he'd believed felt the same. Jack felt sick to his stomach. Someone had gotten to them, had turned people he didn't think anyone even knew about, leaving him blind in a world that he needed to see. And while he could always cultivate new resources, that could only be done slowly and reliably, or quickly with great risk. He didn't have time for the former and the latter probably wouldn't get it done.

That's what big, powerful intel organizations did, took away your options until they funneled you to the kill. Back at Kazimer Wozniak's compound, that had almost worked. Almost.

So now he'd head back to the farmhouse outside Berlin. Then he'd play the one wild card he had left in his hand.

CHAPTER 36

"The Wozniaks are dead!"

Victor Drugal's words surprised Vladimir Roskov so badly that he almost dropped the cell phone.

"What? How?"

"I don't have the details yet. Just that The Ripper went into their compound and killed them all. Kazimer Wozniak, his wife Ludmina, and three guards. He escaped the compound before the police arrived."

Vladimir forced himself to relax the grip that threatened to crush the phone into small, non-functional bits of plastic, metal, and glass.

"Tell me we didn't lose him again."

"One of Wozniak's men put a GPS tracker on The Ripper's motorcycle while it was parked at the docks outside Wozniak's warehouse. We're tracking it right now. He's back in Germany, headed toward Berlin."

The sudden rush of adrenaline brought a grin to Vlad's face. "Okay. Round up a dozen of our boys and get them moving. Wherever The Ripper stops, get him surrounded. I want that bastard alive, but I don't care how badly he's damaged."

"Koenig's not going to like it."

"I don't give a shit whether Koenig likes it or not! It'll be over before he knows what happened. One less complication. Let me know as soon as it's done."

"Okay, boss."

Vlad ended the call, returned the phone to his pocket, and walked to the penthouse window. The Polish Bear, the head of the Polish mob, a man who had seemed as indestructible as Vlad, was dead. Kazimer had been a crucial partner since their criminal organizations had joined forces eight months ago, forming a remarkably profitable relationship for both of them. The vacuum that would ensue after word of his death got out was sure to spark a war for control of Polish organized crime, one that Vlad would have to participate in if he was to maintain the special arrangements Kazimer had put in place.

It was a tragedy, but out of it, some good had come. In a few hours he would have The Ripper at his tender mercy and then he would make sure the killer paid for all the trouble he had caused. And, on a day like this, it was nice to have something to look forward to.

CHAPTER 37

By the time Jack parked the motorcycle in front of the farmhouse, darkness gripped the German countryside. Still wearing his helmet, he walked directly inside and up the stairs to his room. When he removed the helmet, the scalp wound began bleeding again. As it was, so much blood caked the left side of his face that he looked like a car crash victim.

Stripping off his leather jacket and shirt, Jack started a jet of hot water flowing into the sink and set about scrubbing the scabs and blood from his face, hair, and neck. When he was satisfied, he used a washcloth to apply direct pressure to the inch-long cut, then retrieved his first-aid kit and bandaged it with gauze.

The image of Ludmina Wozniak splayed out across the stove—a round hole in the center of her forehead, green eyes wide open and staring as her hair caught fire—filled his mind. He needed a shower, needed to feel the hot water wash away the filth of this day. If only it could wash the filth from his soul.

Jack stripped out of the rest of his clothes and wrapped a towel around his waist. He transferred his wallet and Janet's USB dongle from his filthy jeans to a clean pair, grabbed some boxers and the shoulder holster that held his H&K and survival knife, and walked down the hallway to the water closet. Closing the door behind him, he locked it and stepped into the single stall, setting the water spray as hot as he could stand.

The bar of soap in the ceramic dish was rough. Either it was one of those exfoliating pumice bars or it had been dropped on the floor a few times too often. Either way it felt good scrubbing his chest and shoulders. With the steam building to sauna thickness all around him, he breathed it deep into his lungs and let the tension drain from his body.

He'd just finished toweling dry and pulling on his pants when the sound of the window in his room shattering preceded a shock wave that shook the building. Jack recognized the signature of the weapon. A flash-bang grenade designed to stun and incapacitate. Booted feet raced past the water closet, followed by the crash of splintering wood.

Immediately Jack was in the hallway, his H&K barking twice, each nine-millimeter Parabellum hammering three-hundred pounds of force into the backs of two of the men who had entered his room. But he'd heard a half-dozen running feet so he didn't wait for a response. Launching himself down the narrow stairway, his shoulder slammed the wall at the turn and he rolled into the entryway as two more weapons blazed into the space where he'd just been.

Again his gun bucked in his hand as his first bullet made an eye hole in a black hood and the second round spattered wood from the edge of the counter the fellow's partner had just dived behind. Jack hit the open door at a run, leaped over Frau Gensler's sprawled body, and ducked behind a tractor as a hail of bullets spattered off the farmhouse wall behind him. Then he was around the barn and into the woods beyond, his bare feet flying silently over the rough ground, with the sounds of shouts and loud crashing shredding the night's silence behind him.

Jack turned hard left, ducking through the brush and brambles, feeling the branches and thorns clutch at him with sharp fingers, their claws tearing at his flesh as sharp rocks gouged his bare feet. Three flashlight beams swept through the trees to his right, and although he was tempted to kill the wielders, he chose instead to ignore them. They were serving only to rob his hunters of their night vision and the flash of gunfire would give his location away, sending a spread of runners to cut off his selected escape route.

He didn't have a clear idea how many masked men had been sent to take him down, but it had to be at least ten. Even though he had sent three of them into the ever-dark, he didn't really want to stick around for a drawn-out gunfight that would attract others to the action, including the police.

Something off to his left brought him to a halt. Not movement. A stillness within the night that felt wrong. Moving silently down the bank, Jack entered a stream. At its center it was only chest deep, so Jack took a deep breath and ducked beneath the surface, propelling himself forward against the gentle current as a mental count started in his head.

On a normal day Jack could hold his breath for more than six minutes. Right now though, he was winded. He'd been swimming beneath the surface for just over two minutes and already his lungs were screaming for relief. But based upon where he had sensed that unnatural stillness in the night, he hadn't yet passed it. That meant his lungs would just have to wait. His mental count reached three minutes and still he forced himself to keep swimming, despite the fairy-dust sparkles beginning to appear at the edge of his vision.

When finally he broke the surface, he did so silently. And though he wanted to gulp in great lungfuls of the fresh night air, he merely sipped it, remaining perfectly still along the bank while his heart rate slowed to sixty beats per minute. The distant shouts indicated that his pursuers were cutting a circuit through the woods, attempting to find his trail. But these guys were Roskov's thugs, not professional trackers, and the odds of them finding and being able to follow his trail in the dark weren't good. Then again, there were a bunch of them tromping through the woods and they might just get lucky.

Although the night wasn't cold, the water had chilled him and, stirred by the stiff breeze that had come up after sunset, the chill added to his discomfort. Cold, wet, and exhausted, he could feel the demon fire rise up within, a dim but growing echo of the blood lust he experienced in his dreams. Sensing that he had passed beyond the outer perimeter his enemies had set up around the farmhouse, it would be a simple thing to shift from hunted to hunter. They would not expect him to come back at them from outside.

From its sheath on his shoulder holster, the black SAF survival knife called to him. He wanted to feel that razor sharp blade part flesh and slide through vital organs, wanted to feel the hot, sticky wetness spurt from fatal wounds to cover his arms and chest.

Jack sniffed the night air, and though the nearest hunter was downwind, he could smell the mixture of fear and anticipation that oozed from the man's pores. Returning the H&K to its holster, Jack filled his hand with the black blade and slithered silently back toward that killer. He knew full well that it was unlikely that any of these men had taken part in Rita's killing, but they worked for Roskov, and someone on Roskov's team had taken his sweet time with her. A down payment on her suffering was long overdue. It would have to hold him until he got his hands on the one who had actually done the killing.

Jack paused, his senses attuned with the night. Just ahead, a man struggled to still his breathing, shifting his weapon so that it brushed a branch. When Jack moved, the man heard him and spun. As Jack's blade sliced his throat, the man's finger tightened on the trigger, sending the stutter of submachine gun fire into the night. The silence that followed was broken by the sound of men yelling to each other as they crashed through brush a hundred meters back toward the farmhouse.

Jack relieved the dead man of his weapon and two spare ammunition magazines before slipping into the thick brush ten meters to his right. The men racing toward the kill zone expected him to be running. As he settled into a prone firing position, Jack watched the beams from two flashlights converge on the dead man, then sweep wildly from side to side.

His first shot hit the nearest man in the back of his head, dropping his body atop the corpse and sending his flashlight rolling across the ground, its beam cutting a swath through the darkness. The second man whirled toward him, catching two rounds in the center of his chest. The dual impact lifted him off his feet, slamming him back into a young pine, its low branches catching him, a bloody scarecrow suspended in the flashlight's pale glow.

Gunfire crackled overhead as the others who had been following these two dived for cover, firing wildly into the night. Several rounds struck the dimly illuminated dead man in the tree, making his body lurch wildly but failing to dislodge him.

Lying perfectly still, Jack noted the locations of the muzzle flashes, two from the left of the kill zone and one that answered fire from his right. That shot and its accompanying muzzle flash pulled a volley of fire from the other two and sent an agonized scream echoing through the night.

"Got him!" The German words carried a thick Slavic accent.

"Careful. He might be wounded."

"Check it out. I'll cover you."

"Screw that."

"Damn it, Schmidt. He's down."

"Fine. Then you go get him."

Jack heard the tension in those voices, felt his hunger pull him toward them, and laid the submachine gun on the ground beside him. As he drew the black blade from its sheath and rose to a crouch, a distant wail pulled a memory from his dreams. The cries echoed through a deep canyon battlefield, the sound of wolves moving through the darkness to ravage the wounded, leaping up to tear the flesh from legs that dangled from hundreds of impaling pikes. But this wasn't the wail of wolves or the screams of the dying, this was the distant warble of sirens. Jack took a deep breath and made a different decision. Now, before the police arrived, was the time, but that window of opportunity wouldn't stay open long.

Barefoot and half naked, Jack turned his back on the chaos behind him and stepped into the night's enfolding arms.

CHAPTER 38

"I've got some bad news."

Nolan Trent looked up from his desk at the bald visage of Craig Faragut and frowned.

"Damn it, Craig. What now?"

"The Wozniaks are dead."

"Kazimer and Ludmina?"

"Them and every guard that was on duty in their compound. Five stiffs total."

"Shit!"

Despite the fact that he'd just chewed a handful of Rolaids from the red candy dish sitting to the left of his laptop, Nolan swallowed two more.

"Gregory?"

"All we know is that a man showed up at Wozniak's workplace on the docks. The secretary, such as she is, couldn't remember much about him. Average height, ball cap, and sunglasses. Said his name was Rado something and Kazimer seemed to know him. They left together at around five p.m. local time.

"Around six p.m., the police got a call reporting gunshots at Wozniak's compound on the northern outskirts of Szczecin. By the time they got to the house it was all over. Two guards shot dead outside the front of the house. One of them had apparently been shooting into the house with an Uzi submachine gun.

"The others died in the kitchen. Kazimer and his driver were killed with a Ruger pistol that belonged to his wife. Ludmina had multiple bullet wounds. At least a couple of those were definitely fired from Kazimer's gun. Her body had fallen across the stove and was badly burned."

Nolan, feeling a sudden need to stand, pushed his chair back from the desk and rose to his feet. "This is bullshit. Why would the Wozniaks shoot each other and their bodyguards?"

"We know Kazimer was having an affair with a twenty-year-old ballet dancer. Maybe Ludmina found out about it and got pissed."

"What about the other man? Did the neighbors see anyone leave the scene?"

"That's just it. Wozniak's compound is surrounded by green space. It doesn't have any immediate neighbors."

"Then who reported the shooting?"

"Apparently one of the gate guards made that call."

The deputy director walked to the whiteboard on the far wall of his office, staring at it as he tried to mentally reconstruct the murder scene. After several seconds he turned back toward Faragut.

"The two guards outside, where did they die?"

"The one with the Uzi cashed in his chips by the open gate, about sixty feet from the front door. The other died just outside the front door. Both had been shot with nine-millimeter rounds, not that it helps. Every weapon on the compound, including the Uzi, used nine-millimeter ammo."

"So the two guards shot each other?"

"No. The one by the door was killed at very close range. He had a broken wrist and powder burns on his head. The gate guard was killed by a longer shot. The police report says there were motorcycle skid marks leaving the driveway. We won't know more until the Polish homicide detectives finish their investigation."

Nolan looked directly into Faragut's broad face.

"Was the man from the docks riding a motorcycle?"

"The secretary didn't know and apparently everyone that saw him is dead."

Faragut cleared his throat, then continued. "There's something else. It may not be connected, but I think it is."

"Yes?"

"Late last night, German Polizei responded to reports of gunfire at a farmhouse outside of Herzfelde. They found the owner, an old woman named Frau Gensler, dead at the scene. Someone had cut her throat and thrown her down the front steps. There were signs that several others had died at the site although no other bodies were recovered. But there were lots of shell casings, bullet holes, and plenty of blood. Officially, it's being investigated as gang-related violence. Some of the evidence indicates Russian mafia involvement. My guess is that Roskov sent a team to ambush Gregory."

"Goddamn it."

Although Nolan didn't have anything to prove it, he agreed with Faragut's analysis. This felt like Gregory's handiwork. But how had he known that the Wozniaks had allied themselves with the Roskov? And how had Roskov tracked him to that isolated German farmhouse?

Refocusing his gaze on Faragut's face, Nolan nodded.

"Okay, Craig. Stay on it. Let me know if anything else turns up."

"Will do."

Watching Faragut walk out of his office and close the door behind him, Nolan made a conscious effort to release the tension that had been building in his body. Apparently Gregory had survived another bloody confrontation. If they didn't eliminate the threat Jack Gregory's involvement posed, Roskov's obsession with vengeance could pull Koenig's whole operation down on top of them. One thing was certain. When Jacob Knox learned that Roskov was still muddying the waters, he was going to be very unhappy. But no matter how pissed off Jacob got, he couldn't even begin to approach the meltdown happening inside Nolan's gut at this moment.

Picking up the phone, Nolan dialed his admin assistant.

"Yes?"

"Lindsey, get Vladimir Roskov on the phone, then patch him through to me."

"It might take a while."

"I don't want any excuses. Just get him on the line."

Nolan ended the call without waiting for her response. Considering his mood, Lindsey was probably thankful not to have to continue the conversation.

CHAPTER 39

Janet Price felt an electric pulse surge through her body, a tingle that felt as if sparks would leap from her fingertips into the keyboard that rested on the hotel desk in front of her. After this much time had passed with no contact, she had begun to contemplate the risk–reward ratio of attempting to track down Jack, even though the information she'd revealed to him would make that task one hell of a lot more difficult. But now that wasn't going to be necessary. Jack had posted an encrypted message onto one of the monitored websites.

Centering, Janet enforced the calm that would bring her proper focus, then directed her attention to the decrypted text on her screen.

I have decided to allow you to make a good-faith deposit in the interest of testing our mutual cooperation. It works like this:

First you provide me with the requested information. I will use that to determine your ongoing asset value. Right now, I offer nothing in return.

I want to know the current location and recent activities of Vladimir Roskov. You have until Friday midnight GMT to provide the information. J.G.

The request sounded simple enough, but carried within it a mystery. Jack had tracked down Roskov without NSA help before, so why was he asking for help now? There was no doubt that this was connected with the killing of the Paris CIA operative, a killing patterned after murders attributed to Roskov. The CIA certainly believed that Gregory was her killer and, having seen the video evidence, Janet could understand why. But she didn't buy it for a second. And Big John put the correlation factor at a lowly zero-point-two-three. That meant Big John wasn't buying it either.

Jack had lost his major source of intel. That's what all this data screamed at her. He'd been blinded in one eye. Rita Chavez. She'd been important to Jack. Just how important she'd find out after she sent her next set of Big John priority intelligence requests to Dr. Denise Jennings. But without the bother of invoking that computer super-mind, Janet had a feeling that Rita Chavez had been more than just an intel source to Jack. If that was true, God help her with stopping Jack from killing Vladimir Roskov. Janet had a bad feeling that if Jack did that, they'd lose their only chance of finding out what was really at play here.

So she'd make her move and hit the clock. Janet was in The Ripper's world now, and as illogical as it was . . . she liked it.

CHAPTER 40

Jacob Knox arrived at the farmhouse at six thirty a.m., parking his white Audi Quattro in the gravel driveway, just behind a green tractor that looked like it hadn't been moved in months. The Polizei had finished their investigation of the crime scene yesterday and had taken all their crime scene tape and evidence bags with them. Later today, Frau Gensler's brother was scheduled to arrive from the United States, and after claiming her body and coordinating with the mortuary, he would probably make a trip out to the farm. By then, Jacob would be long gone.

Having read a copy of the official report, Jacob had no confidence that the Polizei would ever figure out what had happened here. Then again, he was perfectly capable of discovering those facts for himself.

The blood stain on the stone front steps showed him the spot where Frau Gensler had died. She'd tried to stop the men who had kicked in that door and they'd cut her throat and tossed her aside as they raced inside. The blood spatter high up on the door frame built a picture in his mind, revealing the exact angle she'd been held as the knife parted her right carotid artery.

Jacob stepped inside and switched on the lights. The entryway was a mess, pieces of the shattered door strewn about, bloody boot prints leading up the stairs on the left, another blood stain farther inside where one of the intruders had been shot.

Jacob took his time, pausing to examine every detail of what had happened in this entryway. Among his special talents was his ability to spot the little things that others, even highly trained investigators, missed. And as he examined the blood stains, the bullet holes in the far wall and in the corner of the counter, the knocked over furniture, and the boot prints heading up the steps, a clear picture formed in Jacob's mind.

Something had so startled Frau Gensler that she had already moved close to the entry door when the intruders kicked it in. But she hadn't been going for the door—she'd been headed for the stairway. From the angle she'd been grabbed and slammed against the wall, no other path made sense.

The action in this room had happened in two waves. The old frau had reacted to something, probably a loud noise from upstairs, and had hurried to discover its source. She'd probably just reached the first step when the door had been kicked in. One of the men killed the frau as others raced past. While Jacob couldn't be sure how many had come through that door, it had been at least a half-dozen. Two of those had remained downstairs.

The second blood stain and bits of hair and bone told Jacob that one of these had been killed by whoever came back down those stairs. An overturned chair and a bullet hole in the wood said that his partner had survived by diving behind the counter. Good decision.

Climbing the stairs, he walked to the room at the far end of the hall that had been a focal point of the action. Its door had been torn from its hinges and hurled back inside the room. As soon as he stepped across the threshold, Jacob understood exactly what had happened here and what had pulled Frau Gensler to her death at the bottom of the stairs. Something had been hurled through the window, spraying broken glass across the floor, bed, and onto the small table.

It had been the opening act in this violent play. In addition to the window, the mirror above the sink had been shattered, as had the two water glasses. Examination of the shards revealed that neither the mirror nor the glasses had suffered direct impact. They'd broken as the result of an explosion. But the limited extent of that damage meant that someone had hurled a flash-bang grenade through that window, just before the assault team had entered the house. The way the door lay on top of the glass merely confirmed this timeline.

Jacob walked back down the hall, stopping to examine the bullet holes in the wall at the top of the stairs. How had the man gotten behind his attackers? Looking back toward the shattered bedroom, his eyes were drawn to a closed door on the right hand side of the hallway. Walking up to it, he saw the large blue WC lettered at eye level. Of course, the water closet.

Opening the door, Jacob stepped inside and flipped on the light switch. The room was typical of these older buildings: a blue tile floor, a sink, toilet, a single shower stall, and a wood bench. A half-used bar of soap sat in a porcelain dish with a single hair stuck to its side. The hair was blond, except for a hint of brown at the root.

Jacob held it up to the light. The hair had dried blood on it. Placing the hair in a Ziploc baggy, Jacob completed his examination of the shower and stepped back out into the hallway. The shooter had been in the shower when the assault had happened. More important, the man had already been injured.

The final details of the events that had taken place inside this farmhouse two nights ago clicked into place. The shooter had heard the attack on his room, had stepped out into this hall and shot two of the men in the back, then ran down the stairs where he killed another man before escaping into the night.

The Ripper.

He didn't need to search the grounds to fill in the rest of the movie. Roskov's men had made the fatal mistake of chasing The Ripper into the woods at night. They were lucky he hadn't hunted and killed them all.

Now, because of Roskov's bloody stupidity, Gregory had been thrown off the track Rita Chavez's murder had set him on. Feeling his teeth grind together, Jacob forced himself to take a deep breath. Then, without so much as another glance around, Jacob walked out of the farmhouse, got in the rented Audi, and headed directly back to Berlin.

CHAPTER 41

Awakening at two a.m. was nothing new to Rachel Koenig. It had become a part of her normal sleep pattern. She'd read somewhere that before electric lights had been invented, this had been the normal sleep pattern for nearly everyone. In agrarian society days, people went to bed with the sun, but after about five hours of good hard sleep, they woke up and spent a couple of wakeful hours before falling back asleep for the few hours before dawn. Rather than lie in bed working to still her busy mind, Rachel switched on the lamp atop her nightstand, swung her long legs off the bed, stood up, and stretched her naked body. The chill in the night air dissuaded her from the Pilates session that had briefly crossed her mind, so she slid into her thick bathrobe. Perhaps a hot cup of tea and a good book would do the trick.

Putting on her slippers, Rachel opened her door and stepped into the hall, the motion detector softly raising the hall lighting to illuminate her way to the elevator. As long as she'd lived in Königsberg, you'd think she'd be used to the odd way Rolf had blended modern gadgetry with fifteenth-century architecture, but it still freaked her out.

She touched a button and the elevator doors closed, preceding a brief ride down to the second floor. There it stopped to release her into another hallway that would lead her to her office and its single-cup coffee machine. Tonight it would serve up a nice cup of chamomile, maybe more than one. As she passed the door to Rolf's office, she noticed that the closed door hadn't fully latched. Pressing her hand against it, she pushed the door open, the room lights rising to greet her arrival.

Weird. Rolf never left his door unlocked unless he was present and, even then, he usually kept it closed and locked. Since he'd been gone for several days, it was amazing she hadn't noticed that the door wasn't completely latched before now. Rachel considered just closing the door to engage the automatic lock, but discarded the idea. What if someone else, one of the staff perhaps, had been in Rolf's office? Although unlikely, it wouldn't hurt to take a cursory look to verify everything looked in order.

Although she'd been in Rolf's office several times, she'd never been in it without Rolf. Empty, it felt huge, as if it had magically grown during his absence. Rolf's desk didn't face the door. Instead it faced the wall opposite the door, where the outside window had once been. The wall had been turned into a huge high-resolution display that Rolf could control from his desk or with voice and gestures as he stood before it. Right now the wall display was in screen-saver mode, currently showing an alpine village in the French Alps.

The other walls were white, as was the door, all completely devoid of decoration. Depending on the level of immersion Rolf desired, he could project imagery on these other three walls using the ceiling-mounted projector, something he'd personally demonstrated just after their wedding, taking her on a live virtual tour of one of his Hamburg factories.

The only two pieces of furniture were the U-shaped glass desk and his office chair. Even the desktop was empty except for the telephone, a wireless keyboard, and a device that looked like a large drink coaster. It wasn't, of course. Another of Rolf's designs, the flat rectangle sensed hand movements in three dimensions, providing Rolf with far greater capabilities than a common computer mouse or touchpad.

As Rachel walked around that desk, she noted that nothing was out of order. There was nothing to be out of order. Rolf abhorred paper. Even his signature was digitally reproduced by a remotely located robotic ballpoint printer. All incoming documents were digitally scanned and converted at that same facility. Rachel paused by his chair, impulsively settling into it, rotating it to face forward as she tried to see this workspace through Rolf's eyes. Strangely enough, sitting here in this sterile environment, she could understand a little of what it felt like to play God.

Her eyes were drawn to a blinking indicator on the phone display, highlighting the text that read, *New Voicemail.*

Knowing she was being stupid, she reached across and pressed the play button. An unfamiliar man's voice, vaguely feminine and vividly disturbing, emanated from the speakerphone.

"Rolf, this is Petor. I tried to reach you on your cell and left a message there, too. I spoke again with Roskov. He's nervous, but he assures me he remains strictly focused on your task. The CIA man is headed to Kyzylorda and that seems to have calmed Roskov some. Don't worry. I'll deal with The Ripper before he leaves Germany."

As the phone began reciting options for deleting, replaying, or saving messages, Rachel felt her mouth go dry. Certain that she must have misheard the recording, she pressed the replay button. Then, as she played it a third time, a new worry crowded its way into her roiling mind.

In addition to other sensors, the room's 3D motion detection system had multiple cameras and microphones that were activated whenever Rolf entered the room so that he didn't have to press any keys to give commands to his networked computers. Jesus. That system would have recorded everything she'd done since she entered this office. Even if she knew the login and password to access the system, which she didn't, she had no idea how to delete those sound and video files.

When Rolf got back and discovered that she'd been in his office and listened to that particular voice message, she was good and royally screwed. Maybe even before he got back if he happened to remotely access the system.

Struggling to control her shaking hands, Rachel made a decision. She rose to her feet and hastily left Rolf's office, closing the door firmly behind her. Hot tea long forgotten, she returned to her bedroom, put on slacks, a pullover, and hiking boots, pulled a suitcase from the closet's high shelf and set it on the bed. Grabbing things from hangers and drawers, she tossed them, unfolded, into the suitcase.

Her thoughts returned to the voice message. How stupid could she have been to believe that Rolf could be manipulated by some Russian thug? Apparently that thought had been scampering around her subconscious for a long time, judging by how the short message had filled in the one missing piece that enabled her to recognize the big picture. It had confirmed her secret fears. Something important enough to kill for was happening and Rolf wasn't just in the middle of it; as with everything he involved himself in, Rolf was running the operation.

Rachel tapped the right edge of the painting that hid her wall safe, the movement releasing the magnetic latch, letting it swing outward on a hinge. Rachel pressed her palm to the scanner, rapidly rewarded by a solid thump as the locking bars withdrew from their slots to allow her access. She opened the heavy door and grabbed a packet of hundred euro bills and ten small plastic cases. While each cylindrical case was only slightly larger than a roll of quarters, it didn't take a lot of gold coins to add up to more than a hundred and fifty thousand euros. Right now, with what she needed to do, cash was queen and gold was king.

Tossing the gold in the suitcase, she stuffed the bills in her purse. Rachel extracted her cell phone, left it on the dresser, and walked out of the room. Two minutes later, she pulled out of the eight-car garage and pressed down on the accelerator, feeling the power of the black Mercedes SEL-600's twelve cylinders thrust her back in the leather driver's seat.

The dashboard clock showed 3:15 a.m., plenty of time to get to the Heidelberg Hauptbahnhof to catch the 9:12 a.m. train to Munich. Once Rolf discovered that she had gone he would have his people searching. Always a big city girl, he would assume she would hide in one of the major European cities. Rachel knew that Rolf had connections in all of them. That was why, by mid-morning, she would be well on her way to disappearing in the sleepy alpine village of Oberammergau. Disappearing was definitely her first consideration.

Reestablishing contact with Jack Gregory would be her second.

CHAPTER 42

Admiral Jonathan Riles stared across the conference table in the White House Cabinet Room at President Tom Harris, barely managing to hide the anger that threatened to break his practiced exterior calm. Riles glanced at the man seated next to him, noting the hint of a smile on CIA Director Frank Rheiner's broad face.

It was an odd setting. To be meeting in the Cabinet Room, sitting directly across the great conference table from the president was odd enough in itself; to be the only three seated at the table that seated twenty just felt strange. It also felt strange to be summoned here and arrive to find the president already chatting with the meeting's only other attendee. The president had greeted Riles and directed him to his current seat, as if his attendance here was an afterthought or a matter of courtesy after the final decision had already been made.

As the president spelled things out for him, Admiral Riles had his suspicions confirmed. He didn't know exactly how this had happened, but it was pure, political bullshit.

"Mr. President. I don't understand what you're telling me. You want me to cease critical ongoing intelligence gathering activity in parts of Europe and Asia?"

President Harris's lips tightened in irritation. "Admiral Riles, you know damn well that is not what I'm telling you. Director Rheiner has made a very good case that the NSA's activity threatens to draw unwanted attention, possibly exposing this critical operation. So, I am directing you to temporarily cease all independent analysis of intelligence data related to Vladimir Roskov or Rolf Koenig."

Riles, feeling the blood pulse in his temples, took a single deep breath before responding. "I can't just turn off part of our data collection, Mr. President. As you know, our intelligence-gathering apparatus is extremely broad based, often deriving critically important information from complex correlative algorithms that automatically search the entire spectrum of available data. There's no easy way to implement the type of exclusive filter that Director Rheiner is requesting without blinding ourselves in the process."

Director Rheiner leaned forward. "Jon, that's not what I'm asking for here. All I want is to have you, for a limited time, while our operation reaches a critical juncture, route all of your data that correlates to Vladimir Roskov or Rolf Koenig through my deputy, Nolan Trent. That way you're not turning off anything, just directing specific information to the people who best know how to make use of it."

Riles looked back at the president, noting the slight lift to his left eyebrow. "I strongly disagree with this approach. This is exactly the kind of myopic, stove-piping of intelligence information that has gotten us into big trouble in the recent past."

"I'm sorry, Admiral Riles. I've made my decision. The NSA will give the DCI his temporary operational window."

"Can you tell me for how long?"

President Harris turned his gaze on the DCI. "Frank?"

"Four weeks is all I'm asking for."

The president nodded. "Okay, you've got your four weeks. Make the best of it, because I won't approve an extension. Gentlemen, we're done here."

Rising to his feet, Riles watched as the president left the Cabinet Room, walking through his secretary's office on his way back to the Oval Office.

"Who will be Nolan's point of contact at NSA?" The DCI's voice carried just a faint note of satisfaction.

Admiral Riles made his way around the conference table, not bothering to look at Rheiner as he responded. "I'll have Dr. Jennings contact him."

Then his long stride carried him into the hallway and, shortly thereafter, out of the White House. When his driver pulled the black NSA sedan onto the Beltway for the first half of the trip back to Fort Meade, traffic had already achieved its usual rush-hour crawl. It would give him plenty of time to stew about this latest political debacle before he got back to his office and relayed the orders.

As Admiral Riles looked out the darkly tinted window at the gleaming white spires of the Mormon Temple, backlit by the sinking sun, he found himself thinking about the Ten Commandments. While Riles did not consider himself a religious man, he had at least read parts of the Bible. He found the Ten Commandments specific in certain areas and broadly applicable in others. The president's commandment to him, on the other hand, had been full of specificity about what the NSA would and would not do with certain intelligence data.

But the president didn't know about Janet Price's involvement. Therefore nothing he had said instructed Admiral Riles to change her mission in any way. At least that was how Riles chose to interpret it. Unfortunately, the order he had been given meant that, for the next four weeks, she was going to be flying blind.

CHAPTER 43

Personality profiles didn't lie. Certainly not the ones created by Petor Kline. A trained surgeon in his last lifetime, Petor had discovered a much more exciting way to put to use his fascination for things that stopped the human body's workings. He avoided using brute force to kill his targets. His long, slender hands weren't really designed for raw violence. But his mind was. Eleven percent of his targets killed themselves. Some succumbed to fatal illness. Many died accidental deaths. Some simply disappeared.

As he watched the black Mercedes leave Koenig castle, he thought Rachel could up his self-kill average. But she wasn't the target, just the extremely enticing bait.

The setup had been simple enough. He'd used her curiosity while taking advantage of her subconscious need to prove her worth to a domineering husband. If he left Rolf's diary open on a nightstand, Rachel could no more resist reading it than she could deny the need she felt to keep her body looking like it had when she'd married him five years ago. The danger of getting caught doing something that would make Rolf furious only sweetened the forbidden fruit. Although Rachel would deny it, she needed that risk of punishment, even needed the punishment.

Rachel liked to believe that she'd been tricked into marrying the famous Rolf Koenig, seduced by the false façade he projected. But Rolf didn't project a false façade. He was exactly the man he seemed, a driven, domineering genius. On a subconscious level Rachel had known exactly what she was getting into when she married him.

As Rachel's taillights followed her twin headlight beams around the bend in the steep, winding road, Petor turned and walked to the elevator. He didn't have to follow Rachel immediately; the micro GPS tracker he'd placed in the seam of her purse would tell him where she was going.

Pausing at Rachel's bedroom, Petor switched on the lights, his gaze taking in the tossed closet and open drawers. He noted the open wall-safe and the cell phone atop her dresser. Rachel wasn't stupid. She would take precautions, ditch the car and acquire other transportation. At this time of night that meant she'd hop a train, probably a high-speed nonstop, headed somewhere far from Heidelberg. No matter where she'd gone, he'd be on her tail in a few minutes. But first, he had a call to make.

Stepping off the elevator on the second floor, Petor walked directly to Rolf's office and pressed his hand to the scanner just to the left of the locked door. The panel glowed pale blue, and then, with a soft click, the door lock released, a temporary access authorization Rolf Koenig had granted him. Pushing the door inward, Petor stepped inside as the room lights rose to greet him. Three strides in, Rolf Koenig's image filled the far wall, the seated industrialist leaning in toward his laptop's webcam.

"So Petor. Your theory proved correct."

"Rachel just left."

"And Gregory?"

"He's the only go-to guy she knows. Once she thinks she's safe, she'll try to contact him, probably setting up a personal meeting. If he comes to her, then I'll deal with him."

"And if he doesn't?"

"Then he'll try to get to Roskov in Kyzylorda. In that case your CIA guy will have to handle him. Either way, we'll know."

"Okay. Make it happen."

As Rolf's image faded out, replaced by a stunning view of the Mediterranean, Petor Kline was already on his way out the door.

CHAPTER 44

"You've got to be kidding me!"

Janet felt the anger flow from her lips through the encrypted cell phone and into Dr. Denise Jennings's ear.

"I'm sorry, Janet. I've been ordered to route all Big John information relating to Vladimir Roskov through CIA. They have the lead on this one."

"Damn it! This is bullshit. Who gave the order?"

"Admiral Riles."

Janet paused, struggling to deal with this new information. It made zero sense. Why would Riles pull her out of Cartagena, fly her halfway round the world on a high-priority mission, only to cut her off at the knees just when she was about to deliver the goods? Jack Gregory had made contact. She had until the end of the day on Friday to deliver the requested information on Roskov's current location or she could kiss the chance of further contact goodbye.

Denise's voice interrupted her thoughts. "I really am sorry, Janet."

Janet thumbed the *END CALL* button, pulled up Admiral Riles's contact information, and pressed *CALL*. She knew she should probably go through Levi Elias, but right now she was pissed and just didn't give a rat's ass about protocol.

Admiral Riles's distinctive voice answered. "Hi, Janet. I've been expecting your call."

"Sir, do you mind telling me just what the hell is going on and why Denise Jennings is denying my requests for mission-critical information?"

"I don't like it either. But this comes straight from the president."

The answer stunned her. Why the hell was the president involving himself in this?

"So you're pulling me out?"

"Not yet."

"You might as well. There's not a damn thing I can do if you cut me off from all my intelligence resources."

This time Admiral Riles paused before responding. "I still believe Jack Gregory is at the center of whatever is happening in Germany. Just because I've been told not to probe into Roskov's or Rolf Koenig's activities doesn't mean you can't continue your Gregory mission. You're just going to have to invent more creative ways to dig up the answers you need. Talk to Levi and keep us informed of your progress."

It wasn't what Janet wanted to hear, but it was all she was going to get.

"Yes, sir."

The call ended and Janet tossed the cell phone onto her bed in disgust. Her wheels had just come off and Riles wanted her to keep him informed of her progress! Leaning back into the reading chair, she linked her fingers behind her head and stared up at the ceiling, replaying the conversation in her mind.

Something about the way Riles had phrased his last response struck her as odd. He'd told her to continue her Gregory mission and to talk to Levi. But he hadn't exactly addressed her accusation that she was cut off from all the NSA intelligence resources, implying that the only information that would be denied was that specifically dealing with Roskov or Koenig. And he hadn't ordered her not to do her own investigation into Jack's Roskov and Koenig connections.

Had he intentionally left open a window of deniability for her to crawl through? In her experience, Admiral Riles always knew precisely what he was saying and how others were likely to interpret his words. While she wouldn't have access to Big John's correlative prowess, she was still free to gather information broadly related to her Jack Gregory mission and make her own inferences, even drawing on Levi Elias's expertise so long as she carefully worded her requests.

Clearly, Admiral Riles intended to comply with the letter, if not the spirit, of the president's order. Janet fully intended to violate them both.

Stripping out of her clothes, Janet stepped into the shower, letting the steaming water wash her tension away. Although it was a little after five p.m. back in D.C., here in Berlin, the nightclubs were just getting cranked up. And even though it was Wednesday night, she felt the need to work out her frustration on a dance floor. She loved cavorting with the wolves that hunted those night spots. Brimming with testosterone, they'd sweep her across the dance floor, writhing to the dance beat as they pressed against her lithe body, little knowing that tonight they danced with death itself.

CHAPTER 45

Thursday found Jack on the move after having reequipped himself, which included the purchase of the powerful red Honda motorcycle he now straddled. It had been two days since he'd posted the encrypted message to Janet Price and so far there had been no response. Although he'd told her she had until midnight on Friday to get him the information on Roskov's location, he'd hoped she'd be a little more proactive.

The morning fog burned off as he passed just west of Leipzig. As much as Jack loved driving on a German autobahn, it couldn't compare to riding an autobahn on a powerful motorcycle. When traffic moved well, like it did this morning along the A9, the slower traffic stayed to the right or moved right quickly upon seeing the flashing headlights of a Porsche coming up behind them at two hundred kilometers per hour. Riding the Honda, with the throttle wide open, Jack hadn't seen anyone coming up on his ass.

As he approached Bayreuth, Jack took the Bayreuth Süd exit and turned southeast onto Nurnberger Strasse, passing a collection of auto dealerships before stopping at a small pension on Oberkonnersreuther Strasse.

Jack removed his helmet and surveyed the establishment. It had several things going for it: it looked nice, it sat in the middle of a well-kept neighborhood just off the A9, and the street address alone was enough to ensure that this wasn't a heavily trafficked tourist destination. Right now, with the dull blade of depression carving its way through his tired brain, he wasn't too picky. This would do.

Carrying his bag inside, Jack booked a room on the second floor, made his way up the narrow staircase, and settled in. Typically German, his room had a double bed, twin mattresses separated by a small board in the center, and a thick duvet atop each mattress. A single would have been fine, but this had been the last available room. It was nice, but the inviting double bed and romantic decorations left him feeling a bit cold. It was probably that he hadn't had anyone with whom to share a bed like that for a long time. Too long.

Or maybe it was the lowering clouds from the incoming storm front that had brought on this sudden chill. Walking across to the white radiator on the far wall, Jack turned the knob to allow the hot steam to flow in. He retrieved the laptop from his bag and set it atop the small round table that occupied the southeast corner, just below the window. After plugging it into the 220-volt outlet to charge, he shrugged out of his leather jacket and tossed it atop the second of the two wooden chairs before making his way to the water closet.

In addition to the sink, the tiled WC had a toilet and a glass-encased shower. All in all, quite a step up from his recent accommodations. Washing his face in cold water, Jack thought he'd better enjoy it while he could, but as he rubbed his face dry with the soft white hand towel, Rita's image swam into his mind, lying naked on their hotel bed, her laughing eyes staring up at him as he slipped into his shirt and slacks. She wasn't his most recent lover, but she'd been wonderful. Too bad he'd just gotten her tortured to death.

Jack found himself staring into his own eyes in the mirror, the pupils glinting red as they always did when his blood was up. He'd first noticed it shortly after his deathbed experience. As much as he was tempted to attribute it to a supernatural cause, there was a more earthly explanation. He had been dead for so long that lack of blood pressure to his eyes had changed them, causing his pupils to expand and contract differently whenever his blood pressure was elevated. The distortion allowed more light than usual into his eyes, illuminating the blood vessels on the back of each eye. At least that was an explanation for the red-eye shine he'd found online. It was the one he chose to accept.

Leaving the room, Jack walked downstairs and asked the proprietor, a ruddy-faced bald man named Fritz, if he could purchase a bottle of wine for his room. Two minutes later, he set the bottle next to his laptop on the small table by his window, removed the cork with the corkscrew Fritz had provided, and poured the white wine into a water glass. Settling his body onto one of the two chairs, Jack lifted the glass toward the empty chair opposite his.

"I'm sorry, Rita."

Jack imagined her glass clinking against his, her lovely brown eyes full of forgiveness. Taking a slow sip of the Spätlese, he let the late-season wine linger on his tongue before swallowing. As the first fat drops of rain began pattering against his window, Jack took another sip. Sitting there staring at the empty chair, lost in his memories, Jack finished the glass and then the bottle.

He awoke in darkness, having lain down on the bed without removing his clothes, boots, or the holstered H&K P30S. The faintly luminescent dial on his wrist watch read 11:17 p.m. Jack's head hurt, not badly enough to make him need an ibuprofen, but enough to make him remember why he didn't drink very often. What he needed was the night.

Leaving his bags in the wall schrank, Jack walked out of his room, down the stairs, and outside. The rain had stopped, but it had left his motorcycle seat wet. Wiping away most of the water, Jack pulled on his helmet, straddled the bike, pressed the start button, and headed toward the A9 and Nuremberg.

Less than an hour later, Jack parked the motorcycle outside the Holiday Inn at the edge of Nuremberg's red-light district and began strolling slowly south along Engelhardsgasse. While prostitution was legal in Germany, it still carried a stigma that led many of the prostitutes to keep secret night lives to protect their respectable daytime lives. In this part of town, some of the prostitutes rented apartments in which they entertained their clients while others worked the bars, splitting their earnings with the bar owners. Others worked at big clubs like the Sauna Bar 3000.

Jack found it neither appealing nor revolting. People were the same as they always had been. Whether the prostitutes worked to support a family or to support a habit, the legal ones were working ladies and men who had a right to ply their trade. That wasn't what pulled him to this part of town. The illegal activity that always surrounded prostitution did that.

Tonight, the smell of danger hung thick in the damp air, pulling Jack along Engelhardsgasse between the Bordell kleines Laufhause and the appropriately named Stars and Stairs. His footsteps carried him around the corner to his left and onto Frauentormauer. The narrow, dimly-lit cobblestone street squeezed between the old city walls on his right and the wall-to-wall apartments crowding in on his left, leaving him feeling like he'd just stepped two hundred years into the past. Jack had walked streets like this many times before. Some were his memories, some just fragments from his dreams.

A sound to his front brought him to a halt. In the deep shadows beneath the old wall, two figures struggled, one sitting astride the other, raining blows on the whimpering figure beneath him. The man on top panted a single German phrase, filled with the same hatred that powered his hammering fists.

"Time to die, faggot."

Jack's kick caught the man in the back, sending him tumbling off of his victim and into the stone wall. When he came back to his feet, he had a knife in his left hand. Despite the depth of the shadows, Jack could see him clearly. Shaved head, pierced nose, ears and eyebrows, tattooed swastika on the left side of his neck. The only surprise was that this skinhead prick was here without a pack of friends.

The words hissed through his broken teeth. "Bad move, asshole."

Lunging at Jack, the skinhead thrust the blade in low, aiming for the gut as he attempted to wrap a long right arm around Jack's neck. Jack shifted right, his openhanded blow catching the man's knife hand just above the wrist, sending the blade spinning away across the cobblestones. Surprised, the other paused, and then threw himself at Jack's legs in a wrestler's takedown.

Jack countered, forcing the attacker's head down as he drove the back of the man's head and neck into the cobblestones. Rolling the stunned skinhead onto his stomach, Jack completed the chokehold that would shortly rid the world of one more piece of trash.

"Please don't kill him."

Jack looked at the blond teenage boy who had risen shakily to his knees, blood dripping from his broken nose and mouth onto the street.

"Please don't kill my brother."

"This shithead's your brother?" Jack maintained the chokehold but stopped tightening his grip. "Why the hell was he trying to kill you then?"

The boy licked his lips. "I'm gay. I'm a prostitute. I'm an embarrassment."

The skinhead tried to spit, then stopped as he felt Jack's grip tighten.

"He may be your brother, but if I let him go, he's just going to come after you again. I know the type, kid. Believe me. He's not worth saving."

"And you are?"

The words punched Jack in the gut. As he fought the urge to break the skinhead's neck, his eyes locked with those of the bleeding boy.

"What's your name?" Jack asked.

"Georg Engel. My brother is Nils."

Jack turned his attention back to the skinhead, moving his lips close to the man's left ear. In a voice that only he could hear, Jack whispered, "Listen carefully, Nils Engel. Your gay little brother just saved your life. You better take care of him. If I hear of something bad happening to him, I'll come for you. And next time I won't be so pleasant."

Then Jack choked him out. As he let the limp body drop to the cobblestones, Jack saw the fear in Georg's eyes.

"He's not dead. One piece of advice, kid. Be gone when he wakes up."

Jack stooped to pick up the knife and tossed it over the city wall. Without another word, he turned and walked back the way he had come. As he looked up at the open second-floor window in which a scantily-clad young woman sat, her red-gartered leg dangling enticingly, he suddenly felt sick to his stomach.

Because he hadn't yet found Rita's killer, he'd gotten drunk, and then given in to his inner demon. As much as he wanted to tell himself that he'd made this midnight run to Nuremberg's red-light district looking for an opportunity to save somebody, for an opportunity to make just one thing right, the truth was he'd come here hunting, thirsting for a kill. Exactly the type of rage reaction that Rita's killer had sought to trigger in him.

As the motorcycle carried him back toward Bayreuth, the rain started falling again, soaking and chilling him to his core. Ducking low to minimize the surface area exposed to the wind-swept spray, Jack shook his head.

It was the perfect start to a new day.

CHAPTER 46

This was the second time Rachel had been to Oberammergau, but she'd fallen in love with the Bavarian alpine village the first time she'd seen it. Famous for its frescoes depicting fairy tale and religious scenes, the seven-thousand-person community nestled in a lovely valley in the Bavarian Alps was as beautiful as any place Rachel had ever seen. Of course, Rolf hadn't been impressed. In fact this was exactly the kind of place that bored him out of his mind. Rolf had to be constantly busy, a part of his nature he could no more fight than a heroin addict could just walk away from the drug. Any place that invited you to smell the clean air and just enjoy the beautiful scenery made Rolf feel like he was drowning. It was what made this the perfect hiding place.

She'd purchased the used Volkswagen Jetta in Munich for seven thousand euros cash. Having parked the car outside a nice pension, Rachel, wearing dark Ray-Ban sunglasses and a knit cap that covered her hair, rented a second-floor room, paying for two weeks in advance. It was a simple space with a double bed, a small dining table, a double schrank for clothes and shoes, and a water closet with shower. The white pine furniture matched the wood flooring. A single radiator occupied the wall beneath her window. With the shutters open, the view of the Ettal cliffs was spectacular.

Going to the water closet, Rachel applied the hair dye that would transform her from a blond into a brunette. It took thirty minutes to apply the dye and another twenty for it to set. When she finally got to step into the shower to rinse and apply the conditioner that would lock in the color, she lingered, letting the hot water unknot the muscles in her neck.

Done, Rachel toweled dry and slipped into a fluffy white bathrobe and slippers, then spent ten minutes brushing out her dark-brown hair. As she felt the tension in her neck and shoulders release, a wave of drowsiness tried to sweep her into bed. But she had one important task to take care of before she could seek the release that sleep in the fresh mountain air offered.

Setting up her laptop, she logged in. It was funny. The pension didn't have phones in its rooms, but it offered free WiFi access. WiFi availability was one of the reasons she'd picked this particular bed and breakfast.

When the computer desktop appeared, Rachel launched the email encryption program Jack had sent her and began typing.

Jack. I know that I have already released you from the job I hired you for, but something has happened that means this isn't over, not for you nor for me. I fear that I have placed you in jeopardy. I have certainly gotten myself into a bad spot. I need to see you. If you are willing, further payment will be forthcoming although, in my present situation, I am unable to offer you an advance. Let me know if you are agreeable and I will tell you where to meet me.

Rachel reread the message, started to rephrase it, and then reconsidered. Jack would do it if he wanted to, not because of her perfect phrasing. She pushed the SEND button and after several seconds a message appeared in the dialogue box.

Message Successfully Delivered.

Now all she had to do was wait.

Yawning, Rachel shut down her laptop, walked to the sink, filled a glass with cold water, and took a long slow drink. Setting the glass on her nightstand, Rachel let the bathrobe fall to the floor, slid her naked body beneath the soft, thick duvet, and felt herself drift into a deep and dreamless sleep.

CHAPTER 47

Janet stared at the computer screen. It was Friday morning and she'd stayed up all night working every lead she could think of to get a handle on where Vladimir Roskov had disappeared to, and she still had nothing. And the clock was ticking. In another fourteen hours, her chance to prove to Jack that she could be a valuable and trusted asset would be lost.

But she'd just gotten a break. This morning's Berlin newspaper, *Berliner Morgenpost*, bore the headline:

Wife of Industrialist Rolf Koenig Missing

According to the story, the Koenig household staff had reported Rachel Koenig missing on Thursday morning. Berlin police were refusing to comment on an ongoing investigation into the matter. Rolf Koenig, currently in Kazakhstan preparing for the launch of the final piece of his company's lunar robotic mining mission, was also unavailable for comment.

She pressed a speed dial button on her encrypted cell phone. A familiar voice answered on the third ring.

"Elias."

"Levi, this is Janet. I need a favor."

She heard the analyst pause before answering.

"What can I do for you?"

"I need you to run two Big John queries for me. The first is for any news within the last two days that correlates to Jack Gregory."

"Okay. And the second?"

"Rachel Koenig has disappeared. There's a police search underway. I want to find her first."

"I'm not allowed to pass you Big John information about Koenig."

"Rolf Koenig is off limits, not his wife. When I spoke to Admiral Riles two days ago, I noted how carefully he phrased his response. I'm quoting, not paraphrasing. He told me, 'Just because I've been told not to probe into Roskov's or Rolf Koenig's activities doesn't mean you can't continue your Gregory mission. You're just going to have to invent more creative ways to dig up the answers you need. Talk to Levi and keep us informed of your progress.' "

The silence on the other end lasted a full six seconds. "You're telling me this information request is only for your Gregory mission?"

"I think Rachel may have been kidnapped as bait for Jack, the same way I think Rita Chavez was used."

"That's a logical possibility. I'll run the priority intelligence request on that basis."

"Levi, one more thing. If at all possible, I need the answers this afternoon."

The analyst's distinctive laugh preceded his answer. "I'll see what Big John can do. If he comes up with anything, I'll forward it."

"Useful or not?"

"Useful or not."

"Thanks, Levi."

Ending the call, Janet set her cell phone beside her laptop and walked to the closet to retrieve her mission kitbag. Unlike the larger military kitbags, this one was roughly the size of a gym bag. Setting the black canvas bag on the bed, she removed the contents, spreading them out on the duvet for easy examination. Selecting one of the five unused identity kits, she opened the manila envelope, setting aside the driver's license and passport, and looked down at her unsmiling image centered above the name on the press pass, Christa Frost.

Janet spent thirty minutes memorizing the details of her new fake life. A reporter for the German news magazine, *Der Spiegel*, she'd graduated from the Deutsche Journalistenschule, more commonly known as DJS, five years ago. She had taken her first job at *Stern*, where she'd worked until recently receiving a superior offer from *Spiegel*.

Real reporters hated intelligence operatives passing themselves off as journalists. Janet understood why. This type of activity put reporters' lives at risk. But it was one of the best covers for someone asking a lot of questions. Personally, she had no problem with it.

By the time Janet finished prepping for the action she hoped was imminent, the bedside clock read 3:13 p.m. Thirty minutes later it read 3:43 p.m. Anxious for Levi's response, she felt like a caged lioness, pacing back and forth as walking meat stared at her from behind the protective bars.

The text message beep brought her back to her cell phone. It contained two words:

Data Delivered.

Immediately, she shifted to her laptop, logged into the secure site, and entered the commands to begin downloading the compressed files. Even though the hotel's high-speed internet connection had reasonably good bandwidth, the download still took forty-two minutes. By the time Janet finished reviewing the data files it was a quarter to six. Strapping on her shoulder holster, she slid into her jacket, grabbed her bag, and headed for the elevator that would carry her to the parking garage.

By the time she entered the on-ramp to the A9 autobahn, she'd made a decision. Although it was doubtful that anyone else, except possibly Levi, would have noticed the Jack Gregory connection in one of the files, Big John had come through. Buried amongst other conflicting data, a Nuremberg police report had jumped out at her.

A young male prostitute had reported that a demon had attacked the man who had beaten him up. Although he claimed not to be able to identify either man, his description of the demon's red eyes struck a familiar chord. The police had filed the report, no follow-up required. But Janet believed that, despite the prostitute's history of drug abuse, last night he'd seen what he described.

Even though nobody had been killed this time, the similarities between this incident and the one in Cartagena screamed The Ripper's name. It was just a hunch, but it felt like a hell of a lot more than that. Jack had been in Nuremburg last night. She'd bet her life on it. The real question was: Why the hell had he been there prowling the dark streets that were home to the prostitutes and the johns they serviced?

The image of another Jack prowling the foggy backstreets of London crept into her mind, along with another question. Had Jack Gregory developed some sort of dark fascination with his nineteenth-century namesake? If so, he was a much greater danger than anyone had imagined. The thought of someone with Jack's special skillset, mixed with that kind of crazy, sent a cold chill up Janet's spine.

When she'd looked into his deep brown eyes in his apartment, she'd seen something, but it wasn't crazy. Something else. She just didn't know what, not yet. Regardless, the knowledge that Jack had been in Nuremberg last night wasn't enough to put her on the autobahn headed to Bavaria. The other Big John data had done that.

A street camera at the edge of Garmisch-Partenkirchen had captured an image of a woman in a silver Volkswagen Jetta. Even though she'd been wearing sunglasses and a knit cap that concealed her hair, the NSA facial recognition software had tagged the face as a possible match for Rachel Koenig, and she'd been driving. That meant she hadn't been kidnapped; she was running. And she'd been on German highway 23, which meant her next most likely stop was the same as Janet's.

Oberammergau.

CHAPTER 48

Rachel's message had come as a surprise to Jack. In part a warning that someone was targeting him, it was primarily a plea for help. Considering she'd already paid him to make this problem go away, he couldn't really back out just because she'd erroneously thought it had already been resolved. Especially since this was connected to Rita's murder.

Pension Enzianhof's wood-shuttered windows and frescos adorned white walls that rose to the steeply pitched roof. Several of the southwest-facing rooms had spacious balconies with traditional Bavarian flower baskets hanging from the railing, each offering a lovely spot for lovers to share the view.

While everything about the place looked normal, it was possible that this could be another setup; it was the reason Jack had been watching the pension since sunrise. None of the places with direct line of sight to the entryway or to the upper-right balcony room where he would meet Rachel had evidenced unusual activity. Everyone he observed looked like they belonged here. So why was his gut telling him something was wrong? Jack rechecked all the positions a sniper might position himself, even those with marginal lines of sight, but nothing specific backed up his intuition.

As he waited for the ten a.m. appointment, Jack's thoughts turned to Janet Price. He'd really expected her to come through with the requested information about Roskov, but Friday night had come and gone without any attempted contact. Jack didn't know what that meant, but after having met the impressive young operative, it probably meant trouble. Someone at CIA was behind an effort to strip him of all his contacts, blinding him for the kill. Had they gotten to Janet Price as well?

Jack glanced at his watch. Five minutes to ten. Well, he wasn't going to find out what was wrong by standing around. With an adrenaline flood propelling him toward the danger he sensed, Jack crossed the street, walked inside, and, ignoring the young couple chatting with the proprietor, climbed the stairs to the second level. He turned right into the hallway, walked directly to the last door on the left, and paused to listen. Aside from the murmurs of the downstairs conversation, the hallway was silent. Jack raised his fist and knocked twice.

After a brief pause, he heard Rachel's voice. "Yes?"

"It's me."

Again a slight pause preceded her response. "Come in."

Jack hesitated. Something about the tone of her voice wasn't right, almost as if it was recorded.

Pulling the H&K from its holster, he reached for the door handle. Then he saw it, the glint from a tiny camera lens affixed to the top of the window frame at the end of the hall. It wasn't a security camera, but something far more advanced. You don't need line of sight if you're watching your target through a high-end web cam.

Jack launched himself back the way he'd come as the blast hurled Rachel's door into the hall. The shockwave lifted him off his feet, sending his body rolling down the passageway, chased by the flames that rushed from Rachel's room. Holding his breath to keep from inhaling the acrid smoke that filled the corridor, Jack regained his feet and managed to stay there as he staggered to the stairway. With the roiling inferno behind him hissing like Medusa's snakes, he grabbed the handrail and descended to the ground floor.

Jack's vision blurred and when he wiped at his forehead with his right arm, his leather jacket sleeve came away bloody. Based upon his empty right hand, he must have dropped his pistol upstairs. Right now he didn't have time to worry about that. Seeing no sign of the proprietor or the couple he'd passed on his way in, Jack hobbled through the exit and out into the sunlit morning.

The yell of a familiar voice brought his head around in time to see a black BMW sedan slide to a stop beside him, its passenger door swinging open toward him.

"Get in!"

Through a red haze, Jack complied, allowing the G-force of the accelerating automobile to close the passenger door for him.

Janet Price, her attention firmly focused on the road, cornered hard, turned down a side street, and then turned again. She eased off on the accelerator and merged into traffic as the warble of multiple sirens faded away behind them.

It seemed to Jack that he only blinked, but somehow they had left Oberammergau and were entering the tiny village of Graswang. Janet turned off the highway onto a narrow farm road and stopped the car in a wooded pullout.

With pain hammering the inside of his skull, Jack watched Janet remove her sunglasses.

"I thought I told you not to look for me."

"Lucky for you I have a problem with authority. You look like shit, Jack."

"I've felt better."

"We need to find a place to get you cleaned up. Then we'll talk."

Leaning back in his seat, Jack let his eyes close.

"Fine. Wake me when we get there."

CHAPTER 49

Janet crossed the Deutsche–Austrian border on the small bridge where the winding two-lane St2060 became the L255, also known as the Ammerwald highway. Except for a sign beside the road, there was no indication that she had just passed from the German Alps into the Austrian Alps. She slowed at the hairpin turn and then accelerated through it, feeling the powerful German sedan sink its rubber claws into the hundred-and-eighty-degree curve.

She glanced over at the killer in her passenger seat. Jack Gregory's chiseled face was filthy, coated with blood-caked soot and ash from the scalp wound. Although his hair was naturally brown, he'd been blond when she'd last seen him. Right now his short hair was a gray mat. She'd seen pictures of people fleeing the September 11th attack in New York City as the first and then the second of the Twin Towers collapsed. Jack was giving a damned fine imitation of one of those survivors.

At the moment he was either asleep or unconscious. Either way, he was certainly suffering the effects of a concussion. When he'd climbed into her car he'd been disoriented, passing in and out of consciousness as she'd sped away from the scene. Getting caught in an explosion tended to do that to you, if you survived the experience.

Janet didn't consider herself lucky to have found him. Last night, she'd found Rachel's recently purchased Volkswagen Jetta parked outside Pension Enzianhof. Having found Rachel, she'd known it was only a matter of time until she found Jack. While it was possible that Jack wouldn't come to the aid of the running Rachel Koenig, she'd discarded that possibility as quickly as she'd considered it. Although certain things about Jack Gregory were extremely unpredictable, he'd never abandoned a mission in his life. Everything she knew about this particular chain of events pointed to a tie between Jack and Rachel. It wasn't a romantic tie. That meant Rachel had hired him.

Janet had been sitting in the parked BMW, watching Rachel's pension since three a.m. Rachel had never left the building, but just before ten o'clock, Jack had crossed the street and walked into the building. It was the meeting Janet had been expecting. She hadn't expected the explosion that followed.

The BMW rounded a corner and a beautiful view of Lake Plansee spread out before her. Janet loved Austria. Salzburg, the Austrian Alps, and its beautiful alpine lakes generated a nostalgia she got nowhere else, not even Switzerland. Perhaps it was childhood memories of her mom serving popcorn as the two of them settled onto their one-bedroom apartment's couch to watch her favorite movie, *The Sound of Music*. Valerie Price had been a most wonderful person. Too bad Janet didn't have similar memories of her father. She'd used her mother's .38 special to pump five bullets into him, the last a point-blank head shot. Happy thirteenth birthday.

Returning her attention to the highway, Janet turned off onto a side road that carried her along the north end of the lake into Campingplatz Sennalpe. Parking the car, she stepped into the main office. Ten minutes later she returned with the keys to a for-rent-by-owner trailer that had become a permanent fixture at this picturesque haven for RVs and tents. Finding the camp space where the gray, blue, and white double-wide occupied a concrete slab, Janet pulled the black BMW under the steel carport and turned off the engine.

She opened her door and stepped out, pleasantly surprised to see Jack open the passenger door and stand erect opposite her. When he looked at her, his eyes held a clarity that hadn't been there before.

"This is it?"

Janet nodded. "Home sweet home. At least for now. Let's get you inside."

He closed his door. "Good plan."

Janet opened the trunk, grabbed her bag, and pressed the lock button on her key fob. She walked to the door, unlocked it, and stepped inside. The trailer's interior was neat and clean, if not spacious. To the right of the door, the living-room couch provided a good view of the twenty-seven-inch flat-screen TV on the opposite wall. Immediately to her left, the kitchen appliances and small dining-room table appeared in good condition. Beyond that, a bathroom door stood open on the right, just before the bedroom at the far end.

Janet motioned toward the open bathroom door. "You get the shower first. You need some help?"

A slow grin spread across Jack's filthy face, his teeth appearing unnaturally white. It was the first time Janet had seen him smile, and she found herself liking it.

"I think I can manage. A couple of Advil would be nice though."

"I've got some in my bag. I'll bring them to you."

Janet retrieved a bottle of ibuprofen and carried it to the bathroom. Finding the door open and the shower going, she set the white plastic bottle on the sink and paused to glance at the closed shower curtain before stepping out and closing the door behind her.

She didn't know what it was, but something about Jack Gregory definitely had her on edge. Bullshit. She wasn't on edge. She was excited. Not just sexually. It was deeper than that. Or maybe it wasn't. There was no denying that the man had a certain aura about him. Part of it was reputation, but the other part was something she didn't yet have a handle on. Whatever it was, she'd put the hobbles on it, right now. This wasn't a man she wanted a relationship with, sexual or otherwise.

Just then, Jack stepped out of the bathroom, a white towel tied around his waist.

"Sorry. My clothes are trashed."

"You're not impressing me."

"Not trying to."

Janet's eyes swept his body. Lean, powerful legs, towel-draped midsection, hard-muscled torso covered with a crazy-quilt of knife scars, Jack's body screamed power and pain. His deep-brown eyes held a hint of the same, along with something else. Cleaned up, the head wound was invisible in his hairline.

"So you're going regimental?"

"I'm not Scottish."

"And that's not a kilt?"

Jack laughed. "The point is, I'm going to need some pants, underwear, a shirt, and some socks before I go out in public."

"Tell you what. I'll drive into Breitenwang and do a little shopping. Clothes for you, food for both of us."

"Fair enough."

"You ready for a conversation?"

Jack looked at her. "How about after dinner? I lost my weapon. Don't suppose you have an extra?"

Janet walked to her kit bag, unzipped it, and extracted a small pistol and two nine-millimeter magazines from a side pocket. She turned and handed them to Jack.

"It'll be a bit small for your hand."

She watched Jack clear the H&K subcompact, insert a fresh magazine, and rack the slide to chamber a round. "This will work just fine. Thanks."

Janet nodded toward the bedroom. "You can have the bed. Nothing better for a concussion than a few extra hours of sleep. I'll be back from town in a couple of hours. I'll wake you for dinner."

Jack didn't argue. Janet watched him walk to the bedroom and stretch out on the bed, and then turned and walked out of the trailer, locking the door behind her.

CHAPTER 50

The news wasn't good. Petor Kline searched the web for stories about the terrorist bombing in Oberammergau, but there were no reports of casualties, killed or wounded. The building that had once been Pension Enzianhof had burned to the ground, but the two guests that had been in the building had escaped, along with the proprietor. They had reported seeing another man stumble from the building, get in a car, and drive off, but except for a vague description of the black vehicle, they were able to provide no helpful details. It was possible that The Ripper's body had been so badly burned that it would take the authorities several days to find the bits of bone and teeth that remained, but Petor doubted it.

Gregory had spotted his hidden webcam, something Petor would have thought impossible given the size of the tiny WiFi device and the dark space in which he'd positioned it. But he'd seen The Ripper pause outside the door to Rachel's room and turn his gaze directly into the camera. If he had entered the room, he would be dead. He should be dead anyway. When he'd started sprinting back down the hallway, Petor had remotely triggered the detonation, apparently a full second too late.

Rumor had it The Ripper could sense the future. Rumor had it he was returned from the dead. Rumor had it pigs could fly. What a complete crock of shit. Petor could name the game the man was playing. He'd chosen a cliché nickname that subconsciously generated fear. Then he let that cliché drive a certain kind of business his way. It was basic marketing 101, but that didn't mean the man wasn't very, very good at what he did. Petor harbored no illusions about that.

Petor shut down the laptop, packed it into its case, and headed for the door. While Rachel was sleeping her drug-induced sleep in the back of the panel van, it wouldn't do to keep her waiting any longer. Rolf's instructions had been very specific in this regard. No harm would come to his wife. Petor was to drug her and deliver her to the Gottfried Clinic, where Dr. Frieda Dortman would admit her. Tomorrow, Dr. Dortman would release a statement to the press that Rachel Koenig had suffered a nervous breakdown and would be undergoing treatment for an indefinite amount of time. In the meantime, the Koenig family requested that the press and public respect their right to medical privacy.

Parked outside Hotel Zugspitze, the blue panel van was backed into a spot at the back side of the parking lot. Petor opened the driver's door, shut it behind him, and moved into the back to check on Rachel. A quick check of her vitals yielded the expected results; she would be out for at least two more hours. Petor removed a needle from his medical bag, pulled two CC's of a clear liquid from a small vial, and turned it up to squeeze the air and a single drop of liquid from the syringe.

Inserting the needle into a vein on her right arm, Petor administered the injection that would add an additional eight hours to her slumber. When next she opened those pretty blue eyes, she would find herself in Dr. Dortman's care. By the time she was ready for release, she would believe that she really had suffered a nervous breakdown.

Petor moved back to the driver's seat, started the engine, and began the long drive from Garmisch-Partenkirchen to Berlin. Once he dropped off Rachel, he would have to inform Rolf Koenig of his mission's failure, something he most definitely was not looking forward to.

He only hoped he would be given an opportunity to make amends for his failure.

CHAPTER 51

Although the heavy downpour stopped around eleven p.m., a steady drizzle continues. It lifts a knee-high fog that swirls through the narrow streets. It clings to my skin, a thick, wet blanket that seeks to quench the little illumination that manages to cut through this night's gloom. My damp cloak brushes my legs as I step away from the corpse but, in thrall to my hammering heart, I barely notice.

Nature is a vicious bitch, a cat that plays with an injured mouse, dragging out the wretched animal's misery right up until the moment that it guts and consumes its prey. I am far more merciful, inflicting a few moments of terror as I strangle the woman unconscious before carefully lowering her body to the ground on my left. Twin slashes across her throat sends her permanently into the dark. The removal of selected organs happens post mortem.

In the distance, a bobby walks beneath a street lamp, his night stick casting a swinging shadow. Stepping deeper into the shadows, the bloody knife clasped firmly in my right hand, I watch the bobby move along Berner Street. The interruption means I won't get to finish the ritual, not with this victim. But I can't just leave tonight's promise unfulfilled. It isn't my way.

Having watched the bobby turn the corner, I exit this dark space the way I entered it. A shadow within shadows, I move out of the narrow yard between numbers 40 and 42 Berner Street, feeling something pull me toward a new target somewhere in the Whitechapel night.

"Dinner's ready."

The call woke Jack, pulling him from the shabby Whitechapel alley into a bedroom that occupied the far end of a campsite trailer in the Austrian Alps. The vivid dream was one he had experienced before and, as usual, it took him several moments to work his way out of it. When the dreams took him, they always felt more like memories than dreams. But they weren't his memories and he didn't want them in his head. He just didn't seem to have a choice in the matter.

As much as he'd struggled to bring himself to terms with Calcutta's lingering aftermath, as much as he wanted to believe these dreams were just PTSD-induced recurring nightmares, he couldn't make himself believe it. Somehow, the deathbed deal he'd made in that nineteenth-century London back-alley had been the real thing and he was just going to have to learn to live with it.

The H&K subcompact lay on the nightstand to his right, but he didn't remember placing it there. He barely remembered crawling beneath the covers. How long had he been asleep? Judging by the gathering twilight, perhaps six hours.

Two soft knocks on the closed bedroom door preceded Janet's voice. "Jack, are you alive in there?"

Jack rubbed his face with both hands, rolled out of bed, and wrapped the white towel back around his waist before opening the door.

"It's debatable."

She laughed and handed him two large shopping bags. "Throw on some clothes. I've got dinner and a glass of wine breathing on the table."

"Five minutes."

He closed the door and dumped the contents of both bags on the bed.

Two pairs of jeans, two black pullover shirts, two button-down shirts—one blue, one tan—a brown leather jacket, a belt, a pair of hiking shoes and a pair of Nike running shoes, plus several pairs of boxers, briefs, and socks. In addition she'd purchased a cap and a pair of dark sunglasses. The second bag had a fully-stocked shaving kit, a Gerber survival knife, a gym bag, and a first-aid kit. Thoughtful girl. Observant too, based upon how well everything fit.

When he stepped out of the bedroom, the smell of pork cutlets, potatoes, and gravy made his mouth water.

For the first time this day, Jack took the time to really look at Janet Price as she carried a platter to the small dining table. Wearing dark slacks over lace-up boots and a navy blue pullover, she'd let her shoulder-length brown hair down. Catching his gaze, she smiled.

"Well, you look better."

Jack walked to the table, leaned over, and breathed in. "Smells great."

"Have a seat. First food, then talk."

"I like the way you think."

Jack finished his plate before Janet had gotten halfway through her cutlet, picked up his glass of Bordeaux, took a sip, and slowed down. Seeing her studying him, he leaned back in his chair.

"I'll wait until you finish."

She set her fork down, lifted her glass, and swirled the red liquid within it. "I'm finished. I had lunch while I was out shopping."

"Okay. Then I have some questions."

Her brown eyes locked with his.

"Fire away."

"You never got back to me with the answer to my Roskov question. Why not?"

She took a sip from her glass, then set it on the table.

"That's the reason I had to find you. I couldn't tell you the answer because I don't know it."

"You're trying to tell me that the NSA doesn't know where Roskov has gone to ground?"

"No. President Harris has ordered Admiral Riles to route all information concerning Roskov and Rolf Koenig directly to the CIA for analysis. I've been cut out of the loop."

Jack didn't like that answer. Why would the president directly disrupt the flow of intelligence information?

"Who at CIA?"

"Deputy Director Nolan Trent."

Finally an answer that didn't surprise him. If Nolan Trent had ever had Jack's back, it was only to stick a knife in it. But how in hell did Trent get the DCI to involve the president in this?

"Did Riles give you any indication what CIA is working?"

"Not directly. But he told me to stay on you. He also implied that the only intelligence data I would be denied was that specifically related to Vladimir Roskov or Rolf Koenig."

"Stay on me? What's that supposed to mean?"

Janet rose from her chair, grabbed her wine glass, and moved to the couch, a series of actions that Jack imitated.

"Like I said the first time we met, Riles thinks you've gotten yourself involved in something much bigger than it appears. This presidential directive has only made him more certain of it. It's pretty clear that people higher up the food chain than Roskov want you dead. Riles wants to know why."

"How did you find me?"

"I didn't. Rachel Koenig's disappearance made the press. I figured someone might be trying to use her to bait you. So I found her, or rather her car. I'd been watching it and the bed and breakfast for several hours when you showed up. It's pretty clear from the fact that the police didn't find any bodies that she was already gone when I got there."

"And when I staggered out of the burning building, you conveniently drove to my rescue?"

"I don't pass up opportunities."

Once again, Jack was struck by Janet's calm self-assurance. She leaned toward him.

"I've been thinking about what this is all about. Assuming you pose a threat to a high-profile CIA operation, they might come after you, but not like this. They've pulled out all the stops on this one. Someone killed Rita Chavez in Paris and framed you. The question is why?"

"To trigger me."

"Sure. But I think it goes deeper than that. That killing was designed to trigger someone else, too."

The realization hit Jack as the words left Janet's lips. "Director Rheiner," he said.

Janet nodded. "It was obvious that you would take it hard, but they made it personal to the DCI. The killer posted the torture killing of a CIA analyst on the web. Not just any analyst, but a close friend of Director Rheiner."

"And Nolan Trent happened to step in to ask for special resources to nail the hitter."

"Convenient."

In his head, another piece of the puzzle clicked into place. Still Jack couldn't see what it was trying to show him.

"But what's the Koenig–Roskov connection? I don't believe Roskov is blackmailing him."

"I don't know. And now that I'm cut off from the raw data on those two, it's going to be a lot harder to find out."

"And that's where I come in?"

Janet stood, walked to the window, and stared out at the moon rising over Lake Plansee. "Riles told me I was going to have to get creative to fish out the answers. It looks like he thinks you're the real bait."

Jack moved up to stand beside her. The moon, its reflection in the alpine lake, the surrounding Alps, Janet standing beside him—all combined to bring a single word to his lips.

"Perfect."

CHAPTER 52

Jacob Knox knew all about patience. It was the key difference between a professional hunter and a rank amateur. Amateurs beat the bush, seeking to frighten hiding game into the open. Even when this tactic worked, the amateur found himself poorly prepared and poorly positioned for the kill shot. The professional studied his prey, learned its patterns, and positioned himself to wait for the game animal to come to him. Jacob was a patient man. But it didn't mean he liked waiting.

His just-finished phone conversation with Nolan Trent hadn't helped that. Either Roskov or Koenig had tried another hit on Gregory, this time in the Bavarian Alps. Once again the attempt had failed and once again, Gregory's subsequent whereabouts were unknown. Jacob wasn't particularly worried that one of these hits would succeed, thus robbing him of the satisfaction of killing The Ripper personally. He didn't think these amateurs had it in them. But they were screwing up his setup. Every one of these attempts distracted and delayed Gregory from following the trail that led to Jacob.

The added delay was more than irritating. The whole point of this operation was to ensure that Gregory didn't interfere with Rolf Koenig's space launch, but as long as The Ripper was alive, that remained a distinct possibility.

He'd completed his analysis of security at Roskov's Kyzylorda warehouse complex. Surrounded by an electrified chain-link fence with triple concertina razor wire along the top, a total of six warehouses provided temporary storage and loading for a variety of goods, some more legitimate than others. Day and night security cameras monitored every entrance as well as the driveways between buildings. Four backup generators protected the facility from external power loss. A tunnel connected Warehouse Five to another warehouse, five kilometers to the southwest, to allow cargo to be shipped out without being seen. Right now the primary purpose of the other warehouses in the facility was to mask the activity in Warehouse Five.

In addition, Vladimir Roskov employed a security detail that consisted of three shifts, each with two guards at the entry gate, two guards at each building, and a rapid reaction squad of five.

Jacob knew that if he wanted to get in, none of these precautions would matter. He didn't think they would bother The Ripper either. But when the attack happened, they would funnel him to Jacob and that would be sufficient. Before any of that could occur, he had to get Gregory back on target.

By the time Jacob's call was patched through to Vladimir Roskov, his irritation had come to a low boil.

"What's the problem?" The growl in Roskov's voice didn't improve his mood.

"I want to know why your people are screwing up my operation."

"Your operation?"

"Damn right. Trent didn't send me here to sit on my ass. I thought The Ripper had already made it abundantly clear that he's out of your thugs' league. I've gone to significant trouble to put him on a trail that ends in a kill zone in Kyzylorda. The last thing I need is your people delaying his arrival while they get themselves killed."

"The Ripper got lucky. I've almost had him twice in a row."

"Almost won't get it done."

"My man is still alive. When he kills Gregory, you won't have to."

"What's his name?"

"That's my business, not yours."

"Then send him a message from me."

"What's that?"

"Tell him to enjoy every moment he's got left."

Roskov's growl changed to a hiss. "Go screw yourself."

The line went dead. Goddamn Roskov. If Nolan Trent and Rolf Koenig could keep the Russian mob boss under control, there was no use wasting any more of his valuable time trying to do it. It was just what Jacob needed right now. One more major complication.

CHAPTER 53

Levi Elias sat next to Admiral Riles at the small conference table in the NSA director's private briefing room, feeling tightness in his throat. His fingers moved across the touchpad to highlight a section of the report displayed on the big screen.

"Sir, something's not right. There are way too many coincidences happening."

Admiral Riles stared at the screen and nodded. "Take me through it."

"Let's start with the most recent sequence. First, Rolf Koenig launches an all-out Polizei search for his suddenly missing wife, possible foul play suspected. Janet was all over that. Thought it was a trap designed to ensnare Jack Gregory. Based upon her request, we identified Rachel's image in a traffic photo outside Oberammergau, Germany. The next day, a bomb went off on the second floor of a bed and breakfast there. Burned the place to the ground. The proprietor and a young German couple reported seeing a man stumble out of the building immediately after the explosion. He got into a black car that sped away before the Polizei or firefighters arrived."

"Janet and Jack Gregory?"

"Looks like, although she hasn't reported in."

"The bomber?"

"We don't know, but since there were no bodies found at the scene, he was there early. Probably set the bomb and departed, taking Ms. Koenig with him."

"Was she in on the setup?"

"Not likely. From everything we know about Gregory, he's extremely good at figuring out when someone is lying to him. I don't think an amateur like Rachel Koenig could have fooled him. Besides, the *Bild* just reported that Rachel Koenig has admitted herself to a psychiatric clinic for the treatment of severe depression. Rolf Koenig's press secretary issued a statement asking the public to respect the family's right to medical privacy in this matter.

"Then there's this. I had a private chat with Dr. Jennings. Big John is registering a significant correlation that could tie all of the following persons and events together: Rolf Koenig, Vladimir Roskov, Jack Gregory, Nolan Trent, and the upcoming launch from the Baikonur Cosmodrome of the XLRMV-1 lunar mining mission."

Levi watched the NSA director lean back in his chair, his fingers steepled in front of his chest. Riles's gray eyes studied the figures Levi brought up on the next screen.

"That's only a little better than sixty-percent probability. Hardly a lock."

"I'd like permission to elevate the priority on this particular search."

"Denied. I'd need a hell of a lot more than that to violate a direct presidential order."

"Sir, we have indications that Roskov is working closely with CIA on this."

"Doing what?"

"I don't know."

"'I don't know' won't get it done, Levi."

Levi swallowed. "That's why I need that Big John priority search."

"Request denied."

Admiral Riles rose to his feet and Levi rose with him. As he watched his boss turn his back and walk out of the conference room, he knew he'd failed to give the old man the excuse to do what he wanted to do. It was a failure on his part. He shouldn't have brought this to Riles's attention without hard data to back up his suspicions. It was just going to make it harder to cry wolf next time.

Disconnecting his tablet from the wireless display, Levi put it to sleep, and began the walk back to his office. It was all up to Janet now. Maybe it always had been.

CHAPTER 54

Having made a fresh pot of coffee, Jack poured two cups and moved to sit across from Janet at the kitchen table. Following his every movement, Janet could feel his thoughts shift to business. His words confirmed it.

"The CIA has gone to great lengths to strip me of a number of my European contacts. I can establish new sources for what I need, but it will take time I don't have. I'm willing to cooperate in your investigation in return for your operational assistance, but let's get something straight up front. I don't work for the NSA, not even as an independent consultant, and I damn sure don't follow NSA rules."

"Understood."

"Right now, I need to know what you bring to the table."

"Is this a job interview?"

"It is if you want to work with me. Otherwise we can go our separate ways."

Janet studied Jack's face. For just a second she thought she saw the distinctive red glint that she'd observed in the grainy Cartagena photograph. But maybe she just wanted to see it.

"My full name's Janet Alexandra Price. Both parents died when I was thirteen. After that I was raised by my grandparents on my mother's side. I graduated high school in Gaithersburg, Maryland, before attending the University of Maryland, where I majored in Computer Science and was a two-time NCAA pentathlon champion. The CIA recruited me through an intern program during my junior and senior year of college. I surprised them by qualifying and training as a field operative as opposed to becoming the analyst they thought they were getting."

"Unusual for a computer scientist to want to become a field agent."

"Computer security fascinates me, but I'd go crazy sitting behind a desk for a career."

"What pentathlon events were you best at?"

"Shooting and fencing."

"Fencing?"

A wry smile creased her lips. "I've always been good with sharp, pointy objects."

Jack nodded. "So you trained under Garfield Kromly?"

"Yes. Garfield first noticed me when I broke your CIA thousand-meter marksmanship record. After that I was part of a CIA group that was put through a special U.S. Army Ranger School class. I was the only woman to graduate."

Jack raised an eyebrow. "Why would CIA operatives need Ranger training?"

"It was a one-time experiment Garfield engineered. I think he used it to evaluate how well select trainees could handle extended physical and mental stress."

"Meaning you."

"I was one of those he was interested in."

"And afterward?"

"I worked as a special CIA field operative for two years. Then I walked away."

"Why?"

Janet's eyes lost focus as the memory of that life-changing decision filled her mind. "Admiral Riles can be a very persuasive man. He was assembling a special team of field operatives to enhance and corroborate electronically gathered information. It was a chance to operate completely off the grid."

"That's stepping on the CIA's turf. If Director Rheiner finds out, the shit's going to hit the fan."

"President Harris issued a number of presidential findings that interpret governing laws in a way that expands the executive branch's ability to deal with terrorist threats. Admiral Riles believes one of those findings gives the NSA director the authority to establish such a team. It's why I don't show up on official NSA employment records."

"And President Harris agrees?"

"Even a president needs plausible deniability. If Riles is wrong, he'll be the one to take the fall."

Jack paused, studying her eyes with new intensity, as if he was trying to crawl through them into her brain.

"Have you ever killed anyone?"

"Yes."

"More than one?"

"Yes."

"Who was your first?"

Janet felt the memory sink its claws into the back of her neck, felt the 38 special's recoil shock her small hands and arms as the weapon repeatedly tried to tear itself from her thirteen-year-old grip.

"My father."

Jack's eyes narrowed. For several long seconds she felt the weight of his gaze bear down on her. The silence grew into a ghostly presence that sought to quench the overhead light and usher night's shadows into the tiny kitchen.

When he spoke again, his voice softened ever so slightly. "You've read my dossier?"

"I have."

"If you have any questions, now's the time."

Janet felt herself hesitate to ask the one thing she most wanted to understand. It might be a deal breaker. Still, she'd told Jack she never passed up an opportunity, and it was God's truth.

"Why did you kill that pimp in Cartagena?"

"Why does that matter?"

"You wanted to know what I brought to the table and I laid it out for you. Now I need to know whether I can count on you to stay on target."

Once again she thought she saw it, that red reflection in Jack's pupils.

"You can't. You're putting your life in jeopardy just by being around me. But you already knew that, didn't you?"

As she looked deep into Jack Gregory's strange eyes, a new understanding dawned. This man walked a tightrope through a violent and chaotic maelstrom that threatened to rise up and sweep him away at any moment. And, God help her, she was dying to step right out there with him. Hopefully that thin strand was strong enough to support them both.

CHAPTER 55

Jonas Aachen didn't like making mistakes. He didn't like having his ass chewed either, especially by the man he admired most in the world, Rolf Koenig. But he'd just been the recipient of a world-class ass-chewing, and he had to admit he deserved it.

It wasn't that his equations were wrong. The problem was round-off error caused by the subtraction of two nearly-equal numbers in the divisor of a single line of native C++ code, the code that controlled the payload trajectories. If Rolf Koenig hadn't caught it, his mistake would have resulted in a three-and-a-half-meter targeting error for the third of the six packages. That error would have produced an eleven-nanosecond delay in the gamma pulse, well outside the two-nanosecond tolerance.

As he stared at the C++ code on his screen, he made the required change, and then spent the next thirty minutes writing a test driver to validate the patch. To Rolf's credit, he hadn't fixed the offending software himself, allowing Jonas to atone for his error. It was one of the many reasons Rolf's people strove so hard to be perfect at what they did. Koenig was demanding, but he always demanded more of himself than of anyone else.

The test finished its run and, satisfied with the results, Jonas checked the change into the source code repository and started the release build that would create a new installation of the payload guidance software. Rising to his feet, Jonas walked across his office to the coffee maker. Selecting a French roast, he placed the K-cup in the brewer and pressed the blinking start button. Less than a minute later, he lifted the cup to his lips, pausing to inhale the rich aroma before taking a loud, slurping sip.

Stepping to the window that overlooked the Kyzylorda clean room, Jonas watched his semi-transparent reflection in the glass hover over the payload that would change the world. His angular face, long platinum-blond hair, and smoke-gray eyes bore a striking resemblance to one of the ghostly twins from that *Matrix* movie.

On the right side of the payload, two white-clad engineers worked to make final adjustments to one of the six Gamma Enhanced Magnetic Field Penetrators they'd nicknamed MagPipes. Each designed to look exactly like one of the nuclear-power generators on the primary power module, these devices were far more dangerous than the components they were destined to replace.

The revolutionary design spoke to the level of Rolf Koenig's genius. First, each device had to match the radiation signature of its counterpart on the primary power module in the assembly building at the Baikonur Cosmodrome, two hundred and fifty kilometers to the northwest of this warehouse. Each MagPipe was actually a gamma-enhanced fusion bomb the size of a welder's acetylene bottle, which only Rolf Koenig could have pulled off.

Each MagPipe contained an array of plutonium pellets, suspended in an explosive gel that performed two functions. It kept the pellets separated, reducing the total radiation output while preventing critical nuclear reaction. And it formed the precisely-shaped charge that would drive these pellets together into one compressed ball for the handful of femtoseconds required to achieve a fission reaction. At that instant, the light from this little A-bomb would fill the case before the explosion had a chance to tear it apart, forming the first stage of three thermo-nuclear reactions. The intensity of the light would crush the long tube that occupied the center of the cylinder for most of its two-meter length, initiating a fusion reaction within the outer tritium tube. That fusion reaction would strip neutrons from the inner tube of lithium-6, transmuting it into lithium-4 and commencing the final stage of the fusion bomb. The resulting explosion would produce the enhanced gamma flux each MagPipe was designed to generate.

When a nuclear explosion occurs at the edge of space, gamma radiation penetrates deep into the atmosphere, ionizing the atoms and sending electrons spiraling perpendicular to the earth's magnetic field lines as they race toward the earth's surface. The intensity of this pulse warps the earth's magnetic field as it achieves a saturation voltage of approximately fifty-thousand volts per meter.

A spread of enhanced gamma nukes detonating over the U.S. east coast would burn out electrical systems over a vast area, but the first three were the key to the unimaginable destruction Rolf Koenig intended to inflict. Those three precisely timed detonations would form a tunnel through the induced electric conduction layer, laying an electromagnetic pipe that would punch through the fifty-thousand volt-per-meter saturation level all the way to the earth's surface.

These phased bursts would be followed by three more detonations to extend the area of peak damage from Boston to North

Carolina, with reduced effects reaching all the way to Miami. While the nuclear explosions wouldn't kill many people directly, people would die in the immediate aftermath. Airplanes would fall from the sky, motors would burn out, power plants would catch fire, transformers would explode, huge currents would be induced in electrical transmission lines, and solid-state electrical components would fry. Even facilities with Faraday cage shielding would succumb to the extended E3 pulse as the earth's magnetic field fought to reestablish its natural state.

The effects on the American economy would be devastating. In the Eastern corridor nothing electrical would work. There would be no fuel because there would be no working pumps. There would be no supplies because none of the trucks or trains would run. The ports would shut down because none of the heavy-lift equipment would work. There would be no running water, no food, no fuel, no heat, no cooling, no transportation for thousands of square miles. The financial system would collapse due to the shutdown of exchanges and the utter loss of banking and other financial records.

The simulations Jonas had run to examine just such a scenario predicted that the EMP attack would plunge the U.S. into deep depression. Many other countries would suffer lesser financial damage. It would be the stroke that would break the world's American addiction. The United States would eventually recover, but it would take at least a decade, and during that time Europe and Asia would not be waiting for them to catch up. The era of U.S. dominance was about to come to a very abrupt end.

Jonas took a deep breath, let it out slowly, and returned to his desk. His one little mistake would have greatly reduced the total damage that they intended the coming attack to produce. Thank God Rolf had caught it in time.

CHAPTER 56

"So who dropped Rachel off at the clinic?"

Jack's question had started Janet down the thirty-six-hour trail that had carried her to the Schoelerpark Residences, a condo complex in Berlin's upper-class Charlottenburg-Wilmersdorf district. She had to admit, if Petor Kline's selection of dwellings was any indication, he was a man of refined taste. The outside of the five-story building, with its many balconies, was so covered in growing foliage it could have been the setting for a modern day Tolkien novel, had Hobbits evolved to live in apartment buildings. It was a fine spot for someone who craved comfort.

Having again been denied access to information that was deemed too closely tied to Rolf Koenig, Janet had been forced to hack her way into a number of not-quite-public German databases to flush out her Petor Kline dossier. A surgeon who had quit public practice to join Rolf Koenig's personal medical staff, the doctor didn't like to get his hands dirty. And while Rolf Koenig was still his employer, a deeper check pointed to a recent working relationship with Vladimir Roskov. It should have taken her only a couple of hours to gather the information, but instead it had cost her the better part of a day.

Thank you, Mr. President.

From where she leaned against a tree in the park that bore the same name as the apartment complex, she watched the empty parking space that would soon hold Petor's silver Mercedes sedan. Since it was a little after six thirty p.m., Janet expected him at any time. Instead he kept her waiting for more than two hours. He pulled into the parking lot at eight fifty-three p.m., just as the sun set in the west, and Janet walked through the parking lot to meet him, her attention seemingly focused on trying to find her keys in her handbag.

As Petor opened his car door to step out, Janet fired a single shot, the tranquilizer dart lodging in the left side of his neck.

"What the . . . ?"

The last word died on his lips as his eyes rolled back in his head and he slumped over in the driver's seat. Closing the remaining distance, Janet leaned over and rolled Petor across the center console onto the passenger seat, slid into the driver's seat, and closed the door behind her. When she pressed the START button, the powerful engine rumbled to life, accompanied by an annoying seat-belt-not-fastened beep. She ignored it and pulled out of the parking lot and onto Wilhelmsaue.

An hour and forty-three minutes later, twelve kilometers west of Cottbus, she pulled the Mercedes into the open door of the partially collapsed barn adjacent to an abandoned farmhouse. When she switched off the engine and opened the door, Jack Gregory stepped out of the shadows to meet her, his body dimly illuminated by the interior car lights. Janet saw her H&K subcompact in his right hand, muzzle pointed down at the ground.

"Any trouble?"

Janet shook her head and smiled. "Kline must have worked late. Decided to take a nap on the ride down."

Jack opened the passenger door, leaned in, and dragged Petor Kline out of the vehicle, letting his unconscious body fall face down in the dirt. A quick pat-down revealed the presence of a nine-millimeter Glock 17 in a shoulder holster. Jack took the handgun, ejected the magazine and checked the chamber before reseating it and chambering a round. Janet accepted the H&K subcompact from his outstretched hand and watched as Jack shoved the Glock into his own shoulder holster before stooping to toss Kline's body over his left shoulder.

The car lights went out as Janet closed the passenger door, momentarily blinding her while her eyes sought to adjust to the sudden darkness. She switched her cell phone to flashlight mode and followed Jack out of the barn and into the dilapidated farmhouse, shutting the door behind her.

A quick glance around showed that Jack had been busy. He'd managed to lower the living room's metal Rouladen blinds common in German houses, completely blacking out the interior from the outside. The few pieces of broken furniture had been shoved against the far wall, with the exception of the weathered dining room table that rested in the room's center. But now, two of its legs had been broken off so that the top tilted down to the floor at a thirty degree angle.

Jack unceremoniously dropped Petor on the floor beside the table, switched on an LED flashlight and set it so that it pointed up to splash its light on the bare boards of the ceiling, the ambient lighting sufficient to allow Janet to switch off her cell phone.

Grabbing the box of supplies they'd acquired earlier in the day, Jack set it beside the table.

He grabbed a large roll of duct tape and, with Janet's assistance, positioned Petor face up on the slanted table. With the sound that only duct tape makes as it rips from the roll, Jack bound Petor's body tightly in place, his feet positioned at the high end while the back of his head extended beyond the table edge to touch the floor.

Janet stepped back to examine their work. Petor's feet had been bound together and secured to the table in multiple loops of duct tape. His hands and arms were bound tightly to his sides, his chest strapped to the lower section of the table with a prodigious quantity of duct tape. Finally, Jack pulled a thick cloth sack over Petor's head, strapping the end tightly around the slender man's neck, before strapping his head to the table.

That done, Jack walked across the room and lifted two of the ten-liter water bottles he had stacked near the door and set them beside the table. Janet glanced back at Petor's body, unable to suppress the shudder that worked its way up her arms and into her shoulders. Although she'd never personally used this interrogation technique, she'd experienced it during her training. The memory wasn't a pleasant one.

Jack's eyes locked with hers.

"Time to wake him up."

Shaking off the feeling that had momentarily frozen her, Janet opened the small bag that held the syringe containing the stimulant that would counteract the effects of the tranquilizer dart. She knelt beside Petor and inserted the needle into a vein in his left arm, feeling her thumb depress the plunger as if it belonged to someone else's hand.

The thought that a dose this large would leave the man feeling wired crossed her mind, but Janet shunted it away. That unpleasant side effect was about to become the least of Petor Kline's problems.

CHAPTER 57

Petor Kline opened his eyes, struggling to remember where he was. When he tried to move, he found he couldn't. Had he been in a car accident? Even his head had been strapped in place so that he couldn't turn it side to side. Once again the possibility that he'd been in a serious accident crossed his mind. He seemed to be bound to a back-board, although it was supported at a crazy angle, his head tilted down as if he were being treated for severe shock.

He blinked his eyes, trying to clear his vision, but it didn't work. All he could see was the cloth of the sheet or blanket that had been pulled over his head. None of this made sense. The last thing he remembered was pulling into his parking spot and opening his car door. Something had stung him on the neck. Not a bee sting, more like a dart.

The sudden realization caused his pulse to spike. Once again he tried to move and again he failed. The cold voice that spoke from above spiked his heart rate even higher.

"Good evening, Dr. Kline."

Petor knew he needed to calm down, tried his best to do it, and failed. He didn't want to ask the questions, didn't want to know the answers, but couldn't stop himself. His voice came out high pitched and slightly muffled.

"Who are you? What do you want from me?"

"I'm the man you tried to kill two days ago."

Shit! The Ripper.

"And I just want truthful answers to the questions I'm going to ask you."

With his mind acquiring a sudden clarity, a new understanding dawned on Petor. He wasn't strapped to a backboard. He was bound to some sort of torture device. His face wasn't covered by a blanket but by a cloth sack that had been fastened tightly around his neck, intended to deny him sight and make breathing difficult. But why tilt him head down like this?

The splash of cold water being poured over the cloth answered his question. The suddenly wet cloth rapidly absorbed the water, plastering itself to his mouth and nose as he sought to inhale. It was as if someone had just pulled a plastic bag tight around his head. He couldn't get any air. He sucked harder, only managing to inhale some of the water.

Like a man in an electric chair, his body went rigid as he fought to free himself, to tear the horrible thing from his face. Feeling his heart try to claw its way out of his chest, he managed to suck a tiny bit of air through the cloth before a fresh flow of water over the sack shut it off. Unable to thrash about, Petor tried to scream, but the sound devolved into a gargling sputter as his human drowning response kicked in.

Then the flow of water onto the cloth sack stopped and he managed to draw a tiny bit of air into his lungs. Desperately, his labored lungs pulled with all their might, and where rewarded with more air, but also with a dampness that left him coughing. When the coughing finally stopped and he was able to draw a deeper breath, hyperventilation sent him into another desperate fit of thrashing against the bonds that wrapped him mummy-tight. Petor was a child trapped in a narrow sewer pipe, his arms pinned tightly against his sides as water seeped in to fill it, unable to wiggle forward or back.

He screamed again and this time he got his money's worth. When he finally stopped, the voice was back, speaking close to his left ear.

"That was five minutes. I'm going to ask my questions now. Lie to me and I'll know it. It's one of my eccentricities. Every lie earns you another five minutes."

Petor felt his jaw clench as his blood pulsed through the veins in his forehead. He was a medical doctor, a skilled surgeon, not some Euro-scum to be tortured into submission by this ex-CIA prick.

"No."

The immediate splash of cold water startled him so badly he exhaled instead of trying to make his breath last. Instantly he found himself transported back into the hell he had just escaped, unable to battle his body's automatic response, even to get out a plea for mercy. He needed air, but it seemed that the harder he inhaled the less air he got. His chest moved but he barely got enough to keep him conscious. When the water stopped, Petor felt his body quake with tremors reminiscent of hypothermia victims.

The Ripper spoke again.

"A non-answer also earns you another session. Do you understand me?"

"Yes." Petor felt his teeth rattle as he managed to spit out the word.

"Good. Who do you work for?"

With every passing moment it became easier to draw breath. Petor gulped in a full lungful.

"Rolf Koenig."

"Tell me about your relationship to Vladimir Roskov."

Petor hesitated before answering.

"Rolf Koenig pays me to assist Roskov."

"What is Koenig's connection to Roskov?"

"I don't know. He doesn't tell . . . "

This time it felt like a whole bucket of water was dumped on his head with such force that it penetrated the cloth, the angle of the incline forcing it up his nose and into his sinuses. He knew this was only an illusion caused by the way the impact pressed the wet cloth up against his face, but as fresh horror filled his soul, that knowledge was little consolation.

The water stopped, the questioning started, the water returned. Always, amid the rising liquid terror that threatened to drown him, The Ripper was there, asking his questions. When Petor Kline began to talk, he told everything he knew about Rolf Koenig and Vladimir Roskov. And, at the end, he only wished he knew more.

Now the sack had been cut free and for a brief, wonderful moment, he breathed in the fresh night air, unrestricted. Then, at the end of a dark tunnel, he saw a distant bright light. But it was only the flash from a gun barrel.

CHAPTER 58

Standing six feet from the table where Petor Kline struggled to draw breath, Janet watched Jack closely. Not quite textbook, Jack used his own waterboarding methodology, one that relied extensively on enhancing the claustrophobic effect produced by tightly binding the whole body. The normal drowning response was triggered when a person felt that first gulp of water enter the lungs, something that dialed the fight or flight reaction to maximum. In the water, even an experienced swimmer, under the influence of that natural bodily reaction, flailed wildly as he fought to break Neptune's death grip. Jack was denying Petor Kline's body that opportunity.

Waterboarding produced the same panicked response, except the person wasn't really drowning. If the person administering the torture knew what he was doing, he could elevate the level of panic and maintain it for an extended period. To do that, it was important to give the subject periodic breaks, not only to perform interrogation, but to allow him to regain the strength required to maximize the effectiveness of the next session.

There were those that held to the belief that, for soldiers acclimated to battle, the longer they experienced it the better they were able to handle their situation. But most scholars who studied the effects of extended life-or-death stress on soldiers had come to the conclusion that individuals had a specific stress tolerance and that the longer they were exposed, the closer they came to exceeding that tolerance. It was as if a soldier had a certain amount of bravery, acquired from nature and life experience. Constant combat drained it and, without an extended break for rest and recovery, the bravery tank eventually ran dry.

Nobody acclimated to waterboarding.

Although Janet maintained her clinical observation of the interrogation, looking for inconsistencies or signs of deception in Petor's answers, she felt a tightness grip her chest, as if her lungs were trying to breathe for him. It was a psychosomatic response, but one she couldn't quite shake. Whether Jack was feeling some of the same thing, she couldn't tell. Certainly there was tension in his face, but his hands were rock steady. Perhaps he was contemplating Petor's fate.

One thing stood out to anyone who had studied Jack Gregory. People who tried to kill him consistently found the same bad end, although the means to that end varied widely. Petor was already a dead man. The only question was how hard he would force Jack to make his passing.

Suddenly Petor was talking, his words filled with real information, his answers long and rambling as the man sought to keep Jack from sending him back into that watery hell. Unfortunately, the more the man talked, the more Janet came to understand that he didn't really know what Rolf Koenig and Vladimir Roskov were doing.

Dr. Kline had been assigned the job of keeping Roskov focused on the mission Rolf had assigned him. Jack was the distraction that Petor had tried to eliminate. But when it came to a deeper knowledge of what Koenig was using Roskov to do, Petor didn't have any answers. What he did know was that Roskov had travelled to his warehouse complex in Kyzylorda, Kazakhstan.

Janet found the coincidence of Vladimir Roskov being in Kazakhstan as Koenig prepared for the launch of his robotic lunar mission from the Baikonur Cosmodrome very intriguing. But not as interesting as Petor telling Jack about a mysterious CIA operative that had contacted Roskov in Kyzylorda. Although he didn't know the man's name, Petor said the man's mission was to kill The Ripper before he could damage their mutual interest.

When Petor Kline finally stopped talking, she could see Jack decide the man had nothing left to give. Reaching down, Jack tore away the sack that covered Petor's head. He waited while the man drew in two full breaths before leveling the Glock at Petor's forehead.

Just before Jack pulled the trigger, Janet saw it, that red glint deep within his pupils. As the gunshot ended Petor Kline's life, Janet's gaze remained locked on Jack's face. When he looked up at her, those strange eyes sent a sudden heat flowing through her veins and, this time, she knew that she hadn't imagined it.

CHAPTER 59

Kazakhstan wasn't known for its high-speed internet service, but the Baikonur Cosmodrome was an exception. Still, it paled in comparison to the direct satellite feed Rolf got from his Hamburg Technautics communications satellites. To minimize transmission delay, he had deployed an array of low earth-orbiting satellites instead of placing them in geosynchronous orbits. His communications software automatically routed data along an optimal route that minimized distance between data start and end points. Since electromagnetic waves travelled at three hundred million meters per second, he could communicate with any point on the earth in less than a tenth of a second. It had only taken the CIA slightly longer to contact him with the bad news.

Rolf Koenig stared at Nolan Trent's grim visage on his laptop as the encrypted video conference came online. The CIA's deputy director didn't bother with a greeting.

"Your man Kline is dead."

Rolf felt his mouth go dry, but denied his face the emotion. "When?"

"German Polizei found his body early this afternoon. My people just learned of it."

"You have details?"

"Dr. Kline was taped to a broken table inside an abandoned farmhouse. He'd been water boarded and then shot in the head."

"Sheisse."

"Damn it, Rolf. I thought we agreed that I would handle Gregory."

"No. I told you your man could handle security in Kazakhstan. If Gregory never makes it here it's a moot point."

Rolf saw Trent's jaw clench, then release. "Let's get something straight. I won't get in the way of your rocket launch, but you better stay the hell out of my lane, too."

"Or what?"

"Or you'll jeopardize the whole operation. I guarantee you, right now Gregory knows everything Petor Kline knew. That makes him that much harder to kill."

That unpleasant thought had already occurred to Rolf and he didn't like hearing the obvious from Nolan Trent.

"Dr. Kline was never in the loop."

"For all our sakes, I hope not."

Rolf damped the annoyance that had filtered into his voice and shifted subjects. "Have you dropped the package?"

"It'll be delivered on the third shift tonight. But behind those firewalls you won't be able to activate it remotely."

"I won't need to. It'll be part of the system, using my algorithm to decide for itself when it's time to take action."

"Okay then."

"Oh . . . and Nolan?"

"Yes?"

"Get your ex-agent off my ass."

As Trent's mouth twisted into the beginning of a response, Rolf killed the connection.

Rolf stood up, placed his hand in the small of his back, and applied what pressure he could to the L4-L5 vertebrae. The polo injury tended to tighten up anytime he sat for more than two hours.

Even more than he hated the clutter of a paper-based society, Rolf abhorred hospitals that seemed better designed to produce resistant superbugs than to cure human ills. It was the reason he had ordered the construction of a state-of-the-art medical clinic and surgery in the upper portion of the Königsberg Castle's dungeon. Unfortunately, even the top-of-the-line spinal decompression unit had not lived up to his expectations. Perhaps, in addition to his other technology interests, Rolf would have to direct some of his genius and competitive drive at that field.

Despite multiple operations performed by the world's best back specialist in Rolf's private surgery, the results had been less than optimal. Today, having reviewed the final payload software patches, he'd been sitting a lot longer than his back found acceptable.

Prior to Nolan Trent's call, he'd actually been feeling very well satisfied. Maybe the two girls the Cosmonaut Hotel kept on call for him could help him recover that feeling. As he made his way out of building 92A-50 and into his waiting sedan, he looked forward to finding out.

CHAPTER 60

For the third time, Jacob Knox watched the Schoelerpark Residences' security camera footage, pausing it as Dr. Kline opened the driver's door to step out of his silver Mercedes. The video quality sucked. It had been captured by a camera on the far end of the building and had been recorded in low resolution to reduce the size of the video files that had to be stored on the server. Another problem was the terrible lighting. The sun had just sunk below the horizon and the southwest-facing camera had been partially blinded by the backlighting caused by the darker terrain against a brighter sky.

The Polizei had found the video was useless in identifying the dark figure who had approached the Mercedes, fired a pistol at Dr. Kline, shoved his body back inside, and then driven away in his car. Then again, the Polizei didn't have access to the video exploitation tools the CIA did, like the one Jacob was using right now.

Jacob moved the timeline slider, advancing a few frames until he had a partial profile of the right side of the shooter's face as he approached the car. Clicking the auto-balance button helped, but not enough. He spent the next half-hour playing with the lighting and contrast settings, before running the enhanced resolution processing algorithm on that frame.

His chair creaked as Jacob leaned back, his hands behind his head. Finally he was getting somewhere. Not a man. The profile was that of a woman. He saved the captured image, then advanced the video until the woman slid into the driver's seat and reached out to close the car door, freezing the image with the profile of the left side of her face. Applying the saved settings from the enhancements to the previous image, he saved his second capture.

Over the next two hours, Jacob meticulously built a collection of images of the woman's head, each from a slightly different angle. Although he didn't have any from the front, the software could form a pretty good extrapolation to approximate the missing details. That done, he launched another portion of the rendering application, one that used the captured images to build a 3D wireframe model of the woman's head and then applied the captured images to build the texture that it draped over the 3D model.

Once again, Jacob saved the results. Manipulating the touch screen, Jacob rotated the head so that he could view it from different angles. Definitely not perfect, but it should be enough to give the CIA facial recognition database something decent to work with.

Jacob composed his request, logged in on the CIA server, and uploaded the encrypted files. Then he settled in to wait. Surprisingly, the wait wasn't long. As he scanned the profile that came back to him, he understood why.

Her name was Janet Price and she was ex-CIA. So what was her connection to Gregory? Further study revealed that she had been tagged as a gifted CIA field agent and had shown great promise. Then, after two years with the agency, she had abruptly quit, citing religious issues, and had dropped off the grid. The problem was that her timeline didn't appear to intersect with Jack Gregory's. Nothing in her file gave any indication she'd ever met the man.

Of course, since she'd left CIA, they didn't have much information on what she'd been doing. Apparently she'd found the Lord and devoted herself to missionary work in Asia and in South America. From what Jacob had seen in the video, she had an irresistible recruiting pitch.

At least now he had some real, high-quality photographs of Janet Price from her time at CIA. Since she didn't yet know she'd been identified, that would let him find her. Since the available evidence indicated that Ms. Price was now working with Jack Gregory, like Rita Chavez, she would have to be eliminated. It was all part of the process of stripping The Ripper of all his support systems, leaving him standing alone to face Jacob and the vast array of CIA resources at his beck and call.

Jacob composed one more high-priority intelligence request, one that would need Nolan Trent's personal authorization.

All asset facial recognition search authorization request. Target: Janet Alexandra Price. Last known location: Berlin, Germany. Highest Priority.

CHAPTER 61

The drive to Salzburg had taken Jacob four hours. He was in no hurry. Once again his penchant for preparation would pay handsome dividends, in this case delivering Janet Price into his hands. And once he was done with her, The Ripper would once again stride a path that Jacob controlled, and he would stride that path alone.

Janet Price surprised him. After she left the CIA, aside from cursory information that fit with her foreign missionary story, she was a complete mystery. But Jacob didn't believe the missionary crap. As a young girl, she had put five .38-caliber bullets into her father.

Not that the prick hadn't deserved it, having just beat her mother to death with his fists. So much for the usefulness of judicial restraining orders. Still, if that trauma hadn't been enough to drive her to religion, he doubted that she would have found it after two years in the field working for the CIA. It was much more likely that she had decided to monetize her skills in service to the underworld, even though he hadn't found any evidence to support that conjecture.

It was a shame he wasn't going to get the chance to ask her that and other questions. Unlike Rita Chavez, she had once been a highly trained CIA field operative. And, even though those skills were likely to be a bit rusty, Jacob had no intention of screwing around with tasers and drugs. The silenced Sig P226 would terminate whatever threat Janet Price might pose.

Nolan Trent may not have been able to tell him much about what Janet had been up to in the last couple of years, but he had delivered on Jacob's high-priority intelligence request. Not only did Jacob know Janet's room number at the Hotel Stein, he knew that she had purchased a single ticket to tonight's performance of *Lucio Silla*. He also knew that she had left the hotel parking garage in a blue Audi A5 coupe at six p.m., allowing plenty of time for a nice dinner before the opera.

Pulling into the Hotel Stein parking garage, Jacob slid the black Mercedes coupe into the first available slot, one level below the street entrance, and turned off the vehicle. A quick press illuminated the green LED watch display. 9:23 p.m. He had at least two hours before Janet Price returned from her night at the opera.

Before he settled in for the wait, he needed to make the required preparations. Grabbing the small duffel bag from the passenger side floorboard, Jacob climbed out of the vehicle and walked the spiral driveway back to the entrance. Positioning a tiny camera and its Wi-Fi broadcast unit just inside the entrance, he checked the signal strength. Good. He'd have to recheck it from the lower levels and, if necessary, position some repeaters, but he doubted he would need them.

Next, Jacob located the hotel's primary breaker box. He didn't bother with the breakers themselves, instead wrapping a wad of C4 around the power cable coming into the box, affixing a wireless detonator to the C4. He had little doubt that the explosion would trip some upstream high-voltage breakers, plunging the entire block into darkness.

Repeating the process on the emergency lighting fixtures on each of the first three levels, he turned and walked back to his car, removed a couple of items, and tossed his kit-bag into the vehicle's trunk.

Without placing them on his head, Jacob switched on the night-vision goggles, verified that they were functioning properly, and switched them off, fully aware that even the dim parking garage lighting would have dazzled him had he tried that test with the goggles properly positioned over his eyes. He wasn't worried. When he turned them on for real, too much light wouldn't be an issue.

CHAPTER 62

It had taken Janet every ounce of persuasion she could muster to convince Levi Elias to provide the identities that would get her and Jack into Kazakhstan with the latitude to move about as freely as they would need to. Unfortunately, setting up those identities required considerable back story and preparatory work, which meant they would have to wait several days before they would be delivered. In the meantime, Jack and Janet had split up, each using identities they had previously obtained to check into different Salzburg hotels. Until the NSA came through, there was nothing to do but wait.

Janet had checked into Hotel Stein, a centrally located four-star hotel, under the name of Judith Kroner. An American from Tampa, Florida, she was in Salzburg as part of her three-week European vacation.

Overlooking the Salzach River, her second-floor room had a beautiful view of the old town's famous Petersfriedhof Dom cathedral and the Festung Hohensalzburg fortress, the latter perched atop a hill less than a kilometer away. It wasn't the largest room in the hotel, nor was it the smallest, but it was nice, with wood floors, khaki-colored walls, and two floor-to-ceiling windows draped in purple. The narrow desk beside the southernmost window provided a lovely spot to clean her weapons.

In keeping with her tourist identity, Janet had outfitted herself in an elegant black evening dress and attended this evening's performance of *Lucio Silla* at the Salzburg Opera House. Now, having thoroughly enjoyed the experience, she was tired and ready to get back to the hotel and crawl into bed for a good night's sleep.

It took her a half hour to make her way back to Hotel Stein's parking garage. Stepping out of her car, she slammed the door and clicked the lock button on the black key fob. She walked to the elevator and pressed the call button. As she waited, a distant explosion echoed through the basement garage and, except for the Audi lights on their one minute timer, all other lights went out.

A scuffing sound to her left brought Janet's head around, sending an electric thrill up her spine. Thirty feet from where she stood, a man carrying a silencer-equipped pistol stepped out from behind a dark van. As he walked calmly toward her, his left hand moved to adjust a pair of night-vision goggles perched atop his forehead. Then, as Janet kicked off her high heels, the Audi headlights went out, swaddling her in pitch-black darkness.

CHAPTER 63

Jack paced his living room. Despite the fact that he had booked an executive suite at the five-star Hotel Lacher, tonight he felt caged. It was as if he should be out there in the night, doing something, something besides waiting.

He'd had a fabulous dinner at the Roter Salon Restaurant. It would have been nice to look across the table at Janet Price. But that hadn't happened. And he couldn't shake the feeling that, after tonight, it might never happen.

Goddamn it! What the hell was wrong with him?

He didn't even know what hotel she was in. It made sense. Operational security. Neither one of them knew the other's location. And they wouldn't know until the NSA delivered the mission package. It was the only way to be safe.

Screw safe!

Why the hell had he agreed to this arrangement? Because it made sense. Because it was logical. Since when had he started being logical? But Janet was logical. And she was hot. So he had allowed her to convince him that this was what they both needed to do. Split up. Lay low. Wait for the package.

It was all wrong. He felt it in his marrow, felt it in his soul. Somewhere out there in this city, in this night, Janet was in trouble. And because he didn't know what he needed to know, he couldn't do a damn thing about it.

Jack focused, trying to attune himself with that extra sense he often experienced. In the grips of his addiction, he felt its directional pull. But tonight, because he consciously wanted it, it wasn't coming.

Another thought occurred to him, a frightening one. Maybe his inner demon wanted Janet to die, wanted him to bathe in the white-hot rage that event would ignite inside him. Maybe that was why he couldn't feel the pull.

Parked in the parking garage, the rented black BMW sedan waited to carry him into the night. Jack slid into his shoulder holster, covering it with his navy blue jacket. He wouldn't keep it waiting any longer.

CHAPTER 64

As the empty parking slots slowly filled with hotel guests returning from their evening outings, Jacob moved his car down to the next level. Using his cell phone to monitor the wireless video feed from the camera he had positioned at the entrance, he examined the make, model, and license plate of each car that entered. When Janet's blue Audi passed the camera, he switched off the phone, grabbed the night vision goggles from the passenger seat, and stepped out of the car.

Moving back into the shadows behind a nearby van, Jacob positioned the goggles on his forehead, ready to be pulled down and switched on in a single, smooth movement. In his gloved right hand, he held the silenced Sig at his side. His left thumb rested on the small device that would trigger the explosion to cut all power to the hotel.

The bright headlight beams swept past and then turned sharply as Janet parked the car in one of the empty slots. Jacob watched as she closed and locked the door, then turned and walked toward the elevator. Wearing a lacy black evening dress and high heels, her hair twisted into a tight bun atop her head, she carried a woman's silver wallet-purse in her left hand. Perfect.

He waited as she reached the elevator and pressed the call button, keeping a mental count in his head. Having taken the ride from here to the lobby and back, he knew the minimum time the elevator required to descend to this level. He also knew how long it would take for the Audi headlight timer to expire.

Jacob pressed the button on the remote detonator. Rewarded by the sound of the distant explosion and accompanying power outage, he stepped out from behind the van and reached up to grasp the night vision goggles. Thirty feet away, Janet Price spun toward him, kicking off her shoes as she turned. Then the Audi's headlights went out.

Pulling the goggles into place, Jacob switched them on. There she was, white hot in the goggles' artificial green glow. As he started to raise the Sig, a sudden flash of bright light wiped away his enhanced vision, dazzling and blinding him as a loud horn blared. Not exactly a flash-bang grenade, but effective. The woman had waited just long enough for him to activate the goggles before pressing the car alarm button on her key fob. Tearing the goggles from his head, Jacob raised his weapon, expecting to see her dodging away through the cars.

Instead she was on top of him. Something sharp glittered in her hand as he brought the Sig around. Pain exploded in his right hand as the object speared through it, sending the gun clattering across the concrete floor. Jerking his hand off the six-inch hair needle, Jacob attempted a left hook that the woman spun to avoid.

Seeing the needle glitter in her spinning fist, Jacob threw back his head, taking a cut high up on his left cheek, a cut that barely missed his eye. Her leg sweep landed him on the flat of his back, sending tiny white lights flashing across his vision. He rolled to his feet just in time to see her dive beneath a Mercedes, her fingers closing around the butt of his Sig.

Jacob didn't pause to think. He just ran. Turning the corner on the parking ramp, he heard the spat of the Sig and felt tiny bits of concrete spray his neck. Away from the headlights, in the dark his hip grazed the rear of a parked car, forcing him to feel his way along as he continued up the ramp.

Three more shots sounded behind him and from the muzzle flashes he could see that she was pursuing. Unable to see him in the dark, she was firing in a spread pattern, hoping to land a lucky shot. Feeling his way around another corner, Jacob saw street lights and put all his effort into getting to that exit before Janet Price found her own way to that last corner.

Outside, he turned right, and merged into the crowd of people that had exited the hotel's dark lobby and gathered on the sidewalk. Plunging through them, he rounded the corner onto Platzl, slowing to a walk as he moved through a narrow alley and onto the Imbertstiege, the two hundred and fifty steep steps that led to the top of the hill overlooking the Salzach River.

Leaving the steps, as he moved into the dense foliage, Jacob heard sirens converge on the hotel he had left behind. He leaned back against a tree, a brief pause to let his breathing and heart rate return to normal. The puncture wound in his right hand was painful and blood dripped from the shallow cut in his left cheek, but neither injury was serious. More than anything, Jacob was mad at himself.

Meticulous preparation and attention to the smallest of details were two of his defining characteristics. But tonight, he'd severely underestimated Janet Price, a mistake that had very nearly killed him.

Shit! She'd almost killed him with his own gun.

Instead of the rusty, ex-CIA agent Jacob had expected, he'd encountered a highly skilled and aggressive killer. She wasn't just Jack Gregory's accomplice. An asset with the special skills that Janet Price had displayed had to be working for some government. But which government? She'd quit the CIA with a cover story, so it wasn't the United States.

Janet had serious sponsorship and that changed the equation. As Jacob headed away from the sirens and left the flashing lights behind him, he made a decision. It was time to step away and do the preparatory work he should have already done.

Next time he'd know what government she now worked for. Next time he wouldn't underestimate Janet Alexandra Price.

CHAPTER 65

Jack turned southeast onto Schwarzstrasse toward the flashing lights and sirens two blocks away. He rolled down the window to get a better feel for how many police and emergency vehicles were involved. At this point it sounded like only a couple of Polizei patrol cars and a fire truck, but it made him nervous. As he got closer, he saw that the Polizei were diverting traffic across the river over the Staatsbrücke, away from a crowd, many in their pajamas, that had gathered in front of the darkened Hotel Stein.

Stopping by the Austrian policeman, Jack hailed him in German. "Officer, what is the problem? I need to get to my hotel."

"You can't stop here. Move along."

Jack nodded and complied. Once across the bridge, he found the first parking place, climbed out of the car, and walked back across the bridge toward the crowd gathered outside the hotel, a crowd that was getting larger as police and firefighters evacuated guests from within. As Jack stepped off the bridge, the sound of additional approaching sirens indicated that a call for reinforcements had been issued and, as they began to arrive, he saw that they were all police cars.

He shouldered his way into the guests that were now being herded farther away from Hotel Stein. Turning to a fully clothed bald man, Jack let concern creep into his voice.

"What happened?"

The man gestured back toward the hotel. "I was in the lobby. We heard a loud explosion and then everything went dark. Someone said they thought they had heard muffled gunshots in the parking garage. Now the police are evacuating everyone."

From the corner of his eye, Jack saw a woman pushing her way through the crowd toward him. When she stepped closer, he breathed an audible sigh of relief. It was Janet. Shoeless, she was wearing a torn black evening gown. Her disheveled hair hung limply over her shoulders, several strands sticking to her sweaty, bare throat.

Before he could ask the obvious questions, she slid her arm through his and pulled him away from the hotel at a steady walk.

"I hope you brought a car."

"Parked just on the other side of the bridge."

"Good. I can't get to my room and I don't really want to answer a bunch of police questions, once they get around to interviewing witnesses."

"You've got blood on your arm."

"Don't worry, it's not mine."

Together they, along with a number of other guests who had decided it would be safer to watch from the far side of the river, made their way across the Staatsbrücke. Once inside the car, Jack headed southeast, paralleling the river on Rudolfskai, not going anywhere in particular, just giving himself some time and space to think.

Janet turned to look at him.

"Have you been following me?"

"No. I couldn't sleep, saw the commotion from my hotel, and decided to check it out."

A wry grin spread across Janet's grimy face. "Ah Jacky Boy, you were worried about me."

"Never crossed my mind."

She laughed and reached over to pat his cheek. "That's sweet, but I can take care of myself."

"I take it you've worn out our warm Salzburg welcome."

She leaned back in her seat and looked at the passing city lights. "Looks like."

As Jack circled the outskirts of Salzburg and then got on the A1 autobahn headed northeast, Janet described the evening's events. She hadn't gotten a clear view of her attacker's face, but he'd been a professional, not one of Roskov's gangsters. To have tracked her down, he had to have access to some serious intelligence assets. That probably meant the CIA was now taking direct action to purge Jack and anyone who might be helping him. It meant they knew Janet's face.

Jack thought the Czech Republic offered the best opportunity to lay low while they waited on the NSA to deliver, and Janet didn't argue. In the meantime, having abandoned another set of false identities and belongings, they needed replacements from a man Jack knew of in Linz. But this guy was nobody's friend.

But first they both needed new clothes and some basic supplies, including some packaging materials. Janet's evening gown had a fair amount of her attacker's blood on it. Tomorrow, after they had wrapped it appropriately, they'd let DHL prove just how fast overnight delivery to Fort Meade, Maryland, really was. If Janet's NSA connections came through, they would know who had ambushed her by the time they reached Kazakhstan.

CHAPTER 66

Twenty-eight-year-old Daniel Jones was his father's son . . . and damn proud of it. His dad had been a great man. More than that, he had been a great American. Throughout history there were men who tugged the strands of fate, reshaping destiny with their actions. George Washington, Thomas Jefferson, Abraham Lincoln, Teddy Roosevelt. These were all great men, but they had been leaders, not shapers. The shapers were those who had been willing to get their hands dirty in defense of great causes: Andrew Jackson, Joshua Chamberlain, George Patton.

These were men's men, ordering soldiers to hold their fire until they saw the whites of their enemies' eyes, ordering men to fix bayonets and charge when they were low on ammunition, driving an army into the oppressor's heartland. These were men who shaped history.

Captain David Jones, killed in action in Somalia facing overwhelming odds, had been such a man. Had he survived America's misguided attempts at nation building, he would have proved it. And even though Dan had grown up stunted and bespectacled, his five-foot-three-inch frame housed a brain that befitted his father's great desire to restore America's lost vision. Tonight, Dan would carry out a task that would have made his father proud.

As opposed to common opinion, America's best days were not behind her, but ahead. And although that path was a hard one, it was necessary that this great country pass through a terrible trial by fire. Nolan Trent had told him only vague details of the grand scheme in which Dan would play a small but crucial part. Dan didn't know how he had come to the deputy CIA director's attention and he didn't care. Nolan had chosen wisely and Dan was now going to prove just how wise that choice had been.

His master of computer science degree from Carnegie Mellon and his top-secret security clearance had landed him this job coding the targeting software used by the land-based portion of the National Missile Defense system. Today, his team would finish installing and testing the latest software upgrades to the missile detection and tracking systems at Fort Greely, Alaska.

What the other members of his software development team didn't know was that Dan had inserted a special subroutine in the final code drop and that routine had been compiled into the executable software they were delivering. Undetectable, the routine would lie dormant until very specific conditions caused its activation.

Even Dan didn't completely understand the code module he had inserted. He just knew that it had come from Nolan Trent and he knew from his brief study of the subroutine that it prevented successful tracking and targeting of a missile that followed a very specific arc. For every other missile path except this special one, all of the Ground-Based Midcourse Defense systems would function normally.

This special trajectory made no sense for an intercontinental ballistic missile. ICBMs were programmed to travel the most efficient great-circle arcs from their launch points to their targets. For missiles launched from Asia targeting the United States, those arcs took them close to the North Pole and over Canada. But this path originated in Kazakhstan and passed over Japan in an initial arc that looked like a satellite launch trajectory, after which the fourth stage would perform an extreme maneuver to put it on course for the northeast coast of the United States.

It certainly was not one of the scenarios anyone would model for an antiballistic missile test. And, as far as Dan knew, there were no intercontinental ballistic missile sites near the origin point, only the Baikonur Cosmodrome that launched satellites and spacecraft.

Dan wrapped up his testing, and then made his way from station to station, reviewing and validating the test results of each member of his software integration team. By this time tomorrow night, they would conclude the final round of testing. Then they would be off to Vandenberg Air Force Base in California to repeat the process.

Feeling a warm glow spread through his torso, Dan smiled. Nolan Trent would be very pleased with the results of his work. And somewhere out there, his dad would be proud of his only son.

CHAPTER 67

Evening found Jacob Knox strapped into a webbed jump-seat in the ass end of a modernized Soviet-era Antonov An-12 military transport aircraft. Modernized was a relative term, meaning most of the gauges worked. But the old airplane hadn't crashed yet, so the odds were good that it would get Jacob to Shymkent's 602nd Airbase in one piece.

Shymkent, known in Russia as Chimkent, huddled near Kazakhstan's southern border, just north of where Uzbekistan, Tajikistan, and Kyrgyzstan came together. Three hundred and fifty kilometers southeast of the Baikonur Cosmodrome, it was as conveniently close to Roskov's warehouse complex in Kyzylorda as any landing spot in Kazakhstan, except Baikonur itself. But Baikonur was way too visible an entry point, so he'd do this the roundabout way.

Jacob stepped off the plane onto the dark runway beneath a star-filled sky he hadn't seen in three years. The flatness of the Kazakh landscape produced the illusion that he stood inside a giant snow globe, the night sky forming the upper dome, countless tiny white flakes stuck to its dark outer surface. The vast dark space within formed a mirror onto Jacob's soul.

The larger of the two men that awaited him stepped forward with an extended hand, the greeting rolling off his lips in slightly accented Russian.

"Mr. Petrov?"

As he shook the larger man's hand, Jacob's answering Russian carried the distinctive tempo and inflection of Moscow. "Yes."

"I'm Goran Dragi. Do you have any bags?"

"Just this one," Jacob said, nodding to the wheeled carry-on in his left hand.

Dragi tossed it in the trunk as Jacob Knox slipped into the back seat and slammed the door, then took the passenger side front seat. Without another word from anyone, the black sedan accelerated, carrying Jacob through the night toward Kyzylorda and the man who awaited him there.

While it didn't have the tightly engineered feel of a European sports car, the Russian sedan had a powerful engine and the driver pushed it to its limit. What would have been a three-hour drive at normal speeds lasted ninety-three minutes. Shades of peach lightened the eastern sky as they stopped outside the fenced warehouse complex, ten kilometers southwest of Kyzylorda. One of two guards stepped forward, shining a flashlight onto the faces of the driver and the two occupants.

Satisfied, the guard stepped back and pressed a button on the control box that sent the gate rumbling open along its track. The sedan rolled forward, passed through the double row of warehouses, stopping at the second one on the right, as a door large enough to accept big rigs rumbled up to allow them entrance. The harsh white light spilling from the warehouse into the vehicle momentarily dazzled Jacob as his pupils fought to adjust to the illumination.

The car pulled inside, coming to a stop beside a black tractor-trailer backed up against a loading dock. As Jacob climbed out of the car to meet the familiar figure who walked toward him, the warehouse door rumbled closed. Extending his hand, Jacob met the other's strong grip.

"Jacob. Good to see you again, old friend."

"Hello, Vlad."

Roskov looked down at Jacob's bandaged hand, then shifted his gaze to the cut on Jacob's left cheek.

"Had some recent trouble, I see."

"Not as much as the other fellow." The lie rolled off his lips as naturally as the truth.

Roskov laughed.

"Just like Chechnya. Ah, those were good days, no? Only war lets you truly know a comrade from an enemy."

Jacob nodded. "Some things never change."

"I'm glad Trent chose to send you. Hungry?"

"You could say that."

"Good. I'll have some breakfast brought up to my office."

Vladimir Roskov nodded at Dragi and the man turned on his heel and disappeared around the semi-truck, followed by the driver. Jacob followed the Russian mobster across the wide concrete floor, between its jumble of shipping palettes loaded with crates and boxes, up a set of steel steps onto a raised steel-grate platform, and then through a door into a room with a view out onto an even larger section of the warehouse.

Stepping up to the windows that formed most of the office's far wall, Jacob stared out at the view that was so different from the loading bay he'd just left that he felt a bit of disorientation. White-garbed workers in masks and gloves worked at automated workstations, directing the robotic equipment operating on the apparatus at the room's center. In addition to the robotic arms that were precisely installing or adjusting components on the Volkswagen-sized nuclear power package, white-clad scientists moved around the machines, observing and verifying the quality of each action.

"Koenig's manufacturing operation is impressive, don't you think?"

"The man doesn't trust anything to outside suppliers. Koenig's businesses build every component used in one of his designs."

"This one won't live up to the world's expectations."

Jacob nodded. Maybe not, but it was going to live up to Koenig's expectations. And that was all that mattered.

The knock on the door turned them in that direction, followed by a voice that Jacob recognized as Dragi's.

"I've got breakfast."

"Bring it in," Roskov said, motioning the man to set it on the small conference table across the room from his desk.

After setting the food tray and insulated coffee pot on the table, Dragi turned a questioning gaze on his boss.

"Anything else?"

"Make sure I'm not disturbed."

Dragi nodded and walked out, closing the door behind him. Roskov motioned for Jacob to take a seat.

"Dig in."

As Jacob seated himself and fashioned a cold cut and cheese sandwich, Roskov filled the mugs with Turkish coffee.

The strong, thick brew had long been a favorite of Roskov's and though it wasn't something Jacob sought out, it was better than nothing. It didn't take him long to polish off the sandwich and lean back in his chair, finally ready for the discussion that was coming.

When he looked up, he saw the grin on Roskov's angular face. "I see you still eat like we're on the battlefield."

"Aren't we?"

"The wet work in Paris was your doing?"

Jacob paused to study the bigger man's face, noting the hint of displeasure in those blue eyes. He took a slow sip of coffee, felt the thickness of it coat his tongue, letting the aroma fill his nostrils, a heady compliment to the sensation storm on his taste buds.

When he didn't respond, Roskov leaned forward. "Did you know that Rachel Koenig had already called off her attack dog?"

"I knew it."

"What the hell were you thinking?"

Once again Jacob took the time for another sip, letting the silence hang in the air between them.

"A man like Jack Gregory isn't the kind of dog that lets go easily once his blood is up. Maybe he would have in this case, but I think not. So I controlled the situation."

"By launching him right here?"

"This way, I don't have to hunt The Ripper. I made sure he'll come to me. And when he gets here, I'll have a very nice welcome waiting for him."

"I want him alive."

"Not happening."

Jacob saw the snarl start to curl Roskov's upper lip and reached across the table to place his left hand on the mobster's forearm.

"But I'll give you his body and, with some CIA video wizardry, you'll have your YouTube special." He smiled. "Hell, after Paris, Director Rheiner will be glad to foot the bill."

Watching Roskov's face as he visualized what had just been described, Jacob saw a grin replace the scowl.

"That works for me."

CHAPTER 68

The NSA had provided Jack and Janet with their new identities and Jack found them quite satisfactory. Drs. Elena and Sergei Kozlov were a Russian geological survey team that would be traveling from Prague to Kazakhstan to investigate possible new petroleum reserves in the southern province of Kyzylorda. Taking on the role of geologists had required some serious cram sessions, and even though they didn't have to become real experts in the field, they at least needed to have mastered the Cliff's Notes version.

Tomorrow, without a gun or knife on their persons, Elena and Sergei would board a commercial flight for the five-thousand-kilometer trip from Václav Havel Airport to Astana. There, in Kazakhstan's largest city, they would meet Janet's NSA contact and pick up their new mission kits. If all went well, they wouldn't be ambushed upon arrival. That would be a nice change of pace.

"Are you going to study all night?"

Seated at the small hotel room desk, Jack glanced up from his laptop at Janet Price, wrapped in a thick, white terry-cloth bathrobe, her blond hair such a striking change that, for a moment, he thought he was looking at another woman. Then he saw the hint of a smile lift the corners of her lips and realized that her beautiful eyes were laughing at him.

"Like what you see?"

Jack had to admit that he did.

"I married you, didn't I?"

"Gramma said it was my cooking."

"Trust me. That wasn't it."

"You know we're wheels up at six thirty in the morning, right?"

Jack turned back to his work. "Almost done here. I'll switch off the desk lamp so you can get some sleep."

Her throaty laugh caused him to glance up again.

"Did I say anything about sleeping?"

Standing there, wrapped in the bathrobe, fluffing her hair with the white towel, she looked damn good. Funny how often he'd found himself thinking similar thoughts these last few days.

As Janet let the bathrobe fall away and leaned back against the far wall, Jack felt himself pulled to her as if levitated by a spell, leaving a trail of discarded clothing in his wake.

Janet's slender fingers slid along the back of Jack's neck, her delicate touch sending shivers of pleasure down his spine. His own hand responded, fingertips barely touching the hollow of her back, lingering there, the nerves so alert that it seemed each contact produced tiny sparks from her skin to his. He felt her ear touch his, the scent of her bare throat filling his nostrils.

Her body moved against his in perfect rhythm, the feel of her full breasts against his chest robbing him of whatever self-control he still retained. Janet's skin shone with sweat in the dim light and her breath came in small pants of exertion, barely audible above Jack's thundering heart. Her bare legs encircled him and her body swayed. As Jack's body writhed within her entangling limbs, Janet's back arched until only his right arm kept her from falling.

With the room misting red all around, Jack felt an amped-up dose of adrenaline course through his veins, fueling the white-hot fire that consumed him.

CHAPTER 69

Standing on the high balcony, I feel the embroidered toga flutter against my bare legs in the night breeze, as bright-orange flames lick the Roman night. It is beautiful and its heat infects me, coursing through my veins with such white-hot intensity that I expect my skin to ignite. As I lean farther over the high stone balcony, two pairs of small, cool hands tug gently at my left arm.

"What mean you, my lord? Think you to walk forth? May we not put your night's fire to better use?"

As I allow the two naked maidens to draw me inside, to gently remove my clothing, and entangle me in supple limbs, that warm orange glow accompanies me into bed.

Jack's eyes opened, but he did not move. He lay naked atop the bed, a lean bare leg and arm draped across him as he passed from dream into wakefulness. Except for the moonlight streaming through the Prague night into his hotel room, darkness prevailed. Janet lay nestled against his right side, her head resting atop his chest, her steady breathing gently tickling his throat.

For the thousandth time Jack wondered if he was going crazy. Maybe he was already there. It seemed that he stood astride a multi-world boundary, one foot planted in the present as the other stepped through times long gone, both feeling equally real. Something was dreadfully wrong with him, that much was certain. He had never feared death, but now he lay here next to this beautiful woman, deathly afraid. A quote whispered at the edge of his mind. A quote Patton had dearly loved. William Shakespeare.

Cowards die many times before their deaths;
The valiant never taste of death but once.

Jack had already tasted death . . . and it had changed him. But it wasn't death he feared; it was loss of self-control. And despite a year of intense effort, one thing had become abundantly clear over these last few weeks. He might never gain control of his inner demon. The harder he tried to suppress it, the greater the ferocity it unleashed upon him when it finally broke free of his restraining bonds.

Either he was crazy or his deathbed demon really had come along for the ride. So he had a decision to make. He could choose which reality to accept. If he really was crazy, then he was good and truly screwed and there wasn't a damned thing he could do to change it. If, on the other hand, he had a demon rider giving him these dream memories and amping up his natural emotions and intuition, then that was a different situation. Maybe he couldn't control it. That didn't mean he couldn't use it. He still got to choose what he did with all that extra juice flowing through his system.

The bright memory of Janet's laughing eyes staring at him as she lay by his side after their love-making filled his head. That look had pulled a real laugh from his lips.

"What?" he had asked.

"I like that laugh. It becomes you."

"It's been a long time since I really felt like laughing."

She'd propped her naked body up on her left elbow, her brown eyes suddenly shining with intensity.

"After my mother's death, I was lost in the dark. One thing my grandfather said helped me find my way out of that dark place. '*This world will try to beat you down. Laughter is ammunition. Resupply often.*' "

As those words replayed in his memory, Jack understood. He'd been fighting his own amped-up nature for the past year, battling the fear that something else now controlled him. But by damming that river of emotion, he'd created the inevitable flood that periodically swept him away. No wonder he was so screwed up. He should have tried to channel its flow.

Somehow Janet Price had revealed a fragment of the truth he'd been searching for. It wasn't the whole solution, but at least it felt like a key that could unlock a couple of doors along that path.

Jack absorbed the feel of the lean killer snuggled up against him. As he held her body close, for the first time in recent memory, he drifted into a calm and dreamless sleep.

~ ~ ~

Through all the centuries of its association with the most exciting examples humanity had to offer, through all the adrenaline fueled lust, love, hatred, and fear its hosts experienced, Anchanchu had never been surprised. Until now. It was impossible, but it had happened.

Despite Anchanchu's manipulation of this host's limbic system, something that should have crushed the man's ability to resist his impulses, Jack Gregory continued to defy the mind worm's will. And every time he did, the futures that rolled out before him shifted, not necessarily in a good way either.

It was the thing that scared and excited the mind worm the most. It couldn't see, with any degree of certainty, what was coming. Anchanchu just knew that this host was somehow bound to future-history more intricately than any of its previous hosts, bound in a way that would either support or pull down the temple of humanity.

Anchanchu sensed that, if it failed to establish firm control over Jack Gregory, there was no way of determining which of those incompatible destinies would occur. It was an all-or-nothing roll of the dice the mind worm was unwilling to risk.

CHAPTER 70

The update Nolan Trent had just gotten from Daniel Jones put him in a good mood, one he hoped would last the whole morning. Rolf Koenig's code module had been successfully installed at both Greely and Vandenberg. The software had passed all performance tests and had been accepted by the government with compliments to the defense contractor for the numerous improvements made since the prior release.

One by one, the items on his and Rolf's lists were being checked off.

The phone on his desk rang and Nolan lifted it from its cradle on the second ring. The caller ID said Knox.

"Yes, Jacob?"

"We've got a new problem."

Jacob's tone siphoned the warm glow from Nolan's body.

"Explain."

"A few days ago, I specifically requested all available data on Janet Price."

"And we gave it to you."

"Bullshit! I requested critical information and I was given crap."

"Think about who you're talking to and dial it down a notch."

"That faulty information damn near got me killed. Don't tell me to dial it down."

Nolan clenched his teeth, biting off the response that tried to crawl from his throat, over his tongue, and out of his mouth.

"Just tell me what happened."

Nolan heard Jacob pause to take a deep breath as the man tried to reassert his normal self-control before continuing.

"I was told Janet Price was a promising young field agent who quit the CIA after two years of service to become a religious missionary in foreign lands. So I have one question. How could she kick the shit out of me in an Austrian parking garage?"

Nolan felt the fingers of his left hand dig into his forehead as he tried to wrap his mind around what he'd just heard. Somehow his agency's top killer had almost had his ass handed to him by a former employee who wasn't named Jack Gregory. When he spoke again, the words rumbled from his throat.

"I don't know, but I'm damn sure going to find out."

"And Nolan . . . "

"Yes?"

"Faster would be better."

Knox ended the call and Nolan had to clench his arms to prevent himself from hurling the phone at the far wall.

"No shit!"

Nolan shunted aside his irritation and dialed his admin assistant. She picked up on the first ring.

"Yes, sir?"

"Get the NSA's Dr. Jennings on the line for me."

"Right away."

Nolan glanced up at the headline on CNN.com.

Robot Moon Miners? Launch Scheduled Next Week.

He and Rolf Koenig were so close to realizing their compatible but very different dreams. To have two very dangerous loose ends flapping in the wind, seeking to entangle a project that had been years in the planning, was frustrating. To have both of those problems fall under his area of responsibility was doubly so.

Lindsey's smooth voice brought Nolan's attention back to the speakerphone.

"I have Dr. Jennings on the line."

"Okay. Patch her in."

He heard the phone switch to the other line.

"Dr. Jennings, this is Deputy Director Trent at CIA."

"How may I help you, Mr. Trent?"

Dr. Jennings's curt tone didn't improve his mood.

"I want all information the NSA can gather on a former CIA agent named Janet Alexandra Price forwarded directly to my office. This request carries the highest priority."

The pause that followed lasted three full seconds.

"I've only been instructed to forward information related to Rolf Koenig and Vladimir Roskov to your office."

"This request falls within that purview."

"I'll have to clear it with Admiral Riles."

"Then you do that, Dr. Jennings. I need the report this afternoon. If Admiral Riles needs clarification, he has my number. I'm sure there'll be no need to involve President Harris again. Am I clear?"

"Crystal." The word sounded like she'd just spit into the phone.

Nolan ended the call. Dr. Jennings was pissed and soon Admiral Riles would share that same feeling. Fine. He could join the club.

CHAPTER 71

The five-door silver Lada Niva wasn't the most comfortable or the prettiest SUV Janet had ever ridden in, but it did have four-wheel drive, a spare, and tools for repairing a flat tire. All of those were important on Kazakhstan's notoriously bad roads.

The flight into Astana and their subsequent meeting with an oil field operations manager from KG group had been uneventful. The oil man had been glad to send the two Russian geologists on their way with the seismic equipment his parent company had instructed him to deliver. He had been especially happy to hear that they didn't want any facility tours or to be shepherded around the countryside by one of his people. They were off to do their geological investigation of potential new fields and out of his hair.

They had one more stop to make on the outskirts of Kazakhstan's largest city, where their contact would deliver the rest of their mission kit before they got to enjoy the fifteen-hour drive to Kyzylorda. While it would have been much more convenient to fly into Shymkent, this was the spot where their contact was.

Janet focused on her tablet, studying the files Levi Elias had forwarded.

"So did the NSA identify your night stalker?"

Jack's voice brought her head up.

"Name's Jacob Knox."

"Knox?"

"You know him."

"I know him."

Janet looked over at Jack, his face giving no indication of what he was feeling. That, and his failure to elaborate, couldn't be good. Knox had been one of Jack's counterparts at the CIA, an asset used for high-profile target eliminations. She hadn't read more than half of the information Levi had provided, but Janet had already learned enough about Knox to know one thing: In that Salzburg parking garage, she had been very lucky. Lucky that Knox hadn't stepped out from behind that van shooting instead of trying to get fancy with the night vision goggles, lucky that he had underestimated her.

But Knox had been fortunate that it had taken her a half-second too long to reach his gun beneath that black Mercedes, a delay that had enabled him to duck around the corner before she could get a shot off. Next time they would both be ready for each other. She figured Jack was thinking much the same thing.

"We're here."

Jack's words brought her vision out of her mind's eye and back to the present.

The house was little more than a shack; its attached garage appeared ready to fall down. The woman that opened the garage door to meet them was exotic. Tall and slender, her raven hair hung to her waist. Jack pulled the SUV inside and the garage door rumbled closed as he turned off the engine.

When they stepped out into the dimly lit garage, the woman held out her hand and Jack took it.

"I am Zhaniya."

Jack inclined his head. "Pure soul."

Zhaniya smiled. "Ahhh. A Russian who understands Kazakh. Such a rare thing."

Janet stepped forward, extending her right hand.

"Elena Kozlov."

Zhaniya shook her hand and then returned her attention to Jack.

"Sergei Kozlov," he said, taking her extended hand in his.

Janet glanced at Jack, half expecting to see that red fire in his eyes. But it wasn't there, something she was surprisingly thankful for.

"Please. Follow me."

Zhaniya turned and led them through a door that appeared about ready to tear free from its hinges. The apartment behind that door didn't look much better: a threadbare couch, a stained wood coffee table, and a kitchenette with appliances that appeared to have been manufactured in the mid-twentieth century.

Zhaniya bent down and tugged on the oval rug beneath the coffee table, pulling the entire thing aside to reveal a trapdoor beneath. She lifted the hatch and stepped aside.

"Sergei. You have the honor."

Without hesitation, Jack stepped onto the metal ladder that led into the darkness below. Before Janet could follow, Zhaniya stepped onto the ladder behind him, her shining black eyes locking briefly with Janet's as she climbed down.

Janet knew her annoyance was irrational, but it was there nonetheless. She briefly considered the possibility that her physical attraction to the assassin might be distorting her perceptions, but discarded the notion.

Shoving those thoughts aside, Janet stepped onto the top rung of the metal ladder and followed the other two down. As she descended, the cellar light came on, a bare incandescent bulb screwed into a fixture in the center of the concrete ceiling. Four hundred square feet of concrete floor, the walls also of unpainted reinforced concrete, the room was no surprise. What filled the shelves and racks that lined the walls was.

Janet felt her pulse quicken as she stepped off the ladder and moved around the room, examining its contents with growing delight. The collection of weapons, ammunition, and explosives was impressive. But the high-tech gear pulled her forward.

Jack grinned at her. "Makes you wish we were pulling a trailer behind the SUV doesn't it?"

"That thought occurred to me," Janet said, running her hand over the latches on an olive-drab, hard-sided case that was a little bigger than a suitcase.

She turned her attention to Zhaniya.

"What's in here?"

"Take a look. My orders are to give you whatever you want."

Janet released the metal latches and raised the lid. Jack's low whistle echoed her thoughts.

"A scanning laser?"

Janet turned to Zhaniya. "Permanently blinding?"

Zhaniya nodded. "Out to three kilometers in green and infrared wavelengths. Tripod mounted and capable of being remotely operated."

"Power supply?"

"A brand new capacitor technology the Russians stole from Los Alamos National Laboratory."

"And you stole it from them?"

"Not me. I'm just the broker."

Janet closed the lid. "We'll take it."

"I thought you might."

Forty minutes later, they had finished their shopping. Several trips to the SUV with their new equipment and supplies and the associated packing of those items took up the rest of the hour.

"Is that it?" Zhaniya asked. "Last chance."

Janet closed the Lada Niva's back door. "That'll do."

"Can I offer you something to eat or drink before you go? Maybe something else?"

Jack opened the driver's side door and shook his head. "Thank you, but we have a long drive ahead."

A sly smile graced Zhaniya's lips as she watched Jack climb into the driver's seat.

"Good luck. Maybe I'll see you again."

As Janet settled into the passenger seat and the garage door rumbled open, she had the distinct impression that Zhaniya's last words hadn't applied to her.

CHAPTER 72

When Levi Elias stepped into Admiral Riles's office, he wasn't happy, but this wasn't his call. It was Riles's ass that was hanging out on this one.

"Yes, Levi?"

"Sir, we've got a problem. Nolan Trent at CIA has instructed Dr. Jennings to run a full NSA query on Janet Price. We are instructed to provide all available information directly to his office."

"Instructed or requested?"

"He's not asking. He's demanding information under the temporary presidential authorization related to Rolf Koenig and Vladimir Roskov. He said you're welcome to discuss it with Director Rheiner if you want the DCI to raise this issue with the president."

Admiral Riles leaned back in his chair, his hands clasped in front of him. His face betrayed no emotion. Neither did he speak.

The uncomfortable silence that followed lasted so long that Levi seated himself to wait for his boss's response. When the Admiral leaned forward again, Levi mirrored his movement.

"Here's what I want you to do, Levi. Tell Dr. Jennings to deliver only the information that matches Janet's original cover story."

"The CIA already has that."

"Exactly."

Although the answer was what Levi had been hoping to hear, he wouldn't be doing his job if he didn't raise the counterargument.

"If it comes out, the president might interpret this as you disobeying a direct order."

"He might. He might not like the fact that I put together my off-the-grid special operations team that Janet Price is a member of. But I believe I have that authority and I'm damn sure not going to disclose anything that puts any of my agents' lives in jeopardy."

Levi rose to his feet. "Yes, sir. I'll inform Denise right now."

Admiral Riles nodded and returned his focus to the daily intelligence update he'd been studying when Levi entered. As Levi turned and walked out of the Admiral's office, he had to admire the man's inability to worry about anything. Riles thought things through carefully, made his decision, and that was the end of it.

A useful trait. Unfortunately it was one Levi would never master.

~ ~ ~

"What the hell is this crap?"

Nolan Trent threw the folder on his desk with such force that it slid off the far edge, sending its contents fluttering across the floor. He didn't care.

Christie Parson raised an eyebrow, but made no attempt to pick up the results of her boss's tantrum.

"It's the information the NSA provided on Janet Price."

"Bullshit. There's not one scrap of new information in that file."

When Christie merely shrugged, he felt his blood pulse in his temples, threatening to make her the object of his frustration. But she wasn't the one he was pissed at and he didn't do counterproductive things like yelling at one of his best people just to blow off steam. Instead he waved her out and punched a button on his speakerphone.

"Lindsey. Get Admiral Riles on the phone for me."

"Yes, sir. One moment."

Less than a minute later he heard her voice again.

"Connecting you now."

Hearing the line switch, Nolan paused to take a deep breath before speaking.

"Admiral Riles, this is CIA Deputy Director Nolan Trent."

"I gathered that. What can I do for you, Mr. Trent?"

The man's calm voice further irritated Nolan.

"As you are no doubt aware, yesterday I requested vital information from your agency. I just received the report and it doesn't have a single piece of information I hadn't already gathered from CIA sources."

"And?"

"And I think the NSA is intentionally stonewalling us in violation of the president's directive."

The pause at the other end of the line lasted several seconds before the NSA director's insufferably steady voice replaced it.

"Mr. Trent. I assure you that I have no intention of stonewalling the CIA's investigation into Janet Price. But let me suggest another possibility, even though it seems farfetched."

"And what is that?"

"Perhaps, this time, the CIA actually managed to gather accurate information without the NSA's help."

The click that indicated that Admiral Riles had just hung up on him left Nolan staring at the speakerphone. A disquieting thought occurred to Nolan Trent. Maybe the NSA director was right.

CHAPTER 73

"Herr Koenig. You're needed in the payload mating facility."

Rolf looked up from his laptop to see the long, lanky form of Gerhardt Balkman, his first shift manager, standing in the doorway to his office, concern firmly etched into his gray-bearded face.

Having seen Rolf rise to his feet, Gerhardt turned to lead him to the source of the problem. Rolf moved up beside him as they walked from the office space into one high-bay and then another. At the entrance to the payload final-assembly bay, they both donned clean suits and entered the room. Rolf didn't need conversation and Gerhardt had worked for him long enough to know it. He'd get his explanation of the problem when he got where Gerhardt was taking him.

As it turned out, he never needed the problem explained to him. Approaching the spot where the nuclear power generator was being installed on the XLRMV-1 mining vehicle, the red failure indicators on the test monitors told the whole story. Stepping up to the control panels, Rolf entered a series of commands, watching as the diagnostic data cascaded across multiple screens.

The nuclear generator had suffered a severe short that had arced past the circuitry designed to protect other parts of the device from such an event. Catastrophic failure. While all the circuitry could be replaced, it could not be done in time for the scheduled launch.

"How did this happen?"

Gerhardt shook his head. "That's just it, sir. It shouldn't have been possible. As the robot arms were moving the generator into position for it to be connected to the XLRMV-1, a voltage buildup caused the primary capacitor to explode, creating an arc across the control circuits and into the frame. We were lucky nobody was touching it or they'd be dead right now."

"Lucky? You call this lucky?"

Gerhardt didn't flinch as he met Rolf's gaze. "We'll just have to delay the launch until we can replace the components and get the next launch window."

"We will do no such thing. I want the backup nuclear generator shipped up from Kyzylorda as fast as you can get it here. Get this facility ready to receive and prep the replacement. In the meantime, I want a team working to figure out how the capacitor failure happened so we can ensure we don't suffer a similar failure with the backup. If you need to pull people in from other shifts and work everyone overtime, do it."

Gerhardt's lips tightened into a thin line. "I'll see to it."

"I'm not going to miss my launch window. Understood?"

"Yes, sir."

As Rolf turned to walk back to the cleanroom exit, he heard Gerhardt's deep voice giving the necessary orders, getting everyone moving. It was a problem and problems required fixing. From what Rolf had seen, the costs involved in fixing the primary generator would probably approach a million euros. That didn't concern him.

Having changed out of the clean suit, Rolf returned to his office.

Picking up his cell phone, he speed-dialed a number. It rang four times before being answered.

"This is Dr. Dortman."

"Hello, Doctor. This is Rolf Koenig."

"Your wife is doing just fine."

"We both know how Rachel is doing. I want you to get her ready to travel. One of my people will be picking her up and flying her to the Baikonur Cosmodrome tonight."

The doctor hesitated before responding. "I'm not sure she will be completely coherent by then. I've been keeping her fairly heavily sedated."

"Coherent or not, I want her on my private jet tonight. She can sleep it off on the flight."

"As you wish."

Rolf ended the call and seated himself at his laptop. As he began composing the email instructions that would get his people in Berlin moving, he allowed himself a small smile. Except for Jack Gregory, everything was going exactly according to plan.

CHAPTER 74

Vladimir Roskov lifted his head at the knock on his office door.

"Come in."

The man who entered wasn't one of his people; it was Wolfram Hitzig, Koenig's stocky lead engineer.

"Yes?"

"It's moving day! We just got the call from Baikonur."

Vlad rose to his feet, cracking his knuckles as he did. "Okay, then. Get the package ready for shipment. I'll have my people position the truck at the loading dock."

"I've already given my team the word."

"How long until it's ready?"

"It should take a little over three hours to secure and palletize it for shipment. After that, thirty minutes to load it on the truck and get it strapped down."

"Good."

Vlad watched as the man exited. Fabulous. He was so tired of sitting on his ass while these scientists and engineers tinkered with their bullshit electronics, even if they were destined to go bang. Shit, he felt like a Goddamn nanny, while The Ripper was out there making a fool of him.

Vlad had begun to think that maybe this man was the arrow that was aimed at his heart. It was a stupid superstition. He knew it. But the image of Gregory's stitched-up, bloody corpse atop that Calcutta nun's surgery table bled into his dreams on a nightly basis. The Ripper was out there, coming for him with an otherworldly presence that he couldn't dismiss via rational thought. In Vlad's dreams, he had seen the man in ages long gone, wading through rivers of blood, always the reaper. And he, who had never known fear, knew it now in a way that made him doubt his sanity.

But he couldn't let anyone know he was afraid, least of all Rolf Koenig. So Vladimir Roskov strapped on his big-boy pants, painted a sneer on his battle-scarred face, and strode from his office in total command of his mafia. And, right now, he was in no mood to be screwed with.

Of course all moods have to come to an end. His in-command mood ended with the arrival of Jacob Knox.

"What the hell is going on here?"

Vlad grinned, although he felt like his lips moved into more of a grimace.

"We have Koenig's delivery order. I'm delivering."

"It's too early. The Ripper hasn't hit this kill zone yet."

Vlad found himself enjoying the other man's discomfort. Lord knows, he'd felt enough of his own discomfort lately.

He reached out and patted his old friend on the shoulder. "Can't be helped. Koenig is driving the train and he wants the package now. You'll have to adjust."

Looking into Jacob Knox's coal-black eyes, Vlad saw only death therein. It gave him a nice warm feeling inside. In the years that Jacob had lent the CIA's secret support to the Russian army's suppression of Chechnya, Vlad had seen that look many times. Surely Jacob's black soul was one that even Jack "The Ripper" Gregory couldn't effectively deal with.

Jacob's growling voice pulled him from his thoughts.

"Fine. Send the package, but keep your entire security force here. We have to make The Ripper believe his target is here. This is where I kill him, not Baikonur."

Vlad nodded. "I agree. But I have to provide security for the package. Plus I have to send the security forces that will be required for the day of the launch."

"We have to make The Ripper believe this is his target. Not Baikonur."

"And we will. Trust me."

But, as Vladimir Roskov looked into Jacob Knox's black eyes, he knew his old comrade didn't. Unfortunately for Jacob Knox, Vlad just didn't give a shit.

CHAPTER 75

With the headlights illuminating a small swath of the endless Kazakh highway, Jack Gregory glanced to his right at the sleeping Janet Price, her head propped against the Russian SUV's passenger window. He had been with many beautiful women. But this one was different in so many ways that he couldn't begin to categorize her. She was a spider, winding him tightly into her web, one more trapped insect. It was a fine characterization, but he didn't believe it. Janet Price was a true spirit, a reliable ally, and a deadly enemy. He could sense it just by being in her presence.

Hopefully he wouldn't get her killed. To make that happen, he'd have to stay alive himself. With the government and nongovernment forces arrayed against them, that seemed less and less likely.

The pothole in the asphalt bounced the car with such force that Janet opened her eyes.

"Would you like me to drive?"

Seeing her questioning look, Jack laughed.

"Don't worry. I've got this."

"Really? Because it doesn't feel like you do."

"Oh, I do."

The smile that curved Janet's lips as she closed her eyes and settled back into her seat warmed Jack. If she was right about laughter being ammunition, then she'd just delivered a fresh airdrop. That was good. He had the feeling that this little adventure was about to get bloody, much more than it had been to date.

Jack felt the danger-lust rise up within him. There was no doubt that death awaited them in Kyzylorda.

CHAPTER 76

The big black semi-truck pulled away from the loading dock inside Warehouse Five and turned hard right, away from the closed steel doors that would take it outside. Jacob watched as it descended a ramp into the tunnel that terminated inside a smaller warehouse, five kilometers to the west. From there, it would make its way to Highway M32 that would take it and its precious cargo to Baikonur. What he didn't like was the fact that it was accompanied by a dozen members of Roskov's security force in two panel vans.

The original plan called for a five-member security team to escort the shipment, but Roskov had insisted on sending more, wanting to pre-position an advance team at Baikonur. Utter stupidity that left Jacob seven men shorthanded.

He didn't know where Jack Gregory and Janet Price were. They had pulled a grand disappearing act in Austria and the

CIA hadn't been able to find their trail since. It was one more indicator of high-level intelligence agency sponsorship, something only Janet Price could have brought to the table.

So why the hell wasn't Nolan Trent able to crack her background story and find out who she'd really been working for the last couple of years? And the NSA was confirming that story. Unbelievable.

Jacob didn't care where The Ripper and Janet Price were. He had no intention of trying to find them. The whole point of this operation was to make them come to him, right here in this Kyzylorda kill-zone. He damn sure didn't want to try to fend them off at Baikonur. The Cosmodrome was in the middle of nowhere and, aside from the surrounding barren landscape, it had no defensible infrastructure. While the Cosmodrome did have a small security force, there were so many ways that it could be attacked that a battalion-size force would have had a hard time establishing a secure perimeter.

As the huge ramp closed the hole in the warehouse floor, Jacob turned his attention to the security inspection he had begun before the shipment had interrupted him. He stepped out of the city-block-sized warehouse into a dreary gray morning, one that foreshadowed heavy rain by noon. It was the first cold day of fall and the dampness certainly didn't make it any more comfortable.

Two hours into his review of how well the restructured guard shifts were implementing his security protocols, the wind picked up. Ten minutes later the downpour began. Because he was dissatisfied with the results of his morning inspection, because employees tended to relax after they'd just been through an inspection, and because he was Jacob Knox, he turned up his raincoat's collar and made one more circuit.

These men had already learned that they might receive a visit from their harsh new master at any moment of the night or day.

But now that he'd had to reshuffle his crews, it was time to ratchet up the pressure.

Of all the warehouses inside the fenced complex, only Warehouse Five hadn't been empty. But it was important to maintain the illusion that all six contained items of equal importance. It was even more important to maintain that illusion now that the package had departed. But all Roskov and Koenig could think about was Baikonur and what was getting ready to happen there.

Stopping just outside the guarded entry-point to Warehouse Five, Jacob stopped and turned to look left and right down the narrow concrete street that separated it from the warehouse immediately to the west. Although he could never be satisfied, the trap was a good one. When Jack and Janet penetrated the outer defenses, and Jacob knew that they would penetrate them, they would find themselves pinned down by enfilading fire from snipers on the rooftops and from response teams that would seal them in one of these alleys with nowhere to take cover. The doors into the surrounding warehouses would be secured by steel bars dropped down behind them. Game over.

For The Ripper, this would be the train platform for his one-way ticket to hell. And on this train, Jacob Knox would be the conductor.

CHAPTER 77

It was 6:58 a.m. here at Fort Meade, almost five p.m. in Astana. Halfway around the world from the black-glass NSA headquarters, Janet would have been in Kazakhstan's exotic capital city for a full day now.

Seated at the head of the small conference table in his executive conference room, Admiral Riles studied his top analyst's hawkish features as he waited for this morning's update to begin. Due to the sensitivity of the subject matter, Jonny Riles was the only audience Levi Elias would have.

Always precise, Levi began speaking as the LED time display on the centermost of the digital wall clocks changed to 7:00 a.m., the others showing local time in other cities around the world.

"Good morning, Admiral."

Riles nodded his acknowledgement.

Levi aimed his laser pointer at the map that filled the monitor on the wall opposite Admiral Riles, sending the red dot dancing in a circle around Astana.

"We have received confirmation that Janet Price and Jack Gregory landed yesterday in Astana without incident. In keeping with their cover, they subsequently met with an oil field manager from the KG Group before linking up with Zhaniya Mustafin on Astana's south side. They're now on the road, headed toward Kyzylorda."

"You've spoken with Zhaniya?"

"Two hours ago."

"So what equipment did they take?"

"Some high-end communications gear and enough arms, ammunition, and explosives to start a small war. They also took a high-power scanning laser that is banned under international treaty."

"How high power?"

"It damages optics and produces permanent blindness at ranges out to three kilometers. Beyond that, it dazzles out to five kilometers, depending on weather conditions, producing temporary blindness and disorientation."

Levi clicked the button and a price spreadsheet replaced the map on the display.

"This might raise some eyebrows."

"I want all those items listed as critical electronic components for the Utah Data Center. It's the black budget so be creative."

"Okay."

"Has Janet given any indication why they need all that firepower?"

"I think she and Gregory just want to be ready for anything. Right now we know that the CIA is protecting Vladimir Roskov, but we don't know why. We've got satellite imagery that shows

Jacob Knox at Roskov's Kyzylorda warehouse complex. Here are a couple of examples."

Levi clicked a button on the remote, changing the display. The NSA director leaned forward. The first shot was a high-resolution electro-optic image showing Jacob Knox standing in front of three guards, his gesture indicative of a man giving orders to subordinates. The next one showed Knox walking between warehouses beside a bigger man, clearly identifiable as Vladimir Roskov. The Russian mobster's head was turned toward Knox and he had a big grin on his face.

The two images piqued Riles's curiosity.

"Seems like Knox has become a member of the family. Old acquaintances?"

"I don't know."

"Find out."

"Yes, sir. There's one more thing."

"What?"

"Janet Price has requested access to satellite imagery of the Roskov warehouse complex."

Riles had known this was coming and it put him in an awkward position. The president of the United States had ordered him to route all intelligence related to Roskov or Rolf Koenig through Trent Nolan at CIA. But a CIA agent had tried to kill one of his people and that same agent was now hanging out with Roskov in Kyzylorda. This CIA operation was dirty. Every synapse in his brain told him that. Riles had sent Janet Price into harm's way and he'd be damned if he was going to betray her now.

"Give Janet what she wants."

Levi raised an eyebrow. "Sir, given the president's instructions, I'm not sure that's a legal order."

Riles knew it wasn't. He also knew that if Levi complied with it, in the eyes of the law, he would be just as guilty as his boss.

"Sometimes a person has to stand up and do what he thinks is right. In my judgment, this is one of those times. You have to make your own decision."

Riles leaned back in his chair and watched Levi's face tighten.

"I'll see Janet gets what she wants."

It was the decision Riles had expected, although he'd been far from certain of it.

"This stays between the two of us."

Levi rose from his chair and nodded.

"You can count on it."

CHAPTER 78

The work had gone superbly, the replacement nuclear power generator unloaded, tested, and connected to the XLRMV-1 robotic mining vehicle with a precision that made Rolf proud. No panic, just well-rehearsed professionalism, the result of uncounted hours spent turning his team's expected actions into habits. All that hard work meant they were back on schedule. The proton launch vehicle had been moved to the pad and erected. Now the countdown had begun.

Rolf had integrated Roskov's security detail into his own, another piece of the puzzle complete. Poor unsuspecting Vlad. He believed that he and the Russian mafia he commanded were a critical piece of Rolf's plan to substitute the real power package with its doppelganger.

The launch of the XLRMV-1 and subsequent EMP attack on the United States' east coast would only be the opening act of a play that would climax with Rolf leading the effort to exploit the untold riches of the solar system. But to do that, Rolf had to come out of this operation alive and exonerated. That meant he had to have a fall guy and just the right window dressing.

On the day of the launch, he would stand before the cameras with his beautiful wife, supremely proud of the experimental mission he was about to send to the moon. Then satellite communications would fail, killing the news broadcasts. Roskov's men would take control of the Baikonur Cosmodrome, substituting a new team for those who were supposed to manage the launch.

After the nuclear attack on the United States was over, Jacob Knox would put a bullet in the back of Vladimir Roskov's head and Rolf's personal security team would turn on Roskov's men, killing them before they could react to being betrayed. Rolf knew that the Kazakh authorities would question him; he was counting on it. During the course of the investigations that would follow, it would become clear that the North Korean government had used Roskov's Russian Mafia to sabotage the original XLRMV-1 power package and replace it with one of their own design.

Deputy CIA Director Nolan Trent, who would be meeting with his British counterpart at MI6 headquarters when the attack happened, would confirm Rolf's account, bringing the curtain down on act two of Rolf's grand play.

As Rolf stepped into the room that he had been given to use as an office during his stay at the Cosmodrome, his attention was drawn to the lightning that crawled across the cloudy sky outside his window. Seven seconds later, thunder rattled the glass in its frame. Two kilometers away, the storm worried him. Not this one in particular, rather the sequence of early evening thunderstorms that were happening earlier every day.

It wouldn't do to have everything in place, only to have the weather delay his launch.

The forecast indicated that the noon launch should be okay, but even short-term weather forecasts in Kazakhstan were notoriously unreliable. If the current pattern would hold just a couple more days, all would be well. If not, well . . . Rolf refused to think about it. Worrying about things he couldn't control accomplished nothing and wasting time wasn't his nature.

As he seated himself at his desk, he glanced at the countdown display on his laptop. T-minus forty-three hours and counting.

CHAPTER 79

The sun rose behind her as Janet drove the silver Lada Niva into Kyzylorda. It was a mid-sized town, population a little under two hundred thousand. For a brief period of its history, it had been the capital of Kazakhstan but, to her eyes, there was nothing particularly impressive about it. Despite its location along the old spice road from Asia to Europe, Kyzylorda was almost entirely forgettable.

This was the likely reason that Vladimir Roskov had chosen to build his warehouse complex ten kilometers southwest of town. The Russian mafia dealt in new brands of spice. The question that worried her was what brand now connected them to Rolf Koenig and the CIA.

Jack slept in the passenger seat murmuring in his dreams. Janet listened closely, trying to make out the words that whispered from his lips. Although she failed to decipher them, they sent that familiar electric thrill crawling up her spine, as if death itself whispered in her ear.

Jack opened his eyes, yawned, and stretched. He sat up and looked around.

"Lovely."

"It's a shame we won't be staying."

Jack glanced at the GPS display, zoomed out, and pointed to a spot southwest of town.

"I'd like to find a suitable place right around here, right in the rice paddy country."

"Have you been here before?"

"No. But I'll know the house I want when I see it. We'll only be there until it gets dark, so it doesn't have to be perfect."

Eighteen minutes later, on the south side of the Syr Darya River, Jack saw it. The house and its attached barn sat at the edge of a large rice paddy, two hundred meters off the M32 highway. The man working to attach a piece of equipment to the back of a tractor looked as ancient as the house. When Janet turned onto the dirt road that led to the front of the house, the man straightened and turned toward them. As they got closer, Janet could see a questioning look on the man's gray-bearded face.

"You're not going to kill these people." The words spilled from her lips, half command, half question.

"I'm not going to hurt these people," Jack said, trying to make himself believe it. "We're just going to inconvenience them for a while."

Jack opened the passenger door and stepped out, a sheepish smile on his face. When he spoke, his Russian was flawless. And although it was no longer the official language of Kazakhstan, it was universally understood.

"I'm sorry to trouble you, but my wife and I are looking for a distant relative's farm. Perhaps you can help us?"

The old farmer wiped his greasy hands on a red rag and smiled. "I know all my neighbors. What's his name?"

The smile disappeared when he found himself staring into the muzzle of Jack's pistol.

As Janet stepped out of the car, drawing her H&K subcompact, Jack motioned the farmer toward the house.

"Into the house."

When the man remained frozen in place, Jack's trigger finger moved ever so slightly into the trigger guard. "I don't want to hurt you, but I will."

"Please. My wife. Her health is not good."

"Do exactly as I say and you'll both be fine."

The old man glanced down at the gun, then looked into Jack's eyes and nodded. When he turned toward the front door, he stumbled slightly, then righted himself and, with shuffling steps, led them to the house.

Janet stepped to the side of the door. With Jack standing directly behind him, gun leveled at the back of his head, the old man turned the knob, opened the door, and stepped inside. Immediately Janet was through behind him clearing the left as Jack swept the room to the center and right. While it was highly unlikely that anyone would be waiting to ambush them in this old farmhouse, making that sort of assumption eventually ended up getting you killed.

"Clear."

"Clear."

The words came out of their mouths almost simultaneously. Jack moved to his right, leaving the farmer with Janet, then ducked through a doorway into what Janet guessed was the kitchen.

"Clear." Jack's voice preceded him back into the living room.

"What's upstairs?" Jack asked.

The old man stared at Jack, a dazed expression on his bearded face, as if he didn't understand the question.

"What's upstairs?" Jack repeated, nodding toward the stairway on the left side of the room.

"Our bedroom, a bathroom, and a guest room."

"Anyone up there?"

"Only my wife. She is confined to bed. Please do not startle her."

Janet watched as Jack considered the request.

"Alright. But for that to happen, you'll have to do something for me."

"Yes?" The hope in that question hurt Janet's ears.

"Listen carefully. We will need to lock you in your bedroom with your wife. Before we do that, we have to search that room for any guns, telephones, or cellphones. Once that is done, we will lock you inside and you must stay there until tomorrow morning. Sometime in the night we will leave, but do not come out of your room until morning. Do you agree to do that?"

The farmer nodded. "Yes."

"I will let you go into your wife's room first, but I will be watching you from the hallway. You must introduce us as Kazakh federal agents, looking for a dangerous fugitive believed to be hiding in this area. After that, Elena will carefully search your bedroom and bathroom. Then we will shut you inside and you will not come out until morning. Understood?"

"Yes."

"Okay then."

Jack motioned toward the stairs and the farmer nodded, then turned to lead the way. The worn boards squeaked beneath their feet as they ascended. Janet let her pistol move with her eyes as a semi-dark narrow hallway opened up before them. The first door on the left stood open, daylight pooling in a rectangle just outside it. Sparkling dust specks floated above it, highlighted by the dark hallway beyond. Ten feet farther down on opposite sides of the hall, two closed doors faced each other. The one on the right would be the guest room; the other would be the bath, which Janet guessed had another door that opened into the master bedroom.

The farmer paused, glanced back at Jack, and then stepped into the bedroom. Janet repositioned herself so that she could see the man lean over the bed and gently touch the gray hair of the woman that lay beneath the colorful quilt, careful not to disturb the oxygen tube attached to her nose. Her eyes fluttered open.

"Anna, do not be startled, but we have two guests."

"Guests?" Her voice was husky, barely louder than a whisper.

"Yes, dear. They are undercover police, searching for a criminal."

Seeing his wife's eyes go wide with fright, the man placed a finger on her lips. "Don't worry. They are here to protect us tonight, but only until the bad man is caught."

Janet holstered her weapon, put on a warm smile, and stepped into the room.

"Hello, Anna. I am Special Agent Elena Kozlov." Sensing Jack step up beside her, she continued. "This is my partner, Special Agent Nuriev."

"So sorry to trouble you," Jack said, a tender smile on his lips. "It is just a precaution."

As the woman looked into Jack Gregory's face, the worry lines in her face relaxed. Then as if the excitement had drained her last vestige of energy, she settled back into her pillow and closed her eyes.

Seeing the farmer sit on the edge of the bed to take his wife's bony hand in his, Janet moved quietly around the room, checking the dresser drawers, the closet, and the bathroom for phones or weapons. Jack walked out of the bedroom and she heard him open the door to the guest bedroom across the hall. He returned as she finished her inspection.

"Can we get you anything before we shut you in?" Jack asked.

The man shook his head. "We have water."

"What about food?"

"I have no appetite. We'll eat again when you've gone."

Janet understood the feeling. As she stepped out into the hall and Jack closed the door behind them, despite not having eaten since they had left Astana, the thought of food made her ill. As Jack retrieved a length of cord from downstairs and bound the bedroom and bathroom door handles to one another so that they could not be opened from the inside, a single desire filled Janet's body. She just wanted the night to get here so they could leave these poor souls in peace.

CHAPTER 80

T-minus twenty-four. Rolf stood at the launch pad gazing up at the huge proton rocket as the crew went through their checklists and Rolf's payload team ran their final series of tests. Even the weather looked like it was going to cooperate. With the sun high in the sky, there was no sign of the thunderheads that had been building for the last few afternoons. That bade well for tomorrow's launch.

Having just finished another of a series of interviews with one of the handful of international news organizations that had sent TV crews to cover this launch, Rolf kept his anticipation in check. With Rachel's arrival, almost all the pieces were in place. Tonight, after midnight, Jacob Knox and Vladimir Roskov would bring in the rest of the security detail and ready themselves for their pre-dawn takeover of the Cosmodrome.

The team just had to keep it together for another day to open entire new worlds of opportunity.

Once the launch happened there would be no stopping it. Despite the presence of an Aegis guided missile cruiser in the North Pacific, the only real chance that the Americans had of intercepting his payload would fail to detect it. He'd written the subroutine that would make sure of that and Nolan Trent had succeeded in getting that software module incorporated into the Ground-Based Midcourse Defense System's tracking and targeting software. The disagreement between what the Aegis and GMD radars were seeing would only add to the overall confusion, further reducing the chance that Aegis would be allowed to engage.

His secure cellphone vibrated in his pocket. Seeing the caller ID, Roskov, Rolf stepped away from the nearest workers and answered it.

"Do you have your people ready to travel?"

"Knox is giving me some trouble."

Rolf glanced around, focused on keeping his voice low and his face calm. "What do you mean?"

"It's Gregory. Knox is convinced he will make his play at the warehouse tonight. Knox wants me to delay our departure until after midnight to provide time for that to happen."

"Bullshit. The plan calls for you to be here at midnight and there will be no changes to that plan. You just get your ass here on time. I'll make sure Knox is with you."

Rolf hung up and dialed another number. It was 7:32 a.m. in London, but he could catch Nolan Trent before his scheduled meeting at MI6. The deputy CIA director answered on the second ring.

"Is there a problem?"

"One you need to handle. Jacob Knox."

"Go on."

"Knox is refusing to depart Kyzylorda on schedule. He wants to give Gregory a few more hours to show. That's unacceptable."

"No shit. I'll deal with Knox. You stay on schedule."

"I'm on schedule. You just make sure your man doesn't screw it up."

Rolf hung up, returned the phone to his pocket, and took a deep breath, letting it out slowly. Then, putting on his enthusiastic face, he headed back toward the car that would take him to the Control Room and his 1 p.m. interview with CNN.

CHAPTER 81

Daniel Jones reached for the ringing phone, his searching hand knocking over the water glass on his nightstand before he found it. Struggling to clear the sleep from his head, he answered it.

"Dan Jones."

"Dan, this is Janice Weston. Sorry to wake you up in the middle of the night, but I think there's something you need to see."

Dan glanced at the clock. "Jesus, Janice! It's three a.m. Can't this wait until morning?"

"As head of the software team, I think you're going to want to look at it before the boss gets in. We need to figure out how this happened."

"How what happened? What the hell are you talking about?"

"I was doing some work on the source code repository tonight and I came across something that shouldn't be there. Somehow a small block of code got checked into the last release anonymously.

I haven't been able to figure out exactly what it does, or who checked it in, but it damn sure looks suspicious. I'm going to have to report it at the end of my shift and I thought you might want to come in and take a look for yourself before that happens."

"I'll be there in twenty-five minutes."

"Okay."

Dan didn't bother to shower or shave. He just slid into his jeans, a pullover shirt, and Nikes, grabbed his security badge and car keys, and then headed for Crystal City. The commute from Reston sometimes took him almost an hour, but this time of night there was no traffic to speak of. The drive took him nineteen minutes.

When he walked in the door, Ben Gerald, the night security guard, glanced at the badge hanging from the strap around Dan's neck, a look of mild surprise crossing his tired features. "In kind of early this morning, aren't you, Mr. Jones?"

"Unfortunately. There was a problem with the nightly build, so I'm the lucky one who gets to fix it."

Stepping into the elevator lobby, Dan pressed the call button. The third elevator on the left opened and Dan pressed button number three. When he walked out of the elevator on the third floor, he entered the hallway on his right and stopped at the door to swipe his badge and enter his six-digit personal access code. Hearing the click of the lock opening, Dan walked into the Sensitive Compartmentalized Information Facility known as the SCIF.

Janice Weston, the only person in the lab at this hour, rose to meet him. Tall, charismatic, and beautiful, she was his opposite in every way except for intelligence. Tonight, as she walked toward him, she looked both intrigued and worried.

"Ahh, Dan. Glad you're here."

"What have you found?"

She motioned toward the workstation behind her. "Have a seat. You're not going to believe this shit."

Dan shook his head. "You know what you're looking at. You drive."

Nodding, she sat down as Dan stepped up behind her. Her fingers moved rapidly across the keyboard, scrolling through the repository's check-in history. She paused, and pointed at the screen.

"See this? The last check-in before the release build was at 3:13 p.m. on the 21st. I looked at it. It was just a minor bug fix. But then as I was getting ready to log out of the system, the last modified time on two source files caught my eye. They were both changed at 6:22 p.m. on the 21st, a little over thirty minutes before the release build started."

"Modified by who?"

"That's just it. I didn't think it was even possible, but someone checked in those files anonymously. It had to be done with root permissions, I just don't know how."

"Have you looked at the files?"

"Of course."

She brought them both up, side by side, in the source code editor.

"I diffed both files against the previous versions. The only change in the one on the left is a single statement that calls the subroutine on the right. Look at this."

Janice highlighted an if-structure. "It does the same thing as in the previous version, except in a very special case. I haven't finished analyzing it, but it looks malicious."

Dan leaned forward, reaching for the mouse. "Do you mind?"

Janice removed her hand from it. "Go ahead."

As his fingers closed around the small device, he pulled hard, ripping its USB cord out of the computer and wrapping it around Janice's slender neck in one quick motion. Pulling with all his might, he dragged her backward, tipping over her chair, and dumping her facedown on the floor. Dan landed on top of her, his legs straddling her back.

Gagging and twisting beneath him, Janice's fingers struggled to loosen the cord that bit into her neck. But as Dan continued to tighten the loop, the lack of blood supply to Janice's brain ended her feeble effort.

Dan felt her body go limp beneath him. Still he continued pulling the looped cord, not stopping until he watched the clock on the wall tick through two full minutes. When he finally did release it, he verified that Janice had no pulse, either in her wrist or her left carotid artery.

Dragging her across the room by her feet, Dan stuffed Janice's body into a supply closet. When he straightened, he paused to wipe the sweat from his brow with a paper towel before shutting the door on Janice Weston.

Without pausing to think about what he'd just done, Dan walked back to her desk, righted the fallen chair, closed down all the applications Janice had been running, and shut down her workstation. He knew he wouldn't get away with the murder, but by the time anyone figured out what he'd just covered up, none of this would matter.

When he exited the lab, Dan paused one last time to survey the room before flipping off the lights.

At the security desk, Ben asked. "Get it fixed?"

Dan waved as he headed for the exit.

"Problem solved."

CHAPTER 82

Rachel Koenig stepped out of the shower onto the red tile bathroom floor and reached for the thick white towel. She knew she was in Kazakhstan, but the house in Baikonur that Rolf had procured for her stay felt like the villa they had stayed at last year in Puerto Vallarta. And now that the drugs had worked their way out of her system, she could appreciate it. Unfortunately the fact that she'd been brought here against her will and that her wait-staff was preventing her from doing anything that Rolf didn't want her doing put a real damper on the resort feeling the place should have had.

Rolf's voice interrupted her reverie.

"I need you ready in forty-five minutes."

Rachel turned to see her husband dressed in an Italian suit, as if they were going to a cocktail dinner instead of taking the drive from Baikonur out to the Cosmodrome.

"I'll be ready," she said, giving the towel a twist, knotting it on top of her head.

As she walked to the right hand sink to begin applying her makeup, Rolf stepped up behind her, running his hands around her stomach from behind, his lips gently brushing her left ear. The gentle, appreciative nature of that touch sent a chill through her body. It felt, for all the world, like one last goodbye.

"I think I owe you an explanation of what is about to happen to us . . . to everyone."

Rachel's hands froze in the midst of unzipping the makeup bag, just for a moment, but Rolf's slight smile said that he had noticed.

"I know that it seems unusual to get dressed up to go to the launch site, but it is important that we be seen together by the news media, if only from a distance, proud parents of my mining robot, celebrating its last night on earth."

Rachel turned to face him. As she looked into those sparkling blue eyes, she could sense the excitement within her husband, so much so that it spilled over into physical excitement. She was sure that, had he not been in such a hurry, he would take her right here on the bathroom counter.

"Won't the press be there for the launch tomorrow?"

"They'll be there; they just won't be in a position to broadcast anything."

"I don't understand."

Rolf reached up to stroke the side of her face with the long fingers of his right hand. "Before tomorrow morning's launch, most of the assembled press corps and all the official launch control personnel will be dead."

Rachel felt her mouth go dry.

"And my dear, your performance tonight will very much determine whether or not you join them. So put on your makeup and the black evening dress that is laid out on your bed, and be ready to wave and smile. Don't worry, I've done enough interviews today that they don't expect us to actually talk to them tonight. But they will get a bit of video as we make our way from our limo to the Control Room."

When he leaned in and kissed her forehead, it felt like she'd just been kissed by her mortician, right before he placed a penny on each eye. Then Rolf turned and walked out of the bathroom, the leather soles of his black shoes scuffing ever so softly on the tile.

Too shocked to respond, Rachel felt her body go through the motions of applying her makeup and getting dressed, while her mind replayed the unreal scene that had just happened. She'd heard the truth in Rolf's voice, had seen it shining brightly in his eyes. This went far beyond her worst imaginings.

Tomorrow, her husband was going to cause the death of dozens of people, possibly many more. But for what purpose? And why had he told her after keeping this secret for so long? She had no answer to the first question and the one that came to her for the second left her shaking so badly that she had difficulty sliding into her high heels.

Rolf was certain that he had all his pieces arranged so that no one could stop him now, so certain that he'd offered her a lifeline. She could climb onboard or get sucked down in the maelstrom that was about to swallow so many others.

Staring at herself in the mirror as she finished doing her hair, she battled back the tears that threatened both her mascara and her life. If it had been a magic mirror from a fairy tale, perhaps it could have relayed the words that whispered from her lips.

"Oh Jack. I need some help here. Where the hell are you?"

CHAPTER 83

Jack watched Janet as she continued downloading the latest satellite imagery of Roskov's warehouse complex. They'd spent the afternoon checking all the equipment they'd gotten from Zhaniya, cleaning and loading weapons, and going through all the photographs they'd been able to get from the NSA. To do that, they'd had to set up the portable satcom antenna that provided the link for their Secure Terminal Equipment, and that encrypted STE link was what Janet was using to pull down the imagery. Some of it was at such high resolution that the downlink took a long time. But those hi-res photos were worth the wait.

One thing that concerned him was the increased level of activity shown in today's imagery versus images from prior days. The sniper positions on the rooftops and in the five guard bunkers positioned at the outer fence corners and at the entry gate were still manned. But a number of vehicles had disappeared from the compound and guard posts at several of the warehouses were no longer manned.

"Got it," Janet said, turning the laptop to give him a better view of the latest image.

Jack pulled an oak chair around the kitchen table so he could sit beside her. Janet let him study the overview until he was satisfied and then, section by section, zoomed in so they could both study the fine details. There was no doubt about it. Something important was happening in the compound. Now, only three vehicles were visible: a white panel van parked near the guard bunker just inside the entry gate, and two others that had been captured pulling inside one of the large central warehouses.

"What the hell is going on there? And why today?" Jack asked.

"That's not the question." Janet's silky voice carried a hint of excitement that indicated that she sensed the same thing that had Jack's blood heated. "The real question is: what is about to happen?"

"Yes. Something's going down, but not right now. Tomorrow."

"I think so."

Jack stood up. "Pack it up. Time to roll."

A scream from upstairs was accompanied by the pounding of fists on a wood door. Jack saw Janet draw her weapon as he felt his own fill his right hand. They reached the top of the stairs at the same time. Jack looked down the hall. Aside from the yells from within the master bedroom, he saw nothing out of the ordinary. But the agony in those cries pulled him to the door.

With a swift motion, Jack's blade cut the cord that bound the door handle closed. Then he was inside, his H&K leveled. The force of his shoulder driving the door inward had sprawled the old farmer on the floor, but not for long. As if in slow motion, the old man struggled back to his feet, almost clawing his way to his wife's bed, draping himself across her lifeless body.

"My Anna," he cried, his anguished brown eyes rising to lock with Jack's.

And as Jack's gaze met the older man's, he felt it drain the life from him, imparting an unquenchable longing and misery.

"My Anna."

Jack felt his gun hand drop to his side. "Jesus!"

To his left, he saw Janet sag back against the doorway.

"Please, sir. Kill me. Just kill me now. Let me follow my wife into the dark."

The misery in the old man's eyes ate at Jack like a zombie. He took a deep breath, walked to the bed, and placed a finger against Anna's right carotid artery. Nothing.

"I'm sorry, but you'll have to do that."

The man sobbed, his old shoulders bent and shaking as he hugged his dead wife's body close to his chest. When he turned his head and opened his eyes once again, the feeling in those eyes was so intense that Jack had no chance of denying his last request.

"My religion forbids it, but I cannot go on without her. I beg you. Send me to my Anna."

Jack heard the sound of the suppressor screwing into the barrel of the H&K without realizing that his fingers were doing it. Had he made the decision that had carried him to this moment or had he allowed something else to make it for him?

He raised the weapon, felt a tremor in his normally rock-steady hand, and hesitated, as each passing second siphoned the strength from his body.

Then, with intense sadness flooding his soul, Jack looked across the handgun's sights, directly into those pleading brown eyes, and squeezed the trigger.

Blood and brains splattered the headboard and wall, but the farmer's head fell onto the pillow against his beloved Anna's. As

Jack raised his eyes to see the shock in Janet's, he judged himself. The results of that judgment were far from favorable.

He straightened, unscrewed the suppressor from the barrel of his pistol, and turned toward the door.

"Let's go."

When Janet failed to respond, it didn't surprise him. Why should she? After all, she was learning what he truly was . . . The Ripper.

CHAPTER 84

Jacob stared at his cell phone, more than half tempted to hurl it into the cement floor and then grind it to bits beneath his heel. Nolan Trent had lost his mind, unwilling to allow Jacob an extra three hours here at the warehouse complex to allow The Ripper one more chance to show. Normally Jacob was the one who did everything in strict adherence with the plan. That was what made him even angrier that his request for an exception hadn't been given consideration. He was ordered to move out with Roskov and the remainder of his men at precisely eight p.m.

Trent had made it very clear that Jacob's plan to lure Jack Gregory to him at the warehouse complex had been given plenty of time and it had failed. The fact that there had been no sight of The Ripper or Janet Price since Salzburg meant they had probably both gone to ground. Even if they hadn't, they were too late to stop what was about to happen at Baikonur. But Jacob risked screwing it up if he didn't stay on schedule. It was his job to stay with Roskov to make sure he succeeded in taking control of the Cosmodrome, and then to shoot him in the head when the time came. Only in that way would all the blame fall on Roskov and his mythical North Korean puppet masters. Then Jacob could kill Gregory at his leisure.

None of that was news to Jacob. But it didn't feel right. Two dangerous loose ends had not been tied down despite all his assurances that he would deal with them.

Putting his cell phone back in his pocket, Jacob turned to walk back across the floor of Warehouse Five to Roskov's office as two of the last three guard vehicles drove into the building, turned into the tunnel, and disappeared. It didn't really matter anymore. His trap had been dismantled.

Climbing the steel steps that led up to Vladimir Roskov's office, Jacob opened the door and stepped inside.

As he had known it would be, except for a small table, the steel case desk, a swivel chair, and Jacob's bag sitting by the door, the small room was empty, having been cleared earlier in the day. Only one more thing to do.

Jacob opened his case, his gloved hands extracting a single thin folder. Sliding open the bottom-right desk drawer, he pushed the folder into the gap behind it, and then closed it once again, a final piece of incriminating evidence for the authorities to find after this was all over.

A glance at his watch showed that it was now 7:48 p.m. It was time to turn out the warehouse lights, stow his gear in Roskov's big black sedan, and move on to the last phase of the operation.

When he walked back down the steps and around the corner, he saw Roskov standing beside the car smoking a cigar. The Russian grinned at him.

"I take it Trent gave you the bad news."

"I got the picture."

"Cigar? They're Cubans."

Tossing his bag in the trunk, Jacob accepted the offer.

"Sure. Why not?"

Taking the cigar, Jacob accepted a light, took a long pull, and held it before letting the smoke out in a long stream. As he climbed into the limousine, he watched Roskov lift his cell phone and issue the command.

"Lock the front gate and pack up. We're rolling."

As they drove into the tunnel, he glanced back, watching the ramp close behind them. With the headlights illuminating the narrow underground road ahead, Jacob pulled the smoke into his mouth, savoring the rich taste of the leaf tobacco. Sitting in the back seat beside Roskov, separated from the driver and bodyguard by a panel of bulletproof glass, neither man moved to crack open a window. With their faces briefly illuminated by the orange glow from a fresh drag on a Cuban, they rode along in silence.

Jacob knew that, at this reduced speed, it would take about ten minutes to reach the small warehouse where this tunnel ended. Then they would make their way to Highway M32 and by eleven p.m. they would reach the spot just south of the Cosmodrome where Rolf Koenig would be waiting. After that, they would get this show started.

In the meantime, Jacob would lean back, enjoy the cigar, and, for the first time in a long while, just let his mind go blank.

CHAPTER 85

Night-vision goggles weren't comfortable to drive in, but they weren't comfortable for doing anything. Having driven the last three kilometers on seldom-travelled dirt roads with his headlights off, Jack was glad to have them. Both he and Janet had their windows rolled down in case they needed to use their weapons sooner than they were planning to. As was often the case in Kazakhstan with fall's approach, the warm day had been chased away by night's cool breezes.

The vehicle lurched over the rough road hard enough that Jack and Janet both had to tighten the straps on their goggles to keep them in place.

"How much farther?" Janet asked, shifting the AS50 sniper rifle so that it rested across her body, with its barrel out the window.

They were the first words she'd spoken to him since he'd killed the old man. Jack couldn't blame her for that. Why had he chosen that house? Had it been because he subconsciously sensed death there? Maybe Anna would have died today anyway, but he didn't believe it. And Jack had killed her husband without even asking his name. He was just a farmer, just an old man.

"I think we can get to within three hundred meters before we have to get out and walk. About a kilometer from here."

Jack slowed the SUV until it felt like it was crawling through the night, finally stopping two hundred meters short of where he had planned, unwilling to take the risk of the vehicle noise being heard by the gate guards.

Turning off the engine, he got out and walked around to open the back hatch. The problem with having a lot of equipment available to you was that you had to pick and choose. As a general rule of thumb, the more important a piece of equipment was to your operation, the heavier it was. That was certainly true of the scanning laser with its tripod and its portable battery-capacitor hybrid power supply.

They had preloaded their packs before departing the farmhouse, distributing the weapons, ammunition, and tactical radios. They'd strapped the tripod and laser to the outside of Janet's backpack and the power supply to Jack's. The good news was that they would be setting up the laser at the over-watch position, two hundred meters from the front gate. The bad news was that, until they got there, Janet would be carrying a hundred and fifty pounds and Jack's load was well over two hundred.

Janet turned to face away from him and Jack lifted her pack into place, letting her slide her arms through the straps and take the weight slowly.

Jack walked around her, double checking the straps and fastenings, grasping and shaking them to ensure there was no give.

"Good to go."

"Lovely," she said, leaning forward to grab the AS50.

Walking back to the hatchback, Jack positioned his pack at the rear edge, straps facing out so that he could kneel down and slide into them, and then lean forward and stand. With a grunt of effort he climbed back to his feet.

“Makes you wish you were infantry, doesn’t it?” Janet’s grin was a bright spot in the infrared lens. “Then you’d get to do this on a daily basis.”

Picking up his AK47 rifle, he nodded.

“It’s always been my favorite part of the job. Right up there with pain and hunger.”

On nearly every deadly non-solo mission Jack had ever participated in, such banter preceded the action . . . a last touch of light to ward off the coming darkness.

Jack quietly closed the rear door and led the way into the night. While the terrain was mainly flat, there were folds in the ground and Jack stayed down in the lowest of these, working his crooked path toward the spot they had preselected as their objective rally point, the spot where they would prep the equipment they would take on their final assault. As the straps of his load bit into his shoulders and chest, he thought of the woman beside him, carrying a man’s load with no hint of complaint, no whisper of fatigue or pain, and he remembered.

Janet Alexandra Price. The first woman to ever successfully graduate from the nine weeks of hell that was the U.S. Army Ranger School, a woman who, as a child, had emptied a pistol into her own father. And yet, Janet was a person who had managed to reintroduce joy into her life, something Jack had not yet accomplished.

At least for this mission, she was his partner. It was a thought that left a nice, warm glow in the pit of his stomach.

CHAPTER 86

Having dropped the heavy packs and clipped the equipment they would be carrying for the assault onto their utility vests, they mounted the scanning laser to the tripod, attached the power supply, and raised it into position. As Janet switched the laser to standby and verified the RF remote controller was working, Jack crawled forward to survey the compound.

"What the hell?"

Jack's voice in her radio earpiece pulled her to his side at the top of the gentle rise. Low crawling into position, Janet looked down toward the Roskov complex. Completely dark, her night-vision goggles picked up no hint of engine or body heat, no roving guards, no snipers, not even at the front gate.

Removing her NVGs, she slid the AS50 into position to look through its infrared scope. Sweeping the scope across the entire compound revealed no sign that it was anything other than completely abandoned.

"Got anything?" Jack asked.

"Nothing."

"Cover me."

Jack moved out low to the ground, moving in quick bursts from firing position to firing position as Janet looked for anything to shoot at. The laser range-finder showed that the front gate was two hundred and thirteen meters from her position, the nearest warehouse, two hundred seventy-eight, the farthest, eight hundred sixty. She judged the wind speed at only six to eight knots, directly into her face from the west. She couldn't ask for better.

Upon seeing Jack settle into position on the near side of the paved road across from the gate, his body white hot in the IR sight, she spoke into the jaw microphone.

"Clear."

Immediately he was on his feet, running across the road, angling at the chain-link fence twenty meters left of the closed front gate. When he reached it, he knelt down, laying the AK47 on the ground to his right as he worked to thread a strand of detonation cord through the wires.

When he moved away, Janet killed the power to the IR sight and looked away to preserve her night vision.

"Fire in the hole." Jack's voice was followed by a loud bang as the det cord opened a six-foot hole in the fence.

As the flash died, Janet switched on the sight and once again swept the complex. The hole in the fence and some of the surrounding ground glowed bright as the explosion's ghost lingered. But, except for Jack's body heat, nothing else stirred.

"Still clear."

"Looks like we wasted our time setting up the laser."

"Looks like," she agreed. "If they're waiting for us, they're inside one or more of those warehouses."

"I'm going for the first one on the left."

"Ready."

Jack sprinted through the hole in the fence, his focus on making it to the warehouse wall as quickly as possible instead of ducking or seeking cover. And as Janet watched him run, she saw no other hint of life or movement. Just weird.

Jack reached the warehouse's east wall and then moved to a crouching position at the northeast corner.

"Your turn."

"Moving now."

Janet slid the IR goggles back into place, adjusted the strap, and then didn't stop running until she reached the warehouse. Leaning back against the wall next to Jack, she took several deep breaths, working on slowing her breathing and racing heart.

"Okay. I'm good."

"Oh, I know."

She didn't need the infrared goggles to spot his grin.

"You'd better."

"I'm going for the door. Cover me."

Janet slid into a kneeling position at the corner, sliding her goggles up and picking up the AS50 scope's sight picture.

"It might be booby trapped."

"I'm going to blow it."

Jack ducked around the corner, stopping beside the small door just short of the huge rolling door designed for truck access. Sticking a small wad of C4 to the lock, Jack shoved in a wireless detonator and moved back a dozen meters.

"Ready?"

Janet again looked away. "Go."

This explosion was louder than the previous and, when she reacquired her sight picture, she saw that the door had been torn from its hinges and flung back into the warehouse. Moving up behind Jack, they went through the opening one after the other, him clearing right as she swept the left.

Empty.

Jack moved rapidly around the left side as Janet held her position by the door, searching for a target inside the building before swinging around to guard against an assault from outside the door.

Jack's voice in her ear carried a hint of frustration that the radio hiss couldn't mask.

"From the amount of dust on the floor, this warehouse hasn't been used in over a month."

"Then why did they have two guards posted outside yesterday?"

"Classic shell game. Make us guess which is important."

"If I had to pick one, it would be the one we saw the two trucks pulling inside in that last satellite image."

Jack stepped up beside her. "I agree. I'm going to need you on the roof. You should have clear firing angles all the way down the row to that center warehouse."

Janet didn't like what she was hearing. "Then I won't be able to help clear it when you get there. It splits us up too much. What if people are hiding in some of these other warehouses?"

"You just make sure I get there. We'll deal with other contingencies if they happen."

"Okay, but I don't like it."

"There's a steel ladder in that far corner. I'm guessing it goes to a roof hatch. Let me know when you're in position."

Slinging the AS50 across her back, Janet readjusted her night-vision goggles and moved off toward the ladder, leaving Jack crouching beside the doorway behind her. She had the distinct impression that Jack felt something was about to go seriously wrong here. If she was paranoid she would be thinking that he was moving her away from him to keep her safe. But Jack Gregory wasn't that kind of man. He expected her to carry her own load and she damn sure would do her own heavy lifting.

She found the ladder where Jack had said it would be, steel rungs mounted a foot and a half apart, set into the concrete wall. When she reached the roof, forty feet above the warehouse floor, she hooked one arm through the top rung, leaned back, and pulled on the locking lever. When it failed to open, she rocked her body outward, giving a much harder tug. Although the lever moved, it took three pulls to get the job done.

Once the hatch was free, Janet lifted it just enough to see out onto the empty roof. She knew no one was up here, but taking unnecessary chances wasn't her way. She opened the hatch and climbed out onto the flat roof. It wasn't completely flat, the center just a few inches higher to provide for water runoff. A foot-high lip rimmed the roof's outer edge with gutter spouts every twenty to thirty feet around the perimeter.

Staying low, Janet unslung the AS50 sniper rifle, crawled to the northeast corner, and moved into a prone firing position. Switching back to the IR sight, she scanned the surrounding rooftops and the alley Jack would be taking to the central warehouse. Satisfied she spoke into the jaw microphone.

"All clear."

CHAPTER 87

Vladimir Roskov exhaled a mouthful of cigar smoke that made the limousine air finally achieve the critical mass that caused him to crack a window. When his cell phone rang, he answered it.

"Roskov."

"Boss, we've got action in the compound!"

Vlad recognized the voice as that of Pavel Krupin, leader of the team of five that had been left to ensure that nobody followed them through the tunnel.

"Where are you now?"

"We are holding position inside Warehouse Five, as you instructed. But we heard two explosions from outside. Do you want us to go hunt down the intruders?"

"No. Stay where you are. If anyone tries to come through that door, kill them. Understood?"

"Understood."

Roskov terminated the call and turned to look into Jacob's black eyes.

"My boys have company."

"I told you The Ripper would come to me."

"We stay on target. My guys will kill him or keep him jammed up so long it won't matter."

Jacob laughed in his face. "You think so? Then you're as big a fool as Trent and Koenig."

Vlad felt a sudden fury boil up inside. For a handful of seconds he was tempted to pull his gun and shoot out those black eyes. But Vladimir Roskov had seen Jacob Knox in action, and that dark memory stilled his hand.

At least for tonight, he'd let it pass.

CHAPTER 88

"All clear."

Janet's voice in his earpiece put Jack in motion. Hugging the north wall, he paused at the gap between this warehouse and the next, double-checked the crossing road, and then continued working his way toward his objective. It practically called to him.

"Roof hatch opening."

"Close it."

The sound of the fifty-caliber rifle was so loud in the shallow canyons between the warehouses that he could almost see the concrete walls vibrate with the echoes.

"Target down." Janet's words sent an electric thrill up his spine.

Moving faster now, Jack crossed to the north side of the street and reached his objective, moving along the south wall toward the access door. He attached a palm-sized brick of C4 and then backed off around the east side of the warehouse.

"Have you got line of sight to the door?" he asked.

"Yes. But I won't have much of an angle to the inside of the building once you blow it."

"That's okay. Watch me and wait for it."

Leaning back against the wall, Jack removed the folding grappling-hook from his utility vest, uncoiled twenty meters of cord, and secured it with an end-of-line bowline knot, followed by two half-hitches. Stepping away from the wall, Jack whirled the hook, launching it up and over the lip. On the second toss, the grapple caught firmly. A minute later, his AK47 slung over his back, Jack climbed over the ledge.

With the hook left in place, he unslung the assault rifle and crawled silently across the roof to the hatch. On the northwest side of the partially opened hatch, the spray of blood, brain, and hairy chunks of skull confirmed the kill shot. The fifty-caliber round had sent the body tumbling back down to the warehouse floor. It didn't surprise him that nobody else had followed the man up.

Jack moved up beside the hatch, took two high-explosive grenades and one thermite grenade from his vest, and set them on the roof beside it. Then he removed his night-vision goggles and set them on the roof. Jack pulled the pins and tossed the grenades through the hatch in different directions. A lone scream accompanied the explosions that followed as the blinding glare from the burning thermite grenade obliterated the darkness within.

Janet's fifty-caliber barked again, its echoes seeming to come from all directions, and Jack swung the barrel of his AK47 into the hatch, sending a three-round burst toward the spot from which the scream had sounded. The answering twin muzzle flashes sprayed rounds wildly, some in his general direction. Jack ducked away from the hatch and waited until the volley subsided.

Now that he knew the precise location of the two shooters, Jack repositioned himself, popped up, and fired twice. His first round lifted the rightmost of the shooters from his covered position behind a forklift and flung him back into the far wall. The second shot punched a hole through the door at the top of a fifteen-foot metal stairway as the man's partner ducked through it. This time Jack did not duck back from the opening, maintaining his sight picture on that door.

As the arm holding the submachine gun swung out, Jack put a bullet through it, sprawling the man backward and sending his weapon clattering down the stairs to the concrete warehouse floor. With the warehouse illuminated by the intense white-orange glow of the hot gasses and flame of the thermite reaction eating a hole in the center of the concrete floor, Jack had a clear view of this room that formed the southern half of the warehouse.

The body of the man Janet had killed lay in a pool of blood directly below the hatch. Besides the two men he had just shot, two grenade-mangled bodies lay near several overturned barrels; a total of four dead and one wounded.

"Status?"

"Four dead men in a big room. Except for a loading platform and a forklift, it's mostly empty. There is one door at the top of a metal stairway in the wall opposite the one in the south wall. I wounded the guy inside."

"You think anybody else is waiting on the other side of that door?"

"I'm not feeling it."

Moving away from the hatch, Jack picked up the NVGs and hooked them to his vest, then moved back to the rope, stepped over the edge, and slid back to the ground. At the corner of the building, he saw the central street was still empty. Moving back up the alley where he'd grappled up to the roof, he ran to the warehouse's northeast corner.

"I'm going in through the back door. Kill anyone who sticks his head out the front or up top."

His ears still ringing from the gunfire and the explosions, Janet's response in his earpiece sounded faint. "Got it covered."

A glance around the corner showed that the warehouse's north wall was a mirror image of the one on the south side. A man-sized door occupied a spot in the wall just to the east of a huge rolling metal door. When Jack reached it, he sensed the desperation emanating from the man that waited somewhere on the other side and fought the adrenaline rush that pulled him in that direction.

He attached a block of C4, hooked it up, and retreated to the corner. Slapping a fresh magazine into the assault rifle, he fingered the remote. He'd do this, not the demon way, but his.

"Going in."

His words entered the mike a half-second before he triggered the twin explosions that obliterated both the north and south doors. Unclipping the NVGs, Jack slid them into place, switched them on, and moved into the waiting darkness.

CHAPTER 89

With his back against Vladimir Roskov's steel-case desk, Pavel Krupin ripped his shirt off, wrapped it around his torn left bicep, and, with his right hand and teeth, tied it into a knot. When the arterial blood flow showed no sign of slowing, he unfastened his ankle knife and shoved it, sheath and all, through the knot. With what was left of his rapidly draining strength, he gave the knife two hard twists, then used his belt to bind the tourniquet in place.

How had it come to this? He'd sent his best man up to the roof, but a large-caliber bullet had blown Nikita's head off as he tried to climb out of the hatch. The ferocity of the assault that followed had stunned Pavel. The Ripper had tossed grenades down the hatch as if he'd known exactly where Pavel's men were positioned. Then he'd followed up with a volley of well-placed shots that had stripped Pavel of the rest of his team and had left him bleeding out inside Roskov's office.

The current silence terrified Pavel worse than the preceding bedlam. Except for the faint glow of the cooling thermite residue, darkness draped the warehouse. Pavel could have switched on the office lights, but that would just help the killer who had probably already descended the ladder into the southern half of the warehouse.

Pavel fought to clear his mind as he gripped the Sig Sauer in his right hand. If he could make it to the switch that opened the tunnel ramp, maybe he'd have a chance of escape. But that meant he would have to go back out into the southern half of the warehouse. The Ripper would kill him before he got out the door. But staying where he was, hiding behind Roskov's empty desk, wouldn't save him either. Having lost the use of his left arm, he couldn't easily change magazines on the Sig. Any second now, The Ripper would blast open that door and roll a hand grenade inside.

Pavel's only other option was to take the door that led to the clean room on the north side. But The Ripper had probably already thought of that.

Pavel knew he was in shock. Not surprising. It was so damned hard to think.

Twin explosions from the north and the south rocked the building and sent Pavel scrambling back into the corner, firing at first one door and then the other. With his breath coming in ragged gasps, he forced himself to stop shooting. He knew he should eject the magazine and slap in a new one, but he didn't dare set the gun down to make the one-handed switch. Somewhere in that darkness, on one side of the warehouse or the other, The Ripper was coming for him.

What if the man had shot him in the arm on purpose? What if he wanted Pavel alive?

A sound from the clean-room section of the warehouse caused Pavel to swivel in that direction, his movement sending an electric arc of pain shooting up his left arm.

What the hell was taking so long?

A new thought wormed its way into his fevered brain. The Ripper had no intention of killing him. The man would keep him alive until he learned everything that Pavel knew, just as he had with Petor Kline.

The metal stairs on the north side creaked under a man's weight and, with his heart hammering to get out of his chest, he made a decision. Thrusting the gun barrel deep inside his mouth, with the taste of well-oiled steel heavy on his tongue, Pavel pulled the trigger.

CHAPTER 90

Captain Steve Cole watched the crew manning the *U.S.S. Lake Erie*'s Combat Information Center with a great feeling of pride. The Ticonderoga-class guided-missile cruiser was a key piece of the Constellation Battle Group, currently sailing one hundred nautical miles southwest of Sapporo, Japan. With so much at stake during this latest round of tension between the United States and North Korea, his ship and his crew stood ready to provide anti-ballistic missile defense against a potential nuclear attack.

As he stood looking at the four Aegis large-screen displays and the myriad other manned consoles, observing this watch finish the latest ballistic missile defense battle simulation, he noted how much this team had improved over the last two months. It wasn't that they hadn't been good before. When he'd taken command, they'd been very good. But the legitimate threat of a nuclear attack on their homeland had narrowed their focus and increased their intensity such that Captain Cole knew that there was no finer crew in the fleet. And that applied to the entire ship's crew, not just this CIC watch.

Leaving the CIC, the captain made his way out onto the deck. As his eyes adjusted to the dark, he gazed up at the beautiful, cloudless night sky, dusted with stars from horizon to horizon. Looking at that black sky, feeling the powerful ship move beneath his feet, tasting the salt spray on the cool ocean breeze, Captain Steve Cole felt like a Viking captain of old, listening for that distant call of battle.

And when that call came, he and his mighty ship's crew would stand ready.

CHAPTER 91

Seated in the back of the black sedan, surrounded by his security detail, Rolf Koenig watched as the small convoy of vehicles approached the roadside pullout where he waited. A glance at his watch showed the time, 10:45 p.m. As the five vehicles pulled off the road and another black sedan came to a stop a dozen feet in front of his, Rolf opened the door and climbed out into the rapidly cooling night.

Vladimir Roskov and Jacob Knox climbed out of the other sedan and walked to the spot where he waited, just outside the splash of the headlights.

The Russian mob boss spoke first. "We've lost contact with the five-man team I left behind at the warehouse."

Rolf stifled the curse before it made it to his lips.

"That's okay. We planned for this. It just means I'm going to have to bump up the launch."

"Bump up?" Knox asked, his strange black eyes giving Rolf the impression that the man had twin holes drilled in his head. "By how much?"

"Six hours."

"That's tight." T-minus thirteen had just become T-minus seven.

It always irritated Rolf when someone bothered to state the obvious. It was especially true when the drivel spouted from the mouth of Nolan Trent or one of his subordinates.

"True, but this will actually make some things even easier. The only difference is that we'll be initiating the takeover of the Cosmodrome at midnight instead of just before dawn. I've already got my people integrated into all the key launch system, Control Room, and security crews and they're aware that I'm about to bump the schedule. I'll send my guys with you to guide you to the link up.

"We'll stick to the original plan, with only a slight change in the launch vehicle refueling schedule. At midnight I'll kill all external communications links, including the link to the Russian Mission Control Center in Korolyov. As soon as that's done I'll give you the go signal. Since the actual launch isn't scheduled until noon, staffing will be minimal. Your teams and my agents on the inside will put the existing Russian Security and local onsite security teams out of commission and will take control of Areas 92, 95, 81, and 200, with most of our attention focused on Building 92A-50 and Launch Pad 24.

"Once I get word that those and the road leading off-site are secured, then I will use my computer to take over the control center and adjust the countdown clocks to the new schedule. The replacement launch platform crew will take the place of the original launch platform personnel and will then begin fuelling the launch vehicle.

"One last time, so you are both clear on the schedule, at T-minus six hours, midnight local time, we take over the Cosmodrome.

"At T-minus five and a half hours, I'll override the pre-programmed launch trajectory, upload new trajectory and engine burn commands into the navigation computers, and reprogram the telemetry and command channels to our new frequencies. Launch vehicle propellant loading will then commence.

"At T-minus one we'll roll back the Mobile Service Tower and go into our final countdown sequence.

"Everybody knows what happens at T-minus zero. Any last questions?"

Jacob Knox cleared his throat. "And if The Ripper shows up?"

"Isn't that why you're here?" Rolf let the satisfaction that response gave him creep into his voice. "Take your team and kill him. Just make damn sure you keep him away from Launch Pad 24 and away from the Control Room in Building 92A-50. That's where I'll be running the show."

The look in the CIA killer's black eyes wiped the momentary satisfaction from Rolf's mind. Turning his attention back to Roskov, he clapped his hands.

"Okay, then. Let's do this."

CHAPTER 92

Jack moved through the hole in the north wall and into the warehouse, scanning for thermal signatures that indicated life. But except for the hot residue and smoke from the explosion that had destroyed the door, the place bore no trace of hot bodies or equipment. From where he moved along the warehouse wall to the left, he didn't have a clear view of the steps that led up to the office from which he had heard the gunshots that had answered his C4 detonations. Either the man he'd wounded or someone else still remained alive inside that room.

In the green IR imagery presented by the night-vision goggles, the large room in which he found himself looked all wrong, with large sections separated by transparent walls and extensive duct work. As Jack moved through it, he passed work benches and equipment he failed to recognize. Reaching a transparent wall, he tapped it with the knuckles of his left hand. Plexiglas.

"How goes it?" Janet's digital voice whispered in his ear.

"Clear so far."

"Ready for me to move up?"

"Not yet. I'll let you know."

Jack stopped beside a Plexiglas door. A large, round gauge mounted on the wall beside it indicated that, when everything was working, this room was kept pressurized. That meant the door probably opened into a chemical or air shower. When he stepped through it, discarded disposable gloves, booties, and masks confirmed his theory.

He spoke quietly into his mike. "I'm in some sort of clean-room complex on the north half of the warehouse."

"Still nothing out here."

Letting the assault rifle follow his eyes, Jack stepped out of the air shower. He was standing in a small open space at the bottom of a set of grated steel steps, the twin of the stairway he'd seen in the other half of the warehouse. At the top of those steps a railed steel platform provided access to a closed doorway that had been pock-marked with bullet holes.

He could feel the presence in the room beyond that door, could sense the man's pain and terror. Jack reminded himself that there might be more than one man waiting inside the room, but he couldn't make himself believe it.

Staying against the wall, Jack stepped onto the stairs, heard the metal creak beneath his weight, and then stepped again. The sound of the gunshot from within the room didn't surprise him, but the utter silence that followed the lone gunshot did. There was a wrongness to it, something that said that the man on the other side of that door no longer cared if he came through it or not.

Moving swiftly to the top of the stairs, Jack fired three shots through the locking mechanism. For two seconds, he paused to listen and heard nothing. Leaning back, he hammered the bottom of his boot into the door, just below the handle, sending it crashing open. A quick survey of the room revealed only one occupant. The man lay sprawled on the floor behind a steel-case desk. What was left of his head lay in a spreading puddle of blood, and though the body was still putting off enough heat to stand out in the NVG's infrared display, there was no need to check for a pulse. This fight was over.

"I'm in. One dead inside the central office. Come on down."

"Be there in a minute."

Just to be certain that he hadn't missed anything, Jack walked across the room and pulled open the south door and surveyed the huge room beyond. Rapidly descending the steps, he swept the south side of the warehouse. Except for the absence of the glow from the now dead thermite grenade, nothing about it had changed since his last look down through the hatch.

"I'm at the south door," Janet said.

"Come on in. Everyone's dead in here."

Janet stepped through the door and walked directly over to where he waited.

"Except you."

"Yeah," Jack paused. "Except me."

Janet walked over to a panel of wall switches and pulled off her goggles. "Might as well see if the lights still work."

As Jack removed his goggles, rows of fluorescent bulbs along the high ceiling bathed the room with light, momentarily dazzling his vision.

"Where the hell did all the others go?" Janet asked.

"I don't think they went out the front gate," Jack said, walking out to a section of the floor where the concrete gave way to a large steel plate. At its eastern edge, tire tracks on the concrete led out onto the steel, but didn't emerge on the western side.

"What is it, a lift?" Janet asked.

Jack shook his head. “I don’t think so. Looks like a ramp.”

“If it is, someone might be down there waiting for us to open it.”

“Let’s find out.”

Jack walked around the west end of the ramp as Janet moved to a panel with a number of switches. “Ready?”

“When you find the right one, just open it about a foot.”

On her third attempt, with a rumble, the west end of the ramp began to lower.

Jack raised his left fist. “That’s good.”

The ramp stopped. As the rumble subsided, complete silence replaced it.

“Kill the lights.”

Janet moved back to the other panel and darkness once again filled the warehouse. Jack didn’t think anyone was down there, but he slid the goggles back into place and switched them on. With the business end of the AK47 pointing the way, he stepped carefully around the corner of the ramp, just far enough so that he had a view into the tunnel. As he had suspected, it was empty for as far as he could see. Moving around to the other side he used the new angle to confirm it.

“It’s empty,” he said, stepping back. “Turn on the lights and close the ramp.”

“Damn it! We missed them.”

As light flooded the room, he snapped the goggles back to his vest, feeling the same frustration that echoed in Janet’s words.

CHAPTER 93

Seated in the lobby of the Marriott London County Hall, waiting for his driver to bring the car around, Nolan Trent got Rolf Koenig's call. Because of Jack Gregory, the launch schedule had been bumped up by six hours. His watch said it was 6:30 p.m.; that meant it was a half-hour until midnight in Baikonur.

Nolan had been invited to dinner at the home of Sir Ralston Kent, the head of MI6, and though he would have preferred to spend a quiet evening in a local pub, this news made him glad he'd accepted the invitation. In thirty minutes, Rolf would kill all communications channels out of the Cosmodrome and the mutiny would commence. Even though this part of the world wouldn't find out what was happening there until tomorrow, the fact that Nolan had spent the evening dining with Sir Ralston and his wife would help his CIA cover-up.

When Rolf's payload reached its target, it would be evening in Washington, D.C. The nation's leadership would be dining or enjoying an after-dinner drink, little knowing that hell would be served for dessert. Although most of that leadership, including President Harris, Vice President Gordon, and Nolan's own boss, Frank Rheiner, would probably survive, they would be stuck like bugs on fly paper, trapped in the nation's capital with no means of communication or transportation.

But they would be the lucky ones. Eventually help would be sent from distant parts of the United States, where things still worked. The leadership would get priority in these rescue efforts. The common people who lived in the northeastern states would suffer the most. With police and first responders unable to do more than walk about, the people would quickly find themselves at the mercy of marauding gangs. And though they would eventually band together to protect themselves, except in rural areas, they would find themselves unarmed, outmatched, and lucky to survive long enough to starve.

The vision tore at Nolan's heart. More than his own life, he loved his country and its people. It was a true shame that it had come to the point where America's only chance of salvation lay in such severe punishment.

Seeing the limousine pull to a stop and his driver step out, Nolan stood up, walked out, and slid into the back seat. Shrugging aside the melancholy that had settled over his shoulders, he turned his thoughts to dinner and a lovely evening of conversation with Sir Ralston and Mrs. Kent. He would savor this slowly, the last evening that the United States of America would reign as the world's superpower.

CHAPTER 94

Janet's frustration continued to mount, along with the feeling that they were rapidly running out of time. The question was, time to do what? She could see, from the urgency with which he moved, that the same feeling was eating at Jack. A thorough search of the bodies strewn around the southern half of the warehouse had revealed nothing of importance.

They'd opened the ramp and gone into the tunnel, finding nothing except tire marks that formed convincing evidence that several vehicles had used it to leave the compound. Janet had no idea where the tunnel ended, but after a hundred meters it turned southwest. Given the isolation of the warehouse compound, the tunnel exit was probably inside a building several kilometers away. While the thing had probably been constructed for the Russian mafia's smuggling operations, the presence of the clean-room complex that filled the north half of the warehouse told her that something far more important than drugs or guns had recently made that trip.

Once Jack had turned on the lights in the north half of the warehouse, they'd noticed something interesting. A ceiling-mounted crane system with electric winches and pulleys ran through a large rectangular hole in the wall that divided the northern half from the southern. It seemed highly likely that it had been used to move a large piece of equipment from the clean room to the shipping area, where it had been loaded onto a truck and shipped out through the tunnel. But what it was and where it had gone, they had no idea.

Now they'd just come up empty in the office. Not completely. They'd recovered the dead man's cell phone, but it was encrypted and, even if the decoders at the NSA could overcome that, it would take time that they didn't have. She'd pulled open all of the drawers in the gray steel-case desk and found nothing. Whatever files had once been here were gone.

With her booted right foot, she kicked the bottom-right file drawer closed, started to turn away, and then stopped. Despite the excessive force she'd applied to that kick, it hadn't closed all the way.

Seeing her kneel down to examine it, Jack leaned in.

"Got something?"

"I don't know. Maybe."

Janet pushed, but the drawer had wedged on something and it took a strong pull to get it free. Reaching down, she pressed the twin release catches on the slide rails, pulled the drawer free of the desk and set it aside. When she looked into the vacant compartment, she saw something that elevated her heart-rate ever so slightly. A green file folder had fallen behind the drawer and now lay at the bottom of the compartment.

Janet grabbed it and set it on top of the desk, mentally crossed her fingers, and opened it. With Jack leaning over the desk beside her, she spread the contents across its surface. Five sheets of engineering drawings. Although she couldn't tell what piece of equipment these represented, she did recognize part of the label at the top of page one.

XLRMV-1 Power Supply Schematic.

Jack's low whistle brought her eyes up to lock with his.

"What the hell is this doing here?"

Janet shook her head. It made no sense, whatsoever, for these drawings to be inside one of Vladimir Roskov's warehouses. Then again, the clean-room setup made no sense either. But taken together, they just might.

Janet returned her gaze to the topmost diagram.

"We need to set up the satcom gear and talk to Admiral Riles."

Jack straightened. "I'll go get the SUV, throw the gear we left behind in the back, and drive it back here."

"Okay. Leave the south garage door open on your way out. Might as well drive inside when you get back. In the meantime, I'll take a closer look at these schematics."

Jack opened the door and stepped out, the sound of his rapidly descending footfalls ringing the steel grating in his wake.

Janet pulled up the office chair, seated herself, and began slowly flipping through the pages, one key question forming in her mind, a question that the NSA should be able to answer. In the past few days, had any part of Rolf Koenig's experimental payload been repaired or replaced? And since the launch was scheduled for noon tomorrow, the sooner she got that answer to that question, the better.

CHAPTER 95

Rolf didn't return to the Control Room in Building 92A-50. Roskov's men would take him and Rachel there soon enough. Instead, he had his driver take him directly to the Hotel Polyot in Area 95, conveniently located between Building 92A-50 and Launch Pad 24. Although this hotel wasn't nearly as nice as the one he'd stayed in until last night, this one was on-site and it was where he had always planned on staying for the last two nights leading up to the launch.

Carrying the case with his laptop and portable satellite communications gear, he stepped out of the sedan, through the door held open by one of his security detail, and into the lobby. A minute later he walked out of the elevator and entered his room. Across from the plain wooden desk, Rachel lay dreaming, courtesy of the prescription dose of Eszopiclone that had been administered earlier this evening. She would cause no trouble.

With practiced ease, Rolf arranged and connected the equipment, and then powered it on. Satisfied with the signal strength to the nearest of his communications satellites, Rolf looked at the digital clock display: 23:57.

In three minutes he would initiate the program that would trigger the shutdown of all external communications from the Cosmodrome. This included the old land line communications, the cell phone links, and all satellite links except those that were routed through his satellite network.

It wouldn't hurt anything to go ahead and trigger it now, but Rolf was a man who demanded precision in all things. So he would wait for it.

When the numbers changed to 00:00, he clicked the button that launched those special programs he had surreptitiously injected into the various networks and computation systems throughout the Cosmodrome. There were no explosions, nor was there any sign at all, except in the Control Room, that the Cosmodrome now stood isolated from the outside world. Even there, it would go unnoticed unless the night shift attempted to check in with the Russian Mission Control Center in Korolyov. Even if they did, periodic communications outages occasionally happened, and were usually corrected within a few minutes.

Having accomplished that part of tonight's agenda, he dialed the number that connected him to Vladimir Roskov.

The rasp in the mobster's voice showed his excitement. "Da?"

"Communications are down. Proceed."

The distant sound of gunfire echoed outside the building as Rolf set the phone down. Within the hotel, he heard the sound of running footsteps, hoarse shouts, and then more shots as Roskov's paid traitors inside the Russian security forces turned on their comrades and then began rounding up the small international press contingent staying in the hotel.

Packing his equipment, Rolf waited for their arrival, knowing that similar actions were taking place at Area 92, Area 81, and Area 200, as the Russian crime boss demonstrated his organization's power and reach.

The sound of his hotel room door being kicked in did not disturb him. Rolf maintained his seat as three heavily armed, stocking-masked men stormed into his room. Within seconds they secured Rolf and his groggy wife, cuffing their hands with plastic ties and taping their mouths shut. Then, as one of the men grabbed the bag with Rolf's equipment, the other two dragged him and Rachel out into the hallway, past a handful of similarly bound reporters, and down the stairs to one of the waiting cars.

Feeling himself roughly shoved into the back seat beside Rachel, pinned between two of Roskov's goons, Rolf glanced into Rachel's wide, tear-filled eyes. Apparently the shock of the sudden assault had managed to overcome the effects of the drugs. He hoped the reporters they had been dragged past had gotten a good look at that face.

The ride to Building 92A-50 was a short one. Upon arrival, Rolf felt himself dragged from the car, noting that Roskov had gone a bit too far in telling his men to make his treatment look realistic. The man with his bag greeted two men who stood guard outside the door that gave access to the stairway leading up to the main Control Room.

When they stepped out of the stairwell, Rolf was confronted with the sight of all of the Control Room night shift personnel and guards bound and gagged, seated with their backs to the walls as two more masked men stood watch. Rachel's guard pushed her to the floor beside one of the bound nightshift crew.

Then Rolf was shoved through the door into the six-by-thirteen-meter Control Room, its monitors and consoles now completely unmanned. The man with Rolf's case set it at a workstation as his guard released his firm hold on Rolf's left arm.

Seeing Rolf, Vladimir Roskov grinned and stepped forward to cut the plastic cuffs that bound his wrists together. With a sudden tug that ripped the duct tape from his mouth, Roskov spoke the words that erased Rolf's rising anger.

"Herr Koenig . . . the Cosmodrome is yours."

CHAPTER 96

Levi Elias's afternoon had just taken a turn for the worse. How much worse, he didn't yet know, but it didn't look good.

Janet Price's encrypted message was marked "EXTREMELY URGENT" and, having looked at it, he couldn't argue with the categorization. Seated here in Jonathan Riles's small conference room, surrounded by specialists with paper copies of schematics spread across the table in front of them, his concern was steadily rising.

The look on the Old Man's face didn't reassure him. For the first time he could remember, Admiral Jonathan Riles looked grim.

Their top engineering specialists had verified that these enlarged engineering drawings were for the nuclear generator that would power Rolf Koenig's experimental lunar mining robot. But these differed from the official documents that had been submitted to the Baikonur International Launch Services, better known as ILS. While the power supply looked like a perfect match to the original from the outside, there had clearly been significant internal modifications.

The problem was that the specifications were incomplete. All the parts within the drawings were symbolically labeled, but the table that showed what each of those symbols meant was missing. Also, since Janet had only been able to uplink cell-phone pictures of the drawings, the quality wasn't what he would have liked. Although it was far from unanimous, a quorum thought this might be the plans for a dirty bomb or a nuclear explosive.

To be fair to those that disagreed with that assessment, the drawings were unlike any bomb design they had ever seen. And without knowing what materials made up the components, there was no way to be sure. It could be a bomb. It could be a refined version of Rolf Koenig's nuclear reactor.

The fact that these documents had been recovered from a facility owned and operated by the Russian mafia disturbed Levi deeply. But what tied his gut in a knot was the answer to Janet's question.

She'd asked if there had been any problem with Rolf's XLRMV-1 payload that had required replacement within the last week. Two days before the payload had been mated with the Breeze M fourth stage, a major problem with the robot's nuclear power supply had forced replacement of that critical piece and the timing coincided with satellite imagery that showed a sudden reduction in manning at Roskov's Kyzylorda warehouse complex, the same facility Janet and Jack had just found abandoned.

Clearly, it hadn't been completely empty. One of Janet's photos had been taken from an angle that showed a dead man's sprawled body lying near the desk, and Levi suspected he wasn't the operation's only casualty.

Admiral Riles's cell phone rang. After a quick glance at its display, he answered it.

"Yes?"

There was a brief pause as the NSA director listened. Levi noted a tightening at the corners of his mouth.

"I understand."

Riles terminated the call, returned the phone to his pocket, and dismissed everyone except Levi. When Levi closed the door behind the last man out, he looked around to find Admiral Riles's gray eyes staring expectantly at him.

The admiral lowered his voice, almost as if he was speaking to himself instead of to Levi.

"The Russian Mission Control Center outside Moscow has lost communications with the Baikonur Cosmodrome. They think it's a technical problem and will be cleared up shortly. It shouldn't interfere with tomorrow's launch schedule."

Levi didn't curse in front of his boss, but he wanted to.

"I hope they're right."

Admiral Riles leaned back in his chair, rubbing his chin with his left hand.

"So, Levi. Is a nuclear weapon sitting on the top of a Proton Rocket at the Baikonur Cosmodrome or not?"

Levi worked up just enough spit to swallow. "I think so."

Admiral Riles rose from his chair, and then leaned over to take one last look at the schematics.

"Damn it. Tell Janet I want her and Gregory to hustle their asses up to Baikonur and confirm."

"Yes, sir."

"Okay then, get going. I'll call the president."

CHAPTER 97

Control Room 4102 wasn't a big room like NASA Mission Control in Houston or the Russian Mission Control Center in Korolyov. On one wall, a heavily armored and reinforced window provided a view onto the room where the space capsule payload was fueled prior to being mated to the Proton Rocket in the assembly area. In addition to that view, this room provided control of the launch and subsequent maneuvers to place the spacecraft into orbit.

Rolf couldn't remember the last time he was so excited that his palms were sweating, but, here in this room, they were so damp they felt as if they would leave puddles on the keyboard. It didn't take long to bring up his laptop and hook it into his satellite communications network. The most difficult remaining task would be replacing the preprogrammed firing sequences and steering commands for the Breeze M main engine, thrusters, and attitude control engines. But Rolf had prepared for this moment and he knew those components as well as he understood his special payload.

The initial arc would take the rocket eastward over southern Russia. During the initial ten minutes of flight, the Proton rocket's first three stages would fall away, leaving the Breeze M to carry the spacecraft the rest of the way. Normally that meant the first burn would end in the vicinity of northern Japan, sending the spacecraft on a forty-minute ride across the Pacific and over the southern tip of South America. Then the second and third burns would put it in a transfer orbit as it again passed over Baikonur.

Rolf had no intention of allowing the Breeze M to make those standard burns. His fingers moved across the keyboard in a blur that brought up a new control panel display. Moving his cursor to a button labeled *BEGIN* UPLINK, Rolf initiated the transfer of a program that would change the frequencies for sending commands and receiving telemetry and replace the Breeze M's firing sequence with his own.

Instead of waiting forty minutes after completion of the first Breeze M burn over Japan, during the following thirty-one minutes the Breeze M would execute a series of corrective burns that would alter the spacecraft's flight path, sending it veering onto a trajectory that would take it over the east coast of the United States, where it would release its game-changing payload.

It was a crazy flight path, one that had no chance of placing a spacecraft into orbit. Rolf didn't care. With Nolan Trent's help, he had arranged for a special subroutine to be inserted into the American Ground-Based Midcourse Defense system, a software change that gave those radars a blind spot along this one sub-orbital path. It ensured that, approximately one hour after launching from the Baikonur Cosmodrome, Rolf's special payload would light up the night sky.

Those east coast Americans had better enjoy the show. It was likely to be their last.

CHAPTER 98

Seated on the cold concrete floor, plastic cuffs cutting into her wrists, Rachel couldn't stop shaking. Standing over her, the stocking-masked man stared down her nightgown at an angle that left little to the imagination, the tip of his submachine gun almost touching her left breast as she cringed back against the wall.

Confusion filled her mind and the remnants of the sleeping drug weren't helping her sort out her thoughts. One name echoed in her head. Vladimir Roskov. The Russian crime lord must be behind this. But these men had captured Rolf, too. If anything, they had handled him more roughly than Rachel. It made no sense.

Rachel had been convinced that Rolf was the one pulling Roskov's strings. Maybe he'd tugged a little too hard. Or maybe he had never been in charge after all.

She was in a narrow hallway, at the end of a line of similarly bound and terrified people, probably the night shift that had been on duty in this building. Rachel took some comfort in the fact that her captors wore masks to protect their identities. Why bother if they were going to kill all their prisoners? Of course, they might still be planning to abuse and kill some of them. An ex-supermodel might be high on that list.

"So, now you can relax."

That was what Jack Gregory had said to her on Heidelberg's Alte Brücke. Damn him. Rachel had felt the man's strange energy when she'd leaned up against him. He'd looked straight into her eyes and made her believe.

Right now, huddled in a cold hallway with a bunch of other poor bastards as an armed prick stared down at her tits, Rachel found that belief worn thin.

CHAPTER 99

The house reminded Nolan of 10 Downing Street. While Sir Ralston Kent wasn't prime minister, he was of noble lineage and old money, the likes of which Britain's current prime minister could only envy. After finishing dinner and thanking Mrs. Kent for her hospitality, Nolan had accompanied Sir Ralston to the drawing room. There, seated in twin high-backed chairs that were angled toward the fireplace, the two men regarded each other over glasses of single-malt Scotch.

The combination of the low fire, the old English atmosphere, and the clink of the ice cubes against his glass helped spread the whiskey's warm glow from Nolan's stomach through the rest of his body. The conversation was light and pleasant, never straying to work topics. Altogether, as perfect an evening as Nolan could recall.

Then his cell phone rang.

Seeing Frank Rheiner's name on the caller ID, Nolan apologized for the interruption and answered it.

"Hi, Frank. I'm having a cocktail with Sir Ralston. How can I help?"

"Find a private spot. I'm about to conference you in on a call from the Situation Room."

"Give me a second."

Nolan turned to Sir Ralston. "Excuse me. Do you have a spot where I can take this call in private?"

"Happens to me all the time. Right through that door."

Nolan nodded and walked out of the drawing room and into Sir Ralston's private office. Seating himself at the teak desk, he put the phone back to his ear.

"I'm ready."

He heard a click and then the babble of conversation from the conferenced group. Then the CIA director spoke again.

"Mr. President, I have my deputy, Nolan Trent, on the line now."

President Harris replied. "Mr. Trent. Let me briefly summarize. I have assembled my national security staff to help me make sense of some troubling intelligence information I just received. Admiral Riles reports that the NSA has gathered information that causes him to believe that part of Rolf Koenig's XLRMV-1 mission payload may have been replaced with either a dirty bomb or possibly even a nuclear weapon.

"Having looked at his evidence, Director Rheiner strongly disagrees. But since external communications from the Cosmodrome are currently down, we have no way to check it. I understand you have a man on the ground in Baikonur?"

"Yes, Mr. President. I heard from him less than two hours ago. He reported the countdown to tomorrow's launch was proceeding normally and he's in an excellent position to have noticed if anything was out of place."

Admiral Riles's voice was calm, but challenging in tone. "Did your man notice that the nuclear generator on the XLRMV-1 was replaced a couple of days ago?"

Nolan kept the tension out of his voice. "Of course. The new one passed all the tests required by the International Launch Service team. Their scientists gave it a clean bill of health. If it hadn't passed those tests, the ILS would have cancelled the launch."

"Admiral Riles?"

"Mr. President, the NSA intercepted the schematics in question from people with confirmed links to high-ranking figures in the Russian Mafia. Combined with the nuclear power supply having just been replaced and the loss of communications with the Cosmodrome on the night before the planned launch, I believe this poses a serious threat to national security."

"And I disagree," Frank Rheiner interrupted. "Mr. President, Admiral Riles has already told us that almost half of the NSA experts that examined those schematics didn't see anything threatening about them."

"The DCI is twisting my words. What I said was that most of my experts agree with my assessment."

"Bob," President Harris said, "you've heard the arguments and seen the evidence. What do you recommend?"

Nolan listened intently, fearing what Bob Adams, the president's national security advisor might recommend. The pause that followed seemed longer than it probably was.

"Mr. President, I have to agree with the CIA on this one. They have a man on the ground at the Cosmodrome and, as good as the NSA is at electronic surveillance, I'll take good human intelligence any day."

"George?"

Vice President George Gordon's deep voice carried its usual, confident tone. "Sorry, Jonny, I have to agree. The NSA evidence just isn't compelling enough to interfere with the launch and provoke an international incident."

"Admiral Riles," President Harris responded, "thank you for bringing this to my attention. But since the CIA has an operative on site, I'm confident he would have reported anything that rose to the level of a national security threat. This matter is settled."

As the call disconnected, Nolan realized he'd been holding his breath and released it. Returning his phone to his pocket, he reentered the drawing room.

"My apologies, Sir Ralston, but you know how bosses can sometimes be."

The MI6 chief chuckled. "I'm sure my people think I'm a pain in the ass. May I refresh your drink?"

"Excellent."

As Nolan accepted the glass and resumed his seat, a smile settled on his face. One more crisis handled.

CHAPTER 100

Although the open Kazakh desert that surrounded the Baikonur Cosmodrome was relatively flat, it was far from smooth. As Janet drove the SUV cross country, the bone jarring ruts, gullies, and rises made it difficult to keep the night-vision goggles on her head. After allowing her to sleep the first two hours of the trip from Kyzylorda to Baikonur, Jack was now taking his turn. To her utter amazement, he seemed to be succeeding.

After passing through the city of Baikonur, Janet had taken the off-road route they had agreed upon, one that looped well to the west of the road that led to the facilities that would be used for the upcoming launch of Rolf Koenig's spacecraft. The route would take them to a concealed position west of Area 92. Unfortunately it had added two hours to their trip.

She and Jack had both agreed that if something bad was happening at the Cosmodrome, it would be directed from the Control Center in Building 92A-50. That was the center of gravity around which all the action would revolve. The near certainty she felt that bad stuff was happening at the Cosmodrome should have surprised her, but it didn't. Maybe she was picking up some of Jack's black magic, just from being around him.

With one eye on the GPS display, Janet maneuvered to keep the vehicle in the low ground. Even though she was driving without lights, she didn't want anyone with infrared equipment spotting the hot vehicle engine as they approached the preplanned drop-off point. One last lurch rattled the suspension as she brought the SUV to a halt and killed the engine.

"We're here."

Beside her, Jack sat up in his seat, stretched, and opened his door.

Janet stepped out onto the rocky ground and looked to the east. Although she couldn't see any of the buildings from where she stood in the shallow wash, lights from the launch platform brightened the sky in that direction. Moving behind the SUV, she opened the hatch. Once again, she and Jack would pack up the heavy gear, same drill as in Kyzylorda, but with one big difference. This time Jack was going in light. That meant that, except for his H&K P30S pistol, all he would carry on the final assault was a healthy supply of nine-millimeter ammunition magazines, two throwing knives, and his SAS survival knife.

It was up to Janet to keep the bad guys off his ass until he reached the building.

She shrugged into the pack with the attached scanning laser and tripod, feeling the straps dig deep into her shoulders. Watching Jack lean into the weight of the laser's power supply, she hitched her pack a bit higher on her back, picked up the AS50 sniper rifle, and moved out. This time they had a significantly longer hike to get to the designated over-watch position, so she didn't even make the effort that some final light banter would require.

Putting one foot in front of the other, Janet noted that Jack didn't either.

CHAPTER 101

Hearing his name called, Dr. Dobrynin spun his thick body in the chair. The bank of monitors back-dropped him, some blank, others showing a listing of the last data they had received before the Russian Mission Control Center had lost communications with the Baikonur Cosmodrome.

"Yes?" he asked, seeing Dr. Valery Kargin's spectacled face staring into his, her thick lenses magnifying her blue eyes to startling proportions.

"Sir, we received a short message from Baikonur, before the line dropped again."

"What's their status?"

"Due to the extended communications problems, they are scrubbing the launch. They'll wait for the next window."

Dr. Dobrynin nodded and rose to his feet. It was the news he'd been expecting for the last two hours. It looked like the famously impatient Rolf Koenig would have to wait a few more days after all.

Putting two fingers to his lips, Dr. Dobrynin issued the ear-splitting whistle he knew his night-shift crew loved so well.

"If I can have everybody's attention, please? That's it for tonight, folks. We're going to minimum staffing. The rest of you, go home and get some sleep."

Turning back to his slender communications expert, he smiled. "Thank you, Valery. You should get some sleep, too."

"I think I'll stay. Until I figure out what happened, I won't be able to sleep anyway."

"Suit yourself."

As he made his way out of the Mission Control Center toward the parking lot outside, Dr. Dobrynin realized just how tired he was. Nothing drained him like missing a launch window. Oh well. A double-shot of vodka over ice would set things right once more.

CHAPTER 102

Jacob Knox watched as the massive Mobile Service Tower slowly rolled away from Launch Pad 24, indicating that the countdown to launch stood at less than T-minus one. A glance at the luminous watch on his left wrist confirmed it: 5:13 a.m. In just under forty-seven minutes the Proton's main rocket engines would ramp up to full throttle, sending Rolf Koenig's MagPipes to burrow their way into electromagnetic pulse history.

In the meantime, he needed Roskov's men to stay focused on their tasks. Two hours before dawn, somewhere out there in the darkness, The Ripper was coming. He knew it was superstitious nonsense, but Jacob could feel his presence. And if he was coming, he would target the main Control Room in Building 92A-50. But Koenig, paranoid about losing his rocket-child, had insisted that Roskov deploy half his team in a perimeter around the launch pad.

The captives had been moved out of the hallway outside the Control Room, down the stairs, and into the changing rooms, an area adjacent to the northwest entry. The need to guard those hostages removed an additional two guards from the available force to secure the outside of Building 92A-50.

Having completed his circuit of the massive building, Jacob was nervous. Since Building 92A-50 occupied the most westerly spot of any of the Cosmodrome's facilities, when Gregory came, his attack would most likely come from the open terrain to the west. It was with this in mind that Jacob had positioned a dozen of Roskov's men in a defensive arc around the building's western side. Even though that left only eight others to secure the remainder of the huge building's perimeter, it was the best he could do.

Launch Pad 24 lay over a kilometer to the east, with a number of support buildings and the hotel complex separating it from this spot, so he could count on no support from the two-dozen men protecting the rocket. Worse, the lights from the launch pad and the moving Mobile Service Tower backlit his men when they moved away from the building. The only good thing was that Vladimir Roskov had positioned himself in the Control Room with Rolf Koenig, where he could keep a watch on the bank of closed-circuit TV monitors that showed the launch pad. For the time being, it kept him out of Jacob's business.

As Jacob returned to the guard position closest to the northwest corner entrance, he flashed the infrared flashlight three quick blips, followed by two longer ones. Seeing his response echoed in reverse, he moved all the way up to the firing position and knelt down.

"Any sign of movement?" His question brought the head of the nearest of the three guards around, the night-vision goggles giving him an alien outline in the near darkness.

"Nothing. Looks like The Ripper's going to miss the party."

"Stay sharp."

The man's harrumph as he returned to his spotter scope told Jacob what Roskov's man thought of him. That was okay. He didn't need to be liked.

Jacob spared one more glance at his watch: 5:28 a.m. T-minus thirty-two minutes and counting.

CHAPTER 103

With an audible click, the power supply cable snapped into the connector at the base of the laser. Hidden behind the largest of the berms that blocked the line of sight between this position and the building that housed the Baikonur Control Room, with Jack holding the infrared flashlight, Janet adjusted the level until the two air bubbles inside the tripod's level indicators remained centered. Satisfied, she switched the laser to green, removed her night-vision goggles, set them on the ground, and began turning the hand crank to raise the laser above the mound.

The shape of a stereo receiver, the device would spray laser energy across a sixteen-degree fan, the single beam passing back and forth so rapidly that it would look like a solid plane of green light to anyone who viewed it from above or below the beam plane. And she wanted everyone to see it. Anybody closer than three kilometers who was unlucky enough to look directly at it would see something entirely different, the last sight they would ever see in this lifetime.

The optics of any night-vision goggles or rifle scopes would suffer severe damage. But the frying of the inside of the viewers' eyeballs would make it extremely unlikely that they would care. The intense laser light-show would instantly fuse their optic nerves, its unique wavelength designed to produce a sudden rise in temperature and pressure inside the eyeballs, bursting some of them in their sockets. At a distance of twelve hundred meters, even stray reflections from the building windows could be damaging.

Beside her, Jack slipped off his utility vest, revealing the black T-shirt with its multiple, tight elastic pockets.

"Ready?" Jack asked, as he checked his knives and ammo, pulling a black baseball cap down low over his eyes.

"One second."

Taking a long, cool sip from her canteen, Janet passed it to Jack and watched as he drank deeply. Then, after returning it to its case on her utility vest, Janet pulled on her own ball cap and knelt beside him.

Jack moved, staying low, and Janet followed. They skirted the mound, then shifted into a low-crawl as they worked their way east, toward the last covered spot forward of the laser.

Without a word, Janet wormed her way into some thorny desert brush so that only the barrel and scope of the sniper rifle emerged on the far side. Flipping on the infrared scope, she scanned the thousand meters from her hide position to Building 92A-50.

"They're definitely expecting trouble. I've got multiple firing positions set up on the west side of the building. Not exactly what you'd expect for normal launch security."

"What's between us and the northwest entrance?"

"I see three firing positions spread out about fifty meters in front of the building. There are probably others."

"Range?"

"They'll probably see it."

"Don't care."

Janet briefly thumbed the infrared laser rangefinder. "Nine hundred twenty-seven meters to the closest position. Wait. I've got movement. They saw the IR flash."

"Let's make sure."

Janet heard the words and turned to look into Jack's face. There it was, that undeniable red-eye shine that she'd seen before. But this time his eyes seemed to reflect an angrier red.

Jack pulled his pistol and stood up tall, his gun-hand hanging loosely at his side as he began slowly walking toward the men waiting near that distant building. With her thumb resting on the laser remote control's central button, Janet watched his dim silhouette glide steadily forward.

She began counting his steps, sweat soaking her undershirt despite the chill of the predawn air. As he reached a distance that put him within seven hundred and fifty meters from the nearest group of bad guys, she saw the first muzzle flashes. Three seconds later the rolling thunder of gunfire reached her ears. And even though they had little chance of hitting him at that range, Jack had their attention.

With her thumb resting on the laser remote's fire button, she spoke a single word into her throat mike.

"Sunrise."

CHAPTER 104

Rolf Koenig watched the bank of CCTV monitors that showed Launch Platform 24 from a variety of angles and vantage points. Atop that platform, the fully fueled Proton rocket vented fumes that showed up clearly, backlit by the platform lighting. As the countdown clock reached T-minus five minutes, the launch vehicle guidance, navigation, and control sent the T-300-second command signal to the upper stage Breeze M, synchronizing lift-off time and starting the Breeze M transition to internal power.

Rolf shifted his attention back to his computer display, the readouts confirming all systems reporting nominal. Excellent. In less than three minutes the Breeze M would send the GO signal. Shortly thereafter, at T-minus two seconds, the six Stage One engines would start at forty percent full throttle, with full throttle commanded a sixth of a second before liftoff.

The sound of distant gunfire caused Vladimir Roskov to jump, momentarily pulling Rolf's attention from the display. There were no windows to the outside from the Control Room, but the shots sounded like they came from the west side of the building. Roskov turned in that direction.

"That's my men firing out there."

"Go check it out."

Without another word, the big Russian pulled his pistol and strode from the room. As the door closed behind him, Rolf returned to his work. Roskov and Knox could handle The Ripper. Regardless, the man was too late to interfere with the launch now. To be certain, Rolf entered a sequence of instructions that would force the system to automatically issue the correct sequence of launch commands on the predetermined schedule.

Standing, he stretched his aching back, and stared up at the monitors. It was time to settle in and watch his rocket light up the predawn Kazakh sky.

CHAPTER 105

"What the hell?"

Jacob looked to his left at the man looking through the infrared spotter scope. "Tell me."

"He's out there, just walking straight toward us."

His friend with the night-vision goggles and an AK47 laughed. "The idiot thinks he's a cowboy. Want me to take some boys and go kill him?"

"No," Jacob said. "He's trying to pull us out into sniper range. Let's see how long he keeps coming."

Jacob spoke into the microphone that connected his radio to the rest of the team deployed around the building. "Gregory is coming. Target him but don't shoot until I give the order."

A hundred meters to his left, someone began firing, and as Jacob turned his head to see who the hell was shooting, other weapons opened up all along the line.

"Son of a bitch!"

Then God painted the sky a brilliant green.

As Jacob ducked down, squeezing his hands over his dazzled eyes, the wail of screaming men replaced the gunfire. Jacob knew that if he hadn't been looking south to see who was shooting, his own screams would be mixed in with those of these other poor bastards. Even that brief indirect glance at the green sheet had hurt his eyes. Now, with his eyelids squeezed firmly closed, the afterimage filled his vision.

The Russian nearest him stood up, his wail of pain and despair rising above the others.

"Shit! My eyes. My goddamn eyes are gone!"

With the sound of a baseball bat striking a side of beef, something lifted the man and hurled him over Jacob. Only after his body hit the ground did the thunder of the gunshot reach Jacob's ears, bringing him a new realization.

Janet Price had broken Jack Gregory's CIA thousand-meter shooting record. And from the sound of the weapon, she was somewhere out there with a fifty-caliber sniper rifle.

Another shot tore the night air. The bitch had turned off the laser and was busy picking off Roskov's screaming fools. Then as a smattering of return gunfire sounded, another burst from the laser painted him so bright that Jacob could see the bones in the hands pressed against his tightly shut eyes.

CHAPTER 106

Jack walked directly toward the northwest corner of the distant building, knowing that it was only a matter of time until Roskov's men started shooting at him. But the men Roskov had with him weren't known for their sniper skills. And even if there were a couple of excellent shooters in that group, he doubted they could hit a man at distances greater than seven-hundred meters.

When they did start shooting, they'd be looking directly back into the waiting laser.

The first gunshots got nowhere close to him, but he heard some of the second burst whiz nearby.

"Sunrise."

Janet's voice in his ear-piece caused him to tilt his head down so that he could only see the patch of ground near his feet, the brim of his ball cap blocking any stray reflections that might bounce back from the building's windows.

When the twenty-second laser burst began, Jack started running, angling his path sharply to the left to remove himself from the previous line of fire should any brave souls try to get back in the fight. And as he ran, he maintained a mental count. When the count reached twenty, the laser light died.

Despite the precautions he'd taken to preserve his night vision, he tripped over a rock, barely avoiding a fall that would have sent him sprawling headlong in the dirt. He shifted his course back toward the northwest entrance that would take him to the stairs and up to Baikonur's Main Control Room.

Jack heard Janet's AS50 answer a new smattering of gunfire. Two shots. He knew very well what those shots meant. Two more dead guys.

"Sunrise."

Once again, Jack lowered his head as he ran, this time closing one eye in an attempt to maintain some of his night vision. Then, once again, the laser's horizontal green guillotine sliced the night.

CHAPTER 107

Once more the spray of laser energy died out. The cries of the blinded overwhelmed the curses of the lucky few who were just scared shitless. Jacob was neither, but he had been surprised and stunned by The Ripper's acquisition and use of the banned weaponry.

With Janet Price out there filling in the gaps between laser pulses, picking off anyone that stuck his head out, Jacob knew he needed to take immediate action to change his circumstances. The only way he could think of to do that was to get back inside the building, away from the long reach of the sniper and her laser.

But the fifty meters from this position to the northwest entrance would expose himself to a world-class marksman. He didn't like those odds. A new idea hit him. She couldn't shoot while the laser was active for fear of a stray reflection blinding her. Assuming the pulses were about same length, that would give him a twenty-second window to make the run for the door.

When the light sliced the night for a third time, Jacob ducked his head, shielded his eyes, and ran. Keeping his eyes directed at the ground, Jacob missed the door and crashed into the wall. Sliding left, his fingers closed on the handle, and he twisted and pulled. Inside, a waiting guard squeezed the trigger on his handgun, sending a bullet whizzing by Jacob's left ear. Then the laser light blazed into the gangster's eyes, sending him to the floor, hands pressed tightly to his face.

Reaching back, Jacob pulled the door closed behind him, stepped over the writhing man, and burst through the door on his left into the now-empty security checkpoint. Continuing his momentum, Jacob ducked through another door into the change area entry. Behind him, he heard the outside door bang open and shut, followed by two rapid gunshots. The blinded security guard quit screaming.

Shit. The Ripper was right on his ass.

CHAPTER 108

The sound of gunfire from below echoed into the Control Room, but Rolf barely noticed it. As the countdown clocks ticked off the last twenty seconds before launch, his eyes were riveted to the closed-circuit TV monitors showing the Proton rocket sitting on its launch pad. At T-minus two seconds, the six RD-276 first stage rocket engines ignited and then ramped to full throttle, the rumble of their mighty thunder shaking the building.

With his hands clenched so tightly that his nails threatened to cut the skin of both palms, Rolf felt tears well up in his eyes as the mighty rocket lifted off, belching a huge cloud of smoke and flame, the brilliant display turning night into day. It seemed that time slowed to a near standstill, the rocket lifting from the launch pad at a snail's pace. But as it continued to rise, its speed increased and its size in the tracking camera dwindled to a bright pinpoint in the night sky.

As the sound of more gunfire made its way up the stairwell, Rolf collapsed back into his chair. He'd done it. No matter what happened from this point forward, he was the only man capable of stopping the automated sequence he'd initiated and nobody could force him to do that in the hour that remained until his payload deployed and detonated over the east coast of the United States.

The thought that The Ripper had made it inside the building finally wormed its way into his head. That's what the gunfire from downstairs meant. Roskov and Knox were having problems holding up their end of the mission. He knew he should be concerned about that, but he wasn't. There was no way fate could deny him his destiny. His planning had been far too close to perfection to allow it.

As the rocket passed through an altitude of thirty kilometers, its speed just over a thousand meters per second, Rolf took a deep, calming breath and focused his thoughts back to its flight path.

In twenty-three seconds, he would get first stage separation. In four minutes, stage two separation would be followed by the payload fairing jettison near Kolpashevo, Russia, two thousand kilometers down-range. Ten minutes into flight, as Rolf's spacecraft approached the Sea of Japan, separation of the third stage would mark the end of the standard mission trajectory.

After that, his precious cargo was in for one hell of a wild ride.

CHAPTER 109

Vladimir Roskov had just stepped off the stairs when he heard the screams that brought him to a halt. They sounded loud and close, just on the other side of the wall. A door banged against the door jamb as footsteps echoed through the far end of the hallway. The two gunshots that followed put a stop to the screaming.

His Sig at the ready, Vlad dared a quick peek around the corner. Finding the hallway empty, he took aim on the opening into the change area entry and stepped out, struggling to regain control of his breathing. Nobody had ever rattled his nerves like The Ripper had, but he'd be damned if he'd shrink away from the man. He, Vladimir Roskov, was the hunter, never the hunted.

Moving forward slowly and silently, stopping just short of the narrow opening into the change area entry, he put his back against the wall and readied himself for the quick turn around the corner.

When Vlad moved, he pivoted around the corner in one swift motion. But quick as he was, The Ripper was quicker, as if he had known exactly when the attack was coming. As Vlad pulled the trigger, he felt the assassin's knife punch through the back of his right hand, nailing it, and the gun it held, to the wall. Feeling the recoil of his own shot kick the Sig from his spiked hand, Vlad stifled the scream that threatened to crawl from his throat.

As Vlad tried to free his hand, the Ripper's side kick buckled his right knee, and if the black blade hadn't held him, he would have sprawled on the floor. Instead, it spun him into a seated position, one hand raised high as blood wept down his right arm.

Seeing the barrel of The Ripper's Heckler and Koch rise toward his face, he looked up into the red reflection in the killer's strange eyes and spat.

"Gregory, you're a dead man."

"So I've been told."

Then, as the distant rumble of rocket engines shook the building, The Ripper's bullet tore his throat out.

CHAPTER 110

Jack Gregory reached up and grabbed the black handle of his survival knife. A strong pull unpinned the dead crime-lord's hand from the wall, allowing his body to slump into the pooled blood on the concrete floor, as the deep rumble of rocket engines continued to shake the building. The sonic boom that followed that fading roar was echoed by distant reports from Janet's AS50. Because of her, Jack wasn't concerned about anyone following him into the building.

With Roskov out of the way, he had one significant threat left to deal with. Jacob Knox. When Jack had looked deep into Roskov's eyes, he'd known the Russian hadn't killed Rita. He didn't know how he knew, but he did. That left Knox. The CIA assassin had tortured and killed a fellow CIA employee, just to get to Jack. The thought poured liquid fury into his adrenal system. Jack knew he was losing control but, for once, he just didn't care.

Suddenly it was as if he could smell the man's lingering scent. Knox had run into the building ahead of Jack and had passed through this very room, seconds before Jack's and Roskov's paths had intersected here. Jack knew, from studying the building plans, that the hallway to the north led to a lobby and medic station, the only way in and out of that area. There was no way Jacob Knox would have trapped himself in there.

Roskov had entered this room from the south hallway, from the stairwell that provided access to the Control Room. He wouldn't have continued coming this way if Knox had passed him. That left the two doors on the west wall, doors that provided access to a series of interconnected locker-rooms, restrooms, and storage spaces. Lots of places behind them to hide and wait for a kill shot.

"Jack? You still with me?" Janet's whispered query through his earpiece partially cleared the red haze in his head.

"I'm in. Roskov's down."

"You need me in there?"

"I've got this. Just keep the others away from that door and off my ass."

"Good hunting."

Jack felt something behind the leftmost door pull him forward, so he took the door on the right. Jerking it open, he followed his H&K into a narrow, dimly lit locker-room. Two rows of sheet-steel lockers lined both walls, a long set of benches separating them. Beyond those, a door in the northeast corner stood open, revealing bathroom stalls beyond.

He knew that the closed doors on the locker-room's east end led to a pair of storage rooms, one of which provided access to a long, east–west access hallway that paralleled the room through which he now moved.

Except for moments when the distant thunder of Janet's fifty-cal swept it aside, a menace-filled silence draped these spaces.

Jack didn't fight the adrenaline flow that rushed into his blood stream to stoke his growing need. His heart pounding with anticipation, Jack's vision misted red.

Yes!

Knox was nearby. Jack could hear the man's cold soul calling to him. Gritting his teeth, Jack glided silently forward. Rita's killer's wait was almost over.

CHAPTER 111

"Captain, you're needed in the CIC."

Captain Steve Cole turned to see tension tightening the corners of Commander James Rodin's green eyes.

Nodding, Captain Cole turned toward the *U.S.S. Lake Erie*'s Combat Information Center.

"What's up, XO?"

"I'll let the tactical action officer lay it out for you."

Captain Cole stepped into the CIC, greeted by the familiar, "Captain on deck."

"Carry on. TAO, what have we got."

Lieutenant Commander Carlos Sanchez pointed at one of the four large displays.

"Captain, we've got a track over southeast Russia. It's on a trajectory that will take it almost directly over the top of us. It's still a thousand kilometers out at an altitude of two hundred twenty kilometers, velocity six kilometers per second and climbing. It'll be here in about two minutes."

"That's a standard Baikonur launch track."

"Yes, sir. Only one problem. Today's Baikonur launch was scrubbed. Even if it hadn't been, that launch wasn't scheduled to happen until six hours from now."

"Who's on the line from the National Command Authority?"

"The National Security Advisor, Bob Adams."

"Put me on."

"Yes, sir."

Captain Cole cleared his throat. "Mr. Adams, this is Captain Cole, commanding officer aboard the *U.S.S. Lake Erie*, on station in the Sea of Japan."

"Hold on for one second, Captain. President Harris is on his way down to the Situation Room right now."

A loud click was followed by the sounds of people moving around a conference table. President Harris's distinctive voice brought the noise level down.

"Captain Cole, this is President Harris. I'm in the Situation Room with Vice President Gordon and my National Security Advisor, Bob Adams."

"Mr. President, we have a track that matches the expected initial trajectory for today's planned launch from Baikonur. It's early and it's supposed to have been scrubbed. The payload will be passing over our heads here in the Sea of Japan in just under two minutes."

There was a very brief pause before the president spoke again. "Bob, what's the Ground-Based Midcourse Defense system showing?"

"They say they've got nothing showing on their Sea Based X-Band Radar."

"Mr. President," Captain Cole interrupted, working to keep his voice calm, "we've damn sure got something on our scopes."

"What about the Russians, Bob?"

"If they're aware of anything, they haven't told us about it."

Two more beeps sounded on the line as a voice announced the addition of CIA director Frank Rheiner and NSA director Jonathan Riles.

"Mr. President, this is Admiral Riles. We have very little time if you want to have the *Lake Erie* try to intercept. Based on our earlier discussion, I think your choice is clear."

"Nonsense," the DCI responded. "As good as the Aegis systems aboard the *Lake Erie* are, we've got negative confirmation from the GMD's SBX-1 radar, and it is optimally positioned for this."

Captain Cole glanced at the display and swallowed. "Mr. President, we're seeing what looks like third-stage separation. We've got sixty seconds if we're going to shoot this."

More voices babbled unintelligibly out of the speakers in the CIC before Bob Adams once again spoke up. "GMD is still saying they've got nothing on that trajectory showing up in their system."

"Mr. President . . . " Admiral Riles's voice rose a couple of notches in volume. "I firmly recommend that you engage this target. Worst case, you shoot down a satellite that wasn't scheduled to be launched."

"And if you do that," said Frank Rheiner, "we'll be firing an antiballistic missile right over North Korea. It could very easily trigger a war."

"Bob?"

"Even if it's real, Captain Cole says the trajectory matches a satellite launch trajectory, not a ballistic missile attack. I recommend we do not engage."

"George?"

The vice president spoke for the first time. "I agree with Bob."

Captain Cole interrupted the brief pause that followed. "Thirty seconds, Mr. President."

As he stared at his four CIC displays, his XO and TAO beside him, the president of the United States of America kicked him in the teeth.

"Stand down."

CHAPTER 112

Rachel Koenig had seen the lean American with the shark eyes talking with her husband. Upon being introduced to Jacob Knox, she had taken an instant dislike to him. Now, staring up into his face as he dragged her roughly to her feet, she liked him even less.

The plastic cuffs that had long since put her hands to sleep bit into her wrists so sharply that they pulled a cry of pain from her lips. The American paid no attention, shoving her away from the others seated along the square locker room's south wall, through a short hallway, and into a clean-room changing area, leaving a lone gunman to guard the rest of the hostages.

When he pulled her to a stop near the north wall and put a gun to the middle of her forehead, she found herself shaking so hard she could barely remain standing. After all she'd been through on this hellish night, after the gun battles that had raged outside and then inside the building, was she going to be executed in the middle of this austere space?

"Do you see that hallway?"

Knox motioned to the short hallway that exited the room on her left. Rachel blinked tears from her eyes and nodded.

"Very soon now, The Ripper will come around that corner. He'll see you before he comes into my line of fire. When he does, I'm going to give him a choice. You can probably guess what that choice involves."

At the mention of Jack Gregory's nickname, a small seed of hope sprouted in her clenched gut.

Jacob Knox leaned in closer. It wasn't clear what he'd recently eaten, but if sharks breathed air instead of water, they would have breath like his.

"I'm going to walk across this room and into that storeroom," Jacob continued, nodding toward the door in the room's southwest corner. "If you so much as twitch, I'll kill you right now. Let's keep hope alive a while longer, shall we?"

Unable to work up enough saliva to speak, Rachel again nodded, then watched as Jacob Knox walked diagonally across the room, keeping his pistol's red laser dot locked on the same spot on her forehead. Stepping through the door, he kept it cracked open just wide enough to enable him to see her and a small portion of the L-shaped hallway he had said Jack would use to enter the room.

She didn't hear it, but movement at the leftmost edge of her peripheral vision caused her to look that way. This time she found herself staring down the barrel of another weapon, this one held in Jack Gregory's two-hand grip. He stood at the corner of the short L-shaped hallway, his body shielded by the wall as he aimed the handgun around it. From where he stood, he would have to come around that corner and advance another three feet before he could get a shot at Knox. Of course that meant Knox couldn't yet see him either.

Rachel glanced back across the room at the open slot through which Jacob Knox aimed his gun at her. Shit. She could almost feel that laser dot steady on her head. There was no doubt that Jack could see it too.

Knox spoke, his voice loud and clear.

"Hello, Jack. Glad you could make it."

When Jack failed to respond, Knox continued. "You've got quite a reputation for being unpredictable. Funny when you think about it. What you really have is a penchant for getting people you care about killed."

Rachel saw Jack ease silently around the corner, inching ever closer to the spot where he could get a shot at Jacob Knox.

"Your brother's name was Robert, right? Maybe it's only the R people you can't protect. First there was Robert, then Rita . . . I took my time with her. But you've seen that video, haven't you?"

Rachel found herself unable to take her eyes off Jack's face. The way the red laser dot reflected in his pupils sent an icy chill up her spine, sapping what little strength she had left.

"And now that brings us to Rachel. You see that laser dot on her pretty face. Fast as you are, as soon as you start to turn that corner I'm going to splatter her little head all over the wall."

Knox's laugh held no mirth.

"Then again, why should I wait for that?"

With rising terror freezing Rachel in place, she saw Jack shift his aim, his bullet spinning her slender body back into the shelves on her right. Then, amidst the fading sounds of more gunshots, the enfolding darkness swept her pain away.

CHAPTER 113

Jacob Knox heard the gunshot as he started to pull the trigger, saw Rachel's body spin away from his aim point as the Sig bucked in his hand, his bullet missing her head by two inches. His surprise cost him a third of a second of reaction time.

Jacob ducked sideways as The Ripper spun around the corner, firing, his first bullet spraying a flurry of concrete chips and dust into Jacob's eyes. The rounds that followed splintered the door frame, only intended to keep him pinned behind the wall as The Ripper crossed the room toward him.

Blinking to clear his watering eyes, Jacob leveled his gun at the doorway and waited. When The Ripper hit the door, he exploded into the room. Having anticipated Jacob's aim point, he twisted his body as he fired his own weapon. Jacob's bullet missed The Ripper's stomach, catching him low on his left side.

Although it caused the ex-CIA agent's shot to miss Jacob's head, it sent Jack into a spin that he converted into a spinning side kick that knocked the Sig from Jacob's right hand.

Lunging forward, Jacob seized The Ripper's gun hand as he drove him backward over a pile of boxes, sending them both rolling across the concrete floor. With both hands locked around Jack's right wrist, Jacob felt Jack's left elbow break his nose. The blow that followed loosened his front teeth and filled his mouth with blood.

As Jack continued battering Jacob's face in an attempt to free his gun hand, Jacob drove his right thumb into the bullet hole in the man's left side. The Ripper countered by gouging his left thumb so deeply into Jacob's right eye that Jacob felt his eyeball pop free of the socket, the nauseating wave of pain causing him to lose his focus on Jack's gun hand.

The gunshot caught him high on the right side of his chest and the scream that it pulled from his lips carried a bloody froth. When Jack pistol-whipped him on the side of his head, Jacob felt his body go limp, but somehow managed to stay conscious.

As strong hands lifted him to his feet and shoved him back against the wood shelves, The Ripper's gravelly voice whispered in his ear.

"This is for Rachel."

The long knife blade penetrated his stomach just below the solar plexus, driven with such terrible strength that it passed almost all the way through his body. As he felt a fresh rush of blood and bile fill his mouth, The Ripper growled again.

"And this is for Rita."

The knee that hit him in the midsection hammered into the haft of the knife, severing Jacob's spine and spiking his body to the two-by-four behind him. As Jacob dangled on the impaling blade, paralyzed from the waist down, partially blinded, and bleeding out, he watched The Ripper turn his back and walk out of the storage room, pausing just long enough to close the door behind him.

CHAPTER 114

Blood ran freely from the hole in Jack's left side, but he ignored it. The bullet had punched a hole in the old Calcutta wound, so he knew it had missed any vital organs. He'd have to do something about the bleeding, but first he needed to get Rachel stabilized.

He'd aimed the bullet just below her left clavicle so the wound shouldn't be too bad. But bullets sometimes did strange things once they entered a body, and shock was nobody's friend. He'd have liked to have just winged her, but he'd needed enough impact to hurl her out of Knox's target line. So he'd made the best compromise available.

Rachel lay face down in a spreading pool of blood next to shelves containing an assortment of disposable clean-room garments. Kneeling beside her he put a finger to her carotid artery. The good news was that she had a pulse and was still breathing. The bad news was that her pulse was rapid but weak and her skin felt clammy, all symptoms of shock.

Ripping her blouse, he examined the exit wound, sighing with relief at the sight of the small hole. His bullet had missed the bone. Grabbing two hand towels and some of the plastic garments from the shelves, Jack carefully rolled Rachel onto her right side and applied an improvised pressure dressing to the entry and exit wounds. As he bound them in place, a sound to his left brought his head around.

At the corner of the narrow hallway that connected the change room to the large locker-room to the west, another of Roskov's men stepped out, his handgun swinging toward Jack and Rachel. As Jack reached for his own weapon, a shot rang out, sending a spray of red mist out the side of the man's head and sprawling him onto the floor.

Without bothering to check the downed Russian, Janet Price, clad in black, stepped around the corner, her H&K subcompact hunting its next target. Seeing Jack kneeling over Rachel, she lowered her weapon and rushed to his side.

"Christ! You're a bloody mess."

"It looks worse than it is. I thought I told you to stay outside."

"I'm not real good at following orders."

"Help me get Rachel stabilized, then you can work on me."

Janet glanced at Rachel and her bandages. "You've done that already. Let me have a look at that side. You might want to keep your gun handy while I'm patching you."

Moving Rachel into a more comfortable position with her feet elevated and towels draped over her shivering body, Jack leaned back against the wall as Janet ripped off his bloody black undershirt. Working with practiced efficiency, she applied a pressure bandage and tied it off.

Janet offered him her hand and he took it, using the leverage to ease his climb back to his feet.

"We can't stay here," she said.

"No. It's been fifteen minutes since the rocket launch. We need to get up to the Control Room and figure out how to stop it."

Jack looked down at Rachel and made a decision.

"She'll be safer here than if we try to carry her upstairs."

"What about the other hostages?"

"I haven't seen any."

"They're in the locker room just around that corner." Janet pointed at the dead Russian. "He must have been guarding them before he decided to get stupid and come check on what all the shooting was about. I don't know whether any of them might be of use to us."

Jack stepped into the narrow hallway through which Janet had just come.

"Okay. Let's find out."

CHAPTER 115

The Washington, D.C., clock on his office wall told Admiral Riles it was 8:15 p.m. Late nights were nothing new to him or to Mary Beth. He'd fallen in love with her while still a midshipman at the Naval Academy and married her immediately after graduation. After all these years of long hours, separation, and hardship, she still loved him enough to put up with it all. And because he had failed to make a strong enough case to the president, there was a significant possibility that Mary Beth, along with untold thousands of others, would be dead in less than an hour. Worse, in his gut, it felt like a certainty.

It made him want to race home to spend those last few precious moments in her company. But that was the coward's way out. It would mean he had given up. It was why he had his entire staff working late, just so they would be ready in case that small chance to make a difference actually presented itself.

When the phone rang, the sense of impending doom seemed to ooze out through the ringer. When he pressed the speakerphone button, his assistant's soft Virginia drawl did nothing to lighten his mood.

"Sir," Barry Whitcom said, "the president and his national security staff are on line one. Conferencing you in now."

Hearing the connection switch, he announced himself. "This is Admiral Riles."

"This is President Harris with my entire National Security Staff here in the Situation Room. We don't have much time, so I'll get right to the point. Shortly after my decision not to engage the rocket from Baikonur, the fourth stage began what would normally be a four-minute firing sequence that would place it in a staging orbit.

"However, the *U.S.S. Lake Erie* reported that the fourth-stage burn has lasted longer than expected and has modified the trajectory to such an extent that it cannot achieve a useful orbit. In fact the payload continues to perform a series of maneuvers that has put it on a track that will take it up over the Arctic Circle and across northern Canada on its way down the United States east coast where it will reenter the atmosphere and be destroyed."

Jonathan Riles visualized the warped trajectory in his mind. Such an aggressive maneuver would consume all the fuel available to the Breeze-M fourth stage.

"Mr. President, that doesn't sound like a navigational malfunction. It would have to be planned."

"All of our experts are in agreement with you on that."

"Then, Mr. President, I strongly recommend you shoot the damned thing down before it passes over U.S. soil."

The president paused and, strangely enough, not one of the people with him in the Situation Room made a sound as they waited for him to speak again.

"Unfortunately, Admiral Riles, our Ground-Based Midcourse Defense system reports negative on the track. None of their radars see it."

"What about NASA or our satellites? What about our allies? Can't anyone besides the *Lake Erie* confirm this thing's trajectory?"

President Harris cleared his throat. "We've had multiple confirmations. Unfortunately, none of those sources is capable of engaging that target. And unless our GMD folks can fix the problem with their radar systems, we just have to sit tight and hope that you're wrong about this being an attack. That is, unless the NSA has some means of remotely hacking into the rocket's control systems."

"Why haven't the Russians sent the self-destruct command?"

"We asked them that. They said the rocket is not sending telemetry on the designated telemetry channels and is not responding to commands sent on command channels."

"Jesus Christ! I'm sorry, Mr. President. I'll have my folks give it a try, but if someone has changed the telemetry and command frequencies, we don't have time to try to find which new ones the rocket is using. We've got forty minutes. I recommend you have NASA, Air Force Space Command, and everyone else trying the same thing."

"Okay, everyone. Let's take our best shot."

Riles hung up the phone. Shit. Take our best shot. They'd already missed their best shot. As he pressed the button to connect him to his admin assistant, he shook his head. Never having believed in miracles, right now he found himself badly in need of one.

CHAPTER 116

At the base of the stairs, Jack turned to face Janet and, once again, she saw his strange red-eye shine.

She nodded her head toward the top of those stairs. "You know that Rolf's two personal bodyguards will be with him in the Control Room."

"That's why I want you to cut through the clean room and out into the payload fueling bay. When you get there, you'll be able to see them through the Control Room's observation window."

Janet lifted the H&K. "Without the AS50 I left behind when I made the run, there's no way I can penetrate that blast window."

"I don't need you to penetrate it, just make them think you might."

"Those guys are top notch; both were Kommando Spezialkrafte before they signed on with Koenig. They're not stupid."

"Just give them a moment's doubt."

Janet turned and moved to the door that opened into the set of locker rooms that Jack had cleared earlier. When she reached the door that provided access to the huge payload fueling bay, she kicked it open, clearing left and right, high and low, as the bang of the door echoed through the high bay. Finding it empty, she walked to a spot in the center which gave her a clear view up to the observation window.

Although the angle up to the higher level limited her field of view, she could see Koenig seated in front of a laptop computer. One bodyguard stood between Rolf and the door, while a second stood just beside the door. Both had their weapons leveled directly at that exit.

Since the room was designed to prevent fire and deadly fumes from entering, the door was sealed and opened outward. That meant Jack would either have to open it toward himself or blow it off its hinges. Assuming he did the latter, he'd have to go for a relatively small explosion to avoid damaging the computer that might be their only way of destroying Koenig's nuclear payload.

Lifting her H&K, Janet aimed at the back of Rolf's head and began rapidly pulling the trigger, concentrating on placing each bullet in the center of the bullet hole left by its predecessor, switching magazines so rapidly that there was almost no break in her rhythm. Good as she was with a sniper rifle, she was better with a pistol. And as round after round hammered into the same precise spot, cracks spider-webbed outward from that central point.

Janet knew that, inside the Control Room, the sound of the bullet impacts and cracking glass would be louder than the muffled echoes of the gunfire. As she had hoped, all three men turned their heads to look at her ongoing handiwork.

Then, amidst a cloud of smoke, the heavy door crashed into the Control Room.

CHAPTER 117

Without hesitation, Jack dove through the smoking hole where the door had been, firing at each of the twin muzzle flashes. He rolled hard to his right and fired again. This time, no answering fire met his. Through the smoke he could see Rolf Koenig seated at a desk, his chair swiveled so that he faced the spot where Jack lay. Both bodyguards lay sprawled on the floor, unmoving.

"Freeze or I'll put a bullet right through your head."

Rolf froze.

Rolling to his feet, Jack shot each of the bodyguards in the head before turning his attention back to Rolf. A movement from the doorway drew his attention as Janet raced into the room.

Jack nodded at Koenig. "Cuff him."

Moving up behind the German industrialist, Janet grabbed his arm and threw him face down on the floor. A handful of seconds later, with his hands plastic-cuffed behind his back, she frisked him. Removing a cell phone from his pocket, she placed it by the laptop before dragging Rolf onto a chair and binding his legs to its rolling feet.

"You're too late," said Rolf, a thin smile on his lips. "I've disabled the self-destruct circuitry. Nobody can stop it now."

Jack watched as Janet picked up Rolf's cell phone and turned to look into his face.

"The hostages said all communications are down, but like your laptop, I'm betting your phone still works."

Seeing his eyes narrow, Jack knew she was right. Dialing an overseas number, she switched to speakerphone.

"Hello, Levi. This is Elena Kozlov. I'm standing inside the Control Room at the Baikonur Cosmodrome. I need to speak with Riles immediately."

"Thank God. Hold on."

After several seconds of silence, Jack heard a new voice come from the speaker.

"Riles here. What's your situation?"

"I'm with Sergei Kozlov and we've taken the Baikonur Control Center back from the group that hijacked it. As you are probably aware, the rocket is already downrange. It's been reprogrammed by Rolf Koenig and unless we can regain control, I fear that a nuclear attack on the United States is imminent."

"How did he override the command channel?"

"His laptop is connected via his own satellite uplink. That seems to be what has been talking to the bird. Right now the laptop screen is locked and password protected."

"Is Rolf willing to cooperate?"

Jack saw Janet glance at him as he stepped close to the chair where Rolf Koenig was bound, her eyes settling on the left side of his scarred torso where blood leaked through the bandages.

"Not yet. I think Sergei would like to discuss that with him."

"Levi and I are in the computer center with Dr. Kurtz, the NSA's top computer scientist. If you can reason with Koenig, the time is now."

Janet directed her unsympathetic gaze at Rolf.

"What's the password?" The words left her lips as a command rather than a request.

"I forget."

Janet caught Jack's eye and nodded. From a belt sheath, he drew one of his two remaining knives and cut off Rolf's left ear.

"Wrong answer."

Rolf's scream came to a sudden stop when Jack grabbed his hair and brought the tip of the knife blade up to Rolf's left eye.

"You're going to give us the password," Janet continued. "Might as well be now before this gets ugly."

"Sheizekopf!"

Jack's hand moved so quickly that Rolf didn't manage to flinch, his stroke sending Rolf's other ear flopping to the floor amidst renewed screams and a fresh blood-fountain.

"Wrong again."

Jack moved the knife down, so that its tip probed the man's groin. Rolf gagged, but managed to spit out his answer.

"pi3141592653E@&!*@*!*@*"

Janet seated herself at the laptop, entered the sequence at the password prompt, and hit the ENTER key. Immediately the login screen was replaced by a set of telemetry displays showing the Breeze-M's altitude, velocity, heading, latitude, and longitude.

"I'm in. We're receiving a steady stream of downlink telemetry."

"Elena, I need you to enable remote access for that laptop and hand off the display to Dr. Kurtz. You will also need to disable the firewall and tell us which of Rolf's satellites he's connecting through."

Jack leaned in close to Rolf's face, his voice loud enough to ensure the earless man understood him.

"You heard the man. Which satellite are you linked to?"

Sparing a quick glance at Jack's knife, Rolf hissed the answer. "Orion-23."

With Dr. Kurtz talking her through it, Janet completed the required administrative configuration and then spoke into the cell phone.

"All done on this end. Let me know when you're ready."

"Any time," Dr. Kurtz replied.

As Janet reached for the ENTER key, Jack glanced at the countdown clock. T-plus thirty-three minutes.

"Handing over laptop control . . . now."

CHAPTER 118

"Okay, David. Tell me you've got something."

Levi rarely heard any sign of stress in Admiral Riles's voice but, at this moment, the sound of tight vocal cords was readily apparent.

For several seconds, as Levi watched the man's fingers dance across the keyboard, he wasn't sure the NSA's wild-haired, chief computer scientist had heard Admiral Riles. When the query finally pulled part of his attention away from his work, he paused and rubbed his hands together, as if debating his next move.

"I have a fully operational remote desktop with administrative permissions on Koenig's laptop. I've verified that the telemetry and command channels are fully functional. Pushing the telemetry display onto the wall monitor now."

The ninety-inch monitor on the wall opposite Kurtz's workstation lit up with a display showing a full earth map with an overlay showing the trajectory and current location of Koenig's space capsule.

Kurtz pointed a red laser pointer at the map, tracing out the rocket's flight path as he continued.

"The first three stages launched it on a standard fifty-one-degree trajectory that should have taken it over northern Japan, and then down across the tip of South America and back up over the Atlantic, Africa, and Russia. But shortly after third-stage separation, the Breeze-M fourth stage performed a sequence of hard burns that drastically altered the space capsule's trajectory. It's now headed over the Arctic Circle on a path that'll take it across Canada toward the United States' northeast coast."

Levi watched as Kurtz pushed additional telemetry output onto the matrix of smaller monitors that surrounded the big central display.

"I see the telemetry," Admiral Riles said. "But can you send it commands?"

"Yes, not that it's doing much good."

"What do you mean?"

"That last Breeze-M burn completed its sequence. It doesn't have fuel to fire again, other than the retro motors that kick in on separation from the payload. That means I can't alter its course. And the self-destruct commands to the Breeze-M and payload are being accepted, but ignored. Koenig must have physically disabled that circuitry prior to launch."

"There's got to be some goddamned thing we can do besides watch it fly to its target which, by the way, means us, our families, and our friends and neighbors. I won't accept that."

Levi rubbed his throbbing temples as if that act would force better blood supply to his brain. "Can we command an early Breeze-M separation from the payload?"

David Kurtz rapidly entered a series of commands on the keyboard, looked up at the telemetry display, and shook his head.

"It looks like that only happens when it reaches the pre-programmed location."

Levi felt his eyes drawn to the clock display. T-plus forty-six minutes. The map showed the space capsule now at the edge of the Arctic Circle, just beginning its pass over northeastern Canada. In another dozen minutes, the lives of millions might be over.

A new thought occurred to him.

"So we can't cause an early separation. Can you spoof the location?"

Dr. Kurtz's eyes widened. "Of course. Make it think it's already over the target. I should have thought of that."

Admiral Riles took two steps closer to the master display.

"Do it."

If Levi had thought David Kurtz's fingers were moving fast before, he had been mistaken. Holding his breath, Levi watched as Kurtz hacked the navigation system while the seconds ticked away.

"Got it!"

Kurtz's exclamation caused Levi to look up at the big screen, the sight momentarily sending his heart into his throat as the rocket suddenly jumped from northern Canada to a spot over central New York. Then he remembered that they were looking at the rocket telemetry showing where it believed it was rather than a display of the spacecraft's actual location.

"The payload's short range maneuvering rockets have engaged. We've got separation!"

Then, as Levi's yell of exaltation was echoed by the NSA director and his chief computer scientist, the data on all the displays froze.

CHAPTER 119

"*No!*"

The utter despair in Rolf Koenig's horrified scream failed to pull Jack's gaze from the laptop display. All of the telemetry numbers remained frozen, the flashing red light indicating loss of link.

Jack felt the stress in Janet's voice as she spoke loudly into the cell phone, trying to make herself heard over the noise from the NSA end.

"Admiral Riles. We're showing a total loss of link with the spacecraft. I'm hoping that's good."

When the admiral spoke his voice had miraculously reacquired its normal authoritative tone.

"Damn right it's good. Whatever that payload was supposed to do over D.C., it just did over frozen tundra. I want to congratulate you and Sergei. Our nation owes you a tremendous debt."

Jack laughed. *No shit.*

Beside him, Janet stayed focused. "We'd settle for an extraction point."

There was a pause as Admiral Riles discussed the matter with Levi Elias.

"Get your ass back to Zhaniya. We'll have something hooked up by the time you link up with her."

"Roger. Elena out."

As Janet ended the call, Rolf Koenig's voice turned Jack toward the bound billionaire.

"Prison or not, money like mine has a long reach. You'll regret making an enemy of me."

"I doubt it."

Jack pulled the trigger, noting the irony of the moment. Rolf Koenig had just passed his vast wealth and its long reach to the wife his men had tried to kill. Stepping around the body, he turned to meet Janet's brown-eyed gaze, glad to see there was no judgment in that look.

With a slight nod of recognition, he turned toward the door.

"Let's go get Rachel and get the hell away from here, before the local good guys come riding in to complicate our lives."

"Right beside you."

CHAPTER 120

The drive that would have taken two hours at rush hour took his driver fifty-six minutes. When he stepped out of the black sedan, Jonathan Riles paused to look across the Washington Mall at the nation's Capitol and monuments, silhouetted against the aurora-lit night sky. As he stared up at the beautiful, dancing light show, Riles wondered what the view looked like much farther north.

Thanks to the work of two magnificent young Americans, the United States remained the great power that so many had sacrificed to make it. It was a tragedy that only he and a couple of his trusted lieutenants would ever know what Janet Price and Jack Gregory had accomplished this night.

Black Ops was a thankless business. And although Jack Gregory wasn't technically a part of the Black Ops community, in his private contractor capacity, he had certainly played a key role on this operation. Riles admitted to himself that he was still hopeful Janet could bring Gregory onto the team on a full-time basis. Those two made one hell of a pair.

When he stepped into the White House, Admiral Riles was met by Bob Adams, the president's lanky national security advisor, and escorted down to the Situation Room. Having had the farthest to travel, he was the last to arrive. As he walked into the room, Vice President Gordon clapped his big hands and the uncharacteristic applause spread throughout the room. Even Frank Rheiner joined in, although somewhat less enthusiastically than the others around the table.

President Harris stood up and stepped forward to meet him, hand extended.

"I've got to say, Jonny," the president said as they gripped hands, "your NSA team pulled our asses out of the fire tonight."

Admiral Riles smiled. "Dr. Kurtz and his cyber-attack team deserve the credit. I just told them what we needed."

"I'll arrange to thank them personally."

Admiral Riles shifted to the meeting topic. "I understand you have received initial data on the impact of the attack."

"Have a seat. I'll let Bob give us the latest update."

For the next hour, Bob Adams presented the latest Pentagon analysis of the size and type of weapon involved and its area of impact. It was very clear that this was an extremely sophisticated EMP weapon of a type none of the experts that had looked at the early data had seen before. While it would take weeks to conduct a thorough analysis, scientists at Los Alamos and Lawrence Livermore national laboratories had made initial estimates that a multi-stage weapon had been able to burn through the EMP conduction layer, possibly generating ground-level voltages in excess of fifty-thousand volts per meter.

Despite the fact that the space burst had occurred over a very sparsely populated region of northern Canada, the strength of the pulse had knocked out an entire section of air defense radar systems and had disabled electronic systems for thousands, possibly millions of square miles. Communications losses had been reported for two U.S. icebreakers and numerous foreign seagoing vessels, as well as over large swaths of Greenland. In addition, three communications satellites had shut down, and it was unclear the level of damage they had suffered.

The electron flux had been captured by the earth's magnetic field, producing incredible aurora borealis displays as far south as North Carolina and echoed in Antarctica as the electrons spiraled around the magnetic field lines connecting the North and South Poles. Though it was much too early to accurately estimate the weapon's effects had it reached its target over the northeast U.S. coast, there was no doubt that it would have produced catastrophic damage.

As Bob Adams concluded his overview briefing, the president turned to CIA Director Frank Rheiner, the tone of his voice just short of accusing.

"Frank. Would you care to tell me how the CIA got this so wrong?"

To Rheiner's credit, the graying ex-senator from Wisconsin showed no hint of the emotional stress that Riles knew he must be feeling right now.

"Mr. President, I have no excuse. I take full responsibility for my agency's failure to properly advise you in this matter. I readily admit that, from the start, Admiral Riles has been right about this and we have been wrong. I offer my resignation, effective immediately."

President Harris slapped his palm angrily on the table. "Bullshit. You screwed up. I don't need a new DCI. I need you to find out where this screw-up happened and fix it. I'm quite certain that there is nobody I could appoint who wants those answers more than you do."

As Admiral Riles stared at Frank Rheiner's tightly controlled expression, he knew that the president was correct. Nobody at CIA would be sleeping until those responsible for badly advising the DCI were identified and staked to the side of some barn for buzzards to pick their carcasses clean. A quick glance over at Vice President George Gordon, his old Naval Academy roommate, told Riles that he was thinking the same thing.

"Okay, everybody," President Harris continued. "We can stall for a few hours, but then I'll have to go to the briefing room and issue a statement. Our job, between now and then, is to develop some plausible cover story that doesn't involve an attempted nuclear attack on the United States. I don't care whether we blame Koenig's robot's nuclear power supply crashing back into the atmosphere, global warming, or a giant solar ejaculation."

Bob Adams leaned forward. "Mr. President, if we blame Koenig's nuclear power supply for this, we could compromise our ability to launch future nuclear-powered spacecraft."

"I don't care. So long as our story is good enough to convince fifty-one percent of the American public, I'll be fine with it."

President Harris turned to his chief of staff.

"Andy, get my press secretary down here, ASAP. She's going to need to have her story straight before I go public. And order some pizza. Gentlemen, it's going to be a long night."

CHAPTER 121

Nolan Trent woke from a short and restless sleep, a dimly remembered dream crawling through his head. The alarm clock beside his bed displayed the time: 6:00 a.m. That meant it was 1:00 a.m. in Washington, D.C. Last night, in the capital of the United States of America, the American government hadn't collapsed. That meant Rolf Koenig had failed. It meant he and his team had failed, something that Frank Rheiner had not been shy about shouting into his ear over the telephone.

As unpleasant as that phone call had been, today was going to be worse. The DCI had relied upon Nolan's information and had made a fool of himself in front of the president and his national security staff. Now, a very pissed-off Frank Rheiner wanted answers. He'd get them, too. Rheiner wasn't stupid. The trust that Nolan had worked years to cultivate had been wiped away in an instant and wouldn't be coming back.

Standing in the shower, hoping the hot water and steam would clear his head, Nolan couldn't come up with a workable scenario in which he kept his job. Worse, he could only think of two that would keep him off of death row, and neither of those alternatives was particularly pleasant. The first, he ruled out immediately. Suicide was a loser's way out.

Option two wouldn't be available until 8:45 a.m. That gave him time to get himself properly cleaned up, properly dressed, and properly fed, before making his way to Kensington Palace Gardens 13 for his morning appointment with the Russian ambassador.

Although Nolan had told Frank Rheiner about this meeting, he'd lied about the purpose. The DCI thought he would be grilling Ambassador Volkov about Russia's failure to notify the United States government when they had first learned that something was seriously wrong at the Baikonur Cosmodrome. But Nolan knew that, when he walked into the Ambassador's residence, he would become the highest-ranking CIA defector in U.S. history.

After shaving and combing his hair, Nolan put on a freshly-pressed, herringbone suit, noting how the dark color matched his mood. Washing his blood-pressure medication down with a swallow of water, he stared at himself in the bathroom mirror. No one had ever loved his country more than Nolan did. It was a truth that made his imminent defection all the more tragic.

But America's loss would be Russia's great gain.

CHAPTER 122

Levi Elias settled onto his couch, savoring the feel of the soft Italian leather. Remote control in one hand, a glass of cabernet sauvignon in the other, he turned on his sixty-inch TV, tuned to CNN, and muted the volume. It had been a hell of a thirty-six-hour workday. Now the media was busy doing what they did best, beating the story to death. And this story was the gift that kept on giving.

When the Kazakh special forces had arrived at the Cosmodrome, they'd found a slaughterhouse. Most of the original security force had been rounded up and executed by a military arm of the Russian mafia. According to news reports, some of the Baikonur security forces managed to mount a counterattack to retake the Cosmodrome, killing Vladimir Roskov and most of his terrorists.

Unfortunately they had been unable to stop the launch of the rocket that had been retargeted at the United States. And if that attack had not been thwarted by the U.S. ballistic missile defense system, it would have formed a dirty-bomb that would have had disastrous consequences for the heavily populated northeast corridor. What a complete load of bullshit. Levi had to smile. The government propaganda machine was in full-throated cry and the press was eating up everything it dished out.

Somehow, in the backwaters of Kazakhstan, Janet Price and Jack Gregory had kicked the shit out of dozens of badass Russian mobsters and a serious CIA killer named Jacob Knox. They'd nailed the hides of Vladimir Roskov and Rolf Koenig to the wall and had given the NSA's hackers a backdoor into Koenig's super-EMP device.

Several hours later, Nolan Trent had paid a scheduled visit to the Russian ambassador and had not reappeared. There was only one conclusion that could be drawn from that. He'd defected. That action had resulted in a formal protest by the United States government, followed by the arrest of Craig Faragut and Christie Parson, two key members of Nolan Trent's team.

Levi took a slow sip of his wine, letting the full-bodied flavor thoroughly infuse his taste buds. As he felt the red wine send a warm glow through his stomach and into his head, a new headline scrolled across the breaking news banner on the muted TV.

"Defense programmer arrested in Virginia. Suspect, Daniel Jones, accused of murder and of inserting a computer worm into a crucial missile defense radar system."

However reluctantly, Levi had to give Rolf Koenig credit. The man had constructed an incredibly intricate plan involving the Russian mafia and the intelligence agencies of multiple countries, just so he could launch an EMP attack on the industrial heart of the United States. The big question was why? Since Jack Gregory had cut Koenig's ears off and shot him in the head, it was unlikely they would ever know. Rachel Koenig was clearly a victim and if she knew anything, she wasn't talking.

Lifting his glass in a virtual toast, Levi imagined the ghostly image of Pamela Kromly settle on the couch beside him. Smiling, she held her ethereal glass out to clink against his, her lovely, light-hearted voice exactly as he remembered it.

"To Janet and Jack."

With tears welling in his eyes, Levi held his glass high.

"To Janet and Jack."

CHAPTER 123

In the two weeks since Rolf had been killed during the hijacking of his Baikonur rocket launch, back at home in Königsberg, Rachel had been busy healing. These last few days, with her left arm in a sling, she'd also been busy with lawyers.

As with all things Rolf had commissioned, his prenuptial agreement with Rachel was ironclad. It clearly specified that, if they, for any reason, divorced, Rachel was to receive a lump-sum payment of one hundred million euros and nothing else. It also specified that, in the event his death preceded hers, Rolf's estate, minus the same one hundred million euros, was to pass to his children. The one thing that Rolf had failed to anticipate or to accept was the possibility that he would die prior to producing any children.

It wasn't that they hadn't tried; it had been one of Rolf's many obsessions. Unfortunately, although Rachel was fertile,

Rolf wasn't. When sex hadn't produced offspring, they'd tried to fertilize Rachel's eggs with Rolf's sperm. Convinced that it was his duty to bring about the continuation of the Koenig bloodline, Rolf had gone so far as to have his doctors attempt to fertilize donor eggs with his sperm. In Rolf's mind, this was just a manufacturing problem, and all manufacturing problems could be resolved. But nothing had worked.

What that now meant to Rachel was that she was the sole heir to the vast Koenig estate, with all its corporate holdings, real estate, and large bank accounts. As hard as it was for her to believe, she was now the single richest woman on the planet.

One of her first directives to the Koenig army of lawyers was to ensure the protection of the Koenig name. Jack Gregory had refused to tell her the details of how Rolf had died, but she'd seen her husband dragged off by Roskov's men. Clearly, he'd been tortured and forced to override his own spacecraft's controls prior to being shot in the head by those same thugs. Rolf Koenig had lived for his vision of proving that robotic off-world mining operations were both viable and profitable. He had resisted while the Russian mafia had cut off both his ears, before finally succumbing to their torture.

Since nobody had come forward to dispute the evidence that supported that scenario, the Koenig legal and political machine had gone after anyone who proposed a different version of events, both legally and in the press.

Her thoughts turned to Jack Gregory. He'd saved her life. For that Rachel had just completed the transfer of a mid-seven-figure bonus into three separate Cayman Island accounts. Considering the tens of billions of euros she was now worth, she'd considered an eight-figure bonus.

Then again, Jack had shot her and her plastic surgeon said it would leave scars.

Turning her attention back to her new office, she looked around. The giant screen across from her desk was fine, but those other white walls would definitely have to go. Yes, a little paint, some fine art, good furniture, and a couple of throw rugs might make this room livable after all.

CHAPTER 124

The seaside cafés of Heraklion, Crete, had a certain whiteness to them. Whether it was the deep blue of the Mediterranean lapping up against the shore or the beautiful sight of Rocca al Mare, the Venetian fortress that protected the inner harbor, Janet couldn't deny the ambiance or its effect on her.

For the last two weeks, she and Jack Gregory had stayed at the Galaxy Hotel Iraklio, making love and recovering, both mentally and physically. She had no doubt that, like her, Jack was a damaged soul. He contained an internal force that defied logical analysis. Janet wanted to understand it, but she didn't.

When she looked into Jack's deep brown eyes, she felt . . . something . . . something she couldn't put her finger on. But in the heat of their passion, she saw in those eyes a flame that reflected the lust in her soul. Jack's inner fire didn't scare her. When she saw the red in his pupils, she just wanted to share the passion that consumed him.

Sipping cappuccino at the seaside café as she stared across the table at him, Janet knew that the time had come to ask him the question. She suspected she already knew his answer.

"Jack, you know Jonny Riles wants you on his team?"

"Yes."

"You and I are good together."

Seeing him raise an eyebrow, Janet laughed.

"Not just that way, but good together. You could lead the team. Totally off the grid. That's the admiral's offer."

Jack smiled a gorgeous, happy-sad smile, stood up, then leaned over to kiss her lips one last time. His soft whisper confirmed her fear.

"Believe me. Long term, you don't want me anywhere around you."

When he turned to walk away along the inner harbor, the tail of his white cotton shirt flapping over his loose-fitting cotton pants, the wind ruffling his brown hair, Janet was certain of one thing.

This time, Jack Gregory was dead wrong.

ACKNOWLEDGMENTS

I would like to thank Alan Werner for the hours he spent working with me on the story line. Thank you to my editor, Clarence Haynes, for his wonderful work in fine tuning the end product, along with the outstanding editorial and production staff at 47North. I also want to thank my agent, Paul Lucas, for all the work he has done to bring my novels to a broader audience. Finally, my biggest thanks go to my lovely wife, Carol, for supporting me through our many years together.

ABOUT THE AUTHOR

Richard Phillips was born in Roswell, New Mexico, in 1956. He graduated from the United States Military Academy at West Point in 1979 and qualified as an Army Ranger, going on to serve as an officer in the US Army. He earned a master's degree in physics from the Naval Post Graduate School in 1989, completing his thesis work at Los Alamos National Laboratory. After working as a research associate at Lawrence Livermore National Laboratory, he returned to the army to complete his tour of duty. Today he lives in Phoenix, Arizona, with his wife Carol, where he writes science fiction thrillers.